Unconscious Escapades

James Hendershot

Order this book online at www.trafford.com
or email orders@trafford.com

Most Trafford titles are also available at major online book retailers.

Print information available on the last page.

ISBN: 978-1-4907-5882-4 (sc)
ISBN: 978-1-4907-5881-7 (e)

Trafford rev. 04/16/2015

www.trafford.com

North America & international
toll-free: 1 888 232 4444 (USA & Canada)
fax: 812 355 4082

Dedicated to page

Dedicated to my wife Younghee with special thanks,
and to my son John and daughter Nellie,
and check in coordinator Heidi Morgan.

Contents

Alpha

Who among us does not find themselves losing the light, which surrounds them only to be one with the darkness that defeats the world as it spins them through the emptiness of the vast unknown? We deny the vastness of this great darkness by concentrating on any light that we can immerse ourselves. While lying in bed, I began to wonder about that realm, which defies the light. I continued to wonder how the power of this darkness could turn our bodies off slipping us into deep sleep. We call our life and visions in this darkness as our dreams. In these dreams, we own castles, enjoy the love of those we consider as angels, climb the highest mountains, sing the greatest hits, and lead the finest Empires. Nonetheless, we rejoice when the light of a new day takes these riches and glories from us, returning us to a world of hate, hunger, pain, and misery. The mystery of the dream world we live in subsequently, much of our existence vanishes from our reality instantly. It is as if a new memory disk is loaded as the previous one stored until the arrival of the next darkness. I realized that in my dreams, I do not eat nor sleep. I wonder if the point of sleeping in my dreams is the point where I live in the world of the light. Is my consciousness in the light as true as my consciousness in the dark? Do I walk in the dark as I walk during the day? Why can I remember a few parts of my night world? One such memory has me traveling above the Earth, without fear and filled with excitement and peace. I remember how beautiful it was, being a part of the firmament. I recalled how this experience is as much mystery as how I lived it. I remember friends talking about a dream documentary that discussed the common dream where people float through the sky. The warning they issued was that if we fall to the ground in this dream, we would die. They suggest this dream is correlated with our heart and the point we hit the ground is when it stops. My primary objection to this is how they can prove this, in that they would have to verify a person was in such a dream and died because of crashing to the ground. This is the comprehensive separation between the dark world and the light world. They do not communicate with each other unless in coded symbols and mind-altering experiences, which in themselves produce an integrity issue of being genuine or being a creation of our mind. Even the Earth that I have walked on all my days is always surrendering to the dark half of its surface. One-half suffers through the light, while the other half enjoys the universe in their sleep. Those who talk about existence in the dark are cast from those who live within the light.

Each day our lives are filled with the conflicts of light verses the dark. In the days of our youth, we believe the light will always be with us. This light will give us all power and ability to achieve our goals. It is solely through the process of thousands of days and nights; we wake up in the final years of our life to discover the dark is our future, a place that holds eternity for us. We gain our hope in the testimonies of those who have faced death and claim they entered into a great light. I hold on to this hope, for I would never wish to spend eternity 'in the dark.' Notwithstanding, I must accept the fact that every light always ends 'in the dark.' We have labeled the realm we do not understand as evil, without God, belonging to the devil. They assert God cannot be 'in the dark.' Is this to say that God is not in space, in the depth of our oceans or in our nights? Can the light of God be confined to the light of stars, which takes thousands of years to reach our Earth? I want to think that God can give us a door of light when we enter eternity is not simply the arrows of light through the universe, but also the darkness it streams through the center. The realization of how fast the speed of light is spurting through the universe suggests it has a working relationship to the dark it passes. As I search through the darkness, I find nothing. I ponder what I find when I search through light. Light, is empty to our eyes, yet logic dictates that something is in it. The items we touch in the light are in the dark as well. Try walking through your house at night and see how long before you bump into a piece of furniture, or even better leave a pair of your shoes on your steps and test if they are still there when you go downstairs at night for a cup of warm milk. I have tried this twice and discovered the wisdom in leaving items off my steps. We physically move our body in the light, yet our mind travels in the dark. The light gives us a world of color, whereas the dark world provides us a black-and-white world. The irony is how this world without color provides our greatest experiences. The overwhelming majority must prefer to live in the dark world where they have no hunger and never grow tired.

The power in the night centers on our dreams. Science tells us that our muscles only need a few seconds to replace their energy. Sleep has no essential biological need. Our program is written, as it demands we sleep or our mind and body begin to malfunction. The need for sleep is a mystery. Mysteries are solved by looking at where they begin, when they go, and where they end. While we are asleep, we dream. Therefore, there must be a relationship between sleep, night, and dreams. Many sleep a little during the day and during that process dream during the day. This schedule conflict with our biological clock and in so places an additional burden on their bodies and mind. Thereby, the sleep and dream element have the direct association, whereas the night is the variable element. Dreams provide us a pathway to a wonderful existence and may even give us the energy to face our life in the light, which for most does not give us access to this pathway to the magnificent. The oddity is how fast it is erased from our awareness when we awaken. I have tried desperately to recall a few of these dreams, yet something pulls in deep into my memory too far for remembering. This oddity may also exist when we go into our sleep, in that we forget most of what exists in our world of light. The sleep world has a few punches of its own, one being what we call nightmares. We discover a method for defeating these wicked foes and either merges into another dream or wakes up, sometime soaked with sweat, believing we have survived against great probabilities and had no desire to repeat the challenge. The dream world may be closer to our life after death than our life we currently live. The similarity is remarkable. Our concept of life in the spiritual world, absent from our body, is precisely what manifests itself in our dreams. I wonder if we are not living through another part of our brain, and part that does not function when we are in the world of light. Another factor about dreams is how common they are among us. Everyone dreams, therefore, it has to be a part of our program. We begin programing our children at a young age not to watch horror movies, or they will have nightmares. Somehow, at least a portion of our dreams is related to the day world. These connections interlock the two realms, thereby allowing our normal life to influence the night world and dream world. Subsequently, I grow abnormally tired. This is strange in that I woke up in the present day at three P.M. It is now almost ten P.M., and I even had a nap today. Nonetheless, in my bed I go and fall asleep. My wife explains to a difficult patient, she had today. She was afraid he would not make it through the night. Her friend lost a patient today on the operating table, so they are apprehensive about another one dying along the things happens in three philosophies.

The stepdaughter

The next thing I know I am talking with my new wife about her day in the office. I thought she worked in a hospital. She awakes and turns on our bedroom light. Presently, before me is standing a beautiful black woman. I guess there can be no ugly people in the dark world. I am currently married to an Asian woman. My dark world has a large beautiful heart-shaped bed with walls packed with paintings and pictures, none of which looks familiar. She appears not to be alarmed so I realize while she is not screaming I am safe. She is so cheerful reminding me about our activities planned for today. I am ignoring her, feeling the confidence that she has this coordinated and with her strong personality, had no doubt she will make sure I am where I must be. I watch her leave our bedroom, dressed like a top executive. A few minutes later, I walk out of our large bedroom and step on a balcony, which connects the doorways to our second floor. I walk down this open hallway on our second floor, observing entrances that reveal wide long side hallways. I am now discovering how big this place truly is. On returning to the front hallway, I look down at the corner of our kitchen on the first floor. My dark world wife had a large group of our household servants providing them instructions for their day. I see a young girl sitting on the kitchen island in front of her and watch her hug the little girl who gets up and departs by the side door in her pressed clean uniform. I secretly ask the servants when school is out, telling them I plan to bring my son to live with us and need to adjust my work schedule. I go to a local machine shop to see if a piece for one of my tools is ready. This bar is special, which connects levers I am currently using vice grips to operate. This has effectively turned a one-hour job into half a day. I walk into this chilly dark greasy shop and approach the man at the front desk about the status on my part. He tells me that one of his best machinists, who took an early lunch and asks me if I want to wait for about one-half an hour after his return. I agree to wait, and he invites me to make myself at home. I stroll to the back of this shop, able to see a few busy bins, yet most exist empty. I realize there are no such things as lights; nevertheless, I can grasp everything, or the telescopic sight highlighting what I am viewing. I find the restroom; I was looking for, enter, and then leave, as the dark world is kind to omit certain unnecessary details. While preparing this in my day world, I realized that since the night world does not eat, they would have no need to dispose of bodily wastes, therefore, would not include such activities. I walk out of the rest room, look over my left, and see a man. I duck back so he will not spot me. He hears a noise and rams his foot into the metal steps. I see a long twisted metal piece eject from the back of his foot. Silently, I walk to the front of this shop and see my machinist and the desk clerk preparing my bill. I pay and bid them farewell, returning to my house. I adjust my security camera, so I can see my wife's daughter come home. I spot her riding her bike into our driveway seeing five larger girls racing to catch her. I find myself praying that she makes it home safe. She races onto our property almost making it to our door as the other girls swarm around and ask her why she did not stop. I open the door and tell them because today is the day she meets her new daddy. She knows who I am and begins crying while hugging me with all her trembling might. The five girls, which two are black, one white, one Mexican and one Asian congratulate her and scramble to their bikes leaving at once. I ask my stepdaughter if dads are truly this terrifying. She smiles and answers me, only new ones with a Mexican accent. I ask her where she got that accent. This little ten-year-old tells me her mother made her learn and speak this accent as protection against her real father. I tell her she needed not to worry about that much from this day forward. She tells me that they have a surprise for me today as well and ask me to follow her to her room. We walk down her barren brick walled hallway. I am filled with guilt that my wife's child would be forced to live among the servants. I ask her why she stays here. She explains her mother was afraid to ask me. This catches me as odd in that she is the one who appears to be the breadwinner. I hold her hand as we walk this hallway, trying to verify she is indeed human and not a machine as those in the mechanical shop I exited earlier today. She guides me to her room where I see a woman servant playing with my daytime daughter, who in the daytime is sixteen years old, yet in this dark world in almost one-year-old. I rush to my Billie Jean and give her a big hug. My stepdaughter tells me we should go to the playroom. I ask the servant if she brings a few goodies for the children. She bows smiles and rushes to obtain these treats for the little people. We go into the playroom; my stepdaughter jumps on my lap, and a servant puts Billie Jean on her lap facing us. We both wrap our hands around her as my stepdaughter is making Billie Jean laugh. I cannot help but laughing with all this positive energy bubbling from these children. I ask my stepdaughter where my son is, who would have been six years old at that time. She has no idea that I am talking about now. Her mother comes walking in this playroom and looks surprised when she sees me sitting there. I tell him to see whom I found. She apologizes for not telling me. I ask her why she would hide someone so special. I explain we must be a family, and that no child of ours will live with the servants. We have extra bedrooms on our floor. I tell the servants immediately to bring her belongings and put them in the best spare room on our floor, which my wife approves. My wife asks me if the sweet next to our room would be available. I tell her that I cannot think of a better room, especially since such a room was created specifically for that purpose. I find myself confused that my wife would be so afraid of me. My daytime wife is eager to defy me on all issues, as would any normal American wife. I give an emotional bonding speech to my family pledging to struggle to keep us together as a family. Suddenly, I appear back in the machinist's shop in front of the steps. A man in a black suit comes down the steps with one of my daughters in each arm and tells me I can only keep one. I am speechless, as he continues by telling me if I do not decide he will take both. Filled now with shame I reach out for the infant, as he tells me, unless I leave this house at once we all will perish. A thought runs through my mind that the best solution for this situation would be that we all perish. Nevertheless, I remember the days when Billie Jean was an infant and how different she was henceforth being a mean American teenager. I grab Billie Jean, too ashamed to look at my stepdaughter and rush out of the house, and with the door almost closed decide to fight and push the door open just as the man, and my step vanish. At least, I got one more look into her eyes, and I hope she saw me coming back for her. I broke my promise too soon. The one thing I could not face would be this child's mother. Fortunately, I woke up reentering my daytime world.

Sacrifice for her mother

By recording the notes of this dark experience, I can still feel many of the disappointments associated with this event. Never in my day world have a made such a life-or-death decision. The shook that my true character may not stand firm and honor my promises shakes my genuine foundation. I ask myself if I made the best decision, in that I can never see myself cheating an infant from her life, even though cheating a ten-year-old from her life, which was filled with being denied and forced to hide from her father. I could never imagine the personality damage that a child would undergo knowing her mother married a man and had kept her a secret. A mother with no ability to support herself may be tempted to deny, yet a woman who was financially successful and whose husband stayed at home should not have sacrificed her daughter such as this. Little comfort can be derived that before I denied her, she was a part of a family for a few hours. I pray she vanished existence knowing I came back to fight for her.

I lay down with my daytime wife as we discuss several challenges of her day, including a code blue today. She brought home a charming glass vase of flowers tonight. I fall into my night world arriving at a hill on my mother's farm in Ohio. I search through the hills that surround me looking for something else to verify where I am. I cannot find anything; nevertheless, I know this bald hill with an oil well beside me. I see a slow wind blow over the world around me as darkness engulfs all but the hilltop I stand. Subsequently, a heavyset man, wearing an expensive suit, with dark black hair greased to his head, and a large cigar hanging from his mouth, begins laughing aloud. He stretches out his hand, and a woman drops to his hands. She wears a blue jean skirt and white tight tee shirt spotted with flowers. I have never seen her face previously, yet do appreciate the long well combed brown stringy hair. She looks at me as she smiles. The old heavyset man laughs aloud once more and asks me if I want to have a little fun today. I tell him I always want to have fun; nonetheless; I cannot see what fun he could find on this hill. He throws the women to the ground. He reaches down and rips her tee shirt off, without any resistance, other than for a show. Her screams are sandwiched with challenging laughs. I look down on the ground at her as she lays there topless. Surprisingly, I know she is bare-breasted, yet can see merely the top of a moving mannequin. She is moving and talking; therefore, she must be a human. He continues to laugh as he rips off her skirt and throws it in my face. I wrap it in my hand and slowly toss it back to him telling him this is funny, yet not as funny as the greatest day in my life. He asks me to explain. I am actually trying to keep him from abusing the woman who is laying on a hill about one-hundred yards from my mother's home. This is not the type of event, which I would want my mother to walk out in her yard to see. He laughs and asks me to tell him about my glory day.

Accordingly, I tell him I was working one day in my office when we had a distinguished visitor come strolling to visit us. He introduced himself as a former President of the United States Nixon and came here today to see me. He saw me on a talk show that our section produces and how I had declared him, the greatest President America ever had. No other President had or has perpetually taped all his activities. To this day, I believe his tapes were his property, and the public had no right to them. If any government employee taped his or her work activities, this is their personal property. There is no need to debate this now, as this argument belongs in the dark world. Any ways, the formal President and I enjoyed a day of picnics and fancy restaurants, with our entire office staff. He behaved as a normal person, and seemed merely to be seeking a non-hostile environment to relax. I think this story upset the old heavyset man who I was sharing it with currently. He took it as me trying to show that I knew someone greater than him. Subsequently, we reappeared in our office building. He flung the girl over his desk, called all in the office to join us, and seduced her at will. She held her peace submitting completely to this rape. I stood in shock at the absolute power he had over this group. When he finished he told her to walk into the office and see if anyone else needed any sexual favors. Everyone returned to his or her desks. I saw her walk up to the two elderly secretaries; we had and asked them. They removed their shoes and told her to kiss their feet. She dropped to her knees and did as she was commanded. I would have thought these two, what I thought was respectable secretaries would have attempted a form of consolation. I later learned that one of them once tried to comfort this girl a few years earlier, yet found herself raped in front of the office group. There was no need to report this to the police, since everyone else in this office would deny this, and he would sue the accuser for defamation of character.

The next phase had her walking through the office was even more surprisingly. As she stood before each male employee, he gave her a flower that was stored in his desk. None dares to speak with her. A coworker later told me that our boss completely owned her and if any talked to her while she was nude, he would have them beaten. When she came to me, I felt bad in that I did not have a flower. I wrote a note to her saying I would bring one the next day. She went back to the boss's office, and he gave her permission to redress. That night as I was driving home, she drove behind me flashing her lights. I pulled over to talk with her. She begged me not to do anything foolish and to do as everyone else in the office does and ignores it. Next, she told me that her mother needed an expensive surgery to survive and that he listed her as an employee and provided her medical insurance. If he canceled her insurance, even her prescriptions would cost more than three times their combined income. She kisses me on my cheek and tells me the price she pays one or two days a month is well worth it. I explain to her that I will not participate actively in these rapes. She asks me why. Accordingly, I explain that I do not want to end in prison because of this. I am officially volunteering now to protect her in the future if she wants me to help her. She asks me not to help her. I tell her this officially removes me from any liability. She agrees, yet asks me why I am worried about prison. Subsequently, she informs me that prisons no longer exist. This sends a chill through whatever I am. Without prisons, how can they enforce their laws? I discover the night world does not have prisons or laws. All who live there do as their situation demands, and when the 'scene' is finished, they vanish. It is getting close to me to vanish, nevertheless; I land back on the hill; I started this episode. I want to take a lesson learned from each event. This event taught me how much a few people will do to save a loved one. The raped woman in this vision is truly a woman by any standard.

Rape of the young girl

I get uneasy when my dark mind is exposed to women being abused. Even though a few might have much power in the courts, nevertheless, many have no such protection. I part of me resents the overwhelming power they currently appear to have, nonetheless, there are so many more who enjoy no such protection. My mind once more drops into the dark world, which remains a continual mystery to the land with the light. I am now walking through the gate where armed guards control who enters our gated community. I bring a few of our young guests to our apartment, and upon arriving, my wife goes down to the gate to bring several more guests to our home party. When my wife arrives, she begins creaming that one of the adolescent girls is missing. I knock on several friends' doors and gather a couple of them to help me with our search. We search through the complex when we finally hear a young girl crying. As we rush toward her, as groups of boys come rushing pass us. I stick my leg out and trip the first one, while my friends capture the other four. We gag them, put them in a storage room, and take our trembling victim back to a safe room where we can question her. She alleges these boys raped her. We take her and one boy to the guards at the community's gate and submit her charges. The guards ignore us. Then a guard tries to arrest me for kidnapping this boy and attempt to release him. My friends jump in and begin to fight for my release, while recapturing the boy. We wrestle their pistols from them, and call our American police, who arrive at the scene. They take the girl to a nearby hospital, where her father arrives with the media. The local police come and take the guards to jail, as we surrender the remaining boys. One of the boys cuts a deal with the police and testifies they raped the girl. My wife calls my cell phone telling me someone is outside our door shooting through it. Our police immediately rush onto the scene and rescue my family and our guests. I report in the media what the community guards did to us. My friends also submit their reports. Unfortunately, the little girl is executed at the hospital before she can testify. The local government at once calls for the public execution of the five boys. I ask the media if they believe this is justice. The media tells me there will never be a way in which the true killers will be identified; their sole thing they know to be real is that someone was protecting these boys. Therefore, when the boys die, the reason the girl was killed will be avenged.

This is a strange form of justice for me to comprehend. It appears the justice in the dark world cuts straight to the determining to motive behind the murder and removing that motive. Although, the murderers did not want the boys to face prison time, we can be assured they did not want an ending date on their gravestones. The police tell me that my friends and family must leave this foreign nation and return to our home nation, where they hope, we will be safe. We decide to send our families back home and to stay here. I know the lone chance we have is to hunt down those who are behind the little girl's death. The initial task will be to find out all we can about our young guest. This will be so difficult in that we have no way into her world. I ask my wife to invite her parents to our house. Her father tries to blame me, nevertheless; I argue that we did not know these boys, and that they only targeted their daughter. I then ask the father how he can blame us, especially how hard we worked to free her and that her death occurred while in the hospital he selected. Her father accuses me of trying to shift the blame to him. I ask him why I would want to shift and blame to him, as I am sure, he would never try to shift any blame toward me. I repeat to his wife how important it is that they study their friends and their daughter's associates. I will have to depend upon their integrity in this situation, especially considering I cannot get within a country mile of these people. The main issue I have is there is no way to tell if this is for real, or if they are setting me up for a disappointment. Nevertheless, the greatest disenchantment is that I may never discover who killed my guest. The frustration in the dark world is the unknown can hide and not at any time again be discovered.

Mountain to the heavens

The range of my emotions when considering the extremes of the dark world is oscillating from high to low. I am seeking something that is stable. I find myself spinning. When I stop this whirling, I awaken on a boat. We are sailing on the wide-open ocean. The sky is a light, peaceful blue, and all on this boat are laughing and enjoying themselves. The Captain is a tall blond-haired woman. Everyone speaks the dream language, which I understand. They fill their conversation with the beauty of this ocean. I am amazed over how relaxed they are currently. One man invites me to join their group. I eagerly join them. Every person is so kind and open, as each talk about his or her victories over previous failures in their lives. When it is my turn to talk, our Captain interrupts us, inviting everyone to view a large island we are passing. One of my crewmates asks her to tell us more about this mysterious island. She explains how this island is so famous for its baffling mountain, which many claims actually go into the heavens. Even the airplanes fly no closer than three miles from it, claiming the thick clouds prevent them from seeing its peak. This enigmatic tale creates an unsatisfying craving in our hearts. We begin begging our Captain to take us to this mountain. She pleads with us not to fall for this temptation, which will lead to our deaths. Our Captain pulls her ship into the dock on this island. We walk among the busy streets, stopping in a few stores. Our Captain tells us not to buy anything, as it will load down our mountain-climbing vehicle. We finally choose our vehicle and climb in while selecting our seats. I now noticed only five of us are in this vehicle. I ask our Captain what happened to the rest of our group. She reveals they changed their mind and decided to shop in the overwhelming number of available stores. She asks us once more if we are sure about taking this dangerous trip.

When she said dangerously, our eyes lit up in excitement. I began to slide back in my seat. Accordingly, the two women I was sitting between each grabbed me and asked if I were too scared for this adventure. I looked at them and shook my head no, and then I told them I was saving my energy for the fights with the monsters who lay ahead. I fletched my arm muscles, as I released a groan of relief and lay back in my seat pretending that I was now sleeping peacefully. The other man in our group fledged his muscles and told the woman beside him that he must also rest. In what appeared to be minutes we were beginning to rise up on our mountain. We began up this early dead mountain of rocks and burned tree stumps. Soon, we were passing people screaming on their way down for us not to go up this mountain.

This caused our group to yell for the Captain to go faster. I scanned the area around us and could find no logical reason for so much alarm. Even I was beginning to believe this was a sort of false panic. Up we went to the top of this mountain. The Captain took us up and slowly over the razor edged top. Our vehicle rocked on the top. We had no choice but to lean ahead while waiting for our front wheels to hit the rocks, so we can go forward into the unknown land before us. We rock our vehicle quickly and begin down into the mystery before us. As we successfully shake our front wheels, to the burned stone below us. Our Captain begins driving our vehicle extra speedily down the slippery mountain, notwithstanding we commence to wonder why she is driving so fast. I ask her to slow down now. She tells us that our brakes are no longer functioning. She believes the sharp razor mountain peak may have cut her break lines. This powerful woman yanks the steering wheel flipping our vehicle. Considering this all-terrain vehicle has no seatbelt, we went flying onto the stony surface. When our dust settled, we discovered the married couple with us now lay dead. Our Captain had a broken leg. I broke a long metal bar that was used as one of the vehicle's supports. I also pulled off a piece of the roofing canvas, and cut it into extended thin strips, using the sharp rock tips that covered our area.

We begin searching for a nearby road; nevertheless, we could not find one. Afterwards, we returned to our Captain to report our inability to find a road. She confesses not to know if a road actually exists on this side of the mountain, nor even to know how to get back once we come off this mountain. Subsequently, I explain to our group that we uncovered the myth that the peak was in the heavens. Our Captain confesses she did not go over at the peak, which was far off on a prolonged ridge. Consequently, when we considered two was already dead, and that we were lost and still had a long journey down in this dark. This puzzled me in that this side of the mountain was dark. We began walking down this steep mountain, pulling our Captain on the canvas I retrieved from our vehicle. As we continue to crawl, I discover a cave. Just as I spot it one of our women, spot a gang of apelike creatures walking pass us. We rush into our cave remaining quiet as the apes continue to pass us. I ask if any among our group wants us to leave this cave. They agree to follow me in this cave. Since the cave drops slowly, our Captain can walk. We continue deep into the cave, while being subjected to strange eerie noises that sent chills through our bodies. We continue walking for a few hours. I tell our group that we must be heading for the other side. Subsequently, our cave ends. I tell them to stay put and begin exploring a few of the side tunnels. Finally, I find one that might work, so I return to the main cave to gather our group. We begin our journey, as we walk through this darker side tunnel. Accordingly, our Captain warns us that our air is getting thinner. If we do not find an opening soon, we will die. One of our women faints, as she falls onto the ground. Now I must carry her, while the other women help our Captain to walk. We are in deep trouble and must find another way out.

The classroom

I am so close to death in the cave side tunnels. This was when life began to flash before my eyes. I wanted to get out of this dark world. Miraculously, I end in a classroom with plenty of air. I am in a science classroom with Asians. The language is no barrier as we speak the dreamland language. I glance around our classroom and notice everyone has a book, except for me. Our teacher continues to ask questions as no one answers. She is becoming angry. I slide over to a boy who is sitting beside me. I recognize he is a former classmate from my high school days, and is even a current friend on my Facebook. The teacher asks a question, in which I reduce to a keyword and request him to check the index. He becomes angry yelling at me to get back to my desk in my row. The teacher asks if we have a problem. I tell her that I do not have a book, and was trying to answer her questions, yet the previous friend beside me turns out to be a jerk. She asks him for his view. He gives no answer, causing the teacher to ask once more. Accordingly, she calls me to the front of the classroom as she walks to her podium. She gives me a book. I thank her and return to my desk. Accordingly, I now lean over on my American friend who betrayed him and promise revenge. The teacher angrily asks one more question, warning us that if no one answers she will keep us in class for the entire weekend. I wonder to myself if she can do this. I see a school handbook and realize this is a resident school, as we have all moved away from our homes to attend this institution. They have absolute control over our lives and can do anything they wish to us. I have never been a slave before in my life.

The teacher asks the next question; I determine the keyword and rush to the index flip to the page and answer our teacher's question. Our teacher jumps for joy. I see our classmates begin to smile. They wad paper into balls and begin throwing them at my former high school classmate. Our teacher does not release us from her pressure cooker yet. She tells us that if we do not answer this next question, she will keep us in her science lab. I know her labs are intensive, since our professor micromanages each of us while in her lab. I cannot believe how much she knows about this material and can answer each question faster than a computer can put it on a screen. She actually lives this subject and has my utmost respect. I feel sad that she never married nor has any children. Occasionally we see her walking around our campus with many of her nieces and nephews' children. Rumor around our campus is that she is exceptionally generous to her family. I know she has much love to give, and for her life since she is married her profession. She asks the next question, which proves to be a difficult one that requires a subjective answer. I find three keywords, make notes in my tablet, and then tie them together. I raise my hand, as our professor's face turns red. We know that if we raise our hand and give a wrong answer she will flunk us from this course immediately. She asks me to reconsider, remembering the consequences. I report that I am ready. She tells me to continue. I tell her this question is answered based on four factors. I list these four factors and the exact response for my final answer, which I give to her. The answer takes ten minutes. Consequently, our professor congratulates me on my answer, as my foreign classmates begin to clap for me. I see nothing but smiles, as they now throw their pens at my former American high school classmate. Our professor begins to smile at my classmates. Apparently, she is proud about the way her foreign students are showing their appreciation for my command of this subject. I can tell she does not support the rejection my American classmate gave me, especially when considering she is a foreigner as well. She tells our class that we will receive three bonus questions and each one that is answered correctly will result in a one-point addition to our final scores. I answer each of these questions, the ending two barely getting my hand up before many of the other students. They were scanning the index the same as me. I think their problems lie in identifying the keywords. We gained three extra points on our final grade.

Trailer court on mother's farm

I discover after class that this was the first time our professor has ever given bonus points. Considering most of my classmates are on the verge of flunking, these three points might allow them to pass. I usually go straight to the dining hall after class. I notice twelve of my female foreign classmates following me. They are trying to be invisible, yet are walking in the middle of the sidewalk. When I turn around to look at them, they scramble bumping into each another. This is so innocent and funny. They sit, in groups of four at the three tables around my table, where I eat alone. I search for a change to say something to them, yet these female students are pretending not to be watching me. I know they are, nevertheless; I am thankful to be having this much possible attention. Sadly, I float out of this dream. This dream was so much better than being in a dark cave in the belly of our Earth. I now drift back to my late mother's farm, notwithstanding her rear yard is packed with mobile homes. I ask my mother why there are so many trailers packed so tight over her farm. Her valley is packed, as is her ridge and her field is packed beside her pond. There must be at least five hundred mobile homes here. Her land is nothing but packed dirt now, as I can see no grass. I ask my father who walks up beside me, and he tells me this is from all the underground septic tanks, gas line, water lines, and advanced electric and communication lines. This must be why I do not see any lines above ground. He explains this is for safety reasons, in that so many lines strung over the area. They fear that if one of the lines was broken the children could be at risk.

My next question is who all these people are. My sister is beside me now. She explains the price of land, and homes is too much for anyone to afford, and with the spike in interest rates, those who had variable rates could not pay their mortgages. One family offered her enough money to buy one-hundred used mobile homes, in which she packed on her farm. She rents these to working families now that she set up all the hookups. It was a risk; however, these living units were rented in the first day at one-hundred fifty percent what she was asking. The next day, as the families were moving in, bank representatives came rushing to her offering loans with a low fixed rate for another four hundred mobile homes and their hookups. My mother's lawyers made the bank promise they will never foreclose on this loan. The bank that reluctantly granted my mother's demands made the loan. My mother was not going to fall upon greed in this financial maneuver. She refused to charge anyone more than the others did; therefore, an increase in rent for the new applicants was out of the question. The local county treasurer tried to raise her property taxes twice what the current code allowed. I notice something that catches me by surprise; none of the homes had under paneling. I asked my brother-in-law why all the homes have no under paneling. He explains they wanted to keep this land open as much as possible for the cats and dogs who roam this farm. They fear that other wild animals would hide in these places and prey on their domesticated animals. This made sense to me, thereby relaxing my apprehensions. I notice a beautiful new seventy-foot by fourteen-foot wide mobile home sitting in front of a row of parked trailers. I ask my niece whose home this is and why it is not parked as the other homes are.

My niece explains they are not able to hook it up as various parts; especially the water fittings and hoses are missing. I ask her how long this home has been sitting here. She tells me for about three months now. I slide under this trailer trying to see if I can find the problem. It is too confusing for me, so I go and bring my father to investigate this obstacle. He rushes under it, first in the front, then in the middle and finally in the rear. He returns to the middle and calls my niece's husband to crawl underneath with him. He shows them a strange cone shaped metal filter and shows them this should be changed at least twice each year, and this would keep their heating and water systems cleaned for decades. My father believes the movers unconnected with the hose the connectors. He uses a tape measure to determine the connector size. Once they find the connector, they can match the hose. He measures the ground hose connector, telling them the opposite end of the hose must screw into this size connector and for them to test it before they leave the store. Subsequently, they ask him where they can find this equipment. He tells them about a store in McConnelsville, Ohio, which is about twenty-five miles west of Caldwell on Ohio State Route seventy-eight. It is just less than forty miles west on Ohio State Route sixty from Lowell, which is around five miles from the hilltop my mother's farm is. Later in the day, my mother comes rushing to my father screaming at the top of her lungs about how terrible he is to suggest her grandchild travel so far for a hose and fittings. He argues back that if they want these parts, they need to take responsibility. He is in no mood to help those who will not help themselves. Notwithstanding, he accuses my mother of purposely withholding any help to keep this new home vacant. She argues this is ridiculous. I tell my niece that her, and her husband need to get this equipment. They tell me this is impossible, considering they have no vehicle. I ask how this is possible. They explain that no vehicles are allowed on this farm, for fear of hitting a child. There is a parking lot about one mile up the road, where everyone who had vehicles parked there. They would walk up the road and get in their vehicles to go to work and return. This still does explain why she does not have a vehicle. I ask her about not having a vehicle. She gives a vague answer.

Gunfight in a mystery village

I eagerly await her response, nonetheless; they remain quiet. I now notice everyone is surrounding me as I hear chants for me to leave. Subsequently, I find myself squirming in my bed. I take 1,800 mg of gabapentin each day for my restless legs syndrome; therefore, I find myself shaking my legs throughout the night as they continue to fall asleep on me. I shake my legs and mysteriously find myself riding a horse with a beautiful woman on each side of me. I do appreciate how my dark world appears most times to give me two women to join in my adventures. I believe this is to prevent me from being alone with merely one, which could run into a danger of becoming romantically involved. Fortunately, I have a weakness when making my advances to a woman for a relationship. She must be alone, because I am too shy to face more than one, and especially twelve in a previously dark adventure. These two women are kind and jolly, as they are excited and laughing. Suddenly, a car rushes dangerously close to us while they are beeping their horns as if to make sure that we knew they were passing us. Our horses spook and throw us to the ground, as I soon discover how muddy, our ground is. We slide through the mud, as our mud soaked bodies became hard to identify. Subsequently, a gang of men come rushing pass us, grabbing one of my women and taking her into their custody. By the time, we realize what is happening; they jump in a van and rush through the log cabin town in front of us. We jump back on our horses and follow the van's tracks through the mud. The mud came in handy this one time.

As we frantically chase this vanishing van, a few men come rushing out to warn us that if we keep up this chase, we will face dangers we do not want to encounter. We look inside their saloon and see an aged actor and actress performing. I recognize them as being in many movies and television shows. Further examination, reveals an entire cast of actors, many who are recognizable with the minor exception of being aged. One of the actors is tossed from the saloon. I jump off my horse and rush to his aid. I tell him we must hurry and find a van that has a woman from our group they kidnapped. He offers us his truck. We put our horses in a stable and plan our exploratory journey. As we begin to pull out, I am in front of this truck checking the fluid levels and putting certain rejuvenating oils on the hoses and belts. Another truck comes rushing by us, blowing their horns, which gives me heads up to stand parallel with our truck. As they pass by us, they toss a taped bundle of dynamite that land on my actor friend's lap. I immediately stick my hand in our truck, grab the dynamite and toss it in the back of the pickup who threw it in our truck. It exploded at once, destroying the vehicle and its crew as the gas magnified the damage. We celebrated our victory until I realized we had no one to torture to discover who wanted us dead. I jumped in the driver's seat with my remaining female and our actor, while we once more began our rescue mission. The people in this village come rushing out throwing things at us. They are cursing us, vowing revenge. Afterwards, they begin making fun of us. With this, our actor friend, named John tells Lucy, my remaining female friend that if they are laughing at us, we may be safe in that they will not chase us. We drive around this village looking for the van, making sure we avoid the street where the people were trying to stone us. I am starting to worry that we may not find them. John tells me not to worry, because they will have to leave sometime. The village had merely one entrance and exit. John recommended we guard this entrance.

I thought this was a great idea. I saw a small country-style restaurant near the entrance and asked John and Lucy to if they were famished. John is a big man, so I suspect he is always hungry. We enter this restaurant and are guided to a table by a beautiful waitress. She gladly takes our order. They have excellent selections on their menu. I notice the live musical entertainment that is filling our room with traditional country music. While eating our humongous meal, I notice Hank Williams with his daughter and Hank Williams, Junior with his daughter singing together on the stage. They are actually singing with great harmony. I find myself enjoying this entertainment. Upon closer evaluation, I recognize the woman who is posing as Hank Williams, Junior's daughter as Miley Cyrus. I am so surprised that she is singing country music. Notwithstanding, when I consider her father is a famous country singer who had an acky breaky heart. I rise to clap for them when they finish their song. John grabs me and pulls me down to the table warning me that it is rude to clap for singers here. Accordingly, since all singers and actors are known professionals to cheer for one would require clapping for all. The question comes up; to how long they should receive their applause. This ruins the purpose they retired here, to get away from all the attention. The patrons begin throwing food and silverware at us. We prepare to exit when I notice that Hank, and her three members are following us. Once outside, I confront him asking if he intends to harm us. We pile into our pickup, with Lucy, Hank Senior and his daughter in the truck bed. I notice certain rifles beside us, and pick one up, loading it with bullets. Just as I finish loading it, we come under fire. I slowly shoot back one aimed gunshot at a time and kill six of our attackers. Suddenly, the police begin chasing us. I am in no mood for this, as they force us to pull over our truck. I get out of the truck and go to face them asking why they are chasing us. They begin reading phony charges and tell me we are going to prison for the remainder of our lives. The police begin shooting at me. Bullets are flying around me. I duck beside a nearby car. Afterwards, I open a door, pull my pistol, and shoot two of them. They hit the ground, yet one points his pistol at Hank. I fire my unused bullets through their heads. This causes the remaining two to begin shooting at me. Hank and Lucy use our rifles, and each knocks off one. I turn around and see the van that kidnapped Susie drives pass us.

I begin firing my pistol at the driver and hit him three times in his head. He crashes the van. I notice John is ripping at the back door of this van. He rips it completely off while Hank opens the driver's door and shoots two other men who are firing at me. He has snuck up behind them killing them with ease. John pulls Susie out of the van. I ask her what they did to her. She tells me her answer will be available once she has proof we will not return. Notwithstanding, I ask her why she is so concerned. Susie reports that a few things are better left in the secrets of time. I explain to John that we must leave this village and ask if he wants to join us. Miley agrees with me that John should go with us. She asks him if he wanted to perform to a real audience. She tells him even an audience that is booing is better than an audience that simply sits there. I agree with Miley and inform John that his performance was extremely entertaining. He should be proud of his advanced skills. They understand, subsequently Miley asks if she can join us. Once we leave the village, Miley confesses that if she had to sing another country song, she would go crazy. I do appreciate my accomplices having names this time. It feels more like the conscious world by them having names. This is the tricky part, how this dark world feels almost like the light world. It is real in my sleep, and in my sleep, my day world is a myth. I ask Miley to sing a song that will put me to sleep. She does a wonderful job, as I fall back into my sleep, waving goodbye to my inspiring vanishing friends.

The prisoners and couple's retreat

Miley does a fantastic job of putting me to sleep. She veers away from her Wrecking Ball thumping to a soft mellow tale. My sleepiness does not last long, as if find myself walking in a hiking club that is walking through the mountains. I wonder, which is better, mountains or log cabins as both provide excellent hiding places for those who wish to attack me. I notice we have a large group of couples, except for two big black men. They appear so out of place among this group. They are also each carrying a large red machine. This red intermittently flashes with black in that one minute it is a pale red, then it turns murky. The two black men are sweating profusely and appear to be on the verge of passing out and dropping to the ground. My wife is laughing and speaking to me informing me about so many fun things we can do. I feel sorry for the two men and ask if I can carry one of the red machines. I carry one for an hour and then swap off with the other man. Surprisingly, these machines are not heavy. I can carry them with ease. I pretend they are a little difficult, so as not to disgrace them. My wife becomes angry because I am sticking close to the trail and not playing in the available terrain. She went rushing to our guide to report this. Our guide comes back and tells me to stay where I am. She has several in her crew retrieve the prisoners. Once we are all assembled, she warns the prisoners that if they do not take back the red machines and promise never to pawn their sentence of on anyone else, she will report them to the court and get their sentence tripled and then put in solitary confinement. She turns to me and tells us I am banned from the tour. My wife looks at her and asks how she can take me from her and the group. She explains that I was only trying to help two men whom I thought needed assistance. Our group leader asks my wife to explain why I aided two known prisoners. I ask her to explain that if they are such bad prisoners, then why they are traveling unsupervised with married couples in the middle of a mountain. I tell her this is the same as saying they have a get out of jail-free card, or at best not a great danger to society.

Continuing to hold her position our guide comments how happy she will be when she witnesses the police taking me somewhere that I can carry many truly heavy packages. My wife slaps this betrayer on her face and tells her that those police will have more trouble than they are expecting, beginning with cleaning up her splattered remains. I ask her if she explains to me why those red boxes are so light. I reveal that she knew this and as such participated in a public conspiracy. She tells me to hold my horses, in that I am trying to make something out of nothing. She winks at my wife and me and tells us we need to start our journey if we hope to live through the dangers ahead of us. Our guide comments the law enforcement knows the red machines are light. They simply want the public to see them suffering and in pain. She explains the justice department's wishes are her commands. I tell her that I will never trust her, and she is a wolf in sheep's clothing. She tosses out a set of golf clubs and a bag of golf balls. As she pulls off, I spot a narrow rock covered valley to our left. Accordingly, I confess to my wife, I need to drive many balls to release our stress. She is worried about our security once it gets dark. I explain that we are in no danger, and with me driving golf balls all over the mountain side, most predators will be apprehensive at best. I drive about fifty golf balls over our hillside, and then I grab two clubs, giving one to my wife. We start down the mountain, walking for about one hour when another vehicle with two men in it and stop to give us a ride. We arrive at the base of the mountain and walk into the local pub. I ask if the tour with the prisoners is back yet. The bartender tells me they just received a call they will be here in about twenty minutes. I order fish and chips for us and relax waiting for the tour to arrive. Meanwhile, I call the police and tell them I want to press charges because she violated the terms of our tour contract, placing us in danger, and making false charges against me. Subsequently, I discover the ranges of charges available in the dark worlds are much more creative than in the real world.

This is remarkable in that police also arrive with the tour guide, as if they are going to battle each other. Then various police dressed in white arrives. They dismiss the police, and give my previous guide a summons telling her, "You have been served." I look at these white police, and they explain my charges will be presented in court. I smile at her and tell her we will have our day before a judge. It is important that people know for reasons not briefed on before the tour, she will cast them out with no means to survive against the deadly predators that roam the mountain. She accuses me of exaggerating this situation. My wife asks her if she remembers, "We need to start our journey if we hope to live through the dangers ahead of us." The guide shakes her head and tells her she believes the judge will be more understanding, especially when considering predators seldom visit this mountain. I tell her this is irrelevant in that it is the reasonable belief such a danger could exist. Just as we are preparing to speak with other people, I decide to build my case by yelling at the prisoners. The reporters, who are covering this return, since the public is still divided over this program, immediately come rushing around us. I accuse the prisoners of faking their struggles while carrying the red machines. The prisoners become angry and attack me. My wife takes her golf club and hits them. I rush to her side and begin hitting them as they attack my wife. Fortunately, the police open fire on them, and cause them to hit the ground. The ambulance rushed them to the prison hospital. After their surgery, they will go to solitary. Lawyers contact us about a settlement with the guide. Subsequently, bleeding hearts from the public is in our yard screaming at us accusing me of harassing a guiltless man. I yell back that if they were innocent, then why were they prisoners. I tell my wife, we will abandon any foolish quest for justice and go for the money from this day.

The spinners

Unfortunately, these dreams have a way of ending it, at their will, and this adventure finished before we could spend our money. I returned to my day world after this mountain challenge finished. My days are now for resting, and the normal search for the things to keep my life rolling. Today, I took Billie Jean to an eye doctor and then took her eyeglass prescription to Walmart and got her two pairs of eyeglasses. I was hoping to get these glasses before she returned to high school next week, only to discover the lab gets three days off, or the remainder of this week as their holiday time. This leaves me spinning in place, at first thankful that I could get her eye doctor appointment so fast, merely to get set back is the easy part of this process, the lab is making them. We purchased Billie Jean a new comfortable set for her bed. I saw the eight-piece number, so I figured it had everything, only to get home and discover it does not come with a sheet, although the package cover shows a bed with a matching sheet on it. Everything must be based upon deception, so with that in mind, we will go back and buy a matching sheet tomorrow. Being civilized, I must give them another chance to rob me. This night, I take a few sleeping pills and quickly drift once again into the world that those who profit secretly through deception are not acclaimed as saints by those who enforce the laws. I awaken in a large open field with a calm breeze floating over me. I look around and see no one else. Consequently, I have gone from twelve wonderful females following me, down to two lovely angels, dropping to one wife the last dream. This time, it appears as if I will be on my own. I cannot see a sun or anything producing light from the sky; however, I can easily see everything. I walk around this green-less meadow. Even though it is not green, it is a lovely brown and has an abundance of wildlife bouncing around in it. This is a rare treat seeing so much energy and excitement bouncing around me. I may be finally in a peaceful, enjoyable dream. I know that such dreams are possible.

Nevertheless, I notice many small piles of dirt forming. I wonder what this is. Afterwards, heads begin to appear from these piles. Next arms and finally complete bodies rise up from underneath the ground. They are men and women; however, even though they are nude, they have no genitals. They rather appear like mannequins, although they can move and have smooth skin. They remain at attention in their individual positions. I presently hear selected peaceful music filling this meadow. This is extremely relaxing until they all rise about two feet above the ground. The music stops and all these people begin spinning in midair. I am so puzzled. They appear not to have any desire to fight or cause harm. They stop spinning, slowly replant their feet on the ground, and look at each other and go through all the functions of a conversation even though I cannot hear any speaking. In fact, they do not even move their mouths. They do move their hands and make the other facial expressions that people go through when talking. Subsequently, they each move to another spot as if rotating one position. Afterwards, they all rise again and begin spinning. They all stop at the same time and drop to the ground. This meadow is still quiet and peaceful. These spinners repeat their spinning three more times. I am beginning to wonder about this oddity. I have never experienced something like this before, and I do not realize how to react. They ignore me as if I am not even in this meadow. Nevertheless, I have no information that would suggest what their function is, or why they were created. I feel that such an existence like theirs would be miserable. This last time when rising they do not spin, but instead continue to rise, eventually going into the clouds. Strangely, as they drift into the clouds, I begin to feel lonely, even though when they are here around me, they ignore me. Finally, I look up in the sky above me and see them returning. They left with nothing and returned with nothing. This time they land on the ground, have their conversation, and then rise about six feet and explode. Blood and body parts are flying everywhere. Now my meadow is covered in red blood. These deaths, just like their lives had no reason or purpose.

Journey to the Jerrilamo

I translate their spinning is as we encounter our challenges and their ascension to the clouds as the highest point in their lives, and return is their decline. It truly is confusing, as I prefer to be in situations that are real and have a purpose. This left me unprepared for the next adventure suddenly comes upon me, except this time I was drifting through space passing worlds as one would pass trees while driving in a car on a Sunday afternoon. Afterwards, I begin the orbit a large planet. I can hear thunder and gushing winds below me. The wind is like the whirling sand-packed desert storm. I find joy in the fact this is the dark world and as not the day world, because in the day world this grinder would chop me to pieces. I fall into this chaotic cyclone and begin shooting like a bullet across this darkening world. In what feels like one hour I finally drop below the wind zone. The absence of the wind stabilized me in one position, causing me to fall to the ground. It was wonderful to be on the ground, although I have no idea what planet, I am on now. This world is the normal pale rock color, and unlike my previous adventure, is absent from any small wildlife. In fact, I can see merely empty houses, buildings, and roads. My eyes can scan cobwebs in the corners. Accordingly, I can just sense that various sorts of life existed here at one time and found myself confused as to why I would be brought to a vacant world. Surprisingly, I keep sinking into the ground. This is initially puzzling, especially since I have not fallen into a surface as I am currently.

I continue sinking into the surface until I find an open area. Upon entering this area, I see an ocean of faces; all packed too tight against each another. I am fortunate in that my body does not reach the crowded floor. Nevertheless, from above I saw many side tunnels all packed with faces. I witness a small group holding hands as they are apparently concentrating on something. My mind then receives a message, which explains that the Jerrilamo communicates only in mind talk and through spells, enchantments, and rituals. They ceased speaking physically when they evolved from their days in the light world. I look in shock when realizing they are all talking with each another. They appear to be shaking now as many begin to vanish. I hear them chatting that one of their enemies is attacking them currently. Their leader calls for them to prepare to fight, as they are presently going to start vanishing them. They published this through their secret channels to make sure they were immediately distributed through the grapevines. At this time, rumors of a large war abounded. The groups began to line up on the opposite sides of the lines, with all facing off against the Jerrilamo. The join around the banner that claims the Jerrilamo are the fathers of evil. The Jerrilamo created slogans attesting to a world of wicked trying to stop their righteousness. The enemies of the Jerrilamo struck hard and quickly, devoting a high percentage of their resources to unleash a powerful blow. The Jerrilamo withstood this massive blast, almost as if they knew about it and was somewhat prepared. Even though they might not have been surprised, they had no defenses strong enough to withstand such a comprehensive invasion. The lone hope for the Jerrilamo proved to provide them a lifeboat, in the opposing forces fell into confusion and disorganization, and in several cases, was attacking each mistaking the Jerrilamo for their allies. I witnessed lights flashing across the caverns before me and striking each many times with both vanishing.

Confusion is the sole companion I have at this time. I see so many lights doing too many different things; therefore, it is impossible for me to understand what is happening. I depend entirely on the words that I hear in my head. I do not prefer to communicate this way. I believe it will always be strange for me. I ask why there is no purpose to any life here, much as the spinners confused me in my previous adventure. Consequently, a wonderful looking royal family with four sons comes floating by me. They appear to be terrified, even though surrounded by a large Army. Their Army shuffles them into a hidden tunnel under their castle. I am still trying to determine how they can have a large palace in these underground caves. Guess this planet is composed differently from the one I have spent my life. This royal family now comes under a storm of burning arrows, nevertheless; they crawl into special chambers surviving this attack. Accordingly, I see a vision of this family being burned by continuous lights. I feel they are innocent and do not deserve to be executed such as this. Next, I appear before them and profess to lead them to safety. Oddly, the family thanks me for my service and prepares to follow me. We drift through the open caves rising to the surface. Once on the surface, I guide them to a nearby hilltop. I hope here we can scout the local area for security purposes. The terrain here is hideous at best. One of the Princes tells me, through mind talk, that once great Empires, which battled each for power and bounty. They destroyed their world, therefore, causing all to perish, making the air and water poison, killing all who drank it or breathed the air. This was when they moved underground and slowly over so many years, they evolved from flesh to energy, or light. I explain to this Prince that it is strange they evolved to light in a world so dark. With no warning, a giant bolt of lightning strikes one of the Princes resulting in his light vanishing. I look at the King and Queen as they begin to cry. I shine some of my light on them, hoping to brighten their dark pain filled hearts. The King reveals we will stay here until the great wars under the surface have finished, and his Army comes to guide them back to their castle. This adventure continues to hide from me what its plot or message is. Meanwhile, I will relax here with a royal family and enjoy a few boring royal topics. That should put me back to sleep rather quickly.

Siberian classroom

Through the light while spinning and flashing around the open universe, I flow as a log in a rushing river. To my pleasant surprise, the colors of the universe are now vivid and even inspiring. I attribute this to the feeling one receives when returning home. I feel the elements of the previous war zone break off me as a crust of mud while walking through a hot desert. I descended through a rainbow of atmospheric layers while each change in color slowed my fall significantly, until a sluggish easy floating glide softly placed my feet on the ground.

Fortunately, the dark world has a large range of temperature tolerance. I see a white snow filled land, surrounding a medium-sized village in the cold northern lands. I believe this to be northerly from the way the colorful lights are reflected from the surface, plus the amount of open land with no lights emitting from other villages. The special lights appearing from possible farms are scarce as well. I walk the streets alone, spotting few vehicles until I approach a large, at least six-story high white brick building. It has a grayish and orange sign not far from the road, which reads Siberian Federal University in English with what I suspect to be the same words appearing in another language on the gray side of the sign with welcome appearing in seven languages on the right third of the sign. The sign also reveals an Internet address on the lower portion of the orange third of the sign. I deduce from this sign that I am not in the United States, and from the university's name must be in Siberia, and that they have the Internet available. Therefore, even though I may be way out in the boondocks, civilization is simply a keyboard from me. With eagerness, I rush into this building.

Upon entering this building, a small group of college-aged girls is saying, "Hello Dmitry," while looking in my direction. Since they are extremely pretty, with their winter coats unbuttoned, I am hoping my name is Dmitry. I casually look around me to ensure they are not talking to someone else, then spin around, and say hello back to them. They laugh and accuse me of being funny again. I walk over to a bright locker that has my name on it and open it. As I open it, the brightness fades, thus I can see this is my locker. I notice my books are in piles of three, with notebooks dividing them. I grab the first book, notwithstanding; three books fall into my hand. I look at my schedule that is taped inside my wall locker. My schedule lists my next three classes being in the same classroom, then the following three in another classroom, while the final are in my last classroom. I appear to have only two days of classes each week, yet each class is ninety minutes. This will be a long day. I go into my first class and notice my name shining from a seat in the second row and walk over to it. I sit in it as they fill in with other girls. I count only four other boys in this class. So far, the situation appears to be just what dreams are made. A girl sits beside me. I notice her name is Ruf and complained to her about these long class days. She tells me that I never complained much about them as a junior and that now I am a Senior I should know there is nothing we can do about this. It is too hard for the government to clean the roads every day, so they clean them twice a week, so we can attend classes. The school saves energy costs by merely heating the school enough to keep water pipes from breaking. She pours me a cup of hot coffee and asks me if I want a little vodka in it. I tell her it would be best if I wait until the halfway mark before beginning to drink. I notice about half the seats are still empty as our first teacher comes in, a tall older thin man, who speaks with a low slow voice. I tell Ruf that it will be a miracle if I make it through this class still awake. She tells me if I do, it will be a first for me. My sole advantage today is this material is new for me. One hour into this class, I look around and everyone else is fast asleep. I look at the professor who tells me not to talk, or he will expel me. I shake my head and join my classmates in their sleep. When our bell rings, which sounds lake machine guns firing; everyone awakens and stands up stretching their arms.

I ask Ruf what is happening. She tells me the next professor is a monster, who kidnaps students and takes them to his dungeon for food. Everyone gets his or her books and red notebook out. I cannot find my red notebook. Ruf tells me to open a notebook. The monster comes in and looks around quickly, then grabs his ruler. He stands in front of me and hits me hand, yelling where my red notebook is. I tell him my walrus ate it. The students remain completely quiet and do not move. He tells me to prepare for him a one-hundred-page report on walruses and email it to him tomorrow before lunch. I copy and paste the pages from the Internet, then translate it through my online translator into Portuguese and email it to him after class. I am betting that not too many Portuguese live in Siberia. These ninety minutes of hell ends. I follow him to the top of the stairs, and give him a hard push from behind. The students move away to avoid him, as he bounces from the steps, I slip back to our classroom and get a cup of vodka from Ruf. He quickly returns to our room to see if I am here. Fortunately, there were many students still in the hallway, so I could slip back in before him. He asks me if I have been here. I told him that he was not important enough to take away my vodka time. He appears to accept this and storm away. I look around at my classmates who are all smiling at me. I wink at them. I ask Ruf about our next professor. She reports this class many students like, as her lectures are exciting and informative. She walks in and asks the class if Dmitry and Ruf are married yet. They all laugh, while Ruf stands up and kisses me telling her she if trying everything. The professor asks me what my problem is. I tell her a few things take more than a kiss. My classmates begin laughing at this. Ruf asks the professor what I could mean by this. She tells Ruf to stop by her office, and she will let her borrow specific books. I can already tell this will be a great class indeed.

The continuous laughing worked up a great appetite for lunch, yet when we broke for lunch Ruf drug me out to the dining room and ask her in front of a cafeteria packed with women what we needed to do to become married. I could feel their tension, and knew if I gave a male macho answer, they would eat me alive. I tell her such a question can solely be answered by a professor, since I do not have her vast knowledge and command over so many books to chance giving an answer that may not be completely fair to the female needs, and I for one always take the feminine need extremely important. The women in this cafeteria backed down, as I reached over to her ear and whispered asking her what she was trying to do to me. She kisses my cheek and tells me she wanted to see how I functioned under pressure. I explain to her that it would be better for her to cast me naked in the worse part of the Siberian winter than in the warm cafeteria packed with hot-blooded women. Ruf goes in our professor's office, while I wait outside with her many girlfriends.

She returns ten minutes later with four books and asks me if women truly did things like this. I tell her that I must first look at the books and see what she is referring to in these books. I glance at the pages and confess that I do not know for sure, we may have to practice tonight so we can determine if there is any validity to these claims. Her friends look at the book and ask if they can join us. I tell them they are all welcomed; however, Ruf tells them to all stay away. I ask her how we will know if we are doing it right, unless we have scientific feedback from impartial observers. Ruf tells me we will find a way and that her friends will not be impartial observers. They complain she is being too harsh. I go to speak as she kicks me commanding that I shut up. We head to our next class, which is, 'cultures of the world.' The teacher enters and gives each of us a baton and began leading our class in songs. They started making cheers to guide us in our songs. All seemed to be happy, so I joined them. I find that when my classmates are happy I am happy as well.

After thirty minutes of singing, the professor begins his lesson. I confess to Ruf that I did not know these songs. She confides with me that, as usual, no one knows the songs. Ruf then asks me if I am feeling strange today. I tell her I must have drunk too much vodka last night. A voice in my head reminds me this class is about how people in other countries live. The next two classes were about law, which turns out to be our major. The final lecture was an art class, which turned out to be interesting. After class, Ruf asked me if we were going to my house first or her house. I told her it would be best if we went to my house first. Ruf tells me to wait at the door while she starts her car and lets it warm up first. Luck had it this was her week to drive. I would have to find a way to her house before next week. As I waited for her to come back into the school, a large group of girls formed around me, as two more rushed out to start their cars. The common practice was for the students to travel in groups on the road in case someone had an accident. Life in this part of the world was harsh, yet by sticking together the chance of survival increased to such a degree that no one would travel in the winter unless in a small convoy of at least two vehicles. Cell phones had too many 'no service' spots to be dependable. I was somewhat surprised as we got out at my house both cars of girls followed us into my house. We had ten guests with us as we entered my house. If this is truly going to be a wonderful dream, and I was, bringing in nine college girls with me my family could not be home. My heart finally started beating again when Ruf cheered that my parents were still at my grandparents. She asked if they were going to be at my grandparents until next week as I told her earlier. I looked at the three books we brought home and my nine test subjects and confessed to her that I hoped that was still true. Ruf asks her friends why they are still here. They plead with her to share the new knowledge she will learn about me. Ruf explains to them; she is too scared to ask me to shame myself for their personal knowledge. I tell her sometimes a man must make a great sacrifice to prove to the woman, he loves that he is willing to give up all he has for her glory.

She begins to cry, telling me she was almost ready to ask me; however, after I told her how much she meant to me, she no longer can ask me for such a great sacrifice. Many of her friends begin to cry. I tell Ruf that we must live with these friends, and if they are important to us, we need to care for them as we care for ourselves. Ruf agrees as her classmates begin cheering. I open the first page, which shows a man with three women, and they are all nude. Accordingly, I hand the book to our classmates and tell them I believe we are supposed to be nude. One of the girls is concerned that we have more than three females, and that it might not work with nine. I tell her to look at the next pages and add everyone together, and then it should balance. Next, one of our classmates tells us that we only have one man. Ruf reveals her mother told her that all boys had the same type of genitals. Several other classmates agree they heard somewhat the same reports. Accordingly, I explain that if they see me, they will know basically, how all boys look down there. Consequently, Ruf declares that no one can see her man unless she is nude. As the clothes begin to hit our floor, I start to believe this is going to be one of the best dreams to date. Then I am hit by the bomb hidden in this blessing. After we all strip, I discover we have no genitals, nor do our breasts have nipples. To my surprise, I am the lone one who cannot see our genitals. They all see a male genital. This does not turn out to be the sole disappointment, which are the women are future lawyers and are trained to investigate every situation in detail. They have me twisted into every position they find in the three books, as they swap between each another as my exploration partner. We work late into the evening, as their parents continue to call them; they report they are working on an important case study. They put their classmates on the phone, which eases the parents. We know their parents will can each other to verify who is where. This is why each gives their classmates' names. The mere size of this group attests, they are being great students. I am actually feeling good with the intense interest they have in this subject matter. I am satisfied their curiosity is replaced with fact, so they will not fall prey to slick talkers. They have knowledge as a secure shield now. They talk to Ruf about forming a new club as a sign of their unity and protection from boys pestering them. They are all going to print on their shirts, "Dmitry's Angels." They will explain to their fathers that this is protection from boys, so they can devote more time to their studies. When asked who Dmitry is, they will answer, "Ruf's fiancé," and that this is her idea. My benefit is having nine girls with my name on them.

Readjustment

I traveled the heavens two dreams early, came back to Earth and had nine angels take my name in a story clean enough to share in a Sunday School class. This dream puts me back in the U.S. Air Force in the mid - 1980s. I am walking with my special girlfriend as we discuss how life we be for us living apart from each other. We are in South Carolina, and I will be going back to Ohio. The sole thing I can think about is graduating from college as I let a special love slip away into eternity. I finish my college and enter the Army working my way up to Sergeant First Class, which is equal to a Master Sergeant in the Air Force. Where this dream shifts away from my real life is rather than retiring in 1995, I go back to the Air Force. The switch can merely offer me an E3 rank, a significant drop from my E7 Army rank. My first Air Force duty has me giving away Air Force flyers in a local mall. Soldiers who knew me, plus a few airmen, which knew me from the late 70s, approach me asking what I did wrong to be punished so severely. I explain to them that I wanted to retire from the Air Force. My first four years of military were with the Air Force, thereby making my adjustment to the Army somewhat of a nightmare. The longing for those earlier days continued to haunt me over the years. I gave up too much for my college degrees, and the Army promotion boards were punishing me for this. The President came up with an early release program for Senior Noncommissioned Officers from the Army with at least fifteen years of active duty. I worked out a deal with higher ups to re-enter the Air Force instead of retiring. The purpose of this early out was to create promotions by opening positions. This was why they could merely offer me E3. I did not realize the tremendous misery this was going to cause me. When they put me out in the open right off the bat, the impact hit hard before I had time to make my adjustment.

I am fortunate on this first assignment in that a female E3 is working with me, and she is kind. I can speak with her openly. The girl can think fast on her feet. One of my past soldiers begins to harass me demanding to know what I did to get a court martial. Her name is Sony, and she tells my past friend that I shot a machine gun, emptying an entire magazine in our Colonel's office forcing the Colonel to hide under his desk. My past friend's face turned red, and he left at once, thinking I was a psychopath. I ask Sony if this is wise. She tells me if I want to keep him away from us. She pulls out a plastic Air Force rifle that we have on hand so new recruits can get a feel for it, or many have a picture taken with these weapons. My next harassment heckles at me for about twenty minutes, until Sony tells him; I raped her in our commander's office. We did not know the commander was taking a nap in his closet. This got the heckler away from us. With this, I call our Sergeant, which we need to be relieved. Sony tells him about the negative attention we are creating. She agrees and puts us on a detail in the company area. When our duty ends, Sony tags along with me to our dining facility. I thank her for the help this day. After we finish eating, we go back to my room and chat. She tells me, which sergeants and officers are creeps and, which ones are kind. I feel fine with this working relationship and agree to meet her for our physical training in the morning. I decide to review my enlistment contract and discover a few benefits. I will make E4 in five months and E5 six months after that. They will give me E6 six months later and E7 when I have two years of additional service. They will give me as my date of rank the day I pinned on E7 in the Army. Therefore, this may not be as bad as I originally projected. I begin to think about this Sony with me now, and realize she is the spitting image of a Lasonia I served with in the Army. I discover the Air Force has now copied many of the Army military training programs, such as Physical Training or PT. I find many of the airmen I serve with having the faces of those whom I formerly served with in the Army. These flashes cause my stress level to skyrocket. My last duties I see myself begin to fade and float back to my conscious. As I continue to float back, I feel myself once more gaining control over my life. The day world offers me control over my life, yet no control over the world around me, where my unconscious gives me no control over the world, or myself wherever that may be. I know that life will offer me new adventures, which are just a few winks away.

Beta

I sat at my computer thinking about the wide assortment of adventures, that my first week of dream analysis provided me. I have experienced many challenging situations that put a strain on my emotions. I struggled through worlds where I had no control, yet can proudly confess to having morality, as I tended to drift toward helping the vulnerable, especially when I was the helpless one. Initially, I found the escapades filled with amazement and excitement. Subsequently, the excitement faded, nevertheless; something pleasant was evolving. I actually am missing people that I am forced by the light world to believe they never existed. This is not something the makes me feel happy.

Seventy-eight and ninety-eight

I became exhausted thinking about the excitements of the ages I just struggled to survive. Each night I prayed before I went to sleep for the normal things, such as enough bullets for my weapons and medicine for my female friends if they get sick.

This escapade proved to be more exciting than my previous ones, or had the potential to be different. I appeared in a football suit as number thirty-three or wide receiver on our football team. We were in second place and needed a win today or our season was finished. The first half I remained on the bench, as our team ran every play. The coach throws a fit with us at halftime claiming we would have a few surprises in the fourth quarter. He told us our defense had to keep us in the game and the score close. Our defense came through for us, with an interception that led to a touchdown. We began the final quarter, and our coach put me in the game. I was to run deep not even looking back. The plan was to pull the secondary back from the midfield. First time, three fell back on me as our Quarterback through a short pass and picked up a hefty gain. A few minutes later, on our next drive, the coach puts me in one more time. He has me rushing down the middle of the field as I did the first time. This time, merely one safety has dropped back on me, and the Quarterback drops another short pass. Unfortunately, both drives were nonproductive, nevertheless; our defense held strong. The coach puts me in the third time, which will be the last possession as our offense is in deep trouble. The latest play we lost most of our yardage because of a backfield mistake. We are on the two-yard line, one yard from the left out-of-bounds line. The coach sends a message to me that this time is for real, so goes full speed, and catches the ball. This time he only sends me deep, with one running back, faking, he is running wide going straight to the right out of bounds line. His mission is to spread the defensive line out. The remainder of the team is to build an iron curtain around our Quarterback. I notice the bleachers are emptying themselves as our fans are giving up on us.

The center snaps our ball, and I shoot through the line. The opposing coach believes we will run straight for the sideline to stop the clock hoping we will have a miracle in our next two plays. He suspects we will try something tricky on our fourth play, so this play; he wants his team to be conservative and just give enough yardage to force us into risking our fourth down.

Once he gets the ball, they will run out the clock. My mission is to change the tide. Meanwhile, through the line I go completely ignored. I can now appreciate the coach's earlier plan of using me as a decoy. They believe I am merely trying to trick them one more time, and this time they are not going to fall for it. As I run downfield, I hear the small audience go Oooooh when they discover the running back has no ball. They now witness me running in the wide open rushing to the touchdown line. I glance back to see if any defenders are near me. I have an open shot; therefore, I look up at the sky as our Quarterback unleashed a bomb. He has put everything into the sky-high football throw. I am worried now the ball may be too high and the defenders will arrive the same time it does. I detect the ball has some speed to it, thereby requiring that I triple time to catch up with it. He has put everything he ever had in this throw. I rush as hard as possible getting my read on this throw. I can solely remember one throws this high and fast, and that was in church camp once as a child when an adult male from the right field. I was the catcher. The ball appeared to sit up in the heavens as I stared at it. A few teammates asked me if I had this ball. I told them I had it as I waited for what felt like an eternity, then I flashed down to me, and I caught it. I knew that if I caught that ball, I would be snagging this one as well. I blocked out the entire world, which was easy considering the world felt as if it had vanished. Now it was the football and me as I was going to catch it. There can be no other possible outcome.

I forbid any thought a failure from entering my mind. Failure was not an option. This was my chance to prove what I already knew, and that was I am a skilled wide receiver. All the hours of running, weight lifting, and painful hours of calisthenics had to have some sort of meaning or purpose. Now was payday. The time to perform was at hand. This darn football was sitting in the sky waiting to see how it could double cross me. It now began its descent. I knew that if I fell short, I could rush back, yet if it were too far ahead of me, I would never catch it. Either way was a risk, nevertheless; the ball was equally important, excessively high for me to read it effectively. One thing was for sure, and this was, the defense was getting closer. If the Quarterback throws this pass too short, I have no chance to catch it; therefore, my sole chance is if he puts it over their heads. With this in mind, I begin a short-distance sprint closing in on the end zone. An untimely wind picks up our football and gives it a sort fling. As this ball draws near, I determine I am going to be just as short. Somehow, I had to stretch my body a few more inches instantly. My muscles were beginning to tighten, as I have pushed them harder than ever before in my life. Within the last split second, I dived using my legs to spring me forward with as much might as I could. The ball came toward me as my eyes and hands tried to synchronize to its projection. I felt the air whirling from the football as it powerfully shot through it. Either the greatest glory or failure was now a few seconds away from us. The ball hit my fingers, and I clutched it so hard I feared the football might explode. Our stadium exploded proving to me that I still had the football in my hands. Both of my hands were locked on this ball, as I hold my arms extended. When the dust settled, my hands and the football were over the touchdown line and in the end zone.

The loud speaker blared out, "Touchdown, Hendershot, number thirty-three." We were now just one point behind with my ninety-eight-yard catch. The clock still read forty-six seconds. We formed our special team and made our extra point, once again stopping the clock. I am almost blinded by the cameras snapping so many flash pics. This was my best catch this season yet again it was my only reception. We simply had to hold ourselves together for one more overtime quarter, and we might have a chance at postseason play. The stadium was once more packed. The gate attendants had no way to monitor who previously had tickets, thus they decided whoever wanted to come in had a right to do so. There was merely forty-six seconds remaining, and then a stress packed overtime quarter. The great miracle shocking reception was now history as it blazed over the nation from the cell phones who had recorded it. This was one of the catches where everyone had time to get their phones out and wait. If I caught it, they would forward it, if I missed it, they would delete it. Nevertheless, if I caught it, this file would remain on the phones until they broke. I limped back to the huddle, according to my coach's instruction. He was a master strategist, and had a vision for his plans. Accordingly, he knew everyone was looking for a sign or a tip, so they could get that extra jump. He told us this was the same as fishing, and you had to know what bait would do the trick. He told us to walk onto the field relaxed as we kicked the ball to our opponents. I believe everyone in the stadium could hear him yelling at us to keep our eyes open and to block the lanes. He did not want a miraculous return. We lined up and began our kick off as our kicker surprised me with a line drive kick straight for the second player from the right out-of-bounds line. This opposing player was heavy set and lagged behind the other players. I discovered after the game that he was their coach's son, and they kept on the team because of his big weighty body.

Our coach studied our opposing team players in detail, and watched hours of game plays recorded on the teams we faced. He mapped out any possible weaknesses. This man would also keep records of other sports they played. The story has it that this player could not catch a ball, thus they put him on special teams and on the opposite side of the field from where he believed the ball would be. He believed we would kick the ball to the left center of the field, to take time to make it to an out-of-bounds line and stop the clock. We had two kickers; one was our backup Quarterback and was excellent at place kicking the ball, while the other was for power. Our opponents believed we were using our placekicker to keep the ball in the center of the field and run down the clock. Our kicker sent a spiraling line drive at the opposing coach's son a few feet to his right, which proved enough for his clumsy hands to tip the ball pass his teammate who guarded the line. The ball spun out-of-bounds at their twenty-two-yard line. The stadium went crazy, although this was more of a stab with a needle, in that we now had twenty-eight seconds to drive seventy-eight yards. Any ways, a long bomb currently would be too great a risk for an interception in that everyone was presuming it. Our coach constantly told us that sometimes in life; you had to give your opponent what they anticipate if you can give it better than they expected. Our coach puts me in telling me I would be a decoy once more and be used if the Quarterback could not find anyone else open. We had to get out-of-bounds at all costs. He lined up three other receivers, and our center snapped the ball. Our Quarterback drops back in his pocket as the four of us spread downfield. Strangely, they rather made me angry in that they ignored me. Once, I was on my own path, I kicked it in and lost my limp. Our Quarterback caught my new sprint and shot me another long bomb. This one was not a high as the one a few minutes earlier, and more of a straighter shot. This one was much easier to read than the first throw, and by being flatter, I did not have to worry about as many atmospheric oddities.

I felt as if I were on top of the world, in this throw was moving with me, because I was reading it perfectly. I was alone in the middle of the field, and the end zone was simply a few feet ahead of me. This football fell perfectly in my hands as I leaped into the end zone. The game was over, and we were going to the playoffs. The lone twelve points I had scored during the entire season came within the latter half of the two-minute warning. Once more, the loud speaker blared out, "Touchdown, Hendershot, number thirty-three." This was the first time I could feel any sort of pain in the dark world, although it was the best pain, I have ever known. My muscles were so tight now. This made me feel great in that I know that I gave it all I had. We won this game because my body won for me. Everything worked as one, my body, the ball, and the world that surrounded me. I am so thankful that I believed the ball would stay in my hands, and it did. I could have never been this high in the sky, nor have I seen two miracles come true in front of me. My fulfillment rested in making these two catches. It was time for me to help our city, fans, and teammates share in this fulfillment. My coach bragged to the media that we had the most dangerous weapon that played football this era. I was called upon twice, and both times failed to drop the ball. My teammates and the press went crazy over my accomplishment, as even veteran members of the press and my teammates assured me they had never seen two plays such as this. I pass this off to the Quarterback, claiming he put the ball in my hands. Accordingly, I profess that when the Quarterback puts the ball in my hands, all I had to do was hang on to the ball. Our Quarterback downplays my comments, claiming he did not have any time to plan his throw; he simply put it in the sky and hoped that I would read it and pull it down into my control. He further added this was the first time he ever passed to me in a game, and especially in a game or pennant clincher.

When we finally finished the massive interviews and celebrating our pennant, I went out and hailed a taxi. I had a vehicle; nevertheless, I was exhausted and drunk, thereby, did not want to end such a great day on a bad note. When I got into the taxi, the driver knew whom I was instantly. Within a few short minutes, I went from an unknown, an invisible face that rode the bench the entire year, to the newest David that destroyed a Goliath. He asked where I was going. I gave him my driver's license, rubbing my throat for him. He understood I was telling him my voice was gone for this day. My true glory came as I entered our home. My children were home with their friends. My yard was packed with neighbors, as everyone wanted my autograph. They downloaded pictures of my catches, and I must confess these images were impressive. They were almost on the verge of appearing supernatural, although they were snapped in a nanosecond. I signed the eight by tens and even agreed to take some new pics with them. These are our neighbors; therefore, they are the ones who live near my family, which is my weak point, so they help keep this strong for me. My daughter was so much happier currently, in that she suddenly was the Queen bee in her social group and the number one requested BFF (Best Friend Forever). Now, she will be setting the fashion. My wife and I hope this will give her a chance to scale back on her hair dyes and makeup. Accordingly, many of my family's friends did not know I was playing football, or if they did, were told I was pending retirement in a few years. They downplayed it, something they could never again be able to master. Overnight, signs went up around our town as the, "Current home of Hendershot." My sister sent me a picture from her cell phone of the Warner sign; a small-unincorporated town then I lived for one decade and had some rental property. This was now also my hometown. I laughed to my wife, that soon we would see signs everywhere that Hendershot slept here.

I cautioned my family not to get their heads too high in the clouds, as this was a once in a lifetime experience. I projected that as fast as I rose, I will fall as well. My wife explains we must be thankful that at least it happened once. Accordingly, I agree with her as I explain to my children and their friends who look at me as if I am a legend. Nothing can ever take away the history I made today, how a team that was ahead seven points in less than two minutes later was seven points behind the other team. My wife reports to me that she was asleep during this game, nevertheless, our phones began to ring, and her cell phone went crazy. She even received text from her Asiatic family and friends. This is another dream that I have an Asian wife. At least, this is not the first time I had this wife. I can see the extreme pride my family has in me, and this is making this the best escapade I have had so far. Consequently, my self-esteem is at its highest. I felt the challenge in making these catches. It was not something that just floated into my grip. I proved something to my coach and myself as well. We were back in training on Monday. I immediately discovered training was different for me. The coach had each Quarterback drill many short line drives to me and the other receivers for quick ten to fifteen-yard gains. He refused to designate a receiver, but instead had our Quarterback throw to whomever was open. Our defense is among the best in the league, and they took it personal when we gained yards on them, pushing them back toward their end zone. We had to work hard to get open and had to learn how to work together. We worked out a few plans and plays where we can trip up the defenders. At least twice each practice the coach sent me for the long bomb, as he also gave our other receivers a few long bombs as well. The coach was opening our offense making it fast and yard consuming. My teammates were working well with me, as I could feel the warmth of their new powerful respect. They were treating me like a superstar. I asked a few why they would treat a benchwarmer as they would treat a superstar. One of the other receivers told me that superstars caught vital ninety-eight-yard and seventy-eight-yard passes in season critical plays. What I lived through in this adventure has proven to me that there is something strong deep inside me.

The hair

I reach up to grab a fine pass from our Quarterback; notwithstanding, as the ball gets closer it begins to fade, as does the world around me. I casually begin to reappear in a command center packed with Generals and maps of the world. These maps are on projection screens and are attached to supercomputers and present complex information in real time. We are surprised by a new sort of photograph that begins appearing on our screens. Oddly, these photographs can solely be seen by a special nuclear committee, which I am a member. We have ten on our committee, which has merely three males. Our females are professional scientists, or members of congressional staffs. It takes a few minutes to figure out that we are in an emergency. I am trying to determine what is happening. I see alarms, flashing; therefore, I recommend to our team that we need to group and reevaluate our situation. Accordingly, I ask for whoever feels they are the least informed in this group. A public engineer named Trudy raises her hand. I tell her that I am going to pretend as if I am a senator who knows nothing and will be asking questions. The group agrees this may be a perfect manner to brainstorm and see if we missed something. I ask Trudy to tell me in one sentence, what our situation is. She explains that we have alarms going off in Asia, and the American continents that we cannot explain. I look at our group and tell them that cannot explain is not an acceptable answer, when we consider we have Generals sitting in the center with us that can push a nuclear release button. We must get the best Intel for them. I ask Trudy to tell me what the reasons an alarm may be warning us are. She reports there may be environmental issues, human issues, or Mechanical issues. I ask if there are actions, we can take to overcome systematic issues. Trudy looks at Mary and tells me that Mary, Director of Systems, and Functions are working this issue. Mary tells me there are seventeen tests, she, and her field personnel can run. They are currently running the final summary test and have identified three sites where Mechanical issues are at play, yet since their initial activation is still unknown.

I look at the group and ask what we are doing about environmental and human issues, since we have to be working each element simultaneously. Representatives from our senator staffs tell us they have Homeland Security, FBI, Central Intelligence Agency (CIA), and the Secretary of State and Secretary of Defense working this issue. So far, they can report that no known terrorist group is involved with these alarms. They also have commitments from allies who are investigating every possible scenario. I thank them for their hard work and ask them if they please would keep us updated. I ask to see our human issues' monitoring screen. Trudy tells us we do not have one. I tell our group, we need a human issue and Mechanical issues' summary board, because we have to continue to look for cause and effect relationships. They agree and start setting it up, which will be completely computer based, and be up in a matter of minutes. I now turn our attention to environmental issues. I ask Trudy to explain why this is listed as a separate and independent issue. Trudy explains that human and Mechanical issues can create the environmental issue. This includes damage caused by animals or acts of God. Even air and water pollution must be considered. I now turn our attention toward solid facts about the alarms and see if we could track it. The initial alarms began sounding off in China. The command center believed this indicated China could be mobilizing. The confusing factor was the sequence the alarms were responding, in they were sounding off south to north in the central part of China, followed by an almost concurrent sounding through Mongolia and Siberia. I ask them what would make them sound off simultaneous, in that a missile or air fleet would not fire off at the same time. Trudy tells us this is what is so confusing. I tell her there is an explanation, and that we must find it.

The CIA began sending of staff pictures from China and Mongolia and Siberian provinces. When I looked at the first one, three of my female committee members began to cough. I ask them if they saw what I saw. We regrouped at another table, and openly discussed what we viewed in these photos. I ask them to describe it first. Their names are Sarah, Janet, and Tricia. Janet reports to me that she is looking at a picture of a Chinese family, with three females standing in the front row. They are fully dressed with one small exception. They have a twelve-inch circular section removed from the front of the clothing centered on their genital area. This exposes their underwear with one exception. They have a four-inch by a five-inch rectangle removed from an area the exposes, their belly button, and the top one-inch of their pubic hair. Sarah asks one of the other committee members to describe what one of these front row females is wearing. This member uses a strange word to describe the color of the woman's scarf. I jump up and reveal to Janet that I told her that was the color. Sarah and Tricia begin laughing testifying to Janet that I indeed told her this. This removes any curiosity from the member who was providing this description. Now the other members were pacified, we began our discussion on why we were seeing this. I was curious why I was the lone male to witness this and why we were seeing the part of their nudity. Sarah believes it may have something to do with our society's view of what is nude and what is not. I confess that one of the joys of my elementary school days was looking at art books that had European artists who painted undressed women, such as Venus or Greek and

Roman goddesses. I tell them it was so great to open a book at school, in public, look at naked women, and be told it was okay. I thought the mystery of the female body was unfolding in front of me. Society fulfilled my need to understand with knowledge.

I remember we had a beautiful young female art teacher, and one day I called her back to my desk and asked her a question about one of the undressed women in a painting. It was a technical question such as why the artist showed light on one area and not the other, as I traced the shade projection from the sun in the scene and how it flowed over the naked woman's body. It was so exciting discussing an uncovered woman with a beautiful female teacher. She was impressed with my attention to detail in this painting and promised to research the answer for my question. I believed my adventure to equalize my skills with Einstein's was moving fine until one day a classmate told me the real female genital was below the pubic hairs. I was shocked by this and had to determine if this was true. I scrapped the money together and purchased a copy of a Hustler magazine, which provided the detailed pictures I was searching to find. Subsequently, the detail and irregularity of this mysterious organ, plus the 'dirty feelings,' which came when looking at them, such as the need to keep these magazines hidden, took away the excitement of this discovery. Instead, I enjoy the social freedom that came with looking at paintings that portrayed the female pubic hair. The Internet era opened this hunger, as when between marriages, I discovered the rich black shiny coal-like look of the Asian feminine genital hair. My appreciation of this mystery patch that sprang up on both sexes around the secretive area added a commonality between the genders in this private part of the body. The smooth hairless skin that covered most of the womanly body also added to the uniqueness of this contrast. Another calming effect was that as a male, I, likewise, had this hair, so it did not feel as 'nonhuman.' The final factor was my subjective belief in this presented something paintable representative of the female external reproductive organ. I can only imagine an artist trying to paint a vagina and attempt to glamorize it as a status symbol.

Either way, seeing these three one-inch patches of hair and discuss it with Tricia, Sarah, or Janet felt good. I suggest that we may be seeing this to prove the power of the source to reveal whatever it wishes to show us, and by not showing it to all told me that this source wanted us to keep it a secret. I explain that by showing this portion, and if I got confused forgetting what the message was revealing to me, I was sure one of them, if not all three, would eagerly refresh my memory as we discussed this tonight. Sarah tells me to study this extra hard now, because once they go, I will need to depend on my memory. I told her she was as cold as this mystery force we currently confront. She winked at me as the Mongolian presidential family. We witnessed the four patches begin to appear on four females in this family, while the Chinese women regained their privacy. I tell my girls, we can report China as off the radar now. They agree, and I walk to our military representatives and tell them to take China off our radar, on to put Mongolia up at the moment and be prepared for Siberia. Sarah yells over to me to put Siberia on our radar. I ask our military Generals if we can add China as our partners in this search. One of the Generals tells me the Chinese assets will prove to be extremely beneficial. The Generals ask me how we are making these decisions. I tell them by accurately assimilating the data from our concerned issues. I return to my group and report that our Generals are getting restless. Tricia winks at me and tells me not to worry; they will be getting a phone call in a few minutes from their boss. She types something on her laptop and pushes the enter key. Tricia asks if we want a cup of coffee. We shake our heads yes, as I ask them if I can see the Siberian governing family. Janet reports that I will like this picture, because this family has seven women. I look at the two pictures and tell them I consider myself so lucky, in that my great group mates will allow me to touch what I see on this screen. Sarah tells me maybe if I promise to be a good boy. I wink at them and promise to be the best little boy they ever owned. Tricia smiles telling me I am on the right track.

We hear the red phones begin to ring. Our Generals jump up and rush to these phones. The call lasts for less than one minute. When they put the phone down, three of them walk over to our desk and inform me the president has just transferred operational control to our committee. Tricia tells the Generals, they need to alert the Navies around the Earth to expect some chaotic through the Arctic Ocean swinging through the Bering Strait around many of the Aleutian Islands. Sarah recommends that we add Russia to our allies in this campaign. I motioned for Tricia and Sarah, in our attempt to map this dilemma. I wanted to see their projection for the direction this force is moving; I also needed a map of all active volcanoes, plate tectonics and anything else they think may be important. Janet asks me if I similarly want her to include the Ring of Fire. I tell her only if she joins me in it. Janet warns it could burn her special patch that she was saving for me. Tricia and Sarah jump up and give her a high five. I reach over and pull her to me telling her I never want anything to happen to that precious work of art, especially now that we are viewing Eskimo families. I rub my eyes and then ask if the latest family is Eskimos. They confirm this, as I furthermore, add that I never knew Eskimos looked that fine. Sarah tells me I think every woman is fine looking. I tell her she has me at a disadvantage in that I solely do not like those without patches, so I cannot presently point out the ones I do not favor. Sarah reveals to us that she does not have a patch. I tell Janet and Tricia this is great news for them in that we recognize who will be doing the cooking and cleaning for us tonight. Sarah defuses this situation by winking at me and confessing anything for me. I smile back and tell her I would love to talk about my art appreciation; however, I believe we need to save the Earth first.

Janet and Tricia appear to start crying complaining that all work, and no play will make James a dull boy. This mystery is bugging me, until more pictures of Eskimo families continue to pop up, as the Siberian and Mongolian pics vanish. I go over to the Generals world map and use one of their computer pens that will draw on an overlay, which projects over their maps. I begin at Qinghai Lake draw a line to Lake Baikal. Next, I continue the line to the Arctic Ocean making a horseshoe down through the Bering Strait moving out into the Pacific Ocean working my way around the active volcanoes currently moving in a straight line to Washington. I report to everyone that we can rule out human and Mechanical issues at this stage. We need to get this information out to the scientists of the world, in that something that is not supposed to happen is getting ready to materialize. I now believe that unless you are on a spaceship leaving our solar system, you need to be concerned about this. I pat the Generals on their backs and recommend they alert the president and put my name on it as the blame name. I ask them for as many aerial and ground reports about the line I have just revealed as possible. Information is our only weapon at this time. I notice my patches are vanishing in our photos. I tell Janet that I think the Eskimos are getting cold. Sarah begins laughing at this. Janet and I glance at each other, as we both are caught off guard by her unexpected recent charms. I track the photos in which the patches are vanishing placing a mark on them. I ask my women if there is any way we can track the times the pictures changed. Tricia tells us she can do this by reviewing the security camera behind us. It is motioned activated, so it should go directly to the movements. She reports to us in a few minutes with the times plotted. The Generals also begin feeding us temperature data and storm narratives along the line I drew. The temperatures were dropping and storms becoming unpredictable. I told my girls that it was just too strange how this phenomenon became noticeable at Qinghai Lake and afterwards heads for Lake Baikal and then goes to the Arctic Ocean drifting around the active volcanoes to the open Pacific and now heading ashore in California. Janet asks why it did not go straight across the Pacific from Qinghai Lake. I show her the hot spots on our computer map, and how this event crossed two strings of active volcanoes.

Subsequently, Sarah begins to scream. We rush over to see what she is witnessing. We currently see a picture with thousands of women, completely nude in it on a California beach. We discern this to be true from a sign on the beach that lists it with a California address. I told my friends we were in trouble, unless we figure this out fast. Janet asks me if I have any ideas. I conclude the lone thing this even shies away from is spirited volcanoes, and unless we come up with active volcanoes quickly, we are history. Sarah screams out I am a genius. Tricia yells again to the Generals to ask if they have any spare active volcanoes they can give to the Pacific Ocean. The Generals come over to me and ask whether I will explain my map. I show them how this event has a problem of the heat from active volcanoes. The manner that it avoided the Pacific from inland Asia merely to come back through the Bering Strait down around the Ring of Fire and now heading above the Hawaiian Hot Spot straight for the center of the San Andreas Fault between the West Coast hot spots. The Generals ask what I think about selected hydrogen or nuclear bombs. I look at our scientists and tell them to give the General the targets since we need to get a few shots in while it is still in the middle of the Pacific. They crunched numbers and picked a place to drop seven hydrogen bombs. They believed the seven would shake this plate shift and vibrate it back into position. The Generals asked how soon we needed to fire them. The scientist asks for about three minutes to plug in the exact coordinates.

Subsequently, I questioned them if they programmed the missile in flight times. They affirmed their programs included everything, as well as real time weather from the closest satellites. They next began their countdown for the Generals, and the huge computer LCD monitor shows the missiles in flight on the digital map. Then the missiles began hitting the ocean. We could feel our building shake, as if on a small earthquake. The Generals asked me what was happening. I explained the bombs had jolted the North American Plate back in place. We noticed that many of the women were receiving their clothing once more. I tell the Generals we should be on standby with another five hydrogen bombs. Sarah looks at our California women picture and starts plotting the positions. The positioning of the bombs in this second round was to give the Pacific Plate a jolt and give the tsunami backlash with a counter tsunami with the goal of causing their impact to drive a force down on the plate tectonics. I looked at our magic pictures with the wonderful pubic patches, nevertheless, to my delight their clothing was returning quickly. Within just a few minutes, there were no more nude women on our screens. We look at the Generals and tell them to call the president; this situation is under control for the time being. Accordingly, we began picking up the papers, staplers, and other desktop items that had scattered over the floor. After the Generals got off the red phone, they asked everyone if we were ready for happy hour. We walked down to their command vehicles and rode to the officer's club. This was wonderful seeing soldiers salute the General's flag. It flew on a small pole above the driver's side bumper. We had a few drinks, until Sarah tapped me on the shoulder and showed me a picture. The picture had three women, and they had a circle with no clothing around their genitals up to their belly button, including the one-inch of pubic hair. My heart stopped beating. Sarah, Tricia, and Janet began laughing. I asked them why all this laughter. Tricia asks me if I appreciate the wonderful features of Photoshop. I ask Sarah if this one of those Photoshop deals. Janet tells me yes, as we laugh. I laugh so hard that I wake myself up. I feel special in that I now live on a planet that I saved.

Fighting corruption

I am lying on the street with blood flowing from my arm. An ambulance approached rushing up to us, and a gorgeous nurse comes rushing out to administer first aid to me. They rush me to the hospital where I am recovering over the next few days. I am watching the news from the television hoping to see a special report about the great robbery I prevented or large group of children I saved. No such victories are reported. I begin a conversion with the nurse and explain that when my head hit the concrete, I believe several memories of tonight faded from me. The nurse, whose name is Rachael chuckles, and then tells me nothing is wrong with being bitten by a little dog. I question her how such a small dog can bite accordingly hard. Rachael winks at me and tells me that if I would not have held on to him so long, and then fallen on him, he might not have been consequently, vicious. She assures me this secret is safe with her. I go back to my home to rest for a few days before returning to work. A couple of evenings later, I receive a frantic phone call from Rachael telling me she has been arrested, and she needs my help and asks whether I will go to a local correctional facility and bail her out of the prison. I assure her I will and call a bail bond company and provide them my credit card information and make the arrangements. They tell me I must be there to pick her up, or the prison will recharge her. I pick her up and take her back to her home. She explains this was a terrible mistake. When she went home, her electricity was out. She later learned that a neighbor had turned off her breaker box. She went home to her apartment and on entering her favorite song began to play on her stereo. When she went into the living room, she tripped over her coffee table knocking everything on the floor. When she gathered the items from the floor, she found two pairs of handcuffs. She used one to hock her secretive guest's hands to her wooden sofa frame and quickly cuffed his outer leg to the frame on the other side. After that, her lights came on, and she discovered the apartment filled with police officers. They arrested her on attempted rape charges. She reveals they told her that she was facing about fifteen charges and that all she had to do was make a false statement about her boyfriend being involved with a drug ring.

I asked her if she made this statement. Rachael swears she refused to make it, and this is why she had to be bailed out tonight. I recommend that we call her friend and at least warn him. We call his number, yet no one answers. Rachael wants to make sure he is okay and asks me to take her to his house. I relieve Rachael by informing her that my sister lives next to her friend on Weaver Street, and I will call her to put him on her cell phone. After a short pause, my sister began to scream, telling us Rachael's friend was dead. I tell her not to call the police, because we will call the State Highway Patrol. I call them immediately, as Rachael begins to cry. She is hurting so much currently. Within minutes, the police come to arrest her for the murder of her boyfriend. I can see where this is really beginning to tear her apart. I feel so sad for her. They ask me to explain why I am here. I tell them I am the one recording this even plus the one who posted her bail. Subsequently, I ask them, who was murdered. They tell me that will be revealed after they arrest her. The police take her away, while I call my sister who reports the State Police have arrived, and the crime scene is being processed by their investigators. I ask her if they would call our police and find out for whose murder Rachael was just arrested. They come and take me to their nearby barracks. When I arrive there, they ask me how I knew this officer was murdered. I explain, just as my sister had, that we were checking to make sure he was okay, considering the police tried to force Rachael into making false drug claims against him. With this, they asked me not to tell anyone what I saw. They were going to exit the crime scene and compare their evidence with what the local police produced.

The police arrested Rachael that evening and the prosecuting attorney filed the charges the next day, and one month later; her trial began. The Prosecution called twenty-two police officers and seventeen local citizens forward as witnesses. We sat there day after day watching the witnesses present their false accounts, rigged lab evidence, and photographs. The defense called at their first witness, the state came in and arrested all the previous witnesses. Accordingly, they presented their evidence in closed chambers with the judge who within minutes released Rachael. Rachael was shocked and attributed her freedom to my decision to contact the State Police. I was her fresh hero, as she believed her life would find a new purpose and once more move forward.

To our amazement, her adventure was just beginning. The police were sent to prison where they spread Rachael reported the local drug dealers and gave the Federal government their entire drug files. They failed to disclose the Feds took all the police records as part of a justice department investigation. Their paperwork was sloppy and just reported enough to cover their tracks in case someone reported them. Another benefit of the dark world is you are not bogged down the details presented by the paperwork trail of the day world. Your mind witnesses the submission of all records as a simultaneous action and not the long tedious sequential process. Rachael was in danger, and the state would not put her in a witness protection program because she was the accused. There is nothing like being guilty before being proven innocent. I got a few weeks of work and asked Rachael where she wanted me to take her. She recommends that we head for the Canadian or Mexican border. I tell her the Mexican border may be better, because there is some form of border control, which might deter a few of their hit men. I ask her if she has any relatives who live in the south. Rachael reports she has a few in California. She merely packs a few things in her backpack, since we do not want to alert anyone.

Through the United States, we drive not stopping, except for an occasional driver switch. Rachael's driving skills are exceptional, and actually better than my skills are. Our meals we purchase from fast-food drive thru's. While I am driving on an interstate, a pickup truck pulls up beside us. Meanwhile, a man from the truck bed and began shooting at us. I hit our brakes and swerve my car to the curbside allowing an eighteen-wheeler to pass between the shooting truck and me. Once the eighteen-wheeler passes me, I spin our car into the other double lane and floor it. The pickup truck bounced off the eighteen-wheeler rendering it stuck in the medium. I remembered we recently passed an exit. We got off at the exit, where I bought a map and traced a back road to the next exit. Rachael believes we might be better off just traveling the back roads. Considering this is her car, and I am going to take an airplane on my return trip, we have the extra time so the secondary roads will be fine. I decide we will keep an eye on her relative's house, to make sure things are secure. We notice no one arrives or departs from her aunt's house. This is strange, yet we are getting restless, so I tell Rachael walk to the door, and I will cover her. She walks up to the door and knocks on it. An older man opens the door and begins shooting her. She falls down on the outside steps. The man tries to pull her back into the house. As he steps out, I shoot him in his head. I suspect he may be a part of a small group. I run around to the back door and fortunately find it unlocked. I slip in and spot two men at the table eating breakfast. They have a small TV blaring, which provides me a chance to position myself and after reloading and collecting Rachael's pistol she had, I pumped three solid shots into each of the men. I reloaded my pistol and searched the remainder of this house, finding her cousin, aunt, and uncle lying undressed in their family bathtub with their throats cut. Feeling the house is secure, I move toward the front door where I see another man preparing to shoot at Rachael. I shoot at him, and considering this is my escapade; I hit him and he falls to his death. I rush to determine if I can save Rachael, however, she is not responding. I start to shake her trying to get a response. Each time I speak her name, she fades. Soon, I am once more alone in my bed.

5:30

Once again, I wake up in my house being single with no children. I walk throughout my house looking for my partner, or spouse. No one else is here; nevertheless, I see a wonderful suit from the drycleaners and a calendar taped to my refrigerator. I look at my cell phone to discover what day this is. Accordingly, I look at my big calendar and see I have two times marked for church today. The first time is 8:30 am, yet I cannot make the second time out because of my sloppy handwriting. Now, I have to find which church I must attend today. I see a few tithe envelopes that have the church's name. I turn on my laptop and Google the church for their address. I hate this as much as anything else does; it is popping up in situations not knowing anything. At least this time I have the time to investigate my situation and try not to look too stupid. I arrive at the 8:30 service, and discover this is a Romanian church. Fortunately, everyone is speaking the dream language, so my only objective is to find my friends here, if indeed I do have friends. Within a few minutes, a group of women come and surrounds me talking nonstop. I listen and catch on quickly that we belong to a special study group, which has an 8:30 class, then a 9:30 service followed by lunch. The special thing about these women is they talk about everything. I quickly figured out which ones had jobs and the two that were students. After our 9:30 service, we were going to one of their homes for lunch and then were going to regroup for a singing show tonight at the church. I guess the lone thing that binds us is our nationality. They act as if they recognize everything about me. I soon discover that two live with me, and was merely staying with their friends last night. These two float back toward me taking their positions on each side. This began to fill in my blank spots, in that they treated me as if I were their younger brother. I truly wanted to figure out what our relation was. I suspect they will remind me, such as if one gives a goodbye kiss or reaches to hold my hand.

They both hold my hands when we walked into our classroom, notwithstanding they also hold our two-college student's hands. Accordingly, I figure we are a close nit group. I soon discover we come from the identical hometown. This makes us inseparable, to the degree the two students live next door to us, and we share the same car, which for a strange reason I had this morning. I figure they have a few activities; they do not want me to accidently to slip to our parents. Our class has nine people in it, and all nine of us slow into the main service directly afterwards. Here, I discover how wonderful my home girls can sing. I realize if I keep listening to them sing, I will never awaken. This is not a terrible thing, for it would like hearing angels singing, notwithstanding, escapades constantly end. I slept through most of the sermon afterwards. We decided not to eat at our church, because the girls wanted to be selected shopping in and eat a fancy Sunday lunch. To my surprise, these girls are fast shoppers; they understand what they want, directly shop, get it, and find the best values. I learn that we come from low-income families whose parents immigrated to the United States. We merged into our high school social networks; the lone exception was that we never invited anyone to our homes. It appears; we have maintained this habit with our current homes, in that if anyone visits, they get the five of us. This is to relax us enough securely to socialize. After eating our lunch, the girls ask me if I take the clothing they bought, which also included a shirt for me, back to our house and return to the church for the special concert today. We loaded up our car and to our house we went. I put everything in our house, and this time inspected to two rooms that had their doors closed. They had enough pictures on their walls for me to figure out where to put their new clothes. I did a questionable thing in that I opened their diaries and caught up on our lives. Each wrote much about me, which revealed to me that we were extremely close. Neither wrote about sex, but instead wrote about their deep love for me. They are dedicated to our life together. I confess to myself that this is truly the best type of relationship. I can lean on them and they can lean on me. I review my calendar once more and conclude the concert must be at 5:30 this afternoon. This gives me one hour to get ready and rush to our church. I look outside and see our car is gone. I see another smaller calendar with time blocks for each day and many blocks color.

Consequently, I notice 4:30 to 9:30 are colored in today, which implies someone has the car. Fortunately, our church is not that far, so I will walk there. I grab a baloney sandwich and rush out the door zipping down our street. I walk for about twenty minutes and recognize I have never been here previous. One thing for sure, I was not here this morning. I find a small community store that is open today, which is not normal for a Sunday. I ask them why they are open, and she tells me they always open for the Sunday afternoon meeting. I tell her I had a busy day and left my address book at my house, and a friend invited me. I sure would hate to miss it. She comforts me while drawing a neighborhood map, and shows me how to follow her directions. As I head out the door, she calls me back and gives me a quart jar of a strange sort of red juice. She tells me to give this to the people at the door and inform them she will bring more when she comes. She winks at me and reports they will understand what to do with it and try not to have too much fun before she gets there. I ask her what she means by, "too much fun." She explains the happiest times are the introduction of the new members. I agree that is usually a sign everyone has been working hard the previous week. She agrees by telling me this is the truth. I leave her store with my 'juice' and proceed with the directions she gave me. She told me I could be there in ten minutes, yet twenty minutes later; I am still walking. I notice it is getting dark now. This is strange for the summer months in it usually does not get darker until much later. Fortunately, I wear my watch when going to work, as it is easier to get the time rather than turning on my cell phone, which naturally would ring instantly. I have my cell phone on currently, yet have 'no service.' I have always had service in our city. I look at my watch and see it is 5:30 P.M. Therefore, I must be late. If I had service, my friends would be calling me by now.

We could be getting a surprise summer storm. Something strange is happening presently. A car pulls up beside me, and the woman from the store asks me why I am way over here. I confess that I have no idea where 'here' is. She tells me to jump in with her. This is the first bit of relief I have experienced since this roller coaster ride began what is currently one hour ago. It is extremely dark by the time we arrive at this church. I ask her why there are no lights on here. She reminds me that it is merely 5:30 in the afternoon. I explain this much walking is not normal for me, consequently, I may be suffering from exhaustion. This woman tells me not to worry; they have nurses and doctors at the place we are going. Accordingly, she hands me a dark black cloth to wipe my head. She holds one of my hands and pulls a small wagon packed with her juice into our 'church.' I have never seen a church with this architectural design previously. It resembles a gothic castle. I wonder why this building has never drawn my attention previously. At least, I am here now. In we go, while several men, dressed in black rush up to us and secure the wagon from my saving escort. We walk into a large lobby, where hundreds of people, all dressed in black is standing around a circular altar in the center of this room. I ask my host why everyone is wearing black. She tells me that everyone is not wearing black and calls for a few of her doctor friends to come over and look at me. They examine me, as best they can without their equipment, in my ears and at my eyes. One of them takes my pulse with his hands while looking at his watch. He tells the other doctor my pulse is one-hundred ninety. He asks me how old I am. I tell him I am twenty-five. He explains that 220 minus twenty-five is 195; therefore, my pulse is high and wants to identify if I did anything different today. I explain that I got lost and had been walking fast for one hour. He shakes his head and tells me to start walking at least three times a week. Next, he puts his hand on my head and tells me I feel chilled. He pulls out a robe from one of our seats and tells me to wrap myself in this.

Accordingly, I ask why they have robes in their lobby. My host explains that many times they have traditional services just as our ancestors did almost 1,000 years earlier. I chuckle and say this would be truly interesting to see. The doctors tell me I am always invited. Next, the other doctor explains that my pupils are dilated and this may be why I am having trouble seeing light and colors. I thank them for helping me and ask them if they think I am in medical trouble and should get to a hospital.

They both tell me I need to rest and that a little of our 'mother's red juice' will revive me. I look at her and report she gets another chance to save me. She smiles and reveals she believes my life will be changed her shortly. Loud organs begin to fill our open lobby, as our doctors excuse themselves and rush back to their seats. I sit down with my host. Meanwhile, a towering strong man sits in front of me, and another sits beside me. Each of these men must be at least seven-feet tall. I suspect there might be something to the diets these people enjoy. They begin repeating a few chants, which I am not concerned because I understand several orthodox churches rely heavily on chants. This must be similar to the service part in my church because I am becoming sleepy. Suddenly, a man from behind grabs me as the man beside me gripped my legs, as the man in front helped them. I try to break myself free to no avail. These men lay me on the altar in the center of the lobby and tie each foot and arm to it. Next, a beautiful woman comes to me and rips off my clothes. I tell her she is so pretty, she does not need to do this to get a man. She tells me to get what she wants she must. Subsequently, she lowers her lips to my neck and bites me hard. This stings me as if a hundred bees hit the same spot. After this, my host comes up to them and begins passing out her red juice. I ask them what sort of juice this is. They tell me it is cow blood and that her son works in a slaughterhouse.

I can now see how this blood drips down the side of their mouths that I am in the wrong place. After they each get a big gulp, they look at me showing their razor-sharp fangs. My guest tells me I am lucky, in that if she did not have this blood, I would be dead, and instead they are going to make me a member of their clan. I question her how she knows if I want to be a member. She explains that all who enter her store on Sunday want to be members and all who enter this palace and do not die are chosen by their master. Once he makes his choice, there is no returning. More importantly, when the Queen has bitten a person; that person will forever belong to this clan. I feel fire burning in my veins and my body beginning to shake as if I am having convulsions. Next, all who surround me start biting me. I ask my host why everyone is eating me if I am supposed to be a member of this clan. She explains that I must convince them this is something I genuinely desire. I realize one thing, and that is I am not in the mood to be eaten, accordingly; I begin shouting this is something that I truly want. I remind them the master chose me, and that it may not be a wise thing to make our master angry. The doctors come over to me and begin to cover me with selected salves and lotions. They explain to me that our species has advanced and with this evolution, we can presently withstand daylight. The bites were to give me the vaccine for these advancements and protection from other viruses and bacteria. They untie me and explain it is time for me to prove my love to the master. They will give me fifty-four lashes from a whip. If I ask them to stop, they will; however, I will fail and go straight to hell. This does not seem fair to me. The rotate the whip among themselves to provide me a solid lash with each swing. I understand the pain must now be beyond the shock level, since I am not feeling it. I drift to sleep, and then what feels as a few minutes later wake up in a hospital. Now this is a first for me after a dream until four Romanian beauties come walking into my room. I notice there are tubes in my nose and pinned into my arms. I ask them why I am here, figuring the blood loss from my beating is the reason. Instead, they ask me if I ate any of the mushrooms from our refrigerator. I told them that I put them in the omelet I made for breakfast. Subsequently, they begin yelling at me, while asking how many times they have told me not to eat the mushrooms until they determine if they are safe. The ones in our refrigerator are poisons and cause hallucinations. I am fortunate that they came back to get me for the concert tonight. I wiggle in my bed just enough to realize I have not been beaten with a whip. The doctor comes in and explains they are going to keep me here tonight; thereby he is going to give me a powerful sedative, so I can catch up on my sleep. Finally, this strange escapade is finished; I hope.

The register

I wake up filled with excitement as a review my last pay stub. Instead of the dreaded layoff notice, I got a wonderful note telling me I would receive a pay raise since I was going to operate our new check out register and 3d printer. We were skeptical about the claims we put in raw materials in accordance with a product menu, and that product will appear fully functional. This has to be the craziest thing anyone has ever told me, nevertheless, the man who owns the company I work in and hold my income security just invested a year's profits in a Twilight Zone fraud. I can feel everyone laughing at me when I turn this thing on and put in copper, iron, plastic or whatever that psycho chart tells me. I do not grasp what will hurt the worse, my coworkers laughing, or our owner crying. That will be the easy part; the hard piece of equipment to master will be this copier machine with these hundreds of buttons and stacks of trays. This is a special machine in that it recycles trash and produces new paper copies. This doubles as a register, using the copier scanner also as a bar code reader. I agreed to come to work three hours early today so my boss and I could learn how to use these things.

Consequently, my boss told me he was going to get my mind on track with a first experiment. We were going to make a radio. He tells me to pull the radio chart and helps me put in the raw materials. It turns out to be a mixture of metals and special oil mixtures. I put them in, check the output tray, push the button and twenty seconds later, results a hand-sized radio. I plug it into the wall, turn to a news station, and catch the morning news. I looked at my boss and shook my head asking how this can be. He explains that all things contain mass, and this is based upon the essentials within it and the density of these elements. Having a machine that can do this will make us the hot spot in town. Now, they can get replacement parts in minutes and have broken cars and machinery back online in most times less than a lunch break. I ask our boss if we can have fun when our staff arrives, in that I will harass him over this machine being a joke and set everyone up for a big kill. He agrees, and then we struggle and fight with his register and copier. They do work, and I must confess that recycling has a fantastic satisfying aspect. Surprisingly, we master this rather quickly. The staff arrives, and the boss tells me to make a radio. I ask him to save us from the humiliation and just confess this is a swindle. He tells me to open our folder, pull out the card for radio, and tell him what ingredients to put into the appropriate slots. I called for a substance in which he gave me. In a few minutes, our slots are filled, and he tells me to push the create button so the 3d printing will begin. I push the button and hear the tray shake. I ask my coworkers if they truly believe a radio will appear. They all begin to laugh. I ask them if they want to sing a song about our crazy boss. Accordingly, I ask my boss if he ever heard that a fool and his money are soon parted. He tells me that if this machine does not produce a radio, I will be fired. I reach down, pull out a radio, and pass it to my coworkers, who are amazed. This is, without question, what they claim is the greatest thing that has ever happened. I believe the enthusiasm that is radiating through our faces.

Subsequently, our first customer arrived, and I scanned in the barcodes. My boss hands me a special remote that looks at the products and gives a total. We are using this as a backup up on our first day. This register tracks our inventory, prepares our orders, and calculates our income statements and tax bills. The trouble is that our totals are not matching on our test runs. We run the two totals against each other in our troubleshooting computer program and determine the remote is producing the correct totals. We double check our start up procedures and see where we made a mistake. After fixing this, I process another checkout customer. I see me scanning the items, yet by mistake; I double scan one item, scanning it across and then once more when moving it to put in a bag. I hit the delete last transaction, notwithstanding hit the button above it that repeats it. The man I am checking out used to tease me in high school about being stupid. Therefore, I just give him the total, while reaching my hand out as if to collect a business card to scan. He hands me the card; I swipe it and give it back to him. I ask him if he needs any of our girls to carry his things to his truck. He grabs his purchases, stacking them on top of each other so high that I had to open the door for him. I followed him to his truck to help unload his items. I scatter the products to make it confusing when he unloads it. When I go back into our shop, I scan the receipt into a text file; remove the duplicate items, keeping the total the same. After this, I sent the file to print from the register, an easy function on this new copier-register printer. Next, I tack the receipt on my board and call my friend's father whom the receipt is here. He asks me to fax it to him. I do and pin the receipt to my bulletin board.

My father asks me if there are any problems with this machine. I tell him the buttons occasionally produce an unwanted response. He tells me there is a learning curve with the buttons and that certain practice will bring us online. Subsequently, I notice one of the middle trays rattling. The boss's wife notices it as well. She tells him our machine is doing something strange. The three of us see the next rattle as it also produces a clanking sound. I clutch a wrench, as my boss grabs a hammer, and his wife clings to a mop. I pull the tray open, exposing a strange creature. My boss hits it in the head with his hammer, while I strike it with my wrench. Our coworkers begin screaming and running. I tell my boss it is pleasant to understand we are with people who have our backs. We continue hitting the animal, which is a raccoon from his waist up and a long thick slimy snake comprising the remainder of his body. The creature continues to claw his way through the small openings of the tray rows getting his upper body in, which merely leaves his ten-foot snake lower extremity that appears to be made from rubber. We beat at it nonstop without creating any appearance of doing harm. I cannot determine how it can be working its way in such a limited space. My boss's wife now has their rifle and hands it to my boss, who orders me to step back and protect his wife. He begins firing at the snake, hitting it each time. The bullet creates a hole that immediately fills itself. This is something like throwing a rock into a pond; the rock goes into the water and disappears, leaving no damage. Finally, the snake-coon vanishes. I see no movement in the two lower trays, nevertheless; I can see our floor wobbling, as if something were underneath it. My boss at once called the copier company and explained our situation. The lone thing they can suggest is the creature may have mingled with the 3d printer and moved into the copier trays to avoid the light. As we try to coax our staff to return to their workstations, an elderly woman walks in and warns us we are in extreme danger.

My boss asks her to explain. She shows us an aged book and various original maps of our town. We discover this building is built over an old cave, which the town sealed because of the deadly creatures that would raid the town at night. She believes our new equipment is sending a subsonic wave that is harming these monsters of the deep, causing them to scout this area and plan for a large invasion. The police arrive at this time, take her statement, and claim she is crazy. We argue we saw this creature and if there are more, we will have a battle on our hands. The police ask where this creature is now. I tell him the creature got tired because of waiting so long for them to arrive. The police angrily storm out of our store. We open our weapon's locker where we keep the rifles we sell and give each employee a pistol, hunting knife, and rifle. Next, we slide the copier and discover a small hole underneath it. My boss begins to drop dynamite throw this hole. We can feel the rumble below us and hear hissing sounds. After this, he drops smoke bombs into the hole, hoping to contaminate the oxygen and to see if any smoke rises elsewhere in our office. None does, so he feels confident this is the lone hole. As we are walking away, his wife begins to scream. I do an about-face and begin shooting my rifle at the walls. These creatures are crawling up our walls, coming out of the electric sockets, crushing them as they enter our area. I have no idea what to do now. Our boss punches a code into the 3d printer and tells us to follow him as he rushes out of his building. Once we are outside, his building explodes. I ask him how he did this, as he explains he installed a side program with the elements to create a bomb and explode, as an emergency safety. His building is burning, and he motions for the fire department to concentrate on the homes that surround his business, since he believes there are children in them. By the time, the fire department makes it to his property the fire is beginning to sizzle. We notice a large hole in the middle of his burned property, which we identify as the hidden cave. With this discovery, he rents two backhoes and asks me to help him fill this cave in with the ashes from his business. We scrape all his soil down about six inches yet still cannot fill the hole. He calls for several cement mixers as we begin filling the hole with cement. We also lay a six-inch cement floor, which my boss plans to build a four-foot underway and his fresh business on top of it. After thinking, we agree it may be better to sell this property and begin elsewhere in this town. As we are walking toward his home early the next morning, I trip in gravel and on my way to the ground wake up in my bed. After inspecting under my bed, I prepare to get my much-needed rest. It is exhausting to wake up in the morning after cleaning ashes all night.

High school job

The sun is shining bright above us, while I can hear the cheering from our small town horseracing track. Once more, I am working on a Sunday afternoon. This is my two in the afternoon to midnight Sunday, as I rotate and the following week will be my six A.M. until two in the afternoon next Sunday. We are busy today, much busier than normal, in that we have the weekend interstate traffic and our localized fairground traffic for the horseraces. Our lot is packed with cars since many local people park here and carpool into the fairground to save parking costs. Our owner has sold them lot passes, which are twenty percent less than the county is charging. He could not charge, not as much, because we would have been hounded by the public begging for a spot. Either way, he did give one space to the sheriff. He did this to create the appearance this was endorsed by the local law enforcement and to help deter any thieves. I look and see my two coworkers sitting on the tail of a pickup truck chatting with their friends. Each pump, even the new unleaded gas pump is filled. We are skeptical about this pump, in that everyone knows this leadless fad will go away and those who have these vehicles will be stuck with junk. Our daytime attendant filled a car with the unleaded last Monday, and the car did not make it to the interstate. We saw it being towed to the garages in town. Our station owner felt sorry for the man when he saw his vehicle being towed and commented it may be best to give this a few years before we test it.

The garage called our station and wanted to understand why we filled it with water. Our gas venders reimbursed everyone's expenses, yet the skepticism about this new gas fad lasting. We believed it would be history by 1975. Notwithstanding, this Sunday afternoon is busy. It amazes me my two coworkers can sit on their butts and ignore so much work. I am trying to keep up with the pumps and make sure we are paid for the gas. This was in the days when the station attendants put the gas in the vehicles. Apparently, I am the lone one that remembers this. Fortunately, I believe the sheriff's vehicle if bringing out the honesty in most people. I notice a large recreational vehicle pull in at an angle to get as close to the pumps as possible. I watch him, and after a while, stroll over and start a conversation with him. I notice the pump clicks off at $116.50. He pulls out a clump of money and asks if I would bring him two quarts of oil. I walk over to get the oil and hear his large vehicle pulling out to get on the highway. The thief was lucky in that there were no cars coming so he jumped on the highway, heading for the interstate. I yell for one of my coworkers that we have a thief to catch. We rush for the sheriff's car, turn on our sirens, and rush for the highway. Fortunately, the vehicle has Pennsylvanian plates, so I realize he will be going north for a while, so I shoot across the on ramp, and northward I fly. About two miles ahead, I catch him. I am glad, because the next exit was only four miles, and he could have taken a back road to throw me off track. I bet he was surprised to see the police catch him this fast. I yell on my foghorn for the four of them to exit with their hands high and stand against their recreational vehicle. I park our vehicle in the slow lane, forcing the traffic to decrease. I leave our lights on so people will recognize somebody is in trouble. The four of them mother, father, son, and daughter line up against their vehicle. My coworker opens the trunk, gives me a holster, and he takes a rifle. I walk up, standing behind the man and tell him that he and his family are under arrest and going to jail. Our judge might be out of the hospital in six months, so we will try to get them bread and water at least twice a week.

His wife and children begin to cry. The thief volunteers to pay for the gas and tries to say he simply forgot. I tell him he will pay for the gas, and then go to the fool's jail. We do not let idiots roam free in our county. He gives me a hundred and twenty dollars and asks me if I have the change. This makes me extremely angry. I start to put handcuffs on him. He asks if there is any way we can settle this now. I tell him we have a minimum fine for stealing of $250 cash. He takes out the money and gives it to me. Accordingly, I tell him this is the smallest fine, and it does not include leaving the scene of a crime fine. I tell him another $535, and we will let him and his family go. He tells me that he merely has $185. I unsnap the handcuff from him, raise two fingers to my coworker who pulls two more handcuffs from his bag, and we handcuff the wife, son, and daughter. I take the $185 and tell the man we will send him a note when the court date is determined. We begin to take the wife and kids to our vehicle. After a few steps, his wife tells me she has the money to pay the fine. I ask her how much she has. She tells me $700. I tell her to give that to me, and I will let them go. She gladly hands it over to me. I release them, split the money with my coworker, and rush back to the station. This time, I park the sheriff's vehicle by a pump on the row closest to the road. My coworkers help me be caught up; meanwhile, our station owner arrives and asks about the sheriff's vehicle being parked in the front row. I tell him this is to create an appearance of security. A car with mashed front pulls up to the unleaded pump and begins to fill his tank. I notice the gas is spilling, so I rush to that pump and stop it. The pump reads $1.23. The man apologizes and gives me two dollars. As I am putting it in my pouch, I notice a $100 bill between the two single bills. This man is big and strong. Fortunately, he is laughing and joking with me. I give him three quarters and two pennies. My boss comes out and asks him if everything is okay. He tells my boss this is a lucky day because I saved him much money. He did not know to stop the pump, and that he put the pump in his tank without opening his tank's spill valve. I was glad he put this pump in his gas spout. I would have made the same mistake. The cheerful man leaves.

Consequently, I head for the restroom to check this money. I take the two ones and the one hundred-dollar bill out only to determine they counterfeit. From a standard distance, they appear normal, yet when I read them; it says the United States of Georgia and other irregularities. I figure he did this in case the Feds caught them. He played on my greed, and I fell right into his hand. I deserved this and am lucky this only cost me two dollars counting the change I gave him. Evening has chased away the daylight as we have turned our lights and station sign. Our boss is still here, so I decide it is time to have fun. I put several firecrackers behind our station with my cigarette to burn down and set the fuse. I set four of them on different points of the cigarettes. Accordingly, I go and sit down beside our boss who tells us he is so proud about the way we worked together in the present day. I was, likewise, excited about the almost $400; I made extra today. The firecrackers began to pop, which really made our boss mad. Initially, he wanted us to stand behind the station and drive these troublemakers off his property. I ask him who is going to pump the gas. He tells us never mind, because he is going home. A car pulls in with one of my previous military friends in it. We chat for a little while, and she pulls out vanishing into the horizon. The station lights begin to flicker before going dark. This is great; we have two more hours and no lights. I sit with my coworkers as we discuss the events of this weekend.

The conversation becomes so boring that I come to be sleepy. Another adventure has drifted into the annals of the dark world.

The exam

I found myself relieved to slip away from the station unharmed. It was so refreshing to get that money and not have to pay for it through suffering. I heard the faint sounds of people laughing, and soon I appeared beside them with a beer in my hand. We stood in a large parking lot with a railroad track built on a bridge over the highway crossing it safely above the highway that ran in front of this celebration lot. People were telling tall tales to each other, as the small six-inch fish turned into three-foot giant sea creatures. I enjoyed watching them wobble back and forth to the dumpster to toss their empty beer bottles into the trash. The law here is that if one bottle is broken or discovered in the lot, then the drink outside will be outlawed. I have seen men who could not walk, make it to the dumpster and back without breaking these bottles. This chance to drink outside is worth its weight in gold, a privilege they would kill to keep. My favorite part will soon begin, and this is when a local country music band sings a few sad love songs. It helps the beers go down slowly and smoothly. Our situation changes as a large group of rough looking bikers come plowing into this lot, laughing while everyone scrambles for their lives. This time they are much more aggressive than previously. The gang does the unforgivable and sends members into the dumpster to throw beer bottles onto the lot. Patrons were leaping in front of the racing motorcycles trying to catch the bottles. It quickly turned into what country music fans always called the mud, blood, and beer. This escalated into a fierce battle, as everyone from inside the club rushed out and more bikers came flooding into the lot. After a few hours of brutal fighting, the police arrived and the bikers, who could, fled at once.

The police took twenty-seven injured bikers to the local hospital about ten miles up the highway. They discovered the raid was on behalf of their gang leader's brother being injured in a hit-and-run accident. The captured members were taken to jail pending their court date that night, and then taken with a National Guard escort to our state prison. The members gave an account of their hit-and-run charge, which everyone ignored claimed the offender to be a state hero. That night, I received a surprise social call from my father, who seldom paid a visit. He asked me if I promised to keep a secret. As every person does, I assured him I would. He then confessed to injuring the gang leader's brother. I asked him why he did this. He revealed that this man brutally beat a son of his friend who attended his church a few years ago. He waited this long to remove any association with him and the event. The past few years he tracked the daily habits of this evil man and could predict to some degree of accuracy his weekly habits. I told him that we could not, under any condition inform anyone. The bikers will rage a war now, for the most part, revenging the twenty-seven in prison currently. Revenge they did, as they unleashed attacks in many regional stores. We soon were placed under a martial law, even though they hit a local college capturing a medical assistants' class and raping seventeen women. This turned into open war, as I saw people rushing out onto the roads as the bikers rode by shooting at them. The extent of this resistance, extended to the ambulance drivers who refused to bring the injured bikers to the hospitals, and even if they did bring them to the hospital, they were refused care. While on one of my country walks on a Sunday morning, a group of bikers comes racing along the highway behind me. By the time I determine who they are, I find myself surrounded by them. They do not look happy at all. I ask them if anything is wrong. These bikers tell me that my still being alive is an injustice. I ask them what I did to make them hate me so much. They answer since I am not with them, and then I am against them. Their leader tells me not to give him any story that I had no part in the recent attacks against them. I do not respond, knowing that anything I say will result in more misery for me.

Subsequently, two of them hold me, while others begin hitting me. Each strike renders a thumping sound, nevertheless; I do not feel any pain. I am wise enough to understand if I fail to show pain and hurt, they will strike harder. Accordingly, I am going through the motions. Because I offer no resistance, they soon grow tired and decide to tie me to a pole and start a small fire below me. Complaining about the boredom here, they pile on their motorcycles and blaze away from me. My lone comfort was the time they spent on my misery; it spared others from such torture. I wiggle my feet, as best I can being bound by rope. I continue to wiggle my feet using them to scatter the wood beneath me. I believe that with no wood, the fire will not burn me to my death. I am fortunate, in that I kick a few burning sticks against the back of my pole. The small fire burns my leg ropes from behind permitting me to pull my feet free. Once they are unrestrained, I press them against my pole and jolt myself upwards, slowly pulling myself high enough to free my hands from the pole. At once, I leap frog from the pole landing on the group about three feet from the fire. My liberation from the fear of burning, now shift attention to my body and possible injuries. Fortunately, I have no broken bones, and my burns appear not to be severe. I will apply lotions to them when I return home. I cannot walk on the highway; however, I can slowly step on the soft dirt of the side ditches. I make it back to a bar on the outskirts of my town and go to cross the bridge. This will be painful, walking on the concrete, so I attempt to pass as quickly possible. Just before stepping onto the bridge, I hear someone call my name. I quickly drop low, peek under the bridge, and see my father. Naturally, I ask him why he is hiding here. He explains the news reported the bike gang knew who the person who injured his brother is.

I offer my house as a sanctuary, explaining that they most likely just passed through and should not return for a while. Our small town sits along a state highway with access to the interstate super routes, and a junction with another road that connects to another major highway less than eight miles from us. Thereby, our tiny town, even though in a remote location is easily accessed from many other places. My father agrees to follow me to my house. I am curious if they raided my town. We rush across the road and up a small hill. I see two houses burning to my left behind a row of trees. There is smoke coming from my side of town. My heart is beating as I feel sweat soaking my body. The pain from my burns has lost its sting and must now join the rest of my body as I can merely hope my family is not harmed. I am actually running now, nevertheless, the faster I run, the more homes I see that are burning. Consequently, my home appears and it is not burning. Two of the three homes that are burning are across the street from my house, and the third one is burning on the hill behind my house. I circle my house working my way to my back deck; spotting no danger, rush in my house. I search our down stairs and rush up my stairs checking the first two rooms. So far, I have found no one. I have just one room remaining. This is when I begin to make promises of never sinning again, giving food to the hungry and clothes to the poor if only my family be spared. I pause before entering my master bedroom. The fear of them not being in here almost cripples me. I finally go in, with my father's push and look around this room. My day changes from dark to being flooded with sunlight, as I discover my wife and our two children snuggled beside her, all three still sleeping. They slept through the intrusion by the bikers. We inspect the other rooms and notice dirty footprints throughout my house. I determine they searched the downstairs and when they came upstairs to check the two rooms at the top of the stairs and while in a hurry, decided the last room would produce no results, and ignored it hoping to find better luck in one of the other homes.

My father and I gathered a portable battery charged radio and found a local station, hoping to hear some news about the gang. We had no electricity since one of the burning houses destroyed a section of the wires. The radio reporter announced the bar town that this war started in was now under attack from the bike gang and fire trucks from a station north of us were on their way to our town. The government is sending troops to contain the gang. They decide that today the war will be fought as a war. My father appears to be depressed and feeling guilty. I remind him he needed not be concerned. So many people in this area have challenged members of this gang. He is not the sole one, and if fact I question those, they even suspect it is him from such a small nonfatal hit so long ago. We finally hear a report the gang claims to have found their person of interest and punishment settled. They continue to fight now because they believe their liberties have been violated. We agree the only liberties they should debate are those offered in solitary confinement at a Federal prison. Someone begins knocking on our door, sending chills throughout our bodies. Accordingly, a voice that I recognize calls out my name. I rush to the door, so they can be inside and not easily exposed outside by any rogue gang members. Once we are inside, my neighbor tells me our town is forming a guard unit. They fear the gang may retreat to this area when they are forced to retreat from this current engagement. We form a force of thirty people, collect every weapon in town, and set up our positions. Fortunately, this town has many hunting enthusiasts. Bow hunting is popular in this area; therefore, we can supplement our bullets and use guerilla warfare with the crossbows. We are caught by surprise as a reinforcement gang enters our town from the opposite direction. Nevertheless, we can inflict casualties by striking from behind with our crossbows. Fortunately, my town mates are excellent shots, as one missed arrow could have blown our cover and forced them to attack us. Considering we were shooting from the hillsides that this highway went through, the arrows did not travel too far once pass their target, and in a few cases hit the wheel of a forward bike causing a crash, providing us with additional easy targets.

Nevertheless, we took advantage of these targets going for the kills. We agreed that a potential prisoner would merely invite trouble and put our families in danger. We have a few game processors who live in our town who are quite handy with their knives. They slash the injured biker's necks as if moving through air. We bring town ten of the thirty-two who went through our town. We spread ourselves to cover the three entrances. The one entry descends off a large winding hill, therefore, making it impossible to anyone to rush in over us. We plant one older couple in a house, about one and a half miles up the hill with hand radios. This will give us enough time to shift our offense and pluck them as they move through the open areas. The twenty-two who made it through our town foolishly tried to sneak back in our town, walking the creek that passes behind my house. They were unaware the creek would send muddy water downstream, which alerted us about the possible intrusion. We dropped a few emergency lines attached to raccoon traps into the stream. As they pass through, the lines snap thirteen of them, leaving them as easy targets during our cleanup. We open fire on the remaining nine, plucking them one by one as if on a turkey shoot. To save on arrows and bullets, our resident butchers sliced the throats of the fifteen trapped bikers. My father and I return to our house, knowing war will soon break out here. The mood was different around our table that night. My son wants to hear stories about his Rambo father, yet my father, and I are disturbed that we are now killers, even though we killed to save the innocent. My son tells us about the other fathers, and how they fought with swords, machine guns filling the bikers with so many bullet holes before they sank in the creek dead.

We tried to give my son the security in knowing his father, and grandfather found strong and clean against evil and dirty. I was fortunate in the one shot I had that brought down a nasty biker. I almost hesitated before pulling the trigger, however, when I saw him point at my neighbor, which was it. He had to go down or my neighbor's wife would become a widow. Killing to save those who are innocent, many of which pay taxes to help fund our military, from other citizens who are breaking the rules is sad, nevertheless, apparently a part of survival. Our generation has enjoyed Homeland Security, a gift; we believed a right, which was instead, as through all the ages, won through blood. Our electricity was restored; thereby we could now watch our TV for the news updates. The battle continued to rage around the town up the road from us. The battle lines were now in the forest covered hills around that village. No house remained intact, as the fighting went room through room in each home on every street. The biker force united and fell on this village, as it was easily accessible from a nearby interstate. The National Guard was breaking holes in the biker's defense and after hours of fighting has trapped these terrorists into pockets. They were pressing the pockets, and finally the local residents were safe. When the dust settled in the late morning hours, all but the leader and his immediate guards were not located. This created much tension in our area, although we believed they went back to their secret place, which remained a mystery to the public. We sat our children down and tried to explain how today was a day we fought to keep our homes and families' safe. We did not look for the fight; we waited until they proved their intent to do us harm. This does not make us great; it simply shows we will fight to keep what we earned through lawful means. We were afraid our children's bragging could invite future trouble in our neighborhood. Nevertheless, they have the right to share the pride they have in their adults. I am puzzled because of all this fighting, which comes in spurts, and then all the explaining and adult interactions that follow it.

Our neighborhood formed into small groups as, we attempted to digest what happened yesterday. The news concentrated around the bar town up the road from us; therefore, we became content with the thrill of our victory and realized the gang would not be out of business forever, and they were animate about getting their revenge. My father asked if he could stay for another week, since he wanted to give things some time to settle. He believed that once a little time passed people would not be so eager to discuss this social disaster. Each day became less jumpy, as we struggled to rediscover a peace that once rested inside of us. I was actually beginning to hear myself talk in my head once more. As a survival mechanism in response to the immense danger we faced, our minds became more attuned to the environment surrounding us. My wife decided to take the children to a fast-food restaurant in our county seat, which is fifteen miles from here, although she had to pass the remains of battle town, as everyone renamed it. My father and I were watching TV when we heard someone knocking at the back door. I went to open the door, yet held back at the last second because I could not see who was knocking. Suddenly, a tall man pops up in front of me with a pistol pointed at my head. My back door had a nine-panel see-through glass window. He cocked his pistol and motioned for me to open the door. I slowly open the door as this man pushes me to the floor. I glance over to my kitchen and notice my father has moved. Accordingly, this gives me a little relief, as I know he could not handle a beating from these thugs. This gang of three rushed in rolling over me. When the lead one entered our kitchen, I heard a shotgun fire as his head splattered over all of us. I looked over to a small opening between my back entrance wall and a cabinet I put there. In this space, I had a few of my gardening tools. I grabbed my dandelion root tool and jabbed it in the stomach of the third man who was trying to scramble over me leaving the house. I grabbed his pistol and pumped the second man's belly with four pistol bullets. At the time, he was trying to shake the headless body of his leader from falling on it.

Consequently, my father could pump another shotgun round in the second man's back that even spread a few additional shots into the first man's back. This encompassed the embodiment of irony, so close to having my mind speak to me once more, merely to be splattered in brain and blood. I could not believe how slimy this crap is. Without any doubt, I shall never again put ketchup on my scrambled eggs. The thought of this almost made me vomit. This war was now officially over and the righteous won. My neighbors came to check out the gunshots, conveniently waiting until my house was quiet, and they spotted by father and me putting bodies on my back deck. I was more terrified of my children seeing this blood bath that I forgot how close death came to kissing my shivering lips. Fortunately, the ambulance and police showed up the same time the media did, processing the scene and providing me names of particular cleanup crews. Ordinarily, they had a three-week waiting list due to all the recent violence, notwithstanding this was the scene of the leader's death, and everyone wanted in on it. They were already waiting at the door and willing to do this work for free, so I told them to work together and get it done fast. The police took away the bodies, with only the media still on the scene with my children got off the bus. We are the famous family presently, and I knew strutting a little was appropriate. I asked the police and the media to use maturity in the way that would be proper for my children and the other young people who hear this tale. I was afraid the local children would want to become raging Rambos attacking everything that moves. My son and daughter, accompanied by every kid in our town were raving about my heroic deed. I tried to pass most of the credit to my father, who immediately spun it back on me. He later told me that it was so prominent for our future generation to respect us. The important thing was this nightmare was finished, and we had survived. I grabbed my children and began swinging them asking if they were ever again going to forget their chores. My son asks me if I want to play catch with our baseballs. Unfortunately, he asks me while throwing a baseball at me. He must have thought his superhero father could catch a ball without looking. Either way the baseball got me in my nose. Once more, I could feel the sting a pain rush through my face; my world became fuzzy fading away. I am so thankful this was merely a dream, and that it finished. Understanding that my night world may be influenced by what I eat in the day world, I am now on a strict diet.

The ring of life

Each day I wake in my life, merely to be reminded my struggle evolves around one issue, and that is to survive the day. Even though the night world evolves around death, mystically life follows, whereas in the day, the fear evolves around death and ends with death. The fear of this zone of death must be guarded as it steals the life from each breath. I believe the joy of the night world is the escape from death. There is no finality in death, yet the confidence of my name remaining somewhere among the living a few decades. I hear so sounds surrounding me that resemble a war zone. Nevertheless, I believed the battle was behind me. Even so, those distant sounds were too near for me to drown. This illusion distilled itself when a mirror beside me shattered. There is nothing more shocking than dodging a bullet in a dream. Suddenly, this battle zone is not such the distant memory as I thought. It is as in the instant water in a pan begins to boil over a fire. One second is peaceful, and then the next a realization the water, which suddenly is hot, will merely get hotter until the agony of boiling chases away the dreams of even a return of winter. No amount of chilling thoughts can appease the penetrating burn.

This sound of battle is new for me. I was, merely last night within a few miles of a raging battle, nevertheless, that was close enough for me even it was solely bikers fighting hillbillies. Nothing against hillbillies, as I would not tangle with them for to do so is as sticking one's head in an open mouth of a starving lion. The air is not solely dominated by explosions, shattering material, but also cursed with the screams of the living, escaping the mutilated bodies that once held their dreams. These screams exploded louder than the bombs that caused them. They bring home the realization that our own screams are merely a misfortunate second in the future. I duck down and trot along the side of buildings as I try to understand where I am and what is going on around me. I am astonished with so many buildings in such disarray flooding this landscape, nevertheless; I have yet to see a person. If it were not for their screams, I would believe no other existed. I try to convince myself that I am alone; however, the constant screams each day and night tell me different. Pain and destruction controlled each ounce of air, which charged through my mouth. The emptiness created by the absence of people and the solitude it brings feels the same as floating in the space of the distant universe. The need to see another person is overwhelming and controlling my ability to concentrate. Everyone in this area is hiding, notwithstanding they are still becoming casualties of this war. Accordingly, I find myself walking around in a daze. Finally, I saw something walking across the field. Subsequently, I froze and then dropped in behind a tree. Careful observation revealed there was a group armed soldiers reconning this area. The men appear to believe they are safe since they are walking in an open area. They would be easy targets for snipers who could hide in the houses and apartments surrounding the park they just crossed. I do not know for sure if these are the bad people or the good people. The lone thing I can do is stay low, and watch them monitoring what they do. Not exactly the Rambo style of fighting, yet I believe it is better not to kill someone who is on the side of the innocent or entitled.

My question is answered soon enough as I see a child running between some houses and the three soldiers shoot at him filling him with over ten shots. The child dies instantly. This puzzles me being the first time I see someone who is alone would be a child who ends as a bag for holding bullets. Next, I hear the soldiers talking and notice they are heading in my direction. I do not recognize what to do, and understand I could end like that little boy who just died. This presents the philosophical question of why I should expect to be saved when that small boy was not spared. The soldiers begin firing at me, and I drop to the ground, knowing that my checkout time would be soon. Subsequently, I heard a noise to my right, turn my head, and see a two-foot yellow ring with golden lights inside. The lights were spinning in circles changing colors the deeper they orbited inside the seemingly endless sphere within it. As I look inside the colors change as those within a rainbow, do. Each loop had small sparking stars throughout them. The energy that radiated from this rainbow hole was as nothing I experienced during all my previous days. I longed for the serenity that was pulling me into this peaceful haven. As I placed my hand inside the hole when the light went out, and I felt something bump my hand. Instinctively, I grab a cold metallic item as it rushed by my hand. Afterwards, I pull it out to discover what is in my hand. I am holding a machine gun attached to a bag of loaded magazines. The sound of the men's feet was now to close for any form of security. I swung myself into the open and began firing this machine gun immediately hitting each. As they fell, I reloaded my magazine and fired once more. I saw the dust splatter on a few shots, and if not for this; I had no other manner, except for the way their bodies fletched since this machine gun had a silencer on it. I placed in a new loaded magazine and walked out in the alley to make sure the three were dead and to hide their bodies.

Afterwards, I walked down this alley to inspect the apartment where the little boy came out. As I was walking, my weapon began to burn my hands, thus I tossed it to the ground. Subsequently, I entered the apartment where the little boy was heading and began to inspect each room, as quietly as possible. Surprisingly, I felt a knife, press against my back. I turned around to discover a group of six, three who was women with knives pointed at me. They were dressed like the boy, so I did not perceive them as hostile and asked them who they were. They answered this town was their home and asked why I was here. I explain this to be the same question that I have been asking myself the previous few days. Curiosity overwhelmed me, thereby causing me to bombard them with questions. I began by asking why the soldiers were killing all they saw. Nobody answered, as all looked at me, as any would have an alien from some other world. I explain there is not much difference between an alien and me in that we both are from other unknown places. There is no benefit for me to argue where I come from, as I cannot remember. The night world continues to turn me into a knight from another world. The stranger they think me to be the more likely they will allow me to stay around them. Strange people are most times not considered dangerous, although nothing more could be from the truth. I follow them down a hallway, when we mysteriously come under fire. There are soldiers everywhere. I look over and see the golden ring reappear. Hearing bullets destroy the vases and furniture that surrounded me as I rapidly forced my hand into this yellow hole and pulled out a green bag that opened as I dropped it to the floor. As quickly as the circling hole opened itself, it closed itself vanishing from this dark room. Fortunately, my eyes were not affected by the sudden light shift. I saw a lit smoke bomb, and tossed it in the direction where most of the shots originated. Consequently, two grenades, without pins rolled out of the green bag. I grabbed them with both my hands and threw them caring solely to get rid of them. I heard them bounce from two walls as they instantaneously exploded.

I hear those who were previously held me at knifepoint cheering. I slowly rise to my feet and notice I have a two-pistol holster attached at my waist. I fear this could indicate hostile forces are still active and thereby wave for them to seek cover. I hear a noise behind me, swing around drawing my pistols and firing perfect shots killing three soldiers. It is times like these; I am thankful I watched westerns as a child. I still have my pistols; therefore, decided to hide in a side room for a few minutes and reload my pistols. Mysteriously, I have an immense fear of not keeping my weapons fully loaded. This most likely is because I recognize these are not the movies where they shoot for hours without loading. I walk back out into the hallway to search the remainder of the units on this floor. My concern centers over how they got on this floor. The units are locked, which does not give me any edge, in that if they entered an unlocked apartment, they have an option to lock the door behind them. Fortunately, the unit manager accompanies me as I flush the apartments. I engage in three confrontations as I flush out the potential snipers. When the third one falls, my weapons vanish as well. This leads me to believe this group is safe as I reassure them; they are secure for the time at hand. Several have asked me where I found the weapons I had. I seriously try to explain they are at the same place I found them, and then casually walk away from them. I realize they are in danger if they are around me. Therefore, I walk back to the alley deciding to make myself an open target, having faith in the ring that was giving us life. I walk in the wide open, believing this as my mission until two snipers begin shooting at me, one hitting me in my arm. There is no golden ring leaving me as an open target with no shield. I hear a few more shots causing me to drop to the ground. My current difficulty is that I dropped in the center of the street as nighttime is quickly approaching. This world begins to fade, as I find myself lying on the floor in the middle of my bedroom. Fortunately, my wife has already left for work and an examination of my body reveals no gunshot wounds.

Direct sales

I wake up in my house in the village I helped save in the recent battle. I have been involved in my share of battles and gun fights recently. It would be pleasant if I had some escapades that were not accordingly blood bathes. I try to stretch my legs in this comfortable bed and notice I am not alone. Soon I determine they are my children, comprising one son and one daughter. Subsequently, I resume resting in my defined space and await morning. When morning arrives, my children tell me they are hungry and want to know if they can go to the hospital with me to see their mommy. I boot my computer and open my password's document. Next, I discover that I have a checking account and open this online. I want to see my sources of income and expenses. Afterwards, I open the scans of my paycheck deposits the bank keeps online and right down the address where I work. This will be strange; nevertheless, I find myself growing accustomed to this adjustment process. While I am laughing with my children, our phone challenges the serenity of our joy as it rings. This turns out to be from one of my coworkers, whose father owns the company where we work. She informs me that her father is filling bankruptcy and closing down his business. Therefore, she invites me to the office we share to collect our personal belongings. We agree to meet in two hours. My mother shows up at my back door and asks me why I am not ready for work. I tell her time got away from me, nevertheless; I will be on my way quickly. As I depart, she asks me if I have any news. Notwithstanding, I reveal the strange phone call I received from my coworker and the potential dissolving of our company.

Accordingly, she agrees to keep a watch out for the help-wanted ads, as I tell her, I will see what my coworkers are doing. I complete this fifty-minute drive and wrestle for a parking space. The back lot is unusually packed today. I walk down the back alley between our building and the beauty college's building. We share this outside smoking area. After entering, I walk up our stairs, which led to the owners' offices and then pass the meeting room. I can hear the laughter and celebration coming from the meeting room. I peek back in the owner's office, which is packed with the field managers laughing and joking. Even the co-owner's office is packed, which is strange in that few enjoy this office. As I walk into our training room, everyone appears to be overjoyed. They are singing songs and behaving crazily. I see the coworker that called me walking down the steps from our office. I ask her to tell me what is happening. She apologizes for the wrong information she gave me on the phone. I am to be the sole one dismissed today. I ask her if she knows of any reasons. She believes the owners want to promote a sub-owner's wife. I tell her it is time I moved on to something else. Training people for direct sales is getting old. The pressure from the rejection they face each day, plus the chaos created by the income fluctuations gives weeks of feasting followed by weeks of famine. They were a special group of drug addicts, convicted criminals, and others who life had tossed a few bad breaks. Together, they had formed a sales force that feared no social boundaries. These people worked hard, pleading, begging, and did whatever it took to make their sales. I had grown fond of them over time and tried to help anyway that I could. I noticed that it was extremely late in the day, a time when these people should have been in the field looking for people to sell their merchandize. I asked our office manager why everyone was still in the office. She explains that no one is going anywhere until deciding whom the new owners will be. This hit me as I ask her if I was the only one to be fired.

She explains that no one is fired; it is simply a few who are aligning themselves in groups contingent on who takes the reigns of this company. I walk back to the owner's office, merely to be stopped by his wife, our co-owner. She invites me into her office and asks if I understand what is happening. I begin by saying outside the fact that her daughter told me I was the lone one to be fired; everything else is merely mumble jumble to me. She explains that no one is fired; they are eliminating who they can before the dust settles. Accordingly, I ask her why they are selling this business. She explains there is no money in this field, and they are getting out before completely sinking in red ink. I marvel how they are pitching the profit potential to the eager sub-owners who can solely see themselves making all this 'perceived money.' Such are the ways of the greedy to steel from the needy. Apparently, they purchased a farm in the hills of Pennsylvania and plan to hide out there for a while. She tells me this in total confidence. All will believe their previous owners are in Hollywood retired. If this is what they wish to rely on, then I will not take away this source of hope for them. I smile and walk away from this sad place, a place where the sheep are about to be slaughtered and the wolves have begun their blood hunt. I decide it is time for me to find a position in place where I graduated from high school. As I walk out of this workplace, I wave goodbye to those who notice me. I see a few that I would never trust and have always fought hard to avoid. Today, the succubus are braless and have their fangs sharpened. They will leave with their pockets filled with money, and the promises that many great sales will occur the next week, with these commissions flowing their way, as well. I at no time really hated these girls, for at least were out there with these boys trying to scrape sales from a challenging and hateful public. I knew, as I walked out the door this time that I would never return. I felt fortunate for the lone thing that was hurt in this dark adventure was my feelings.

Gamma

Concentrating on myself is driving me on roads that are going nowhere. Actually, they are going up, down, right, and left. The point I am trying to emphasize is the going nowhere would more accurately be defined as going in circles. Round and round I go, where I end, I do not know. I find my assortment of night escapades to encompass a vast range of challenges. My day life continues to flow along a conservative route, which is instrumental in keeping out of jail. As the day gives me rest, and feeds my mind, the night takes me through a myriad of roller coaster style adventures. I find myself excited as the lights go off and reality fades.

Two stars

My world returns as most things reappear. I am in Army BDU's (Battle Dress Uniform) walking around our headquarters with other soldiers picking up cigarette butts. Once we finish, we return to our offices where we work on our computers, which entails more foolish compliance than actual production. Our position and status are determined by what is on their shoulders. It is not so bad, as long as each in their position treat others with respect. Our current situation at work is good, yet at home is the opposite. The few factors I know about my home life are that once more, I have two small children, this time my wife is in the hospital, and one of her sick friends is helping me watch my kids. I work a part-time job with my Army pay to keep up with my wife's medical bills. I notice my relearning curve is functioning faster in this adventure, as I am almost up to speed with this situation. It is more of a hanging on for a better day sort of existence. The days are met with challenges that rush in quickly and harshly, and the slow process of defeating them. I use the term defeat loosely, as I do not feel the urge to destroy or take in possession. My urge is to spare the pain and suffering of my little ones, if such a thing were possible. The thought of raising these children alone is not as terrifying as it once was. My spouse has turned into a heavy ball and chain that attempted to hold my head under the water forbidding air to enter my mouth. I allow myself to sink until my feet are firmly on the bottom, and then push with my strength until my head bobs above the water's surface. I work toward a shore where I crawl over the ground, sliding through the mud. Somehow, special tools appear where I can work off this neck chain. For the first time in so long, I see myself trying to stand.

The lost weight takes my complete family away while I escape into the barracks. I find myself living alone in a room, empty and trying to discover what the new meaning of my life will be. I spin daily, and hope I can land on my feet. This proves to be a challenge alone I can no longer face. This is compounded by my decision to stop smoking and avoid coffee. My equilibrium, had cause for being out of balance, so this was the time to forge ahead into a new sense of whom I am. I soon discovered I could not walk on this tightrope without leaning to one side. I found my balancer in bourbon, which took away the horrifying urges from my nicotine withdrawals. It was now as if I were breathing in the bourbon instead of the nicotine. This was keeping me in balance currently, nevertheless; it was a delicate balance to maintain. I had nothing else to use as a crush, and my life was open enough to take certain bold fresh actions. Accordingly, this would be a time for building a new foundation. My grammar held be back from continuing my education; therefore, I decided to search another avenue. A new tool was emerging in our workstations; an item called a desktop computer. We had other office tools, such as workstations that were part of large centralized computers, yet we took these as glorified typewriters. We shied away from these desktop computers, which had things called a 'mouse' and were supposed to do these great things in the future. They had already evolved into the second, of what would turn out to be almost endless new generations of possessors that were faster and handled more tasks, combining photo albums, banking, TV, movie, libraries, and music into a new age of perfection and mobility. They could even replace telephones. Each stage offered minute upgrades, which seemed like giant leaps for humanity, and guaranteed enormous leaps in credit card balances. I find my spare time to be a luxury of the past, as this computer is solely dedicated to doing everything; it is not supposed to do and never to do what it promised to do. Years later, one of my military supervisors claimed that computers were possessed by the devil. I thought about this and if it applied throughout the years of misery inflicted on me by computers. I could think of no argument that could refute his claim.

I stumbled over the limited world of new software programs that seemed merely to change with an increasing cost and copy protection each week; I saw a grammar detection program that apparently would work with a word processor I was using. This was a time where everyone was creating the same programs with small variations. The learning curve for each one was the function that kept their followings. I loaded this grammar program and soon believed it knew what it was doing, therefore, I talked a friend into joining this night school program and shortly thereafter was on the road to a beginning. My divorce ended in my favor, as I reestablished a home with my son and settled into this fresh dimension in my life. My social life plummeted, because of my intense interest in computers, graduate night school, and new stress from my workplace. This stress came through a new leader who was military gung ho, which is not bad within itself. It hurt at the time, yet as I have told my children so many times, someday they will appreciate it. I can now appreciate what he attempted, yet as with most crusaders who try to bring change, we suffered our clashes. I rather feel sorry for the man now as I look back on it. I enjoyed the extra-perceived attention from my coworkers as we created this misery. We had a wide variety of female senior Non-commissioned Officers (NCOs), which was safe dating material. The military has a hidden rule concerning this, even though I secretly entertained female officers at my house. I still kept my distance and minded my manners, as I did not want any unneeded troubles. I could generate this on my own. This was the beginning of my star problems.

A female lieutenant and I were getting along fine, both professionally and soon personally. I managed to keep control of the personal part, which forced her to expand our small private network to include one of her friends, whom I later discovered was active-duty Army as well. She worked in an intelligent unit on our post, and thereby kept a low profile, rarely seen in the open air. After our first night sleeping together, I discover she is a promotable captain. This makes her a field grade officer, which is bad news if she gets angry with me. I ask her why she did not tell me. She reveals that a male colonel is trying to date her, and she does not want him as a special friend. This overloads me with stress, which is compounded when my lieutenant friend discovers how our relationship escalated without providing her an opportunity for a relationship. I asked her why she ignored all my advances. She confesses she did not know these were advances. She was learning about me, and I was learning about her. We were different races and did not want to offend each other. I reassure her that if I can get out of the relationship with her captain friend, I will gladly come back to her. A few months later, they confront each other and fight in public. Two female officers fighting in public caught the eyes of the higher-ups. My name eventually surfaced, thereby pulling our commanding generals into this scenario. They were disturbed that two of the three in this event were from their command. The generals did not want the news of two women fighting over a man, especially in that it was officers fighting over an enlisted male. We had three generals on our top floor, a three-star, two-star, and a one-star. The two-star was appointed this task; in that they believed, the damage caused by a mistake would be too risky for their one-star who tended to have anger issues. We were summoned up to the top floor as he first brought the three of us into his office. The lieutenant and I were careful to respect the promotable captain considering the general could regard her as not merely field grade, but also career orientated. It was touch and go, as we, for the most part, tucked behind her, and let her take the lead.

The two-star first asked for a history of this crisis. The captain explained the lieutenant matched her with me. She claimed the lieutenant told her she had no romantic intentions with me and that she believed we would make a good couple. Consequently, she begins to cry, telling the general that she gave her heart and life to me, wanting to start a family and have a house. She trusted me with all deepest love. I saw a small tear pour down the general's cheek. The captain continued that she planned where we were to have our wedding ceremony and presented to the general a page from a magazine showing the rings she wanted to get. The general asked her to have a seat and then question me for my part of this story. He began by asking why I targeted female officers. With this, both the captain and lieutenant told the general, I was not a prowler. They explained this was a mature male and female interaction. They had received flowers, and their doors were opened for them when they entered a car or a home. Both contended I had treated them like ladies. The general looked at me and claimed I had melted their hearts with promises and romance that I could not continue. I knew not to say anything that would make him angry. He wiggled in his chair and then asked why I ended the relationship with the captain. I presented a note she had written me explaining she was ending our relationship. The general read the note and, after shaking his head, asked the captain what her problem was, in that she wanted me to, I go that she received what she asked. The captain explains to the general that she changed her mind a few weeks later and ordered the lieutenant to leave me. I did not know of this part and even wondered in my head if this was the motivation behind the establishment of this interracial relationship. The two-star ordered us to behave as ladies and gentlemen always when in the public. The next time we were called to the floor it will be in front of the three-star who would be sending a few of us to prison.

Subsequently, we went back to my house, after getting my supervisor to release me for the day. Their question was if any of us got into trouble. Everyone was generally happy we made it through the star grinder. We went back to my house and agreed to have dinner together. I grabbed a roast I had in the freezer and tossed it and several potatoes in the oven. The two women finished preparing the meal as we ate together and drank selected wine. Considering they had to drive home, and I might have to take my son somewhere when he came home, we kept out drinking to merely one small glass each. I felt excellent the captain was on favorable terms with us. We agreed to stay friends. The lieutenant agreed to farm me out to her for special occasions like when her family visits. Families want to see someone, which meant I was stuck with all the hard social responsibilities, except for soldierly events. I, being present in military ceremonies would bring back memories of our two-star encounter. The lieutenant and I decided we would tell my son about our relationship, and she would move in with us. The deal was when she was in uniform; she would stay clear of our house and change clothes before returning. I was so far behind in my social skills, having fallen into the clutches of my computer. I learned how to buy components, and then assembled computers, building one for my son and one for my woman. My spreadsheet and database skills improved as we worked on joint projects. We were having a wonderful time as a family unit, as it was special to have someone to help me with my son. We were enjoying the now and therefore, were not planning. This came to a crisis when I received orders to go overseas. The lone way we could keep this housing unit was to get married, and she did not want to marry as, deep down, neither did I, considering I recently escaped my divorce. I allowed the Army to put my household goods in storage, took my son back to my hometown, and bordered the plane and up into the sky we went. My world begins to fade with the light going out.

Coon hollow

Remarkably, my world begins to reappear as this time I am floating over a narrow country road with tree-filled hills to the left and a hundred-foot wide level field to the right. The flat field starts as a section of a large cornfield that runs along the two hundred-foot entrance at the junction of this road known as Coon Hollow. I float up the road toward its other entrance wanting to discover the complete road before establishing a landing point. I pass a few old crumbling buildings that I remember passing when traveling this road during my childhood. Next, I pass my grandfather's farm, though it appears as it did when it was new and not the ravished decay it was the last time I saw it. The primary difference is the grass is cut, and junk cars that are now restored. My uncle's house he built at the creek fork in the cornfields between the road, and the bottom stream has yet to be built. Instead, there is a crispy log cabin beside a tree with many branches. As I continue looking beyond the forked creek, I see a beautiful white house with flowerbeds bursting with splendor. I always called this area the Biggly farm when I was a child and explored the small rivulet that ran beside it. I swoop back to the right burn who makes up the fork that joins in front of the restored cabin. I now return to the dirt road that connects the residents of Coon Hollow. I continue to pass a house that has no porches, which is strange for this area. I remember a little girl catching the school bus with her once when I was staying with my grandmother as a child. This house looked glamorous with its fresh white wash. I notice they have a wooden roof with no walls where they sit outside. This appears to be what they use as a porch. I will test the merits of this concept on my way back from the top of the hill ahead of me. Coon Hollow road curves to its left at the base of a high hill that forms the beginning of this valley. The farm at the base of the hill still looked cared for when I saw it as a child. The farm looked majestic as it looked down upon it. I decided this would be the best place to live in the early days of Coon Hollow.

I walk up the path that leads to the side porch to this two-story golden-yellow house. The path leads back to their fresh black barn with an advertisement for chewing tobacco. These old timers living with chewing tobacco in their mouth as the hot, dry summers make smoking a fire hazard. I am fascinated by the lovely white board fence they have, which marks the boundaries for their personal yard. I look around the barn, which it extremely well kept. The people who live here are hard workers that appear to have pride in this area. I never knew much about them, yet I can see they have many sons who are working with the horses in the field plowing. Afterwards, I scan the area and so others working around the yard, vegetable garden, and one chopping wood. I notice how strange it is there are no electric or telephone lines. This is truly another place in time. Consequently, I would suspect they would be depressed, not having all the modern luxuries; nevertheless, they are not missing what they do not know. Continuing, I wave at a family member working on the front porch who does not respond. Apparently, they cannot see nor hear me. As I walk down to the road, I hear someone say bye to me. I spin around and see an old woman waving at me. I wave back at her, telling her I said hi the boy on the porch, and he ignored me. She explains that her son cannot hear because of a childhood illness. She asks me my name, and I tell her. She asks me if I am staying with Jacob and Barbara. I know of a Jacob as my second great grandfather, thereby if they are under forty that would make this before the Civil War. I explain my journey started in New Jersey, and I have been walking for many moons and ask her if she would tell me the current year. She tells me last she heard it was 1852. I ask her if anything special has happened recently. She explains that a man from nearby Germantown brought a book back called Uncle Tom's Cabin by Harriet Beecher Stowe. I ask her what this book is about; as I am sure, there are plenty of cabins in the area. She believes it is about people trying to help slaves gain their freedom. I ask her why no one will do anything at the federal level about slavery. The old woman tells me that there will be doing something someday, yet for now, the big fight is to keep it out of Ohio, especially knowing Virginia is but a few miles south. When she told me this, I remembered that West Virginia and Virginia were one state during this time. This elderly neighbor tells me they are establishing a local military unit to help fight the South if they invade Ohio. I felt sad knowing they did not know the extent of the death and destruction this war would bring. They would discover this in due time; therefore, I wished her luck. I later discovered that four of the seven men from Coon Hollow to die in the Civil War were from this family. The world would invade Coon Hollow with the sting of her misery taking her greatest product, and those were the future generations. I consider myself fortunate in that my ancestors fared much better in the wars. I walk down this path, observing the road does not have gravel on it as I had always noticed as a child. The road has various creek bedrock that appears to have been hammered into the road. A young boy named John comes up beside me and asks for my name. I ask him his name first and if Jacob is his father. He confirms my suspicion; I am talking with my great grandfather. I saw him once as a man near his death when I was a child. This is one of the most amazing moments in my life, and I want to cherish it. I tell him my name is Bill Clinton. He tells me this is not a good name and that no one with a name such as that would ever be famous. I agreed and changed my name to Clint Williams. John tells me this makes much more sense. I explain I just arrived from New Jersey and plan to live with various relatives in Marietta. John tells me that Marietta is too close to Virginia for him. I ask him what he dislikes the most about Virginia. John tells me it is the dead slaves who drown trying to swim across the Ohio at night and were misdirected into the Muskingum River.

I could see where at night this could be a problem. I always thought this mouth was large when looking at it as a child from the Ohio side. The rivers did not have any conservation dams at that time and was dependent on mountain waters when it flooded. These seasons made this river virtually impassible as it overflowed its banks. I ask John how they got these rocks to stay in the road. He tells me they wait until it rains and dug holes in the mud and tossed rocks in these holes. When the roads dry, they pack the mud back to level the road tops so they do not hurt the horses. This was a community effort in which they kept the roads safe for their horses. I saw that by them, allowing nature to help in the process, the road was holding strong. Notwithstanding, I used to hate the way the dust would fill the air in this hollow when a car drove by on the hot summer days. This was a sizzling day, yet it did not feel as dry as when I stayed here in the summer. We continue to walk down this small road, with freshly planted crops to my right and a sturdy wooden fence to my left. I ask John about barbed wire for fencing. He tells several places, do that in the west, nevertheless, they prefer to make this area resemble the homeland, and that in Germany; the landscape is bounded by white fences. This makes sense. He adds that barbed wire cuts animals and hurts hunters when they are trying to hunt. It is also easier for deer and bear to bypass. I tell him that I believe a bear can still bypass a wooden fence. He agrees, yet adds that he is not as angry when passing through boards as he is when being cut by barbed wire. I agree with him on this issue, especially considering I would not want to be in the area such an event occurred. We continue walking to the next house, which is the one that never had a front porch. I ask him who lives here. He tells me the Davis's. They are from England and tend not to mingle much with the Germans in this area.

Accordingly, I ask him if this could be the reason, they do not have a front porch. John explains he believes the reason they have no foremost porch is that they built their house too close to the road. Their mother decided she did not want a door along the side of the house as they originally planned, so they built a door, with a few steps down the side of the house facing the road, which enabled them to walk straight from the house to their wagon. He further adds they spend so much time outside; they constructed a special meeting building without walls. I ask him why they did not make it closer to their house. John informs me their son told him this was because their butcher and process their livestock and their mother preserves much meat rather than salting it as most everyone else did. She cooked many things that created odors or smoke, and they wanted to keep this smell from their home. They also sang songs outside when their relatives joined. Their father drank wine and moonshine when his friends visited. The boy told John that his mother did not allow any drinking in the house. The Germans in this area were not too fussy over religion. If there were a church in the locality, they would attempt to fit in with the congregation. The English were different as they had many conflicting denominations that were constantly fighting among themselves. Some tried to influence the local government in Ohio, yet always found themselves not in line with public opinion. John tells me that religion can still be a touchy issue, yet history reported so many abuses because of religion and with the Salem trouble, and he did not mean Lower Salem, which was merely a few miles away, Americans burned as witches this put a foul taste in most people's mouths. They joke over Southern pictures of the plantation owners standing proudly in front of their large churches, yet use money earned from slavery for their version of the Lord's work. It was growing apparent the lines were forming against the north and south, as each was trying to lay their claim upon God. To see such a young child speaking so harshly against this told me that his parents and church most likely were preaching hard against this. Notwithstanding, I am against slavery; however, being this close to the borderline and within a decade of the war is too near for comfort.

We kept walking considering John and the other people in Coon Holler were not openly social with the Davis family. They, nevertheless, waved when passing each other. John waved at the family, especially since three of their boys were playing in the front yard. They asked him who I was. John told them I was his friend from New Jersey who was moving to Marietta, so he could be with his relatives. This news spread quickly throughout Washington County giving credit to Coon Hollow. I realized that between each hill was a small creek flowing in the larger stream that poured into the bottom meadows. I can never remember so many wild flowers growing everywhere. This surpasses any paintings I remember of Ohio's landscapes. I cannot ever remember being under such a spell in this Hollow, although I remember getting close one night looking at some family pictures with Grandpa and Grandma when they still lived in this special place. I wonder now if that might have been the seed for this escapade. It is so strange that I consider this place as my home while I am walking through my history. Everything is accordingly alive here, with no knowledge or worry about tomorrow, and a keen insight into their family history. Their families survived the famines, wars, plagues, and other challenges that hungered for their lives. Life in this hollow demanded all work together to survive. Any who tried to cheat these laws were cast away. John explains if he does not do his chores, Jacob will give him a powerful whipping. I ask him if he has a little spare time now. He reassures me all if fine. I look over in the sloping valley to my right and see a pleasant looking small farmhouse with a large barn. John tells me the Parson's live on this farm. I remember hearing once as a child that my grandpa bought the Parson's farm.

Nevertheless, I turn the opposite direction, walk toward the bottom meadow, and follow the northern stream from where the two streams join. We pass a wooden house, which is located near where my uncle built his cabinet shop. He told me once of a tale the people who lived in this house had much money and hid it underground somewhere in this area. We pass them while heading for the stream. A young man and woman are pumping water from their well. We wave at them, as they enthusiastically wave back, asking John if we want a drink of water. We thank them for their kind offer and continue walking. The water in the stream is crystal clear, although I can never recall the water being bad, as it is so close to its source to become polluted. It generates that wonderful splashing sound as it fights against the rocks in its bed, a sound that it continued to share with the world when I was a small boy exploring the wildness of the untamed wilderness. I created this in my mind while listening to the hidden words deep in the dirt and rocks. I believe myself to be special now that I hear a few of these sounds as they come into our world. There are no doubt the words and noises made this year will echo through the halls of time for future years. We walk across the stream and immediately come upon a rock path that leads to the house up this small hollow. They have gone to an extreme extra effort to make this entranceway special. I ask John if this is permissible, and he reassures me these people are among the kindest neighbors possible. They enjoy the privacy offered by this separate adjoining hollow. The one thing I always believed so special about this hollow when I explored it with my uncle when I was a child is the widest collection of huge round rocks spotted throughout it. I remember these stones appeared as if they were dropped from the sky, as they were, likewise, out of place. I never found another hollow with such large stones looking as if they were guarding against intruders in my journeys around the world for the next fifty plus years of my life.

These rocks not merely elicited excitement from me, John as well ran over to play with them. They had carved several small holes on the backside of these rocks, which permitted them to climb on them. I followed him up the rock, and we stood on top beating our chests as if we were supermen, a superhero that was still pending discovery. He yells at me to keep an eye out for Indians. That is the big challenge facing America at this time since most of the wild Indian fights were in the west. We hear a certain awful screaming from one of the older men; therefore, John and I rush to see what the commotion is. We see a wagon with a broken axle. The old man is mad because he ordered it from a new company called the Studebaker Brothers Wagon Company. He argues this is the first time he had a modern wagon break, and that it was a miracle; he got it here from Lower Salem. He will take the broken axle back tomorrow and demand a little boot for his time and labor. They pass around their moonshine jug and start-taking drinks as four men, coated in coal dust come up to join them. I ask John about these miners. John reports they dig in three mines along the hill on this side of the meadow. I remember seeing these mines once as a kid, although we were forbidden to go in them. John explains they sell the coal for the steam engines and save a little for heating their homes. They hunt for dead trees for their firewood, as wood is needed for their buildings and fences. Coal keeps them warm in the winter and provides them a little cash for the markets, although they seldom get that many store bought goods. They believe food from stores is dangerous for their health. As I think about his words, I recognize there is more truth in this than he realizes. I marvel at how many terrible disease cures were found, nevertheless; new ones came in with a vengeance. Accordingly, the sting of death chases throughout the ages. These people do not appear to worry so much about death, which could be they flirted in this fashion close to death so many times; their ears grew deaf.

We cross back the stream and head toward what would later be my grandfather's farm. John explains they just moved this house from the other side of the hill. I asked him how they did this. John reveals they took the house apart, brought the boards here, and nailed everything back together. We keep walking toward the little stream that runs pass the house and through the meadow joining just before meeting the hill to our far front. I remember building a sizeable dam in this small stream once when a kid. I look up at the well-groomed landscape around this large two-story house. It appears so much larger from this viewpoint. I look up the stream and see many small houses built beside it. I ask John, how many homes are along this stream. He tells me last count was eighteen. It looks as if it was a small town. I heard tales about this, but never believed it. I ask John if there are any graveyards in this area. He explains that most people now are buried in the church at the end of this road; nevertheless, many were buried on top of this hill in the olden days. I guess early settlers in this area lost a few battles with the French and the Indians and buried their dead, while the few survivors headed back east. I remember finding this graveyard once as a child and telling my grandparents about it. They explained many told tales about this graveyard, yet outside talking about it, no one was ever interested enough in searching for it. They believed it was better to leave sleeping dogs alone as enjoy the tales they created on this land and forget about those who settled before they had adequate security. I merely had one more tale to clarify. Accordingly, I asked John if they had any ghosts in this hollow. He shares a story that a man whose wife had died of illness went to the barn beside the road and hung himself. John continues by alleging that on the anniversary of his suicide, this old man travels Coon Hollow looking for people to talk. If any who sees him do not talk with him, he will tie a rope around their neck. Darkness falls before we can make it back to the house. I look down and see a man walking on the road. I wonder if this is that anniversary night. The man looks at me, and I begin running, crashing into a tree. My world begins to fade signifying my Coon Hollow miracle is now lost to the ages.

Our replacements

I begin to appear in a bed with no shoes or socks on my feet. Accordingly, I find myself enjoying this rest, while I look at my wife. I enjoyed my previous adventure, being alive over one-hundred seventy years earlier. That time appeared so peaceful, although I merely enjoyed a sunny day's walk sightseeing. I was not as the ones who worked the coal mines, fields, roads, but instead one who stood upon a rock beating my chest, fighting made belief Indians, who had merely a few years earlier battled to hold this land. I wake up in a world free from many of the evils of that time simply to be slaves to new forms of death and destruction. Such are the advancements of humanity, enhancing death along beside life. The stillness of this contemplation is shattered by the sole intruder who may legally enter a home without fear of respect, as our phone begins ringing. Worse than an alarm, as it demands comprehension, I reach over to stop its unforgiving rings. I begin with the standard hello and how may I help you. The voice asks to speak with my wife. I ask this person to identify herself. She requests I told my wife that Gina is calling. I relay this message to my wife who grabs the phone and begins talking in another language. I previously believed that all night language were the same language. Furthermore, I have no idea whoever Gina could be. They talked for about thirty minutes, after which she hangs up the phone. I ask her with a curious voice who this was. She ignores me. Accordingly, I wait for a short while and ask once more. Subsequently, again, she ignores me. She casually gets from our bed and goes to the room beside us. I leap from this bed and rush into this room, once more questioning her about the phone call.

Notwithstanding, she continues to ignore me, which makes me extremely angry. I begin yelling demanding to know what the conversation was. She refuses to answer me and leaves our house. I follow her to a McDonalds. She enters this building and walks into a back room, as if a normal practice. I try to follow, nevertheless; two tall man grabs hold of me forbidding my entry.

I struggle unsuccessfully with these strong men as they toss me to their side. I vow to return and pass them. One of them swung at me hitting my mouth; accordingly, I struck back clawing his face. I realized he would not fall by my strength, thus my sole hope would be identification if we were to meet in the future and our sides equally matched. This scrape gains me an unwelcome kick in my stomach, which provided me with an unwanted nap. When I awoke, confusion filled my eyes at first I believed I might be in heaven. Surrounding me was four blond-haired women, one tall, one with curly hair, one with short hair, and the final one wearing glasses. They tie me and toss me in the back of their van. I attempt to reveal that my wife is in McDonalds. These women tell me to be quiet and things will work out in our favor. Accordingly, I smile in that they did not tell me to shut up or kick me to the floor, so decide it may be in my benefit to hear what they have to say, after all I would not want them to think I was not a gentleman. I sit back deciding I have trusted those who were much uglier in the past and therefore, this time could do considerably worse. I wonder how they can fight without me to protect them. I see a case where I jump in at the last minute to rescue them. I reassure them that if they get into far over their heads, I will be here to save them. They smile at each other and tell me to duck down and keep out of view. I see the lights of a large truck as it pulls in beside us. The drivers leap out and rush to the rear while assisting in unloading a trailer load or chairs.

This time I have a full view of the unloading process. Something is so wrong in the chairs go into the open lobby and appear to vanish in plain sight. I have been around long enough to know the chairs are not supposed to vanish in public view during the middle of the day. Either way, the five of us stared in disbelief questioning if what we saw was real. Two of the women take off running, while the other two leaps in the truck behind where the driver sleeps. Guards came out, seized the van I am tied in, and took me to prison. They ask me why I was in the back of the van, and I tell them the driver accused me of taking chairs. The guards throw me into a prison cell in one of the lower dark floors. I hear a little noise shortly thereafter as I see them bringing in two of the women, the two who tried to escape from the McDonalds. I joke with them, after the guards leave, they must not be too great in that they were caught. The women inform me they allowed themselves to be captured so they could find and rescue me. I ask them if a rescue were better if the three of us were outside these cells as compared to being locked inside them. Accordingly, they ask me if know how to get out, and if I do not to be quiet. I look at them and tell them this is the last time they will tell me to be silent, or they will be kissing my fist. I ask them if they understand what I am saying. They both confirm they understand and begin jiggling at their cell locks. Within a few minutes, their doors come flying open. Once they are outside their cells, they stand in front of mine and ask me if I am ready to hit them with my fist. I wink at them, explain that I am a married man, and as such no longer enjoy knocking sense in women. These girls tell me they will save me this time; nevertheless, if I get mouthy again, they will have to show me how they handle bad men. Immediately, I complain they would think of me as not being a wonderful man. They kindly ask me not to make so much noise as it could alert the guards, and they are not in a mood to watch the guards whip my bottom. Meanwhile, they opened my cell and invited me to solve this mystery.

Likewise, we must first secure the two members currently in the loading truck. I ask them if these women are captured and thus be in a prison such as, we were, or if they are still working undercover somewhere in the structural network of our enemy. My favorite of the four women, the one who wears glasses that I call Sharpshooter, clicks on a program in her laptop and detects their locations. The tall woman who I call Respect because we must look up to her, comments their two teammates are moving in different directions. This suggests they are scouting the facility or facilities. Respect claims we must return to their base and prepare to a rescue. They ask me if I want to join them. I remind them my wife could be held as a hostage and as such, I have a spousal responsibility. We loaded up with their war-fighting equipment. I asked them if we are fighting local criminals or the Iranians. They smile and say it is better to bring back extra equipment than to die from not having enough. We loaded our supplies and began heading for the GPS source of our detector. We arrive at an old church and begin planning our entry, yet run into an unexpected result. The other two members went back into the truck they arrived. Respect volunteers to contact them. She enters and within one minute, the curly-haired woman whom I call Curly comes running back in our direction. Sharpshooter made a strange bird sound and Curly shifts and heads directly for us. She passes, swings around a tree and low crawls back to us. Sharpshooter asks her where Respect is and why she did not return. Respect tells her Shorty (the short member) kept her, so she and we both could have a complete picture of the current situation. They are planning to hijack the drivers and discover a few more drop off points. Our mission is to invade this church, free any prisoners, and disable any offensive sources they may have. We linger until the truck leaves with our members waiting to hijack them and then proceed into the church. Our entry into this church proves to be different from what we expected.

Meanwhile, we enter a side door and move with caution into the church. Once inside, the church vanishes as we find ourselves now inside a myriad of dark tunnels. I count twenty-two possible paths. Sharpshooter asks Shorty if they knew about these tunnels. She reports they did not encounter this phenomenon. Instead, they entered a series of organized tunnels and heard people screaming for their freedom. Sharpshooter shocks me by claiming we must be in a series of normal tunnels as well and will merely inspect tunnels that are perfectly horizontal and then shall first inspect the ones that run north and south. I ask her why she decided on north and south. Shorty tells me that most churches considered the underworld as evil and thus would purely have gone from north to south. South will be our best choice. I ask them why South is our optimum bet. Sharpshooter asks me why all men are so stupid and then explained this way we would be going north when returning, a concept that follows they would be heading for heaven. I surmise this must mean that if they go south, they are going into hell. They agree and recommend we discuss the philosophy of this doctrine after we save any prisoners who may be currently suffering. They turn on their biosensors, and into the southern tunnel, we search. Soon, they hear something as we drop and point our weapons. Two guards pass up to us, likewise; we fire our silenced rifles and drop the seven in this team. Shorty checks their communication equipment and takes a radio. She does this so she can monitor their transmissions. I ask her if this could also permit them to trace our movements. Sharpshooter tells me we will deal with that later. For now, we need all the help we can get in finding these needles in this haystack. We search through so many empty rooms. I ask them why they believe there are so many open rooms. They believe this could be preparing for a large abduction.

Soon thereafter, we find an elderly man that Shorty and Sharpshooter speak with for a while and then stab him causing him to die instantly. I look in shock to them while they explain to me that this man is not human. I ask them how they know this. Shorty reaches down and cuts the top of the man's head removing his scalp. She reaches in, pulls out a folded plant, and hands it to me. I stare at this plant in my hand and ask her how they knew this. Sharpshooter shows me a small handheld device she keeps attached to her ammo belt. The top of it is dark black. She points it to the man, and the top bulb turns red, as well as vibrating lightly. Sharpshooter reveals she simply turned her waist to the man, and it began to vibrate. Next, she looked at Shorty, who also had one of these detectors, and they winked at each verifying both devices detected this was not human; therefore, they executed him. They may not execute unless both can verify, which their backup safety procedure is. I compliment them on their timely work. We return to our search and rescue or remove. Our search of this hall turns up futile; therefore, we return to the entrance and then search an adjacent hall that is also running north. After a few empty rooms, I ask them why these abductors would think as the founders of this church did, and argue they may have put these north tunnels to hide their abductions. Sharpshooter recommends that I search the southern tunnel if I feel so strongly about this. I tell them I will check the southern tunnel directly across from the first northern tunnel; we failed to find anyone, except for two hostile encounters. I proceed back to the entrance, meanwhile I begin to hear noises behind me, and so I hide in one of the side rooms. Surprisingly, I discover Shorty and Sharpshooter are following behind me. I step into the hall and call their names. I am wise enough to understand the danger of scaring or tracking them. They hide in the side rooms as I had originally done. I walk by calling their names as quietly as I can. I pass the rooms I suspected they were hiding. I thought they were too ashamed to confess that I might be right. Shorty opens her door and immediately acts happy that I am safe. She confesses they were worried I would soon fall to my death and decided to return for my safety.

I saw no reason to humiliate them, so I thanked them for returning to save me and asked them if they could stay with me. Sharpshooter tells me they will this time, but for me not to make a habit of challenging their advanced recon skills. I agreed to save face for us and pull us back together as a team. This is much more important, as bragging rights would be formalized after our victory. I know that dealing with women is different from dealing with men. We reunite and enter our first southern tunnel, immediately discovering research labs and large open cavities. We bypassed these, as Shorty said we must first find if any human containment facilities existed. We found one such area stacked with hundreds of bodies decaying. The smell was so toxic we began to vomit. I could think of no reason my wife would be spared from this, thereby any verification would merely give this beast time to kill more people. We decided to begin our destruction program. Shorty began setting timers on her explosions as we quickly worked our way back to the surface. They also added some smoke bombs to make locating air vents when returning to the surface. Once back in the church, they fired these bombs. We felt the ground shake and began searching outside for any smoke signals. We found three and dropped explosions in them. About one hour later, we get a call from Rescue to meet at the McDonalds immediately. Sharpshooter sees a truck parked along the road and enters the door with her knife exposed. A few minutes later, she opens the door and invites us into the cab while she is pushing the bodies out of the other door. We leap into this truck, while Rescue and Shorty leap into our van. They follow so we will not be lost in one vehicle as this allows us to defend on two positions. This also provides us with a faster escape vehicle. I am simply happy this event is back on track, and as we get closer to the McDonald's, when Shorty calls, they are going ahead and will wait in the back part of the upcoming attack point. They say attack point in case our radios are monitored. Sharpshooter tells me to brace myself and be prepared to jump out just before we hit the lot. They tell me I must swing around and protect their back encase someone tries to ambush them. I think this is odd; however, Curly acts as if it is standard and volunteers to help me. I think nothing about this, until a few minutes later, I find myself floating through the air with Curly beside me. As we crash onto the ground, I hear a tremendous explosion and the ground shake. I look to where the McDonalds was and see a huge ball of fire and smoke flooding the area. Curly tells me we must find Sharpshooter. We walk a few feet, hear her crying, and rush to her rescue. She tells us her leg hit the concrete and broke her leg bone. We brace her leg and Curly gives her a shot of morphine for her pain. She gives me binoculars and tells me to protect Sharpshooter while she rejoins Rescue and Shorty. We soon witness fire trucks and police rushing to the scene, as our van slowly pulls up the road beside us. Shorty rushes out, opens the back of the van, and helps up for Sharpshooter in the back, where Rescue is waiting with a first aid equipment. Once they have her inside, they strap her down, as she offers no resistance. Curly reveals a prisoner and secures this person. She surprised me when she cut off both legs and arms, and tossed them outside our van. What amazed me more was that no blood flowed from his torso. I look at Curly and ask her what is going on. She tells me we are in for one strange story about what is happening in our town. Accordingly, I hear a crunching sound as Rescue and Shorty are resetting Sharpshooter's leg. I watch tears fall down her cheeks and her face turns red from the pain she was holding inside herself. I move over and lift the top part of her torso and hug her as tight as I can tell her she is the strongest woman I have ever been blessed to hug. When I kiss her declaring my pride in her strength, I receive a response that I did not expect.

Accordingly, as my lips depart, her closed lips, she begins to cry aloud. In shock, I ask Curly if I did something wrong. Shorty tells me everything is okay, considering this is the first time she has been kissed by a man. I look at Sharpshooter and thank her for saying I am a man. She laughs and denies saying such a thing. I tell her if she recovers quickly, I will let her kick my butt. Sharpshooter declares she will take all the time she wants to recover and then kick my butt. I tell her she must catch me first. Rescue apologizes and tells us it is time to hear the confession from the torso they captured. I tell them that if he talks from his hands, we are screwed. She asks the thing that we call X how they make the chairs they are unloading. X tells us they grind human flesh and then blend it with sand and wood chips. I ask them where they get the humans. X reveals they rob graves, as the flesh is better for them purposes since blood invited to many bacteria. This gives me hope that my wife is still alive. I ask him what happened with the people they abducted in the McDonalds. He reports they are put to sleep and taken to the address on their driver's license, which is solely done to buy a little time before they destroy all on the Earth. I ask him how they plan to do this. He explains this is the source material for the household items they manufacture. Within three years, they planned to have them distributed throughout most of the world. They will finish within one year. I ask what is so special about these items. He explains that when they release there sister gas, it will activate these household items killing all plant life on Earth and cause current viruses and bacteria to mutate. Eventually, all plant life will no longer exist, causing all living animals and humans to starve if not already dead from plagues and diseases from the mutated bacteria and viruses. Once the planet is cleared from all forms of existence, they will bring their people from their dying planet.

I thank this man for telling us this information. Curly asks him how we can prevent this disaster. X refuses to answer. I tell X that these women are dangerous, yet since they spared my wife if I help him protect their vital places will he save my wife and I and help me punish these women. He agrees to pardon my wife and I. I wink at Curly, while turning my head away from X. I explain to X that I can purely help him save his people if he takes to the place where I can protect them. If he takes me to the wrong place and that place falls, he will be responsible, and I will report him. I show him a recorder that I am recording this conversation. He tells us to go up the hill to a large white church. I yell at Rescue to drive and to go only where I tell her. I beat my chest when I tell her. She rushes out saying she will obey me, and that I am her master. We pull into the church lot where X tells me the sister gas is in the tunnel under the church. I pretend like I am looking under the ground and tell X there are many tunnels under the church, and he will be the cause of the death of his race, and he tried to deceive their prophesied savior. He immediately begs for forgiveness, saying he did not know. I ask him how he could not know; in that I appeared at the most crucial time and made those who tried to destroy them obey me. Who else could have this power? He agrees to take me to the entry of the eastern tunnel. Fortunately, X knows a shortcut, as we enter a small building sitting near the back of the lot in front of their fence. I was glad we did not enter the church in that it most likely was filled with smoke, and he would expect his savior to enter the tunnels. We enter the building and drop down into a tunnel, which opens into ten more tunnels. He looks and spots a small white rock in the wall. Next, he tells me to look over four tunnel entrances and for us to go through that one. I am so glad he is light, even though I feel accordingly awkward carrying a torso with his head about one foot below mine. I want him to see what I am seeing.

We travel a few minutes until we come to a yellow room. I walk in holding him as he becomes angry that no person is here, guarding the heart to his world. He confesses currently to understand why the savior came now. I explain to X that we must leave him here in the back room. This will both protect him and give him a chance to alert others if this room is attacked. I look at him ask that he stays on his toes for our species. I set him on the floor, so he cannot look out the office windows. Curly begins to unpack the explosives as Rescue and Shorty join in placing them. After a few minutes, they whisper to me that we must leave now. We rush out and when we make it to the entrance of the tunnels, the explosions shake the ground. Rescue quickly sets two more, and tells us to get back to the surface. Once on the surface, the last charges blow the entrance to shreds. We rush over to the church and set a few charges in it. The church blows up sealing the tunnels below it. We can merely hope that we destroyed the sister gas. We get back in our van and take Sharpshooter to the nearest hospital. While entering, we see three men lying dead on the sidewalk. Rescue stops our van, gets out, and cuts the man's arm, removing it from his torso. There is no blood. She rushes back into the van, notwithstanding; we try to determine why these aliens are dying. We notice one man lying on the ground kicking his feet. Rescue stops and rushes out to this man asking him why he is dying. He claims that the sister gas kept them alive and when it was destroyed the atmosphere changed. Within one month, they shall all die. Rescue returns to our van and gives us this report. We take Sharpshooter to the hospital where the police immediately rush upon her to thank her for great sacrifice for the human race. I ask one of the police officers if he can take me home. Rescue and Shorty tell the police they would not have succeeded without my great wisdom and I. Curly asks me if she can go with me, and afterwards return. I told her that would be good, because my wife would frown if I brought back another woman with me. In the car, she compliments me in figuring out that X was a fool and could be manipulated into thinking he was saving his people. She asks me how I knew about their savior. I confess I did not know and was shooting in the dark, as even if he did not know of one, I would have to convince him. Most civilizations have some sort of savior. It falls within, the hope of the righteous. Curly reports she was so amazed when X recognized me as his manifested savior and by using their obedience as proof of my power was astonishing. Curly kisses my cheek as our car pulls into my driveway. I look over and see my wife looking at me. I jump out of the back seat, shake the police officer's hand, and thank him. My wife looks relieved as she confesses she thought I was in trouble. My heart begins to beat normal once more, as this world fades away, and I wake up telling my wife that I do not feel like going to church today.

The rich and the poor

I appear in a busy street hearing a man, dressed in a tuxedo in front of a limousine calling out my name. I walk over to him, as he opens the back door and tells me to enter. As I am entering, a young thirteen-year-old black girl asks me if her mommy and she could ride with me. I tell them yes and ask my driver to seat them in this vehicle. The mother begs her daughter to forfeit this ride, yet the little girl refuses and jumps in my car telling me not to worry; her mother will follow, as she did. Her mother slips into the seat beside her daughter and begins apologizing for her daughter. I assure her it is okay, as I would enjoy some conversation on our way home. Accordingly, I tell the mother to tell the driver where they live so we can take them home first. They introduce themselves with the mother telling me her name is Margaret and the daughter revealing her name is Mia. Mia tells me they cannot go home, because their apartment building burned down today. Margaret tells me they will get vouchers tomorrow morning. I ask them about their furniture and clothing. Margaret reports the owner's insurance company will give them money to get what they need within a few days. I tell them this is terrible, and I will keep them for a few days and when they get their money, my driver, who was also black, would take our truck, and help them get their new property to their new home. I ask our driver if he thinks this will be acceptable. He tells me if I say it is permitted, then it is okay. I am thinking this may be a wonderful escapade.

We pull into my house, which is a giant mansion. Mia asks me if I live here. I tell Mia that we will go exploring in this mysterious castle if Margaret can keep up with us. My driver pulls up in front of my home. Margaret, Mia, and I get out and walk up to the front door, which opens as an elderly man named Joe opens the door and invites me into my large reception lobby. Once we are in, I ask Joe what my family is doing. Joe tells me that my wife is shopping with my daughter, and my son is still at his college. I introduce Margaret and Mia to Joe after explaining how their apartment burned down today. Joe reports that he heard the news about the Madison Apartments burning and that the people were temporarily homeless. This eased me, as now I knew Mia was telling the truth. I could smell smoke on both Mia and Margaret. Nevertheless, I can only imagine what they have suffered today. I ask Joe to tell Mia and Margaret more about this house and estate. Joe begins by telling them this estate sits on 2000 acres and has forty-eight buildings. We have ten spare guesthouses empty currently. This is the main house that has two-hundred rooms. Each room has a bathroom. The rooms are grouped in chambers, as each chamber has five rooms and a large dinning and family room. The house has a master dining hall for entertaining royalty and celebrities. Mia asks Joe if any Presidents have eaten there. Joe tells her that eleven Presidents of the United States have eaten here. I tell Mia that I stay busy. Margaret asks me if it is secure for them to be here. Joe tells her that if I have invited them; they are safe. I tell Joe to tell everyone that Margaret and Mia are my guests. Joe waves for a woman standing at the door to come to him. Joe introduces Margaret and Mia to this woman and asks her to notify the staff; they are guests from our master. I reveal to Joe that I am uncomfortable being called a master. Joe assures me the staff appreciate the great kindness they receive from my wife and I.

Joe continues by telling us the house has four swimming pools in the lower basement and game rooms on the upper basement. Mia remarks that she never heard of a two-story basement. Meanwhile, as we continue walking I notice the doors are closed. I ask Joe to open the doors for us, so we can explore as part of our adventure. Mia smiles and claims this is going to be so much fun. Joe tells us not to touch anything because my wife will become extremely angry. She has decorated each room according to different themes. The theme of the room we entered was early American. It was packed with everything, to include closets with dresses and suits of that age. The furniture matched that period, as did the curtains and blankets. The lights were electric, although the bulbs were small, so the originality of the piece resembled a candle. We walk around the five rooms in this chamber, which Mia asks why the rooms have no computers or TVs. Joe reminds her that TVs were not invented in this era. Mia asks what the people who stay in this chamber do for socialization. Joe talks us to a small library and sitting room. This is where they can sit and talk or read, and live according to the colonial American lifestyle. The walls were packed with beautiful paintings. I ask Joe how anyone could afford this much detail. Joe reports that nothing in the other eras or cultures is bought; instead, we invite artists to paint and women to make the dresses, blankets, and curtains. We even bring furniture makers here to make the furniture. Most work for little money in exchange for a family vacation in one of the chambers. My wife also allows them to place their name somewhere on their products. Joe reports the estate and furnishings are insured for one point five billion dollars.

Accordingly, I tell Mia we need to wipe our feet before going in these rooms. Joe reveals that each era or culture has one exception to their period, and that is a modern bathroom. Joe qualifies this by adding that many of the Asian bathrooms have some modifications, yet at least two rooms in that chamber will have American style latrines. I open a double door and discover a washer, and dryer tucked in a tight room. Joe clarifies that all chambers have a washer and dryer and a method to cook food. This chamber has portable cooktops and ovens. He demonstrates how this chamber would prepare their food. I continued looking through the rooms. Joe confesses that my wife has been busy building the best possible home in the world. I was realizing this dream had me on top of the world. I did not care so much about that, as I was enjoying Margaret, Mia, and the way Margaret, and I was entertaining Mia, who kept us a part of what she was doing. Joe took us to another chamber, which was an American Indian chamber. We entered as I noticed this chamber had the walls that faced the chamber lobby missing. These rooms had large tents in them. The walls of these rooms were completely painted as landscapes. This gave an outdoor feeling. I open a tent to look in and see a woman jumping up screaming at me. I look at Joe, who comes over to the woman and informs her that I am the master. She tells Joe that my wife said she could stay here for one moon, as she was the one who designed this chamber. She threatens to tell my wife. I inform her that I do not care if she tells my wife, because if my wife gets angry, I have a spare wife and daughter. I point at Margaret and Mia, who shake their head in agreement. The woman apologizes and then asks me if I honor my wife's promise. I tell her I will if she gives us a tour of this chamber and explains why she created it this way. We compliment her on the detail and comprehensiveness she added to this historic chamber. The center of the lobby had an electric log fireplace. The floor in the chamber's lobby had one inch of dirt packed over it, so it would feel like we were in the wilderness. She turned off the lights and small lights resembling stars on the ceiling, with a large glow to look like the moon. When she turned the lights back on, we were staring at each other in amazement. I ask her if she would like to stay an additional moon, and if so she may have to share it based on whomever my wife invites. She accepts my humble thanks.

As we leave this chamber, Margaret asks me how such a house is possible. I tell her that so far I have seen a creation by people expressing their love in their skills. I look at Mia and ask her if we are ready for another chamber. Mia tells me she wants to see all of them. The next chamber was Indian culture from India. Mia asks me why we call Native Americans Indians. I tell her that I do not know, but it does bug me. Joe tells me this house has forty chambers for the two-hundred rooms. We explore a Chinese chamber, Japanese, Roman, Egyptian, Italian, Middle Ages, Renaissance, French, Russian, and then British. Each one was decorated in detail with paintings, furnishings, and the theme for that culture or era explored and enhanced in perfection. It was almost as if the books that report these themes came to life from the pages to these chambers. I was extremely hungry and asked Joe where we can eat. He agrees to guide me to our master's dining room. I ask him if this is where I usually eat. He reveals that I generally eat in my room or at my office, as our cooks prepare my meals and bring them to my office. I ask him why they go through all that trouble. Joe explains this is because my wife is extremely fussy about what I eat. Margaret claims this is so sweet. Joe agrees and tells me I am lucky she is accordingly concerned for my health. This is not a common practice for the wives of my social class. I ask Joe where he eats. He reports this estate has wonderful servants' dining area. I tell Joe that in keeping with the spirit of our exploration, I want to eat in the servant's dining hall.

Joe guides us to the servant's dining hall. While walking in the hallway, I receive a call on my cell phone. I answer it because it is from my wife. Her voice is familiar, resembling my day world wife, so I pretty well know how to handle this. She asks me what I am doing, which is her standard introduction question. I tell her I am walking down the hallway with Joe, and two new friends I made today. We are going to eat in the servant's dining hall. She reveals the food, there is excellent as she eats there regularly. The same kitchen makes the food for all the open dining areas in our home. She asks how old my friends are. I tell her one is named Margaret, who is the mother of Mia, her thirteen-year-old. They are both black and lived in the Madison Apartments, which burned down today. My wife tells me her church is making food for those who are homeless and hungry from this terrible disaster. She continues that she was to go shopping today, but her church friends called her to the church for this emergency. My wife tells me our daughter is in her foreign language speaking class, and our son is eating with a female friend. She asks to speak with Joe, who takes out a table and his pen and switches the phone to the external speaker. My wife tells him what I can eat and what to make sure I avoid. She also tells him to have Mary get my dinner prescriptions and to make sure I get my insulin shot. Once she is finished, he gives me back the phone. I thank her, and ask her to call me when she gets home. She tells me to make sure I clear with Mary where my guests will stay, as they will be with us for a short while. She continues by telling me some Dutch royalty will be visiting us this week. I ask her if we have a Dutch chamber. She informed me she finished that chamber three months ago and has already received an award for the comprehensiveness of her representation of the Dutch culture and fashion. We sat down, and Joe collects our orders. Mia tells him she will take what I am eating. Margaret looks at today's menu and places her order. I tell Joe to get some extra food because he has worked hard today. Joe places our order and soon the chefs deliver our meals to our table. We feast as I ask Joe where I usually eat my dinner. I think Joe believes I am asking these questions for Mia's curiosity and plays with me perfectly. He tells Mia that I usually eat in my chamber, or I eat in my office. My wife is extremely concerned about my diet, and what I ate. She would have the chefs prepare the food to her health specifications and delivered to my office.

Accordingly, Margaret claims this is consequently, sweet. Next, she asks me why I am being so kind to them. I ask her how anyone could be cruel to Mia. Joe laughs and claims I got her on that one. Margaret reports that everyone is wonderful to Mia except for her father who is in prison. I tell Mia not to let this hold her back. Simply shake it off and focus on her world and enjoying the love from the good adults involved in her life. She agrees. I look around this dining hall and notice the perfection of the elaborate wood trim. I ask Joe about this, and he explains that one of the Chef's sons did all this work, plus many other rooms as a school project for his high school. My wife used other students who requested projects. This has worked out great for the school and our estate as the students have their work portrayed and name listed in our comprehensive computer maintenance database. We toured my estate exploring the guest homes and other structures, such as gymnasiums, theaters, museums, arts and crafts centers and galleries. Mia tells me this is too much not to share. Joe explains that these are shared with royalty and executives from other companies. He explains to Mia that many times, the image of whom you are dealing with is more important than the person you are dealing with is. Margaret reports to Mia that sometimes you must show your thirsty opponent the well before giving them a glass of water. They will know that much more water is behind the water that is saving them at that time. Joe explains to Mia that my company deals fairly with others; therefore, many companies compete to deal with us. This saves money in that instead of selling our services we concentrate on providing them above the table.

We are the sole American company that has a five-star rating from the European Union, China, and our Central Intelligence Agency. The signs to all our business entrances declared just those who 'Will not lie, cheat, or steal' may enter. Any who break these rules for competitive profit are fired and any company we deal with who breaks these rules is forever banned. I tell Mia that it takes more money and effort to cheat others than to ask them what they are willing to pay for our service. If they refuse to give us a reasonable amount, we simply terminate the meeting and put them back on our waiting list. Word spreads quickly, as we also demand arbitration for any arguments. There are so many thieves in the markets today. I tell her I get angry when I think about it. The best defense is to keep away from them as much as we can. We have a protected profit margin that keeps us and those who deal with us both in business. Taking more today, merely leaves less for tomorrow. The best method to gain is continually to improve our products and to make the upgrades economical and profitable for our involved in the transaction. We also demand that all who deal with us be certified. This is to make sure they understand what they are doing and why they are doing it. I look at Mia and warn her never to deal with fools, because they will destroy you in the long run. Run from fools. I look at Margaret and tell her to keep Mia away from fools and drug dealers. Drug dealing is against all of my trade rules, in that both do not gain in the transaction and that as such; someone pays dearly for this imbalance. The limited profits today will lead to great losses tomorrow. Margaret assures me that Mia would never deal drugs. I tell Mia this is not enough; she must avoid those who deal, especially if they think she has negative information; they will silence her. Evil takes all when the innocent comes too near to it. You cannot put your hand on a fire and keep it as well close and not be burned.

Mia asks me how she can do this. I tell Mia that Margaret, and I will help her. Joe asks if he can help as well. We immediately invite him, as I tell Mia Joe may have more time than I do. Joe warns us that he will need me to run interference with my wife sometimes. I wink at Joe and ask him if he thinks our two minds can get passed a woman. Margaret tells us this will be only possible if I add her and Mia to our team. Joe smiles and tells me he thinks we may have a chance now. Mia asks me if it may not be better to tell my wife what we are doing. I agree this will be the best way and thank her for adopting my business policies to real life. My cell phone rings with my wife calling to tell me she is home currently. I invite my gang, with Mary to join me as I meet with my wife. Joe leads me to my chamber, and once we are on the top or fifth floor; he leads us down the wing that has my chamber. Halfway down this hallway, two house cleaners come out to stop us. They remind me that only family may proceed further down this hallway and ask me to wait for my wife in the master chamber's waiting area. We enter this magnificent chamber, which reminds me of a sizeable round church lobby. The ceiling to this room projects through a large round silo that exceeds forty feet above this estates roof with another dome resting on top. This room is made with stone walls as Joe tells me it has additional steel beams attacked to a supporting two feet thick steel frame to hold it in place. It will never fall, even if the house were to burn completely. The walls have a solid white marble finish, with carved stone statues erecting from it. There are twelve open rooms along the circle diameter. Each room if packed with statues and paintings, all copies of the greatest works in history. Four rooms are eastern civilization; four are western civilization, and the remaining is what she has labeled as 'the middle civilizations.' This area is a wonderland, as I notice it has no furniture, including the absence of chairs. I ask Mary about this, and she explains the design concept was that no one would ever wish to sit in this wonderful area. She shows us enclosed steps that proceed up the outside of the silo to the dome, which has a seating area in front of some powerful telescopes.

I ask Joe and Mary how such a structure, as this is possible, as I quickly believe it to be worth more than one point five billion dollars. Mary comforts me in that we have three policies, each for one point five billion dollars. We simply tell everyone it is insured for one point five billion dollars so as not to be over boisterous about the value and be seen as bragging or greedy. Mia asks Mary how often we share this home. Mary tells her there are always at least one fifty rooms occupied by guests, clients, employees, academic awardees and such. One of the house cleaners enters this chamber and tells me my wife demands the guests return to the fourth floor. I tell this domestic servant to tell my wife, we will be waiting on the fourth floor in the Dutch chamber. I am actually extremely angry at this point, yet maintain my cool. I tell Mia we are going to stay in a place where real royalty will be visiting this week. A few hours later, my wife arrives with ten servants asking that we leave this chamber immediately. I remind the servants that I am the master and order them to leave. I hate placing them in this position, yet I also refuse to be treated as a guest in my house. I have preached to Margaret and Mia this entire day that I am a pleasant person and have decided that they will be disrespected by my family. The servants step to the side and lower their heads. My wife is wise enough not to push them into challenging me. Next, my wife comes to me and asks to speak privately in one of the rooms in this chamber. I agree and into a private room, we go. She tells me she is angry in that I brought guests to our exclusive floor. I tell her that so many people have worked to give us this home and therefore, there should be no place off limits.

She argues that we must maintain a certain degree of social classism so to maintain order and respect. I ask her how a little girl and her mother can disrupt this. She tells me I have a choice to make, as I inform her not to give me choices. She storms out with her group, as I ask Joe what is his favorite chamber. He tells us about a futuristic chamber that is amazing. He has been staying in a room in that chamber for about three months now, and knows there are still two rooms available. I ask Mary if they are at the same time vacant. She pulls out her portable tablet and pushes a few buttons, afterwards telling me that two new people came into it today; however, three people departed. Mary tells us we are booked. She will contact housekeeping to set us up with what we need to settle in as if we were home. I tell her something must happen soon as I do know that I had to get up early in the morning to head for work. We entered this chamber, as Joe invited Mary to stay in the one remaining room. She confesses to already having booked her room. This is an important event with a master sleeping on the fourth floor. The futuristic design is amazing. The walls are made of metal, as would the inside of a ship. The walls also have windows that have large-screen TV that show deep space with stars blinking. Joe explains we can program it to circle the sun, or any planet in our solar system or deep space travel as it is set on presently. Every household item is sunk in the walls and ejected through remote controls. The chamber portrays alleged life in the twenty-sixth century based upon projections of famous science fiction writers. I take the first wet air shower in life. It was so wonderful, as the water mixed with soap cleans my skin, hair, and then rinses my head before it almost instantaneously air-dries me. This is too good to be true and the best cleansing in my life. I can merely wonder how excited Mia and Margaret are now. Even the music in this chamber is futuristic. Joe told us this music was created solely for this chamber, as no other copies are available. There is a secret sound wave playing at pitches human ears cannot detect. However, once these are copied to another media, the sound wave activates releasing a loud hissing sound.

I wonder if such a precaution was worth it to preserve this. That did not matter. In the morning, I asked Mary if any of the guesthouses were open. She booked one for us. Accordingly, I asked Joe to help get Margaret and Mia set up in a new apartment, and if he did not finish, bring them back to this guesthouse. My family driver took me to work, where I received an angry visit from my wife. We argued and I finally agreed not to take anyone else to the fifth floor. I did this to get her out of my office. My secretary asked me if everything was okay. I asked her if I did enough to help the poor and hungry. She reminds me that our enterprises donate thirty-seven percent of our earnings each year, and that does not include how much our eleven thousand employees donate. This made me feel extremely well, yet I still have some concerns. I ask her if I treat poor people fine when I see them. She laughs and claims Joe told her once that I brought home more poor people than children do stray pets. I tell her that I do hope so. She tells me to relax in my office, and she will get the chaplain for me. I ask her if that is what I need. She reports that after working this close to me for five years, she knows more about me than even myself. I tell her that on days such as today, I agree one-hundred percent with her. The chaplain arrives, and she brings him into my office. She then returns to her desk, calls me on our intercom asking me if Rev. Martin, and I would like coffee. Rev. Martin, thanks her and asks for two lumps of sugar. Rev. Martin asks me how he can help me today. I tell him that I helped a mother and her daughter yesterday, and it felt wonderful. I think something has been empty inside me for so long. I never knew the loneliness being rich could make someone. Rev. Martin told me the important thing was always to keep love as my goal and I will pretty much be on the path to happiness. As he stood up to leave, a bright light shined in my face, which made my eyes blurry. Subsequently, as my eyes refocused I discovered the world was dark around me, and my giant estate had vanished. I breathed a sigh of relief.

The neighborhood

I will miss the wonder in Margaret and her daughter's eyes as we explored the chambers and the creations within my estate. That place was now deep into the dark world. I gain comfort in knowing there is a place, which respects all the ages, and cultures. I currently found myself floating over a string of houses lined on a circular street with a large park on the inside. I stroll over the park first discovering wooden playgrounds, toy cars, castles, a pleasant merry go round, with a basketball and tennis court. I would think there would be children playing in such a joyful place designed for little people. My curiosity is soon fed as I witness three school busses pouring into this neighborhood each stopping an equal distance from the others. I notice these children are not dressed as children in my day world are clothed. The homes that have more than one child entering them, which is all that I see, are dressed in the same uniforms per family. Each family, which is blessed with multiple children, has their own style or design, as if family crests of some sort. This is not strange enough to post it as odd, nevertheless; it is sufficient to elicit curiosity. I hear some screaming to my left as two families, each with seven members came out and began fighting with their hands. I see them slapping and scratching before they started kicking those who fell to the ground. I watch them fight for one hour, then stop and return to their homes. I find this strange as well. Next, I see a group of five women begin walking through the neighborhood. Suddenly, they start running in different directions. Four returned to their homes, while the fifth one continued running until she was ambushed and taken inside a red shed. I see her clothing tossed out and hear screams begging for mercy. Shortly thereafter, her screams stopped, and the men returned to their homes. Nonetheless, because I am not familiar with this place, I elect not to explore why things are happening.

Accordingly, I am now walking along the circular street and notice I have a white shirt and red pants. I did not choose this style; therefore, it must be selected by this escapade. Otherwise, this is someone playing a sick joke on me. This is extremely different from my tuxedos I wore while dinning in my estate the previous adventure. Meanwhile, none of the neighbors seemed alarmed by my red pants and ignored me as I walked by them. I stroll up to a set of folding tables arranged as a yard sale in a driving lot. I looked to see what they were selling; nevertheless, all I could see was cats and dogs dissected with their body parts spread over the tables. Some empty vegetable cans were filled with a red liquid I believed could be blood. This was appalling, representing acts I could not conceive. What caused me to vomit was how the children came out and bought the animal parts and ate them raw. Some children would throw a creature body part in the air, then drop to the ground on all fours and fight over the beast flesh. I foolishly believed this would be the nastiest thing I could witness until I walked up to a multifamily barbeque. A vehicle pulls up to a group of people who were circling around an open grill. Two men exit the car and deliver a cooler to the grill, where they remove from the cooler an infant. Afterwards, they run a thin pole through this small body, and then place it on the end holders, where they attached a turning wheel and rotated the flesh, roasting it completely. While the infant was roasting, I saw two of the men pay the deliverymen money. With this, the vehicle drove out of the neighborhood. I floated higher to observe where this vehicle went. I was relieved to see the vehicle vanish into the roads of the city surrounding it. Next, I saw the children line up against each other forming two large forces, and then begin to throw stones smashing into the bodies of their foes. I saw children dropping and the ground turn red with blood. This was the final step for me, as I closed my eyes, hoping to end this horrifying nightmare. I slowly open my eyes, noticing how quiet the world is present. I see this world fading, as I seldom rejoice the same as I am now.

Loudest screams

Reflecting on the hell that I just witnessed, attention came to me, except for the fifth woman in the shed, the remainders of the atrocities were committed in silence. I could hear the bones crushing when the young people were hit by stones. This would prove to be in contrast with the next zone that unfolded before me. The Earth focusing before me now reveals a beautiful mountain valley. The bright white ridges drop into a lively green valley, with a stream flowing through it. The grass recedes as it moves toward the ridges, replacing itself with a wide selection of wild mountain flowers. The valley is spotted with weeping willows alongside the stream as its waters sparkle over its bedrock. I witness an eagle flying across the sky and see three deer running through an emerald meadow. I discover a small pond to my right tucked between its weeping willows and six people playing in the water. As I move in closer, I determine it is three men at one side of the pond and three women on the other side. The outer branches from the willow form a curtain for each side. I determine they are swimming unclothed, which considering the boys are separated from the girls by the green inclusive hanging branches. A short while later I see them emerge as three couples, dressed in contemporary blue jeans and pullover shirts. They walk to another group of fruit trees, where they pick and divide fruit to eat. I notice a man jump, grab some leaves, and run to hide behind a tree. I can guess with accuracy what he is doing, based on the speed that he exited and the sigh of relief in his face when he returned. The more I watch them, the further I believe they are humans. Notwithstanding, I will need to watch them more since I will take nothing for granted.

Accordingly, I notice they use their hands much while talking. They walk to what appears to be one of three huts. The men walk into their respective homes, and each brings out a stringed instrument, such as guitars and violins. They join in a group and begin singing various songs and dancing. Subsequently, they begin doing line dances, with the men taking turns playing their instrument, so they can form a five-person line dance. They are skilled at these ceremonial pirouettes, twirls, sways, and turns. Their laughter ends when a tall man, wearing a black robe begins beating his drum. The three couples form a line in front of him. He gives each one rock and pins a target on a nearby tree. They each throw his or her rock at the target. Once finished, one of the men rushes before the tall man and drops on his knees begging that he be spared. This sudden change in behavior catches me off guard. The tall man motions for the two remaining men from the couples to tie their tribe member to the tree in front of the target. Once this man is tied, which took longer than normal as the man being tied was screaming and begging for mercy. His female partner was begging the man in black as well. He picks up a violin and begins to play a sad depressing song. Next, he takes his knife and cuts across the strapped man's lower belly. The screeches of his screams were sending chills through my body. The torturer puts a long rag inside the lengthily stomach cut to soak up the blood. Subsequently, he grossly pulls out this man's intestines. The man's eyes and face turn red, as if in unison, before he faints. Afterwards, the man in black who I will now call Mr. B takes his knife and cuts the near-dead man's heart out. Initially, Mr. B used his knife to cut open from the skin, then his hands to break and separate his victim's chest bones, finishing this procedure by using his knife to cut out the heart. Mr. B takes this heart and eats it raw, while the five other people tremble, yet remain stationary. I wonder why they do not fight back, nevertheless, to offer no resistance while a friend is gutted, and heart cutout is pushing the limits of what I consider moral.

Mr. B goes back to beating on his drum. He is playing it much louder than he performed the first time. The remaining five people line up standing at attention. I suspect he is beating his drums louder to intimate his victims, and suppress any possible resistance. He stops pounding his drum and beats on his chest, then points at his small audience. They begin beating on their chest and screaming. Mr. B walks in front of a man or a woman kicking each person as he passes. The victim must not lose his or her balance when he kicked them. They have their eyes closed for this phase of the judgment. Likewise, as he kicks the last man, this man falls to the ground. The remaining four forms into a huddle and stay put, quiet, and at attention. The last free man and three women tie up their friend as Mr. B sharpens his knife in front of him. I rush to tackle Mr. B because I cannot see another man be dissected while alive. Unfortunately, I have not manifested yet in this event, thus am like a ghost. I need to figure out a method to manifest myself, meanwhile; I need to discover any possible defensive opportunities in the event. I cannot save this man or any others depending on how many hearts Mr. B wants to eat. I find a small path that leads up to the top of the ridge. I find two dead men, with arrows in them and collect their bows and arrows. Fortunately, I can hold and carry these four bows, and about three bags packed with arrows. I lug these down to a weeping willow that stands alone about thirty yards from the nearby forest. Upon further investigation, I discover a hole in the ground. Considering I am currently, a spirit I zip into this hole to see where it went. I resurfaced about one-hundred yards up the hill heading for the top of the ridge. This would be a perfect escape route if I can get the couples into it. I store the bows and arrows here. To bring them any closer would endanger the group's escape. My lone mission now is to fix it, so they can see me.

Accordingly, I return to the terror feast of Mr. B, to find myself sickened by the sight of another man with his intestines hanging out, and chest burst open. Mr. B is eating his second heart; there is no way I can handle the remaining man standing with three women watching his cannibalistic abuse. I begin hitting a tree beside me with a thick stick I picked up from the ground. This turns out to be an apple tree and apples begin hitting the ground, and the remaining four lunch boxes of Mr. B. Mr. B looked at me and asked who I am. I tell him I am a curse sent to destroy him. Likewise, I throw an apple hitting him in his head and causing the half eaten heart fall on the ground. Mr. B drops his knife and lunges for the raw heart covered in dirt. He vigorously wipes it as clean as possible. I look at the man and tell him to get the girls over to the willow in the meadow. He hesitates, and I wave my knife at him and ask if he wants to feed me today as well. He starts to run as I toss apples at the women to speed them, so they can catch up with their remaining man. I turn to Mr. B that is chewing the remains of the heart he is eating. I strike him with my longer stick first hitting his head, knocking the raw heart flesh loose from his hands. I instinctively hit him once more with my stick striking him hard in his skull. He rolled over, at which time I immediately started stabbing him repeatedly with his long knife. Finally, I took this knife and cut his throat, yet no blood poured. This convinced me that Mr. B was dead. Accordingly, I ran to find those whom I rescued, having just a set of tracks to follow. Later, I notice one set of heavier tracks going toward some rocks. I pull out my knife and concentrate on all that surrounds me. I feel a slow breeze crosses my face, and the aroma of fear. This odor was familiar with the smell that drowned the air this afternoon while Mr. B was enjoying his last day of killing. I felt it ironic that he would be sweating more over me, one who is trying to save them, instead of the one who was eating them. Such are the mysteries of life.

Notwithstanding, I knew something was about to happy and I had a feeling this would not be what I intended when I rescued these people. As I approached the hanging branches, I heard a crunching sound as a stick pushed its way through just above my head. I grabbed the stick and pulled it forward as I wedged my knife up between whoever was coming through the hanging branches over me. This mystery ended as fast as it started when I saw Mr. B's knife thrust through the third man of the couples. I could not determine why he had tried to kill me. Subsequently, I heard some screams and looked up to see three women, with bows, pointing arrows at me. Someday, I will learn that it might be better to leave those with broken hearts alone. As for now, I immediately shoot into the opening under the weeping willow and rush for the hole that I discovered. I make it in, brush away my final footsteps, and roll a few rocks into the opening that I had collected earlier today when I was preparing this for a possible escape route from Mr. B. These women are much better than I expected, in that I see the arrows flying in here now. Accordingly, I run through the tunnel making it to the top of the ridge. I reach the top and immediately go to work to seal the exit. Knowing the tunnel descends to the valley's floor, I begin to roll large stones into the exit. After I roll the third stone, I hear a scream. Notwithstanding, I have no intent on killing these women; however, if one were to be injured the other two would stay beside her until she recovers. With this in mind, I begin rolling parts of dead trees over the exit. My goal is to prevent the light from entering the exit; thereby the women would be crawling in the dark, which is something that I would not enjoy the least. I decide to make a run for it now, figuring it would be better to stay on the ridge until spotting an area that may be secure. Accordingly, I run for a few hours, when I realize my hunger is too intense. My attention begins to fade causing me to trip over a loose stone. As I hit the ground, everything fades and then soon returns where I find myself awakening drifting back into the day world.

Casanova and the cutup

The thought of having women chasing me with bows and arrows was not the adventure I was seeking. My escaped usually rotate from deadly to peaceful. I hope this rotation continues. I appear in a classroom, with gray cracked walls and creaky wooden floors. I look up to the ceiling above me and see a peaceful cover of smoke. I find it much more appealing than a traditional bone white cracked pasted cement. I look around at my classmates who seem to be disciplined as each time the teacher speaks they write just about every word she says. This is a Biology class of some sort, and the words are long. I struggle just trying to add a few highlights along the way, as sweat begins pouring down my face. This is a something I have wanted to solidify since my 'B' performance years earlier. The thing I remember most about the second time in took Biology was the dedication of the instructor, who did not have fingerprints due to the chemicals he used in preserving the samples for our class. My first attempt was microbiology, which combined with personal problems and illness causing me to lose two of the five weeks of classes and barely passing. The one main memory was the method the woman instructor defined intercourse as 'the transfer of genetic material.' She left a bad image in my mind about that activity. I take out my handkerchief to wipe my forehead; nevertheless, a female classmate sitting beside me grabs my handkerchief and finishes wiping my face. Our instructor stops and asks her if I am okay. She tells her I could use a drink of water. The instructor gives her a glass with water in it, and she braces the back of my head, puts the glass to my mouth, and tells me to drink. I gladly accept this water as it not solely refreshes me, but actually revives me. Our classmates cheer when I pick up my pen signifying I am ready to take notes once more.

Nevertheless, a few questions linger in my mind concerning what just happened. I am confused that our teacher gave my classmate the water to give to me. The teacher did not stop the class when I wiped my head, but instead when my kind classmate wipes my head, everything stops. My classmate has the complete loyalty and support of my classmates. A classmate behind us congratulates her by saying, "Great work, Brenda." I look at her and tell her thanks, as well. She stands up and says, "Anything for my man." Our class, including instructor begins clapping. This is so surprising, yet at the same time; I feel secure in that I can see she is here to protect me. She passes me a note that professes the depth of our relationship. She is beautiful, as most women of the dark world are. When our class finishes, we retreat to a cafeteria to eat our lunch. Our table is packed with other classmates, all who are laughing and eating without a care in the world. Brenda is feeding me as if I was a child. I notice the other girls give her sole dominion over me, as they answer my questions in the strictest respect, with one eye on her at all times. This does not pose any real problems for me in that I can feel all the other boys in this cafeteria staring at me with envy. Consequently, I must be where they want to be, as strangely, I am the sole male intermingling in a relationship with a female. Nevertheless, both the male and female instructors treat us like royalty as we always sit in the front of the classes surrounded by Brenda's following. Brenda does not intimate me with her power, but instead struggles to defend, comfort, and promote me. A bell rattles the walls around us as the students jump up and rush to the classrooms. I jump behind Brenda and follow her to the next classroom. Brenda stops me and asks me if I am okay today. I probe her please tell me why she is asking me this. Brenda tells me I must be having one of my 'brunette' days, grabbed my hand, and pulled me the opposite direction to another classroom. She takes me to another room and tells me this is my class and to meet her back at the cafeteria when this class finishes. Afterwards, I walk into this classroom noticing an empty seat about six rows to the rear of the wall between this class and the hallway. I walk into the class, when a few classmates point back to the vacant seat. Seeing no other empty seats, I slip into this seat. I wonder what is so special about this seat.

My answer comes to me quickly as a female student sitting beside me scoots her chair over beside me. A girl sitting behind us asks this 'Brenda' to pull me over more toward her, so she can see the chalkboard. This Brenda is white compared to the other Brenda, who is black. Both are beautiful, yet this Brenda does not have the same degree of control over her classmates, considering how all the girls in this class wink at me and continue to flirt almost to the point of harassment. One such girl walks pass us and leans over to talk with a classmate in front of me. She is wearing no underwear. I ask Brenda if this is right. She immediately leaps over her desk and rips the girl's dress off declaring that if she is going to show herself to me, then she will show herself to the entire classroom. The boys begin to cheer and parade her around the class. A few minutes later, the instructor tells them to cool it. The boys put her dress back on, and escort this student to her desk. This classroom also is not segregated as the first one was, as the boys and girls are intermingled. I was surprised how they both joined in celebrating their nude classmate being paraded around the class. This confused me, so I asked Brenda why everyone is supporting this girl now. Brenda explains that in this class, we stay together; this is why my other Brenda does not know about us. I was comforted in that she knew about the other Brenda; therefore, I believed this could help me get certain important information about our situation. I ask her how she honestly feels about this other Brenda.

Accordingly, she tells me the other Brenda has powerful friends who will do anything to keep their power. She explains we began our relationship first, then one year into it; Brenda B decides she wants me, and suddenly a few of our friends started to disappear around us. Brenda B offered to help protect our friends if Brenda W surrendered me to her. I ask Brenda W why Brenda B would need to ask another woman for a man. Brenda W tells me this is because Brenda B only wants what she selects, which is usually what someone else has. Brenda W tells me that we must never allow Brenda B to suspect our friends, or we will suffer. Brenda B also adds that we must walk on the needles at the class party tonight. After class, Brenda B has another boy in the class to walk me to the cafeteria where I was to wait for Brenda B, who was late. I ask this boy, what I should do, and I told me if I want to keep my friends alive, I had better wait beside him. Brenda B shows up and my friend waves good-bye and immediately leaves. Brenda B asks me how the class went, and I probe her how any class could go fine. She accepts this and asks me what I want to do now. I tell her all this studying is baking my brain lately, so I plan to follow her for the remainder of this day. Brenda W looks at me and asks whether this will only last for today. I smile and ask her purely if that is what she wants. We go back to our dormitory, in which I discover Brenda B and I share the same room, even to the extent that our names are posted on the door. This happens to be segregated dormitories, by not only sex but also race. Accordingly, this even makes the reach of her power more visible. I can understand Brenda W and her friend's fear for Brenda B. I do enjoy the manner; she has decorated our room, and it does look comfortable, as I can see she has asked me for input. I walk over to our bed, take off my shoes, and lay on the bed. Brenda B asks me if I want to stay in bed for the remainder of the evening. I tell if she wants, and we have nowhere to go. She tells me we have a class party tonight, and that we need to get ready for dinner, as she does not like it when I drink on an empty stomach. We clean ourselves with a shower and redress for tonight. After a lovely dinner at our reserved table in the dining facility, we head for the party. Upon entering the dancing hall, I see a few of my second classmates tied to chairs with their throats cut. This is so unexpected.

Consequently, I ask Brenda B what is going on and why these people are dead. Brenda B asks me if I was sitting beside Brenda W in our class. I told her I was, and thankfully; she saved me from another girl who exposed herself to me. Brenda B thanks me for being honest with her; she knew how Brenda W had protected our honor, and this is why she protected her during this last unfortunate episode. Brenda B owned us; therefore, any missing around with Brenda W was blood, and I do not want anyone else's blood on my hands. The memory of this boy and girl sitting beside each and laughing during our last class is frozen in my mind. Brenda B yells for me to duck as a tall man swings a long sword above my head. I push her back and roll over kicking the man in his genitals, causing him immediately to fall. I grab his sword, and cut his leg to prevent him from escaping. I leap to my feet and scream that no one swings at my Brenda B and lives afterwards. I ram the sword into his chest multiple times. The reason I made this sound as if I were protecting Brenda B was that Brenda W told me they were under her control. I knew this man killed the two students tied to the poles, yet by declaring I was protecting Brenda B; she would not be alarmed by my actions. I acted so confused about everything this day, because I was muddled. Brenda B asked if I were okay, as I inquire why that man pushed me when he had a sword, he could have stabbed me. Accordingly, Brenda B confesses that she was the one who pushed me. I ask her what I did to make her want to hurt me. Brenda B explains she did not want to hurt me; she was just startled that a man was approaching me with a sword. Thereby, I ask her if I did the right thing here because I was so afraid for her security. Brenda B tells me I did fine. She looks at the waiters and tells them to get this body out of here so the dancing can begin. The lone comfort I can take is I punished the killer of those two innocent children, and I will avoid contact with Brenda W. I know it is not right to mess with people's feelings and my lone way to help these people was to stay under Brenda B's wings. We enjoy a slow dance with Brenda B, finally resting my head on her shoulders and closing my eyes to enjoy the music. The music and this world begin to fade as I wake up once more to be an unknown face in an unknown world.

Delta

I altered my activities to avoid any memorial trips into the other zone. This zone is giving me my share of challenges. My love life qualifies as a contender for the most ambitious roller-coaster ride available. This entire process is, consequently, mysterious, as I still cannot believe so many worlds can exist inside my head. It is so unbelievable that so many people can live inside those noodles that float inside my head. I am in these places, and people are sometimes violent, on occasion loving while at other times exploring and even obeying. There is a strange law that controls this realm, which is accordingly real when I am there, yet something brings me back and slowly erases these events. It is merely through meditation upon immediately waking up and recording these events is what gives me that thin fishing line to drop into the lake that holds this life somewhere deep inside me. I noticed that people we label with mental illnesses might have lost that depressive power to shut down this wonderful universe trapped inside me. This is a series of questions we shall never find the answer for, yet worthy of the struggle. I wonder if the events of our dreams may not be a prelude to our existence after death. My flesh has nothing to do with this mystery realm of the night. I travel to these mysterious places spread throughout our worlds and history completely absent from my body. Using this as a foundation for my theory once we die, we simply do not return to the world of flesh. It is this world of flesh, which often harbors our pain and the bad things happening to us. We are subject to so many boundaries and restrictions, as barely few can be the kings, queens, and billionaires. The miracle of this other realm is we each have our chances to be billionaires, to visit those of the past and even in the future. The insane may actually be the sane ones in that they bring something back from the unconscious, thereby leaping back and forth taking parts of the other realm into this realm. I can merely wonder how their challenges in the mystery realm function. I suspect they may not know about their sanity when dreaming. Naturally, there is no current method to explore other people's dreams. Accordingly, I simply understand we must dream to function normally in this realm. Maybe the riches in our dream castles permit us to accept our station in the physical world. These are questions, which lend good for philosophy; however, will not provide the knowledge to control the mortal world. The exceptions come from a few short tales about great men who dreamed amazing new creations.

The classroom

The world surrounding me once more begins to appear. Familiar faces form in the seats beside me. I find myself in yet another classroom. I wonder now if my brain is telling me that I need more education. This just does not seem fair, in that I spent twenty years attending college, most of which was in night school. Either way, I recognize most of the students around me as my high school classmates. Nevertheless, I cannot determine who most of the other pupils are. A few months earlier, a former high school classmate posted our ten-year high school reunion, which had many people in it, few that I could recognize. Considering that photo merely changed them ten years, fifty years later should make most of them unrecognizable. In the world of weird, another strange factor is the classmates; I recognize look the same as when I saw them last. It amazes me that such images can be graved inside extended strands of noodles for so long. When I reconsider these images, the details are vivid just enough to give me a name, which turns the identity into a living force. This appears to be our first year in high school, which was a year of adjustment for me. Our middle school was segregated by academic level as A, B, and C. I finished our middle school in the A group for math, B group for the remainder subjects except for English in C group. This gave me friends in each of the three groups, which worked fine considering our high school was segregated by program choice, such as college-prep, general, and many others. I enrolled in the college-prep program my first year. At first, I was honored that each teacher called my name out initially, when our classes primarily assembled until each made me sit in front of the class closest to them. I later learned my previous year teachers warned them about my disruptive classroom behavior, as I had set a record for most whippings from a principal. Sitting in the front row in high school destroyed my record of poor academic work as I now sat confronted with excellent grades. Academic performance was considered somewhat a sign of weakness in the eighth grade, yet this began to change in the first year of high school in the struggles for excellent grades were now competitive.

In the classroom, I am sitting in now was freshman science. I remember the instructor was tough, yet would toss in a joke occasionally. He gave us much homework, which helped keep me busy at night. This class day had a substitute teacher, which gave us the time to play. She divided us into small groups to work on a project. My group had a popular cheerleader, a Chinese girl, and two other boys, who, although smarter than me were much uglier. We depended on them solving our mission at hand, while I talked to our two girls. I was naturally curious about Asian, as we always considered them the ancestors of our Indians. She really was not much help, in that she was born here thereby developmentally in the same environment as we did. Next, we got our cheerleader, who enjoyed talking as much as she could, to chat. Likewise, speak she did, and even at this it was interesting. We agreed for the three of us to meet on the baseball field behind the school after classes today. My two male group members declined their invitations. I really was not excited that much about meeting with them; nevertheless, I was acting normal while in this group, and they asked for this small discussion meeting after school. I was excited to be seen around them, as they hung with different gangs than I did. We met and talked for about thirty minutes, when I invited them to my house, which was a three-minute walk from this field, which almost touched it and was directly visible. We lived in a large house that we remodeled. It was first class; therefore, I could invite them with pride. It had a large front porch that stood in front of a corner of the house. We had a long swing that usually seated our family of six when we joined, although seldom. I sat on the swing with these two classmates, and we chatted a while, when the neighborhood kids joined us. Soon thereafter, my friends returned to their homes, and life went back to normal. Consequently, when we meet in class the next day, the Chinese girl invites me to sit beside her at the sports assembly. Our cheerleader will be performing; therefore, will meet us after school. After school, we meet and decide to form a club that will investigate local legends. This sounds so exciting. We will ask the cheerleader's grandfather about any old legends or tales in our community.

The next day we meet in the class, believing things were normal. During this class, a group of seven men, dressed in black, rushed into our classroom as the first man thrusts a sword into our instructor, immediately killing him. My Chinese classmate and the cheerleader both scooted their chairs behind me. I remained stern, not wanting anything bad to happen to them. The men spread throughout the class selecting boys and girls and bringing them to the front of the class, where they were undressed, tied them, and then began cutting them with knives. I could feel blood splashing on me. Upon finishing with these seven, they selected seven more and began the process. I knew we had serious trouble because we would be in the next batch or the last batch. Now was the time as we had enough, as I expected the seven tied, once untied would fight as fiercely. I took my book, stood up and threw it at one of the men cutting a classmate. I leaped forward and grabbed his knife stabbing him at once. Next, I stabbed the man beside him reducing the invaders to five. The five began to turn toward me. My cheerleader was yelling for the remaining students to begin throwing books and whatever they could grab hold. I looked around at my other classmates and told them we cannot let these five killers hurt anyone else. The books, scissors, bottles of glue, and other strange items to include a few boots came flying toward the front of our classroom. I took a few hits yet seized this opportunity to stab two more of the murderers. This gave me two knives that I tossed to my classmates. Fortunately, we had a few football players in this class as we rushed the remaining three killers. They got one of the football players, forcing me to stab another of the invaders. Fortunately, the final two fell at the hands of my classmates. We freed the second group of classmates and began tending to their wounds. Two of the original seven were still living, and my classmates worked hard to begin comforting them. We made sure our seven intruders were dead. I now discovered I had two sidekicks, a cheerleader on one side, and my Chinese angel on the other hand. This was fine with me, as they gave me courage, I did not know I had.

I tell my classmates that we must now explore our school to see if any other classes are in danger. One classmate argues that we must stay hidden and escape when they leave. I ask him what will happen when these seven do not return. Surely, someone knows where each group was sent and when they do not return, where to begin looking. Under this situation, we would face their consolidated force, which would make sure our defeat. Leastwise, our greatest battle will be the next one, yet once we secure that, we would have double the weapons and at least twice the fighters. We must move fast, because more are dying while we debate this. We fortunately merely faced three more battles completely freeing our school. Once the school was liberated, the police and ambulances arrived. I did not want to talk about this after school, and was glad that one of the classes I had saved my sister in it. Accordingly, every time I would see her from this moment onwards; I would know my actions saved her life as well, even though all the lives we saved were valuable. My cheerleader friend invited us to her house where her mother took us to her grandmother's house to ride horses. The three of us rode up the hills and through the woods to a pleasant pond fed by a small stream. We attached our horses to the chains they had planted there so they could feed on the available grass while we talk. We sat with our feet soaking in the pond, which felt fine. My Chinese friend boldly blurted out how proud she was to be a part of this group, which is the best group ever. My cheerleader tells us that if she had taken her normal seat, she would have been in the first group. I smile and tell her we were cheated in that we would have seen her unclothed. She kisses me and tells me that I will see her someday, and I get to pick the day. My Chinese friend kisses me and tells me she extends the same repayment as well. I ask her repayment for what. They look at me and answer the repayment of their lives. I tell them I simply did what I had to do to keep our club alive. The cheerleader tells me our club will never stop, and the three of us will be as one until the end of days. I look into their eyes and determine this is what I really need in my day world, without the bloody battle first. Another torment is the rare kisses, which appear in my mind when they are finished. I must search for a tool that will allow me to focus completely, nevertheless; a certain degree of separation is needed when considering the mountains of violence.

The warehouse

My 'world' reappears in a large, two street long Air Force warehouse, alleged to be the second largest building in the Department of Defense (DOD). This was my first permanent duty station in the beginning of my military career. The inside of the structure felt as a separate world, a world that enclosed the repair parts for so many planes that soared throughout the sky the surrounded the Earth. I was fortunate enough to be promoted as among the exclusive after normal duty hour's teams. We formed unique bonds, which permitted us to work as a single unit and most times of the same mind. Our workload at times was easy, which gave us time to study, play cards, and socialize. I attended two colleges and had a serious relationship with a female coworker. She helped provide me extra time during our duty hours to study, so we could have more time together for our relationship. We worked rotating weekends, which gave us time with our former 'day-shift' friends. Cindy was my special friend, and we spent most of our time on base, or visiting remote plantations and other public places out of the main stream. Our interracial relationship was challenging, yet surprisingly; the black race objected the most considering Cindy was black. She felt in danger when we enjoyed our recreational activities without friends. I understood this, and was so proud of my white friends, both male and female who accepted our relationship. My Cindy rewrote the book of beauty when she wore a bikini during our many visits to the beach, a cooling activity during the burning hot days of summer. She eagerly supported my studies and ensured I was prepared for each exam and monitored my homework assignments. She motivated me to perform beyond what my environment had constricted me.

We now commenced our seven A.M. twelve-hour Saturday shift, which was the beginning of an exceptionally slow weekend. Cindy and I huddled together as she assisted me with my university assignments. I so much enjoyed the way we worked with each other and often begged her to take the classes as well. She constantly refused, claiming she could not pass the exams. I wholeheartedly disagreed, attributing her reason to lack of confidence and the negative effects inflicted on her by society. This was sad, because she had so much inside her mind, and I felt like her 'White Knight,' and we would face our life together side by side. I enjoyed explaining how and why the white people behaved in the movies; we watched. Most of the time, it was not the race-specific behavior, but instead country or rural behavior. Cindy grew up in the inner city, nevertheless; I found myself envious of her world, with so many things to do so close. My childhood found me walking long vacant streets, which for a time before satellite TV and no Internet appears anomalous, yet we found things to do inside the house. Cindy found security in socializing among large groups. Contrarily, we had too few people to form sizeable gangs, as nine times two or eighteen were the largest number, and that would be for a baseball game, although seldom this fortunate as most times we had less than ten to play. We always figured a way to play. Those days were gone, or for my escapes may reappear but not in this episode. One of the random responsibilities each team had was to make a security round throughout our warehouse. Cindy and I would walk this parameter, taking approximately two hours. We physically touched each door and touched electrical receptors. We simply touched their casings for heat, which fortunately we never found a hot one. Others on our team performed the second round, most times on our bikes we used to flash around the warehouse finding the parts we had to deliver. Cindy and I routinely would pick up any loose trash, which most times was a Styrofoam cup the wind entering the warehouse blew.

Cindy and I assured our team leader the warehouse met our routine standards. Our sister shift team took over at seven PM and when we relieved them in the next morning, the warehouse was filled with beer bottles and other trash from a large party they had. Their team leader told Cindy and I to clean this mess. We told her she had to have her team clean it. We would leave it where it is if she did not clean it. She looked at our leader and threatened her retaliation if we did not clean it. He told her we were not going to clean it. They argued for about twenty minutes. She turned from him; centered on Cindy and I, told us she was holding us responsible. We did not clean their mess, which made her furious when she came to relieve us. She called our deputy commander and claimed we had made the mess. The deputy commander arrived as she greeted him and escorted this leader to where the trash was located. She reported she had warned us to have our party trash cleaned before leaving. This was why she called the deputy commander because she did not feel it her responsibility to clean other people's trash. She also had a concern about other's drinking on duty, and possibly driving while intoxicated on the runways. Our team leader argued this was not our mess, and we found it when our shift began. The deputy commander decided it was our mess, using the theory that we were the ones with our hands in the cookie drawer. I asked the commander to give us drug tests to see if we had any alcohol in our system. Everybody from both shifts tested clean for alcohol; thereby the deputy commander ruled the blood tests of no relevance. The main thing it proved was we did not drink while on duty. He demanded that both shifts clean this mess again and warned he would have the military police check our warehouse after our shifts. This added to the friction between our teams and the base law enforcement.

Cindy and I called the sister team's supervisor the 'wicked witch,' though we did not call her this to her face. The next day, we discovered another married member of our team was dead. The police said someone broke in and killed our teammate and his wife, stabbing them over one-hundred times. They next slashed the throats of the two sleeping boys. The police found a note, which said, 'I promised revenge.' The remainder of our team, including our team leader, went to the commander and told him we suspected the 'wicked witch.' Unfortunately, she had already spoken to the commander and warned him that we may retaliate against her by making false accusations. She believed our team member who died was murdered because he threatened to reveal the truth about their mystery. We were shocked in that our commander was clearly on her side. Accordingly, fear overtook us and we decided security had to take precedence. We purchased maze to be used as our emergency frontline weapon. Stopping her from killing us was our sole defense, as we had to catch her in the act. Consequently, we decided to make every effort to stay close to phones. These were the days before cell phones. This pretty much puts the beach forbidden for us. I had a phone put in my room, and in those days, this was expensive. We also filled small empty lotion containers with bleach as a backup weapon. I knew she was coming after us. Likewise, I believed she would hit us when we were together, playing on our confusion and lack of concentration when with each other. Accordingly, the 'wicked witch' caught us while we were sleeping. I heard her picking the lock on my door to gain entry into our room. This gave me time to pick up my emergency bag; I kept beside our bed and gave Cindy her maze and bleach, allowing both of us to be protected. My room bag had steak knives in it as well. The 'wicked witch' quietly walked up to our bed with a bat in her hand.

When she went to swing it, I rolled out of our bed shooting my maze at her face before I grabbed her feet dropping her to the floor. Cindy jumped from our bed and squeezed the bleach on her face. This forced both of her hands to her face, causing her to drop her bat. I tied her feet with an extension cord that I had stashed for this purpose. Cindy wrapped the wicked witch's hands, as I hit the witch in her stomach repeatedly to keep her from challenging Cindy while she secured her. After securing her, I called the police that came and processed this crime scene. This shocker was when they processed the 'wicked witches' home and found enough evidence of her extensive obsession with Cindy and I. She had pictures, from an instant Polaroid of where we ate, partied, and even a few of when we were sleeping. This scared me, in knowing she had been in my room when we were sleeping and taken pictures. The police allowed Cindy and I to read the witch's diaries. Her motive was revenge against society because her white boyfriend died in a car accident eight years earlier. She believed someone had damaged the brakes and steering in his vehicle, which caused him to drive his vehicle into an oncoming big rig truck. This confused me; I believed that if she was serious about, she should have tried to help us instead of hating us. Cindy and I felt guilty that our relationship had caused the death of a coworker. Our commander sent us to social workers for counseling. Cindy and I returned to the beach as our getaway world. We stayed beside each other as much as possible. Surprisingly, we enjoyed a night of dancing to my music in our room. This is a rare treat for me in these violent ordeals. Then sadness overtakes our relationship, as I foolishly decide to leave the military and complete my education in my hometown private college. Family problems forced me to terminate our relationship. As this part paralleled my real life, the part that was different I saw her reaction. Years later, a friend told me her heart was broken when I terminated our bond, and she cried extensively. I now saw her crying and felt lower than dirt. I should have stood by her side and hold fast to my heart. Strangely enough, a fresh relationship motivated me to break up with Cindy. This new partner a few years later broke my heart. I knew this was payback. I try to convince Cindy about my regret in what I did to her; nonetheless, she began to fade into the darkness. That episode is done and I accept my much-needed rest.

The juror

My life of being in morality and obeying the law and a few encounters with those who I believed were protecting and serving. My first terrible encounter came when the place I worked was robbed and a deputy asked me if I kindly stopped in the next day and answer a few routine questions. This was the original time I was trapped by the lying and deceit used by law enforcement to force innocent people into confessing to crimes they did not commit. In the spirit of cooperation, I walked peacefully into a small torture chamber where this deputy accused me of major crimes and threatened to prosecute me for all these other crimes if I did not confess to a little crime. I knew they were so far off concerning this minute crime, since everyone worked accordingly hard to ignore to truth as I proved. If they were this blind, then the evidence was on the wall. They believed what they want to and against this mentality; any holding on to the truth would bury me in their lies. I brush this horrible memory from my mind each time I hear how to police protect and serve. I do believe several do, yet I believe most take the easy way to solve a crime and depend too much on their divine intervention with our more unfortunate mere human abilities. I am always so amazed how they can stand in court and claim their way to be the method a crime was committed, and even without evidence, gain convictions. I find confusion how they can lie every step of the process, and declare themselves the holders of truth, yet their victims must endure countless hours of unending bombardment without notwithstanding a slight flinch from the truth, and until they confess the lie the police want; they will suffer and even face the loss of their liberties for life.

This episode is free from all that lying and deceit and falls within the few events that searched for justice. Sadly, when an evil encounter justice, it does not fall in fear of the law, yet instead there are the few who make the sacrifice to punish the wicked. These people face a changed life, in the wicked control the world they exist, and as such; they have no protection, especially once the law no longer has a need for them. I believe I would have great difficulty in facing a vicious man in a courtroom, as the courtroom is the safe haven for the guilty. I wake up in my bed beside a new wife, one I have yet to know. Her name is Charlene and has a warm soft voice. She reminds me we have another busy day today. We must appear for jury selection. I ask her to review this case with me, so I can ensure she understands. Charlene tells me this man is accused of killing or ordering the deaths of thirty people and runs the largest drug ring known in the United States. I tell Charlene that to sit on this jury would be a death sentence and that if you were discovered to have swayed your decision; you would face prison time, while the punishable man will walk. You need to say that he is guilty and must go to prison. That is the only justice, because the police would not have arrested him if he were innocent. She promises to say this. I am called first, and the lawyer asks me how I feel about this case. I tell them this man ordered the death of my friend's father, and I will help see him punished. Next, I rise, point at this man, and beg that they allow me to sit on this jury to make sure this guilty man is punished. The defense rejects me. Charlene is next to be questioned. The judge warns her not to play games with this court. I can see she is getting nervous, since she is easy to intimidate.

The defense began asking Charlene questions, and based upon her timidness, acted nonchalant, so as not to tip off the prosecution. They detected her influenceable disposition. Therefore, both sides accepted her. She was extremely excited and chatted nonstop on our way home in my car. When we sat down at our dinner table, I looked at her and asked why she was so stupid. I shook my head and quizzed her why she had to disobey me. Charlene challenges me by declaring she had to obey the judge, as it is the law. I ask her if that man who killed so many and sells drugs will obey the law. I reveal to her; he will beat these charges, and if he cannot, any jury that convicts him will live in fear the few remaining days they have. Even if the police can control him, they cannot control his people, who are never more than a phone call from him. Charlene demands for me to reveal how I know this. I tell Charlene it is the law of the ages and that anyone who has any intelligence knows this. Continuing, I explain to her that the reason his defense accepted her was because they feel, one way or another; they will get from her what is needed. Charlene pleads I tell her why I am being so cruel to her. I repeat to Charlene, I am talking about everyone on this jury. Accordingly, I remind Charlene this was completely explained to her last night. Charlene tells me she cannot lie. I explain to her; she did not have to lie, all she needed to do was be outspoken about her belief. Consequently, I ask Charlene if she believes he is guilty. She confesses that everyone knows this man is in the wrong. I smile and ask her why she did not tell that to the judge. Charlene explains they did not ask her. I rebut with my concept that by withholding the truth, she is, in reality, telling a lie. Charlene informs me this makes sense to her. She begins to cry asking me what she can do. I tell Charlene that because she has jumped out of the frying pan and into the fire, I will need to stay beside her continuously dumping water on her. We hug each other, nevertheless; I know she in deep trouble. What constantly tortures my mind is this could have been avoided.

I attend each day in court, watching in the audience while Charlene sits on the jury. Accordingly, I find myself wondering if there is anything in the world more boring than court. Each lawyer strives to use the biggest words, speaking the longest, and saying absolutely nothing. They ask a question, make an announcement, which the opposing lawyer objects, the judge either sustains or overrides and gives order to the jury. After a long day of nothing but long presentations and massive information dump on the jury, the judge called for a recess. I listened as the judge told the families of the jurors that they would be kept in a hotel guarded by police, who will also inspect the food they are served. Subsequently, we will not be permitted to talk with them until their verdict is given. I can merely watch her the first two days, as I did not want to exhaust all my vacation time. I believe Charlene will need me more after the trial. The trial finally ends, and the jury deliberates and ends a hung jury. This is no surprise in that they realize four of the jurors refused to accept his guilt. Charlene was one of the jurors who pronounced him guilty. Naturally, they selected a fresh jury for the new trial. Consequently, even though the man charged with these crimes was to be tried again, he did not look kindly to those who did not declare him innocent. That night, we got our first taste of his revenge. Charlene and I were sleeping. Our reunion night was filled with a dinner and dancing. Accordingly, we finished our evening with wine and comedy on TV. Around two A.M., three men came into our bedroom and began stabbing us with their knives. I had a remote control for my stereo and turned it on, raising the volume. The sudden noise scared them, as night killers fear loud noises. They rushed out of our bedroom, as I dialed 911 on my cell phone. Additionally, I rushed outside my apartment and pulled the fire alarm in the hallway. This sounded a large horn warning everyone to go outside his or her homes. I figured the more people who were rushing outside would see these criminals. Accordingly, I pulled the sheets from our closet and used them to dress our wounds. Looking at my belly, I see my white tee shirt, is covered in blood. Fortunately, I do not feel my three stabs, although this blood loss is making me sleepy, as my world begins to fade and return into the world of my conscience.

The nasty boys

Once more, I am faced with a reality issue. I believe that when I fade from an event, all elements of that dimension also disappear gradually. It begins when I enter and depart when I exit. Leastwise, I hope this is true, since it appears each night; I face or suffer, few times alone, leaving a mess behind me. I have encountered courageous defenders of right against the coward monsters of evil. My world takes focus once more, on a bright sunny day. I open my front door and pick up my newspaper. Subsequently, I look on the date and see it is Monday, fortunately a holiday as it is filled with Labor Day sales. This delights me as; I do not have to deal with coworkers today. My newfound skill of performing effectively as a fool among others now is developed to perfection. Nevertheless, as a fool I have adapted to so many situations blending in without any major detection yet. This is the same as jumping in a speeding car on the interstate and driving the car perfectly within a fraction of a second. It seems so impossible; nevertheless, I have done it almost nightly recently. After a while, it begins to feel second nature. I take 'my' newspaper to the table and begin scanning through it. I noticed my son plays on the local high school basketball team and scored twelve points yesterday. This explains why our house is quiet now, as I am sure, we kept late hours last night. I stroll into our kitchen and make a bowl of cereal. The crunching sound this cereal makes is rattling my head; therefore, I suspect we may have added several spirits to our celebration last night. The milk from this cereal soothingly coats my stomach. I may have a chance to comprehend what is about to happen this night, although I do believe a few extra glasses of milk may help me not to vomit if I get my normal dose of blood in this episode.

Later in the morning, my wife and three children come to our family room, as we have what turns out to be our routine check-in before the children go their separate ways, having school and social activities that consume their time. My wife hands each one small bottle of juice and egg sandwich as they rush to our front porch to sort through the children waiting to join them. We laugh as the three gangs go off their separate directions to fulfill their objectives of the day. So much excitement and enthusiasm flowed from their bodies. As if we could see their energy, flowing out in colorful halos that spun on our porch. Then, as fast as it started, they were gone. I looked at my wife and could see she also felt the tremendous vacuum that just took the life from our porch. Stillness brings with it emptiness, which stops time and delivers fear as we now frantically attempt to regain what was in our minds a few minutes earlier. We go into our kitchen; I turn on our radio, while my wife makes us coffee. Our first cups are instant coffee, mixed in our hot water. Meanwhile, I set up my coffee maker to have a pot ready for this day. Accordingly, I tell my wife that today may be busy with us. She questions me on how I know this. I tell her it is simply a gut feeling. Notwithstanding, she tells me we must clean our house, because we do not want others to think, we live like pigs. She hands me the vacuum sweeper, and tells me to clean the upstairs. I obey without question, since my big mouth that put me in this situation. We get everything looking clean, and retire to our living room. I guard my words as we make small talk about her week. Naturally, I ask her many questions to keep her talking so I do not have to chat about my week. Soon, we both drift into a peaceful weekend afternoon nap.

Notwithstanding, our nap is broken by the piercing ring of our doorbell. My wife goes to the door before she calls me to greet these visitors. I stand beside her and say hello to this group of two men and one woman. My wife was overwhelmed when she saw them, as this is rare for our closed gated community. I ask how we can help them. The men tell me they belong to a new church in the area and want to share this great news. Two more men walk on the sidewalk and yell over for the girl on our porch to join them. The men on our porch ask if this is okay with us. I tell them we do not care. She joins the other two men, while our group explains they find it is better at the door to have both males and females. I inform them about my understanding. We join in my living room, where they begin talking about the Bible. I throw this deep ancient Jewish folklore on them. I argue the initial few verses in Genesis that God created the heavens and the Earth, and subsequently they were void without form. I tell them my belief is there was a first Earth, then it was destroyed, and the Earth reformed. This set them on fire, especially as I hold to my belief. We agree to disagree on this issue when I unleash my second issue on them. I argue that Adam had more than one wife. The Bible initially declares that God made a man and woman in his image. The next chapter talks about how God did not think it was good for Adam to be alone, so he puts Adam to sleep, takes a rib from him, and calls her a woman because she was made from a man. This almost drives them crazy as I argue there are clearly two women created here. The truth is that it does not matter who is right on these two issues as they are historical and not doctrinal arguments. In other words, someone should be able to make it to heaven if one accepts or rejects these two issues. I use them, as theological tools to stress there is a need to concentrate on the attention to detail when reading verses.

The complete context must be analyzed as well. The story is comprehensive and even more amazing, than we gave it credit.

Afterwards, things began to settle down, and start to become bored with this visitation. I try to move to the finishing stage, yet find myself continually agreeing while hoping they get the hint. Finally, I cannot take it anymore, stand up, and ask them if they are truly this rude. I question them if they have not noticed I stopped discussing topics with them and hoped they would get the hint and leave my house. One of the men asks me if I want them to leave. I tell them to leave now. They rise to the feet and explain to me that demons are making me behave this way. They ask me if I believe in demons. I tell them I do not want to talk about demons and leave now. Unexpectedly, our room becomes dark. I wonder if my wife turned off the lights, until I remember we did not have any lights working. I ask them if they know why our room is dark. One of the men report that we need to get the elders quickly, before it is too late. He starts dialing on his cell phone and tells the man who answers his call that we are in trouble, in that darkness is over us presently. Next, he asks me for our address for their elder's GPS. Accepting that something strange might be happening, I eagerly give him my address. A few minutes later, my doorbell rings as one of my visitors opens the door and invites them inside my house. I welcome them, and remark how fast they made it here. One of the elders confesses they were afraid we would be lost by the time they arrived. I asked them to explain why they thought we would be lost. They open their Bibles and begin quoting verses. Suddenly, our room becomes dark as eerie sounds fill the air surrounding us. My wife at once faints, which comforts me in that I do not have to worry about her suffering any serious psychological effects. A wind starts blowing in my house. I ask the elders why there is a wind blowing in my living room. They tell me to stay seated on my sofa and be prepared for some other possible environmental effects. I can merely imagine what they are talking about, nevertheless, I think it is better that I do not save any strangers hanging around us any ideas.

Afterwards, I see candlelights appearing at random throughout my living room. With this, the elders tell us we need to get to their church as quickly as possible. I ask them what we should do about my wife. They tell me that once we leave, the darkness will leave, and she will be safe. They ask me if I have an extra Bible. I tell them we have plenty of Bibles; therefore, they advise me to put them beside her. I grab two and put one on each side of her. I follow the two men and two elders as we walk to their church. They do not want to be in a vehicle in case our world starts spinning or environment plays various tricks on us. Fortunately, the apartment they are renting for their church is merely two blocks from my house. These are truly ground routes. They turn on our lights as we enter, notwithstanding, the room turns dark and began to heat. Accordingly, I now understand we have much trouble ahead of us. After this, two bright red and yellow faces appear, both spotted with many horns spread throughout their heads. An elder asks them to identify themselves. One identifies himself as Baalberith, while the other identifies himself as Naamah. The elders challenge these two demons and subsequently trouble rains on us. We each are lifted off our feet and spun in circles and then dropped. We wobble on the floor as if we were drunk. The elders grab their Bibles and begin quoting scriptures. Meanwhile, the two men begin praying aloud. I know something is not stable and cannot remain quiet. I begin praying, repeating various phrases from each. Naamah and Baalberith issue stern warnings that if we do not deny God, they would persecute as until our deaths. The five of us declared our loyalty to the Lord. Although I did see myself as a Holy Roller type, I was smart enough to know that something righteous had to be more powerful than two monsters who were threatening us. Our crises lasted for over ten hours, although when it ended we only lost two minutes in Earth time. The elders told me these demons had taken us to a place beyond the limits of time and space. Finally, we witnessed hundreds of angels rush to our aid. It felt as if I was being sucked into a funnel as I return to my home. Supposedly, each member in our group returned to their respective homes. A now had some time to process in my mind what had happened. I was no longer a virgin in the spiritual encounter's realm. Next, I begin slightly to shiver as my world fades away and daylight returns. I was so relieved to see the daylight, as darkness was currently not a peaceful experience for me.

The Star leapers

I remain in my bed throughout the morning not getting up until early afternoon. The memory from seeing so many angels in the sky brought a strong sense of security and more importantly peace. I describe the sense of security as feeling safe about the environment surrounding me, and the sense of peace as the internal armistice within the forces of the mind, spirit, and soul. This element balances the inside with the outside to maintain this balance. This felt as a dose of a strong psychotropic drug that is addictive on the first experience. Accordingly, I now felt a hunger that was starving me and steeling my mind. I believed my life would not begin once more until I was with those angels. This compulsion was destroying me. I remember laying on my bed, and a voice telling me, or creating the feeling that transmitted this thought, explaining this could not be, and I had to let these angels go. Their mission is to bring peace, not torment and by me being tormented by their memory was abnormal. I had to let them go. Like all addictions, the victim knows they are wrong, yet the road that leads to the right appears to have blocks making that path no longer available for travel. I remember the elders praying and starting fishing in my mind for words that group spoke. I started speaking some of these words. Consequently, I wished I could pull them into my true reality, as the emotions attached to these angels had leaked. Fortunately, I felt something reach into my mind and sink the angels back into my invisible world. This scared me, yet now I had a tool that could free me.

I recognize the importance of closing the doors between these realms.

After keeping busy with the remainder of the day, I hit the sack around midnight. The day had no snags, and almost highlighted by a movie until I remembered I had no gas. After finishing shopping in town, I was in a hurry to get back to my house. Even though the gas station is not far from my house, the time to get the gas would make me late for the movie. I hated leaving early, as that would put me in the theater bored before the movie began. A new practice, I currently adopted is praying before I sleep. A found a pleasant one on the Internet that begins, 'now I lay me down to sleep; I pray the Lord my soul to keep…...' I figure this should not be to Earth shattering and keep me on a margin. Last night convinced me that help could be a welcomed treat, especially when trying to hold onto my sanity. I close that chapter in my life and move on to my next chapter. I feel my body turn itself off as I drift away into the world where the poor are rich, and the weak are strong. I start hearing the beautiful music of harps fill the air. Looking around, I do not see who currently is playing them. I am wise enough to know that someone or something is creating this music. Tonight my first mission will be to solve this mystery. I walk through the substantial castle opening rooms, notwithstanding, each room the music the music grows louder, until finally I open a door and behold a large room before me. The room is packed with at least one-hundred women, dressed in their bikinis playing a stringed instrument. I scan over them trying to determine, which has the better beauty, the bikinis, or the music. This is a tough call, and finally compromised the way we do in this realm and elect to maintain the combination. I compliment them on the harmony of their music, causing a wave of laughter to flow over the room. I ask whether they will play another song. A woman wearing an orange bikini explains they must now play in their home. The castle floor begins to fade, and two women grab my hands while the castle completely disappears. We are floating in the sky. I hope this episode is not finished, as there are still so many musicians to congratulate and with any luck share some stories.

Notwithstanding, the lone thing I can see is the damp fog from clouds. We are surrounded by this fog, as it appears to be thick enough I can walk on it. I keep my eye's alert so as not to step into a hole, although this is consequently, heavy I cannot see that far. My escorts tell me while I hold their hands the sky will hold me. They begin playing their music, and the fog starts to lift high into the sky. I look below me and see great flat stones, about a yard in diameter covered with unique engravings on them. I stare out across the sky before me, and it looks like a pond with large leaves over its surface. The sun is horizontal with us presently and scatters its yellow waves across the stones. The waves strangely dance to the music from my escorts. I soon find myself jumping from stone to stone having more fun than I have in a long time. Occasionally, I will ask for a break and sit down to rest. The sky is clear now permitting me to gaze on the mountains and valleys below me. I consider myself lucky in there is no wind. I ask one of the musicians who put her harp on a stone above us and drifted down to sit beside me on my stone about the effects of wind at this level. She reports there are no winds up here. I am so relieved to hear this. She tells me her name is Georgia, and that she died in late 1778, when shot by a British soldier. I ask her if the reason I am here because I also am died. She does not believe this to be the case, yet warns me she does not know for sure, as such matters are above her need to know. Georgia explains that I am not wearing a white robe, as most men who dwell in this realm do. With this, I ask Georgia why she is not wearing a bleached robe. She explains members of the harmony orchestra do not wear white robes; in they must have a physical part to create the music. She touches me and verifies that I still have some corporeal attributes.

Accordingly, I ask her if this flesh component cannot present many additional risks this jumping across stones in the lower heavens can offer. Georgia tells me when I am falling simply to look up, and I will begin to rise. She adds that I am never to look down unless seated on a stone. I question how I can travel to stones below the plane I was currently playing. Georgia reveals I must make such a drop as an airplane would. I need to look out at a slight angle get the level I want and then swing around to reach the position I want to be. Georgia tells me not to worry, as soon it will come naturally. There is a question, which has been bugging me. I ask Georgia if I can ask a personal question. She tells me I can; nevertheless, she feels it is too soon for me to tell her I love her. I agree such a statement would be equally important soon. Afterwards, I ask her how she died. She tells me it happened when she stopped breathing. I clarify by asking her what her cause of death was. Georgia tells me she was walking pass a neighbor's farm when she accidentally stepped in one of his raccoon traps. I give her a strange look, as she continues by telling me, the neighbor was away fighting during the war, and the trap was buried in snow. When she fell, she hit her head on a tree, knocking her unconscious. It was during the coldest part of winter causing her feet and hands to become frostbitten. This prevented her from breaking free from the trap. During this part of winter, few walked through the forest paths, as wild animals hunted for something to eat. She became a meal for a pack of wolves. I ask her about the pain. Georgia tells me the wolves began by eating her feet, as she could not feel anything here thus offered no resistance. This caused her to bleed to death before they began feeding on the other parts of her body. I ask Georgia if she had a family. She reveals she had two sisters and four brothers. The brothers and her father were fighting throughout the war. I asked her how old she was when this happened. She tells me she was twenty years old. I ask her if this was not old still to be single. Georgia tells me many women were at the same time spinsters, because of the trouble in the colonies, the young were afraid to start their lives until there was peace throughout the land.

Georgia reports she has often looked on the people below and watched how they live. They can merely see those who do not sin and are righteous, because those who are in the heavens do not know evil, nor can they look down until their age has passed. She has no idea those who are related to her, as so much has changed. She questions me on how I like what I am seeing now. I tell her that I never complain when around so many beautiful women. Georgia warns me not to lose focus of where I am. Georgia tells me it is time to practice some flying. I agree when she orders me to jump. I leap into the air, instinctively looking down as I drop quickly. Fear floods my mind, until I recall Georgia told me to look up to the sky. I lift my head up and instantly stops falling and start rising. I in next to no time pass Georgia, who tells me not to go too high. At this time, I practice my landings, which soon gets much easier. I start jumping and playing on the stones once more, yet even this begins to get boring. I realize it would not be wise for me to become involved with any of these beauties when considering they died. I am not quite up to relationships with dead women, as this would take time to become adjusted. Though they are beauties, the stereotype pasted in my mind of the dead forbids me from enjoying their company beyond what is honorable, especially being under the eyes of Saint Peter. I do not want to make him find difficulty in allowing me admittance later. Accordingly, I believe that anyone who was to break their saintly hearts. Another issue is the stories about their deaths. Georgia's story was heartbreaking, as it, shows the bullets and battlefields are not the lone soul collectors during wars. I begin to wonder if this might not be a taste of hell, in that to have so many beautiful women in bikinis with no other competition, nevertheless, to be at war in my mind destroying any impure thoughts as they arrive. I feel as a diabetic in a cookie factory.

Slashing

Consequently, I jump from a stone as I have so many times already; each time my heart loses the thrill as it had previously. I notice these women are losing their initial infatuation, as well. This causes me to ask Georgia if it is time that I departed.

Georgia explains they feel I am holding myself back from them and thus do not want to be with them. I tell her it is not so much that as it is I am not ready to join the dead. She understands and volunteers to take me back to the surface. Georgia takes hold of my hand as we drift off into the open air. We slowly glide into a pleasant small village in a valley below us. Georgia reveals to me living among the dead is not as bad as the fight not to join them. Accordingly, I tell her that when I do join the land of the dead, I so much hope that I can stay with them. Georgia tells me they would wish this as well. My feet lightly hit the ground as an arrow goes flying pass my head. I ask Georgia if I am joining them sooner than later. To my avail, Georgia is gone. I decide it might be wise for me to run now until I can discover what is happening. I notice the arrow that missed me hit a tree, and as I run, pass, I break the end of the tree. A few more arrows pass me until I notice a hill before me. Up the hill I go, this time painfully with my legs. I understand that if the going gets rough, I must be going up or to a better place. Suddenly, I hear men yelling for me to hurry. They anchor their muskets against trees and begin shooting. I hear someone scream behind me, which gives me the energy to run faster until I reach these strangers. I noticed there were five men in this group, all with muskets and dressed as colonials. They fire another volley and tell me we need to run for their fort. I get up and follow them. We make it to a nearby river, where they have some small canoes. In we go, while one hand me an oar. I begin oaring quickly, as both of our canoes become caught in the river's currents to our delight. The men have now reloaded their muskets. I ask them why they do not have rifles. One of them looks at me, questioned if I took a blow to the head while in the forest, and then asks me what the weapon he has is. I tell him it is a musket.

A group of arrows comes flying over our heads. Three of the men brace and fire their muskets, hitting two of the 'Indians' on the bank. I look at the men and ask if they had just shot the Indians. They are busy now reloading their muskets, as they try to keep at least two ready to fire in case they are hit by an ambush. Afterwards, one of the men asks me if I am Solomon. I tell him that Solomon is not my name and asked why he thought it was. They tell me because of all the wise questions I keep asking them. Accordingly, I get the hint they believe me to be an idiot. I request they forgive me for these questions in that I drank too much rum yesterday and did take a fall on my head earlier today. I explain I was really asking what tribe these Indians belonged as I hand the broken arrow to them. They look at the arrow and tell me these are Chickasaw, and they are not too happy now, especially considering I just crossed some of their sacred ground. I dress up my next question by explaining I have wandered through many forests for a long time and was wondering if they knew the current year. They look at each other and then ask whether I will tell them where I got that rum. I agree, and they tell me the year is 1778. Georgia dropped me back on Earth in the year she departed and pretty much in the same general territory. I confess I found the rum on a dead British officer two days earlier. It was such good rum, that it took me two days to drink it. I told them he was a dead British officer to get a feel on which side of this war they belonged. One of the men tells me the British do not know how to make good rum. Afterwards, another remark the soldier must have stolen it from someone, as the British are known to take what they want. They ask me, which side I belonged. I tell them that I was working hard to stay out of this fight, as I have been asked by both sides to join the other side.

This gets a laugh from them as one man confesses he understands why they would say such a thing. A few hours later, we go ashore under what appears as a cavern that hangs over the bank. In we go as they light some torches braced along the entrance. We row about ten minutes into this tunnel created by nature and finally stop at a sandy shoulder. They tie our canoes to a few posts they placed. We then began our journey through the cave network. A few hours later, we emerge at the surface. This has proven to be a strange day for me, as I descended to the surface merely to ascend to it later. I ask them how they learned about this confusing underground cave network. One man informs me the Indians taught them, and they use it to escape from them. Now, I wonder who Solomon is. I have to take a shot at it, so I ask them how they expect to escape from Indians if they are obtaining these routes from the Indians. You may fool them today, nevertheless, there will be a critical time they will remember it. They laugh at me and tell me I am not as smart as I think I am. I know one thing for sure; it will be in my interest to get away from them fast. We walk into their fort, and notice the front gate is open. They rush inside merely to discover their families are pinned to the outside of their homes by knives. Their clothing is dripping with blood, as they no longer have their scalps. These men split up moving to stand in front of their families. Next, they fall to the ground beginning to cry. I rush back to the front gate and close it. Afterwards, I go through opening the doors to the homes and buildings inside this fort to see if any killers decided to hide inside this fort. Fortunately, I did not find anyone. I find beans and boil water, as I know the men who lost their loved ones today would soon need food. They would need a strong shoulder to lean on, yet unfortunately; I was the lone shoulder in this region.

They cry throughout the night, nevertheless, when I wake up in the morning, I discover the beans are eaten. I scrounge for something else to prepare, and find where they keep their salted meat and locate their jarred vegetables and prepare a large pot of stew. I feel so sorry for these men, as I also realize my vacation from the blood was short lived. Something is different this time, in that I can feel the pain these five men are suffering. Empathy now controlled me; their pain was my pain. The irony of this is how just one day earlier, I despised wanting nothing more than to depart from them. The killing of innocent children and women burns a fire for revenge. Soon, we discover these savage killers could not accept the fort's gates were closed. The sky within the fort rained arrows, forcing us to hide under tables, as the arrows would cut through the straw roofs. We positioned a few tables on our fort corners. We filled ten horns for each of gunpowder and gave each man five muskets. Later that day the hills surrounding our fort became covered by Indians. I knew our muskets would not repel such an invasion. We needed another weapon, which I believed a few small barrels of gunpowder spread among the Indians and then ignited would give us makeshift bombs. I suggested we took three horses, tied a barrel to their backs, and afterwards send the horses into the Indian force. Once inside, we would shoot the gunpowder with our muskets causing the explosions. We sent the horses out among the Indians, who allowed them to mingle among them. These colonists were sharpshooters and easily blasted the gunpowder, which terrified the invading Indians while those who did not explode ran as wild animals trampling over each as a stampede crushing any who stood across their path. Victory was ours today. I warn my comrades the Indians will return. One-man comments that I must have turned on my brain, and that they are indebted I did. At first, I believed he was being sarcastic until he added the thankful part. I tell them there is no way that merely a few may live or die now, because the Indians will kill us unless defend this fort. One man asks why, we just do not escape. I tell him their wives and children did not flee, nor should we.

Accordingly, it is easy to give such great speeches when I know I will fade out before I die. I remember something Georgia told me that I tried to forget. She tells me my last episode will be the one where I die, as I will have that terminal split second dream as life leaves my flesh. Either way, I plan that to be another time. I ask these men if they have any bows. They tell me the general store has a few. I advise them to start gathering the arrows covering our ground. These men ask me why I believe arrows will do better than the muskets. Notwithstanding, I remind them we do not have time to reload. We will have every musket prepared for one shot, yet after that, we must continue to fight, as the Indians will not stop and wait for us to reload, nor will they fall for our Trojan horses loaded with dynamite. We need to have hatchets and knives for hand-to-hand combat as well. I tell them we will eat a large meal tonight and will cook food to eat in haste tomorrow, since we will need as much energy as possible to fight a long hard fight. The next day these Indians throw a curve ball at us. Our sky rains with burning arrows igniting the roofs to their buildings. I tell them we must form an inner fort with their wagons and dig a ditch surrounding it filling it with water. The heat from the burning fort will evaporate the water quickly, although we will try to pump more water. We must spread the few kegs of gunpowder we have as well, if not for anything except to prevent one massive explosion. We must strategically place these several barrels to blast the areas that are burning the hottest. The rain of fire continued as the smoke began to thicken above us. The inferno heat puts us to sleep one by one. I witness arrows drop into their sleeping bodies and question if I should not have concurred with their exodus plea. The fire still burns too high for the invading Indians to enter. I feel the thick smoke enter and burn my lungs as my world begins to fade. Nevertheless, I sense myself floating almost expecting to see Georgia. Next, I hear her voice tell me not this time. I fall into my realm of sleep.

A different ending

Notwithstanding, I find delight in returning to the later part of the twentieth century. I am curious about why I did not return to the twenty-first century, nevertheless; I am free from the Indians, so I believe I can learn to appreciate this. I actually return to a fort I once served while in the Army. This fort was extremely different from the one I just witnessed burn. My life changed so much during this assignment. Subsequently, I left an assignment with an Infantry Division due to the medical needs of my first wife to a garrison between Baltimore and the District of Columbia. I soon found myself facing a threat from Maryland that if I did not remove our children from my wife, they would take them. This forced me to seek a divorce and take these children back to Ohio. I secured a two-year assignment with the local Army headquarters, and moved into the barracks. While in the barracks, I found a crutch to replace the family life, I had enjoyed throughout my Army career, and that was in a bottle of Jim Beam. This life crisis caused me to look at my vices and forced me to stop smoking. I was a heavy smoker, even though I ran daily. This turned out to be excessively much for me to undertake, yet I remembered how our children suffered because of the second-hand smoke that flooded our house. My wife and I smoked too much for our children to escape suffering. When I brought back these children for our beginning, my house would need to be smoke free. Even to this day, I shiver when thinking about how this addiction was killing me without mercy. My nicotine withdrawals hit me like nuclear bombs demanding that I surrender my life. This was where the Jim Beam came into play. Initially, it was a relaxer, or something to take the edge off and help me sleep. When I stopped smoking, there was no sleep. I was in trouble, yet committed myself to no smoking, as our society had turned against smokers.

Notwithstanding, I discovered the Jim Beam helped me through these nicotine withdrawals. My withdrawals were not like those of others, and would be at times lasting more than twenty minutes. My compulsive personality was not going to allow this oral fixation escape. Two cans of Diet Coke would make me three drinks, on ice from the two ice-cube trays from my small refrigerator. This was enough to knock me out for the night. Bourbon offered me the luxury of a limited hangover. Among the habits, I gave up was drinking coffee, as the caffeine magnified my nicotine withdrawals. Thinking back about my accomplishments during that year, I shamefully confess my personality was no less than cruel in some cases. I blinded myself to my faults focusing the blame on the innocent. Therefore, I painted an innocent black secretary as my enemy. Thinking back now, I cannot believe how foolish I was. This woman was an angel, as I did leave us on good terms. The point I need to make, is that even to this day I have never met another woman with a body as perfect as hers. She is what wakes men up in their dreams soaked in perspiration. Racism had nothing to do with my unfair treatment of her, as my significant other was a black female and the supervisor, I hated was white. He was and I still believe is a creep and was instrumental in getting my significant other discharged. I always believed they pushed this as a punishment to me. I most likely should have prevented this from getting personal, yet it did. Now, I had to develop a plan for an exodus from this headquarters. A Sergeant Major friend whose wife is Korean talked to me about going to Korea. He pointed out that an unaccompanied assignment to Korea was merely one year, and this should get me a stateside assignment. This sounded so much better than Germany, which would require a two-year separation from my son.

Accordingly, while working on my active-duty officer assignments at the main personnel center I joined my coworker that handled the enlisted assignments. He introduced me to the soldier who determined my assignment. I explained to him that by a fluke, I had yet to serve overseas. Consequently, I wanted to be on the level with him and confessed my recent divorce and custody of my son. He agreed that Korea would be good for me, as I had experience with an Infantry Division and asked me how soon. Thereby, I told him within a month would be excellent, as my son would be on his summer vacation. The next day, I get a phone call from our local personnel office; I was on orders for reassignment. I confirm this is to Korea; however, she informs me I am on orders to Germany. Subsequently, I call my assignment manager that I spoke with the previous day and reveal to him; I just got a call that I was on orders to Germany. He comforts me promising to fix this, as he did fix it. I tell my Sergeant Major friend who is now in Korea that I am on my way. I clear my quarters, split my household goods, as most goes into storage, and what my son wanted went to Ohio with him. A few days later, and I am on a plane to Korea, the other side of the world. As part of my preparation, my coworkers told me Korea was 220 and as such, our 110 electric devices would fry if plugged into them. They also tell me there are no fast-food restaurants.

I go hog wild on hamburgers my final two weeks in America, gaining weight, as I quickly exceed my maximum allowable weight. My comrades tell me that Koreans have no rhythm and are shorter than Americans are. I almost completed my Master's degree, merely needing to touch up my final paper. I decide to prolong my graduation date, to make it as current to such an extent practical. I arrive in Korea; my Sergeant Major friend gets me assigned to the Personnel section for the Eighth United States Army, which is a wonderful assignment. The Army puts me in a local hotel, until they can get me a room in the Senior Noncommissioned Officers. I explore the city that surrounds me.

Due to the massive size of Seoul, which I was fortunate to be assigned was the center hub for South Korea, and since the Olympics was modern and even helping in forming the future of the world. I later learned the United States had over eighty installations or duty stations spread throughout South Korea. Many soldiers lived without modern conveniences. This was not the case for me, because all I had to do was walk about fifty feet, and I was in Itawon. During my first day of in processing, I buy a bottle of Jim Beam and Diet Coke for my nightcaps. I use the ice cubes from the hotel, which turns out to be a mistake. Accordingly, I make my first drink Friday night, and that was it. I get diarrhea and vomit everything from my stomach. It is not until late Sunday night, that I can stand on my feet, as I have crawled to the porcelain queen constantly. I gave up on my weekend, Saturday, and debated calling an ambulance; however, I did not know how to use the Korean phones. I was in another world and was sicker than I had ever been before. During the next five years, I never had any form of reaction to Korean food and solely drank bottled water. My job had limited responsibilities. This provided me plenty of free time. The Army gave me an extra thirty dollars each day to cover additional living expenses. I find a store that sells bootlegged software and copies of their manuals. Programs I previously only dreamed about, such as AutoCAD, Clipper, etc. Within the first small block was a McDonald's, Kentucky Fried Chicken, and on the corner a

Burger King. Their prices were reasonable, and their food tasted the same as in the States. I discovered the advantage was there were many small Korean Restaurants providing me a chance to experience their culture as well. I needed something to fill my time; therefore, I began an intensive exercise program. My room was small, yet had everything I needed such as a refrigerator and a TV I bought at the Army Exchange and VCR, so I can watch movies. This was before the DVD's.

The first one-hundred days were rough, as my exercise program greatly reduced my weight and allowed me to get my highest possible score on my PT test or physical fitness evaluation, consisting of push-ups, sit-ups, and a two-mile run. My initial luck in getting a date with Korean women did not go well. I was surprised how the Koreans were matchmakers. Therefore, I needed to get involved in an activity with them, so we could become acquainted. An American College offered a computer associate of science program. I knew this was exactly what I wanted, in that my compulsion with computers, a compulsion that would evolve with me. Each class, I met fresh Korean nationals and enjoyed some Korean culture with my new guides. I finally meet a special woman and interview for a high-level military job. I remarried, brought my son from the states, and began my new life. We had a son, and then a daughter. Accordingly, I gradually began smoking once more, although never allowed to smoke inside. I did this to help me develop our family reunion without any major mood swings from me. Drinking Jim Beam was on the line of allowed by my ration card. The next few years spun by quickly, as I receive a computer associates degree and a promotion. Given a preference, I choose to take my family to Maryland. I purchase a new car and with my family, we fly into Detroit, thereafter we drive to Fort Meade. I become suspicious now, as our hotel visits and activities are bonding so wonderfully. This is the dream I have longed to enjoy. So far, there is no blood as my wife is discovering America. The public transportation network for DC is centuries behind Seoul. We must fight traffic and find a place to park. My driving skill in the big city is poor, as I feel I could be putting my family in danger, nevertheless; they are hungry to explore. She has that right, thereby; I will dance on this limber branch to provide her a great experience. She showed me Korea and shared her culture with me; as a result, I need to communicate my culture with her. The major problem I face is the American culture is transparent, in that everyone is free to access it.

I get the position I held many years previously before going to Korea. The position had evolved to include both the enlisted and officer assignments, now came with a secretary who was the angel who forgave me before leaving. I ask her if she is going to keep me in line. She is no longer married, although I am now married. I ask her to trust me completely and tell what I can do to help her through this transition phase. My second duty day finally reminds me things can change quickly. I find myself completely upside down and everyone else is normal. This shames me, as I walk with my feet planted on the ceiling. Everyone is looking at me as if I have something weird controlling me. My secretary asks me why I am breaking the law of gravity. I tell her I am having a strange day indeed, and this is something I do not know how the reverse. She told me her aunt knew several spells. She might know how I could return to normal. I cannot go outside; because, I fear, I would float to the heavens and never be able to come back. My secretary informs me her aunt told her what to do. She gives me a kiss while squeezing both of my ears. I slowly drop to the floor and reverse myself as normal once more. I thank her and ask if I might need some extra juice to cure myself completely. She winks and promises to ask her aunt tonight. This is making me look as if I mess around with magic, which would label me as odd. My secretary tells me not to worry about my image, as I am clearly the victim here. I ask her how she knows this. She reports her aunt told her. Afterwards, I tell my supervisor that I need to go home and try to shake this. He agrees and offers to drive me home. Accordingly, I ask my supervisor if it were not wise to have my secretary drive me to my house, considering she was the one who dropped me back to the ground. Everyone agrees and she drives me home, as I introduce to my wife and kids. My wife serves us some Korean barbecue.

My secretary leaves, and my troubles return. Long nails begin to protrude through the floor. I lead us to our upstairs, which the floor currently nails free. We cannot go downstairs, since the nails are mixed with strong and weak. The frail nails buckle forcing the foot into the sturdy nails penetrating it. We cannot challenge them. We sat in our upstairs family room. The light begins to flicker as small fires start flaring. Subsequently, my wife begins to fade. I chat with her as if everything was normal. Consequently, I am puzzled in that my two sons and daughter remain visible. My oldest son falls into a black hole that emerges under him. Therefore, I rush over to grab my two little ones, while the black hole expands to suck us inside. Once inside my son and my daughter fade from me. I look to my right and watch my oldest son fade thus joining my family. I am usually the one who fades as this new twist adds to my constant state of confusion. Suddenly, this hole becomes flooded with people dressed in so many costumes of the ages. I see knights, Kings, astronauts, soldiers, priests, etc. Accordingly, many distinctive people, and as we go deeper into this hole, it becomes more crowded. We soon become silent as we can hear screaming and hollering from those below us. This feels as if we are dropping into a giant blender. Consequently, I can sense the twitching from the men surrounding me. As a result, I recognize there are solely men in this black hole. The loud noises below us are now louder and getting closer at an alarming rate. I priest beside me tells me not to worry; he has been through this before now. The men in this hole are receiving their new bodies. He looks at me and explains that because I am dreaming, I will fade back into my true reality. He asks me how this episode faired. I tell him it had a different ending that my life had. In my day world, I retired from the Army and remained in South Korea for five additional years. Presently, I feel myself being pulled toward the left. Our row dropped out of the black hole, after which they were sucked into another black hole. I felt something lifting me out of this group, while they began to fade. This was a long episode, yet refreshing. I hold fast now to my victories over alcohol and cigarettes.

Free inspection

A road begins to appear before me. The trees have replaced the men who crowded me previously. I am driving one of my high school cars, with a hole in the muffler to add a performance sound when I blast my way up the hills. The rural areas surrounding my hometown comprise the foothills of the Allegheny Mountains, a vast part of the Appalachian Mountain Range, an economically challenged area. Popular pastimes for my friends and I were to buy beer, fill my tank with gas and explore the country roads. This was an exciting adventure, which always added some surprises to it. We were blessed with an endless max providing so many paths to reach the destinations. Original comprehensive local routes were connected to state routes and now interstate routes added that third advanced layer. The slower dirt roads add a touch of history to this area, since I can hear history, yelling from the ground and aged buildings spotting the landscape. I often fantasize what life was like in those days. We consider life back then as just about dark ages, yet most of their photos show them laughing and their stories profess to happy times. My grandmother rode a horse to school. They lived without cell phones, computers or tablets, and the Internet. I remember searching through microfiche to find dates reports and articles, because now my children simply Google it. The information can even be copied and pasted into their word processors, whereas I had to take a physical copy and typed through a typewriter. This was not that many years ago, yet long enough for me to have forgotten what happened to my irreplaceable typewriters, once a household fixture for the creative. That was during the era when men of power did not know how to type, yet today, if one wishes to be considered normal, he or she had better know how to type. I remember a field-grade officer 'slash' lawyer informing us his next assignment had no secretary, but did come with a keyboard.

Computers even made it to the foothills of the Allegheny Mountains, now on almost all farms, homes, and businesses. I look around in my car and can see this was before the time of computers. Everyone used his or her brain more as human memory was the primary memory available. I notice a fork in the road ahead of us and recognize the valley below us. There is an elderly ran a greenhouse on this road, loaded with so many flowers. They specialize in bulbs, which is wise, in that they benefit from the gorgeous flowers they can sell throughout the year by transplanting, or store the increase in bulbs for sale the next planting season. I notice a high school classmate that I was always too shy to talk to her. This must be a dream, in that she is here beside me, and we are out in the country. I notice my car engine wants to sputter now. Subsequently, I tell Laura that I should inspect it before something big breaks. I get out and lift the hood. I notice one of my spark plug wires is loose, so I snug it back in place. I check the other wires. A few were working their way unsecured. My best suspicion is the miss from the loose wire weakened the other connections. I start my car, immediately notice the smoother engine, and increase in power. While watching the speedometer go up, I notice my gas gauge is below a quarter of a tank. Throughout this day, I have estimated our usage based on the miles I drove, yet with the depleted miles per gallon; my estimates are wrong. Accordingly, I am going to see whether a farmer will sell me gas. While we continue riding around, I am trying to work my way back to the state routes. There is no set art to get out of the boondocks, just try to proceed toward places with more houses and fewer barns. I also knew to stay on roads that follow streams that get larger, most times by feeding creeks.

Laura asks me if everything is okay. I tell her I think I have a few distant relatives somewhere in the area who is famous in our family for cooking country food. Laura smiles and confesses this does sound wonderful. Fortunately, I see a mailbox with my last name on it. Laura and I knock at the door, and I introduce myself as my grandfather's descendent and tell them that I remember my grandfather talking highly about them. I was shooting in the dark on this, as we can be no more than thirty miles from his farm, so somehow these elderly people had to hear something. One possibility is they may be too ashamed to tell me they do not know. A young couple usually does not send out to many alarms relative to danger; therefore, they welcomed us and gladly showed off some of the family cuisine secrets. The meal was wonderful, highlighted with farm potatoes and gravy, corn, beef from an animal raised on their farm and hillbilly treats. They also taught us a few old country ballads. As we are leaving, I ask them if they know of anywhere that sells gas. The elder man tells me there is a local garage about two miles up the hill just pass the thick trees. Laura writes the directions in her notebook, and we go searching for the garage. Fortunately, there is a small hand-painted sign with an arrow signaling the road to take for Billy's Garage. We drive up the hill and through the thick trees with branches that hang over the road. This small section is definitely eerie. Laura adds that it feels as if these trees are designed to keep certain people away from the garage. I agree with her, seeing the trees close the road behind us. I tell her this is most likely a defense system, since his garage is far from any law enforcement, rather by itself and must protect himself. The road becomes rocky, as it is covered by multiple layers of gravel. I figure when it rains, the water may drain over this road and make it too muddy to travel, leaving him stuck on his hill equally important exceedingly far to get practical help. As we continued, his house and garage became visible in a well-kept meadow surrounded by trees. We get out, walk to his door, and knock.

Consequently, a middle-aged man and woman answer the door. I begin to stutter while I introduce ourselves. The reason I am stuttering is this couple stands in front of us completely nude. Finally, the man excuses himself, slips on a pair of shorts and comes back to chat with us, while his mate puts her bikini over her privates. Bill tells us the reason they moved so far out and lived privately is they are nudists. He claims his neighbors who visit him join them in their nudism. Laura reports to Bill that we are not ready for this; however, someday, do plan to visit a nudist colony. She believes the more people involved would take the individual pressure off her. Bill's mate, who is called Pam, tells us this is okay, since the three men who work in their garage are not nudists. Laura asks Pam if these men take advantage of every opportunity to visit with her. Pam confirms they do and this gives her a cheap thrill. Bill asks us if we need any work on my car. I tell him I have a few projects I plan to work on at school; however, nothing urgent. I explain we were visiting one of my relatives who lives within two miles up the road, and asked them if they knew where I could get gas. They sent me to him. Bill tells me he can sell me five gallons; however, he must charge me one dollar per gallon, because he has to buy the gas in town and bring it back here. I ask him if I can buy three gallons. He agrees, nevertheless, reveals he keeps the gas in his garage. Pam tells Bill he should show us his garage. Pam also informs us Bill is so proud of his man cave. I smile at Bill and tell him we would feel honored to get a tour of his garage. We walk toward the front of his building, and he opens one of the bay doors. I peek in and notice a sparkling clean shop with walls covered with tools. He has three bays. I see each bay has a hoist, with two of them currently being used. Accordingly, Bill tells me to pull my car on the open hoist. We lift it, and we discover my exhaust system is worn, although; it is still functional.

Subsequently, we wiggle my wheels to inspect my front-end parts and visually search for fluid leaks. Everything checks out, so Bill tells me, he will put the gas in my tank. He drops the vehicle and puts his gas hose in my tank, and the hose stops when his meter says it was three gallons. I give him three dollars for the gas. Bill becomes extremely angry, telling me I owe him more money. Laura asks him why he believes we owe him more money. Bill tells me in owe him seven dollars for his under vehicle inspection. The three men who work in the garage surround us, notwithstanding two of them capture Laura, and begin tying her hands and feet. I begin fighting with them, when Bill shoots me with a sleeping dart. When I am awake, Laura and I are nude and chained to the special poles in this secluded room. I do not know which building we are in, because his garage was as clean as his house. Our clothes are folded and placed on a chair in the corner, while our personal things, such as my billfold and change, Laura's purse has all its contents spread out on the table. Bill enters and tells me our combined cash was five dollars and ten cents. Pam comes back with the three men angry because they tried to get five dollars from my relatives, yet they only got three dollars, so they beat the old couple, breaking their leg and arm bones and trashed the inside of their house. I really felt bad but asked Bill since he has over eight dollars our account should be settled. Pam tells me they had to add a collection charge. My relatives were so innocent, treated us like royalty, and then currently, may not be able to recover. They most likely are dead. I felt a fire burning inside me. I worked the rope that tied me to the pole. Bill came in front of me and stuck his pistol in my mouth. I slipped my hands out from my rope, and hit Bill hard in his face, causing his hand to release his pistol as he went down. I grabbed this pistol pulling it from my mouth, immediately shot Bill in his head and one of his employees who was watching. After that, I was at once untying Laura gave her the pistol Bill's employee had.

When I opened the door to our room, I discovered we were on a long hallway, most likely on their second floor. I motion for Laura to follow me as we work our way to the stairs. I am not going to check the rooms, because if Pam and her two men want to hide from me; I would head for my car. I hear a creak in a room that I pass. I motion for Laura to open the door as I am positioned to shoot. She opens the door and standing in front of me is one of the employees. We caught him by surprise as his pistol was on his dresser. I pumped two bullets into his head. Accordingly, I always aim at the head because I do not like it when I shoot someone, and they sneak behind me and shoot. When I hit their head, they are in serious trouble and seldom do they move. I collect his pistol, which is the same as Laura and mine. This leaves Pam and one remaining employee. We proceed quietly down the stairs. I walk into the living room and notice the sofa move slightly. Consequently, I run across the living room jump on the sofa while leaning forward, the last employee pops his head up, and I pump two bullets into his head. When he jumped on the sofa, the energy pushed the sofa back to the wall forcing the man to pop up. That was all I needed. We can lighten up some, although I would like to kill Pam, even though I know that with her living here alone, she will not last long. We go into the garage, collect our belonging, taking back just the things that were ours. I made one exception, and that was I filled my gas tank before we departed. I told Laura that is our collection fee. I visually take one more scan to see if Pam was visible. She was hiding; therefore, we got inside my car, and went for my 'relatives' house. I had to see if they needed any help. Laura and I enter my relative's house. We discover them in two separate rooms unfortunately dead. Pam and her men broke their arms and legs. This caused them to bleed to death, which for them was a blessing. The looks on their faces signal they were in deep pain. I am so sorry; nevertheless, they were the people who directed me to Bill. I walk over to Laura and put my arms hugging her. She slowly fades until I find myself holding air. I hear a light noise in the next room, so I grab two of my pistols and run into the room. Pam appears; meanwhile, I begin pumping bullets into her, starting with her body and then get four shots in her head. This room begins to fade until I find myself in the black. Then a small light reveals I am in my day world bed. Notwithstanding, I hope we meet again, my special night-world heroes. Laura and Georgia will be hard to forget.

The long bus ride

Suddenly, a jolt bounces me from my seat, followed by a thump when I return to my place. I fade into a crowded bus filled with other teens. I look for signs this could be a school bus, yet can find no signs. The poor suspension and awkward interior design lend me to believe it is an older bus. We are riding during the night, which suggests this could be a commercial adventure. I walk to the back of the bus to urinate, when someone sticks their foot out and trips me. As I fall to the floor, everyone starts laughing, therefore, I bite a man's foot that is trying to pin me to the floor. He screams, which adds to the laughter on this bus. I get back on my feet and proceed to take care of my personal business. When I come out, a thug takes a swing at me. I duck and come up swinging. I land a solid hit on his face, causing him to start crying. Accordingly, I am impressed with my fighting skills, and I knew the projection of strength was required to survive presently. I return to my seat quickly, since no feet were in the aisles to slow me. I issued my reserved smile to appear friendly, yet at the same time the strong, ready to fight if need to type. I take my seat, with no one sitting beside me until the next stop when an elderly man enters and takes the seat beside me.

Subsequently, it is difficult to determine how old he is, although his long white, then beard implies he is not young. He asks me if I know why everyone is so loud on this bus. I tell him that I believe they are simply young people acting rowdy. He agrees, explaining that when children are sent to war, they tend to release as much as they can before they report for duty. I confess to him; I have spent the last two years in prison and have not kept up with the latest news. He understands and reports that America is at war with Brazil and Portugal. I shake my head and question why we would be at war with Brazil and the Portuguese. The old man, whose name is Robert reports he believes it was the oil companies that instigated this conflict, so they could save their reserves and use Brazil's reserves as well. Robert adds that Portugal joined to keep England and Spain out of the war. Argentina and Chile joined Brazil making this a South against the North battle. No other nation in Latin America granted the United States any military rights, thus the battle must be fought from naval cruisers who cannot use the Panama Cannel to move from the Atlantic to Pacific. This was confusing me to the point where my mind was becoming groggy. Things were just too different from what I was accustomed. I have traveled the years and the world, yet this has the spirit of war in the air. These young people do not know they are entering a meat grinder. I saw movies about how society drums up the enthusiasm to travel in foreign lands defending justice and gaining the honor of those of the opposite gender. They brand this as a matter of national honor, whereas, in reality, it is an issue where the extremely rich are sending the souls of the youth of the poor to die to generate more wealth for them. This is the story of the ages; thereby denying this era will be better than any era before it was. It was saddening that it was not going to be fine, yet I am not the first to be distressed by this, nor will I be the last one.

Finally, the bus enters an Army fort, and my watch tells me it is four AM. I look once more at my wrist, rather surprised I have a watch, since they traditionally do not feel well on my wrist. I joyfully tell Robert we will soon be losing all these rowdy young kids. Robert looks at me and laughs claiming he thought I had enlisted as well. I ask him why he thinks this. He tells me the binder I have in my arms has colored papers in them like the folders all the other young people on this bus have. I open the folder and find enlistment papers with my name on them. Horrified, I look at the bottom of the pages and see my signature above my typed name. This is trouble for me. It appears that I am going to have a few challenging weeks ahead of me. Nevertheless, I look at Robert and tell him I am going crazy. Robert pats me on my back and informs me he had second thoughts when he answered America's call in the First World War Now, I knew big trouble was coming my way because if the First World War was the previous war, then this meant I was going to the second

World War, which was a terrible war. This is not something I want to go through as it contained many of the worst disasters in modern history. The bus stops and Robert stood up, walked off the bus as three soldiers got on, and started screaming and yelling. I have been through this before, as certain things go with a military uniform and remain the same. They formed us in a straight long line and began whipping us into shape. I always wondered where they got so much energy to yell and be accordingly stupid for such a prolonged period. They decided to start our training with a run in the dark; therefore, off we went. This was strange, in that we were running in our public clothing while holding our enlistment papers. Fortunately, I came wearing tennis shoes, as my feet have always been uncomfortable in dress shoes. I felt sorry for the boys from the west wore their cowboy boots. The thumping sound those boots made when it hit the concrete road easily kept us awake. The sergeants kept yelling; we were chasing Hitler and needed to run faster. This was extremely different from Brazil and South America. Consistency in my episodes appears no longer to be a given.

After our run, the sergeants took us to our barracks and told us to select a locker and bed, make our bunk, and be in formation in twenty minutes. They march us to our breakfast, chop off our hair, and issue our uniforms before giving us a little sleep time. Strangely, I wake up in an Army officer wearing sergeant stripes responsible for editing training manuals. I quickly detect the primitive training styles and update them with a few less middle age European death traps. Knowing they will not accept a major overhaul, I annotate small changes. One important addition I argue for is that running be done wearing tennis shoes instead of their current boots. This change would not take place immediately, as it had to go up the chain of command first. My highest possible contribution was finished within hours, notwithstanding, I went to the restroom, where I vanished and reappeared with my current family looking for a new vehicle. This is an odd jump through time, yet it is a relief, as I totally was not in the mood to fight Nazis, especially because I knew how evil they truly were. I have discovered today that we are looking for my car. I decide that excellent mileage, small, yet convertible for moving smaller household items. The first two visits do not work out as fine; however, the last lot made me a deal I could not pass. Subsequently, this small vacation did not last long, as once again I was back training with my military class. We were preparing to take a PT test. My competitive nature forced me to strive for the best score I could obtain. Unfortunately, I barely passed, nevertheless; my scores were consistent with the rest of this group. To our misfortune, the sergeants decided additional physical training was needed, followed by a long ten-mile hike. This training was tougher than I had ever been through before, yet I figured it would help me for the rough times ahead. This dream is my first multi-event episode. This kept me on my toes, as I never favored being caught by surprise.

Subsequently, I fade and reappear on an airplane as we are preparing to jump into Nazi held territory. I have no idea how to jump or what to do. The sergeant standing in front of the open door is reviewing the important things we must do, showing us, which strings to pull in their correct order. I notice everyone goes through the motions with the sergeant, and for my benefit, he continues this process repeatedly until we reach our drop zone. Suddenly, he begins to herd us out of the plane. We jump into the dark night, which starts to light up with bullets flying in the air. A few artillery shells explode in the air surrounding the airplane we just jumped. Fortunately, our plane races away, as it had enough time to escape. I hear a few men around me scream as they are hit; nonetheless, merely ten men were killed from our group of seventy-five. There was a sister platoon that jumped from a plane ahead of us. We secure our gear and begin our mission of fighting for the villages along a route that our main force will advance. The first village has a strategically distributed Nazi platoon. We fight from house to house, trying to keep as many civilians safe as possible. To our horror, once the Nazis discover we are trying to spare the French civilians. They began to use these civilians as bait. This shocked the village, actually causing several to join our side. We fought like cats and dogs as blood and screams changed the history of this place for centuries to come. I look over the field and see four Germans ordering the French into a tight group for execution. I begin to focus them in my sites, when I notice two French girls, one on each side of me. I look at them and put up four fingers with one hand and then use my other hand as a pistol, and flicker my thumbs, each time dropping a finger. Next, I point to me and afterwards to them and say 'help me.' They shake their head yes, and I focus my site on a German. We fire, and two Germans drop. I at once switch to the next one, missing, yet my French partners kill the third one. The French wrestled the rifle from this last German and shot him in the head. Finally, they collect the weapons and begin running to another house to hide. We know soon the Germans will herd everyone into the streets and start shooting. Now, we must execute each German, who walks in the street. It is a sad thing when we must behave as executioners to save innocent people. Our fighting becomes easier since the Germans are walking in the open. Their need for revenge is too intense thereby they lose all perspective. The town rejoices how these Germans are walking to their slaughter, yet we know that unless our main force reaches us soon, we will pay for brief independence. My mind becomes flooded with all possible alternatives as I fade out of this disaster into my daytime world.

The blazing sounds of gunfire fade out, as I find myself appearing in a wonderful king-size bed. I get up and walk around this room, spotting a light switch beside the door. Accordingly, this tells me I am not that far from the modern era. After flipping my light on, I realize this room is decorated with riches, walls highlighted with paintings in hand carved frames. The trimming and doors are works of art as also the wooden figurines that complement the two stone life size sculptures. Even the lamps are wonderful creations. I particularly like the wall of books and absence of TVs and other room electronics that have taken over my house in the day world. Notwithstanding, I sense this is a room I spend much time reading and resting. Thereafter, I walk out into a grand hallway. I walk this passageway passing interior designs, which bypass that of royalty. I arrive at the end to see grand circular steps. I peek over the railing discovering endless steps up and down beyond any ends I can detect. This place is larger than most cities. My need to explore drives me to continue up, until I cannot climb any more, thereby I walk into the adjoining hallway. When I pass the third row of bedroom doors, a house cleaner comes out of a room asking me why I was taking the stairs instead of the elevator. I tell her the beauty of the steps always takes my breath. She reports that this mansion has over one-hundred floors, and that seldom does a member of the owner's family make it this high, and we are just on the eighteenth floor. I confess to her that I was making sure the steps were clean and looking for a maid who would prove her loyalty to the family. She promises her everlasting support.

Accordingly, I ask her to show me the things she likes the best about my home. She grabs my hand and rushes me to the elevator. This was something I wanted to know because one-hundred floors would be a challenge to climb each time I wanted to go outside to our wonderful land. A special thing that identified the elevator doors was the silver doorknob compared with the regular golden doorknobs. Every tenth floor the elevators switched to being horizontal where they would take another lift tunnel. This was because the original builders were too afraid of a one-hundred-floor drop. I tell her this is wise indeed, since that is a long way to go down to the ground. Thereafter, I follow her to many special rooms she shows me. I wonder how she remembers all these rooms; nonetheless, she explains once you have seen inside them, you never forget what you discovered. Later in the afternoon, she takes me to the first floor, so she can give me a tour of the outside beautiful landscapes. We walk into the front lobby, packed with domestic servants who stand at attention when I enter. I tell them to relax and do what they are supposed to do. My special house cleaner Jill, recommends we go and look at my car fleet in the basement. Upon entering, I notice my high school classmates are racing cars, crashing into the parked ones as if they were toys. This angers me, and I ask Jill how I can stop this. She runs over and pulls a lever that reads 'owners only.' The alarm sounds and the cars immediately stop, except for one. There is always the one who does not get the message. I go to stand in front of this vehicle, which appears to be a tan Blazer I once owned. Consequently, when I notice who is driving it, my heart stops as I begin screaming. The driver is my three-year-old daughter, who is standing in the seat with both hands on the steering wheel. I yell for her to push the brake pedal, explaining it is the second one from the middle. She has no idea what I am saying, therefore, Jill runs along the driver's side, as I rush to catch the passenger door when it passes. I grab for the door and miss the handle. It appears these are not the movies, nor even a successful dream event.

I bounce from the side of this Blazer, hitting the ground. Next, I jump up to try to get the bumper then maybe lift the back hatch coming in from behind this racing machine. The brick basement wall is quickly approaching. I fail to hold onto the back bumper, as the razor-sharp rusty edges cut my hands. The Blazer rushes away from me too far to catch before crashing into the wall. It crashes followed by an extreme explosion. The thought of my baby burning alive cripples me, causing me to rise to my knees before dropping my face into my hands and crying as a baby. Jill comes over in front of me and asks why I am crying. I lift my head to scold her before cussing her to no end. If she is a servant her, then she should have known my daughter. I look up at her and just before the first word escapes, I freeze in shock. I cannot believe what I see. How could such a miracle occur? She is holding something extremely important to me. Jill has my daughter in her hand. I ask Jill to explain when she started performing miracles. My daughter tells me they were playing jump catch. Jill, noticing my confusion, explains that my daughter and her play jump catch in her room, where she jumps and Jill catches her. Jill reveals she yelled, and my daughter took her hands from the steering wheel and dived into her arms.

I give Jill a stern look and tell her that just cost her the job she had. Jill looks saddened and offers no resistance. I ask her if she understands why she can no longer work as our maid. She reports I do not have to tell her, unless I want to do so. I explain that she cannot be a member of our family and a servant at the same time. I am adopting her as my older daughter and sister to the daughter I almost lost. I tell Jill that because of her, I go to bed tonight with two daughters rather than just one. Accordingly, I ask Jill to call the police, as I want all who were destroying my vehicles charged. Jill calls our home security team, and they apprehend those who were destroying my vehicles. I inform Jill this would be a good night for us to attend church. Jill looks at me strangely, as this house begins to fade. I am exiting this event much earlier than I wanted, yet such things are beyond my control in the world deep inside my soul.

Epsilon

Recording these night adventures left me exhausted many of my days presently. I must now deal with a wider range of emotional issues. I truly do not know when to show my love, as I fear that those, I care for could suffer. Even though I do not, or so far have not, suffer any physical pain, unfortunately I must endure watching others in misery. I steadfastly argue I would much rather suffer than watch those I care about in anguish. The fear of my infant daughter, who is almost finished with high school now, crashing into a brick wall and burning to death, has me even shaking during the day world currently. When I awoke in the morning, I must think hard the first few minutes while I fish deep in the waters of my mind to retrieve the highlights of these escapades. The drama of watching my daughter just three years old rushing to her death is a fear I am experiencing difficulty in suppressing. The multiple visits within an event append an additional variable, which I must adapt. I will figure a way to use these jumps to enhance my experiences. This next event was different in that it contained elements from other dreams, although the roles and situation varied.

The church

My surroundings began to take focus placing in sitting in a giant church. This building has European designs, creating a feeling of advanced architecture. The large windows are designed with Biblical events that created a feeling of the Bible being alive surrounding us. I am wearing a tuxedo, sitting in the front row alone. Looking around, I see everyone dressed in formal attire. A group of men, all dressed in black tuxedos, except for one who is wearing white tuxedos. Accordingly, I am wearing a black tuxedo, which makes me wonder why one would be so different. I soon learned the answer to this question. He sits beside me and asks me if I think my best man looks special. Smiling, I inform him that it would be impossible not to look unique when one is wearing white as all others are dressed in black. If he is the best man and sitting beside me, then I must be getting married today. This place is packed indicating that we have many friends and relatives. I will simply go with the flow, as the roles for the groom are straightforward. Stand in front of the preacher, and kiss the bride afterwards. I can merely hope she is pretty.

The bridesmaids line up on the left side of the stage, as my men line up on the right. My best man remains beside me; therefore, I will merely follow him. The music started, and a young girl walked up the aisle scattering flowers on the floor. When she passes us, she goes to the other side and sits. The organs play loud now as the bride walks down the aisle. I stand with my best man, watching my bride come to me. He has a white veil over her face; thereby I cannot determine who she is. Her father gives her to me. I think how ancient this custom is, a woman is given to a man by her father. The priest calls out asking if any object to this union. Two men in the back of this high-class rich person's church stand up and begin shooting their machine guns. Fortunately, they were shooting at the ceiling, which did no justice to the ceiling. Subsequently, four police officers in plain clothes stand up and begin shooting. Providentially, as can be experienced in church, the defenders were conveniently located close to these men. They fell quickly, as the officers, or those we believed to be officers carried the two dead men from the chapel. The priest calmly asks if anyone else objects, cautioning the audience the church still has some executioners planted in attendance. Everyone laughs, yet a thought goes through my head about the possibility my bride could be part of the mafia. The priest tells me I may kiss the bride. I lift her veil and recognize her at once. I am about to kiss Jill. I feel so awkward in I recently adopted her. I kiss her for currently, knowing that we have many ceremonies throughout the remainder of this day, and now two men have already died for our union. We proceed to our reception in a special vehicle. Once inside, I ask Jill to add to the romance of today by reminding me about our relationship. Jill explains she fell in love with me the first time we met in college. She reports that her father visited us on the campus and approved an association for us. We did not dare date until we had his permission. Jill informs me how happy her family was with me and when her father told us to get married. Jill reminds me we will change into clothing that is more casual and dine on this extraordinary food. As we walk to our special vehicle, a few tall men stop us and reveal we have a small delay. Several unknown people have blocked junk cars around our vehicles. Additionally, they cut all the tires so the vehicles could not be moved. We had to wait until the tow trucks pulled the vehicles out one at a time. Her father gave the tow company the junk cars as part of the towing costs.

Accordingly, our convoy zips to the large restaurant, and our flock pours in to enjoy the food and alcohol. One hour later, the flock is rejoicing and everyone is offering toasts. Jill warned me not to begin drinking until the toasts started, or I would be drunk on my face as we left for our honeymoon. I trusted her wisdom, as I additionally took smaller drinks during the toasts. The band began to play dancing songs, as the couples flooded the floor to enjoy a revival in their romances. Suddenly, all the lights went out as Jill grabbed my hand and told me we had to hide on stage behind the drawing curtains. I willingly rushed with her, considering we were close to the stage. The other couples began rushing for doors, as they were trampling over others. We pass by no people, since we are going in the opposite direction. Consequently, we barely make it behind the curtains as the lights once more appear. Suddenly, we hear machine guns firing throughout. I can peek through a small hole in the curtain and witness blood flying everywhere. This creates more terror as the survivors' stampede for the closest door. Jill guides me through a panel behind the curtains where we crawl into another room. From this room, we rush down a tunnel, which puts us underground. I hear water. Jill explains this is the water system, and is self-contained from any sewage pipes. Actually, I was not worried about this, considering people are dying above us, either way this system has a sidewalk, which we can run. We continue to run until we see a yellow door. Jill stops and opens the door. We enter a comfortable room, packed with our relatives. When we enter, I ask her father how he knew this. I explained the FBI had given them the tip; the mafia puts several contracts out on many of our attendees. Considering these people were asked not to participate, nevertheless, elected to join, they knew these actions were putting people in jeopardy. Our families, and close friends slipped out during the couples' dances. This feast was well advertised and warnings that only invited people could attend. Notwithstanding, the ballroom was flooded with these wedding crashers. Jill's father asks me what else he could have done. He complains unless he plants men with weapons and forces people to obey his requests, they will not listen to him. The lone thing we must worry about now is to get back into his property where we will be safe. As we begin to walk across town in this underground water system, my world around me begins to fade. Once again, I have been cheated from my reward. I go through the wedding ceremony and reception; however, was cheated out of the honeymoon. I wonder if I am being punished, yet either way returned to the day world.

Escape from my station

I fade into a large mowed meadow surrounded by military-style aged redbrick buildings on two sides and a sizeable new bright; clean redbrick office style building connecting the two sides. The continuous rows of windows on each floor identify this as an office building. I recognize this as a building I previously worked while on active Army duty. When standing in front of the building the row of older buildings on my left was General officer quarters whereas the rows of buildings to my right were intelligence buildings. I knew this from an interview I once barely wiggled out of for a military position. My adventures in this large headquarters were now about to take a different course as a new episode becomes a part of my night world. I arrived as a staff sergeant and departed from this assignment as a Senior NCO. This time I was a PFC standing behind a long portable table with a black female PFC, whom I knew as Sonia during my day-world duty assignment in this location. We are processing thousands of reserves who have been camping in the large meadow before this headquarters. I ask Sonia if she knows what is happening. She explains we are preparing for a new war in Europe. Throughout the day, the soldiers I had previously served with come up to me and offer their condolences concerning my court-martial. I ask Sonia why these men believe I was court marshaled. She becomes angry with me telling me now is not the time to play stupid. Another Private who is working with us follows me to the restroom and once inside asks me why I am being so cold with Sonia. I dangerously confess that a drug I have been taking is causing my memory to play tricks with me. Furthermore, I ask him if he brings me up-to-date, so I can make things right with Sonia and myself. He revealed that several other soldiers were harassing Sonia and threatened to harm her. I came to her rescue and got in a fight with them concerning this issue. The others lied accusing me of assaulting them. The military court believed them and reduced me to E-3 and forcing me to remain in the military. Sonia counter sued and won a joint assignment for us.

I return to our desk, apologize to Sonia for my failing memory, and ask her to forgive me. A few minutes later, a couple of Sergeants came to our desk and began harassing us. Strangely, a Senior NCO that I had trouble with comes to our defense. He demands these Sergeants report to our sections Colonel, where he marches them. The Colonel orders their immediate discharge and calls Sonia and me to his office demanding that we stop causing trouble. I never liked his Colonel, although I wisely at no time made this known to him. Sonia told me to remain calm, as we would have our time to get even. We continue our work throughout the day. Late that evening a Major General with several officers comes rushing into our lobby. The reservists had harassed us most of the afternoon, yet the harassing had a strong tint of teasing with it, and when considering there were few women in their unit, Sonia whispers in my ear this is to be expected in that these men are going to war in Europe. The soldiers do not present a real concern for me, so we simply try to keep them from alerting anyone else who may pass in the hallway. Several members have asked us if everything is okay. Each time, we pretend to be busy with our paperwork, such as assembling packets. I told them I did not want to lose any more stripes for fighting or called to the Colonel's office for causing trouble. This proved instrumental in our defense, as a member of our Chaplains Division overheard our explanation, and immediately told a Chaplain who raced up stair and told our Lieutenant General who called the reservist Generals to meet him in our lobby.

This Commanding General waited on the stairs on the second landing, and through radio, contact with his subordinate General timed their arrival to be in unison. The Commanding General overheard much of the harassing. He sent a few privates, with small camcorders to pass by the entrance secretly recording these events. This later provided evidence we were working while these reservists were pestering us. When the Generals entered the lobby, everyone jumped to attention. The three-star told his two-star to secure his troops, and he would tell him what punishment to issue. Presently, Sonia and I stand in front of the three-star who asks us to follow him to his office. Additionally, he orders one of his colonels to get our supervisor and to tell him to send replacements to this station and at once report to his office. Furthermore, he wants the Chaplain observer to join us. Our supervisor immediately joins us in the General's office, arriving with the Chaplain's clerk. Surprisingly, he stands beside us, and then smiles at me. I am relieved that he does not appear to be angry. Further thinking leads me to believe he is holding his feelings considering we are standing on the carpet that is redder than blood. Our supervisor tells us to let him do the talking, and that we are not in order. The three Generals who work on this floor come walking in now, as the three-star sits with his deputy commander on his right and Chief of Staff to his left. They ask the Chaplain assistant to tell us what he heard. He reports he heard the reservists picking on us, and the reason we did not resist was they had reported a previous harassment and told by their Colonel not to cause any more problems. He also heard us talk about telling the truth once earlier and getting a court-martial for trying to defend themselves. The Generals turn to my supervisor and ask him if he knows anything about these privates being told not to cause any more trouble for complaining. He confesses that he witnessed a few reservists harassing us and took them to our Colonel, who discharged them and then told these soldiers to stop causing problems. He tells the Generals that he cannot claim to know what was in the Colonel's mind, unless he was trying to toughen them up expecting some sort of retaliation from the reservists.

The Generals ask me to explain why I felt had suffered a wrongful demotion. Sonia speaks up immediately telling the Generals that as an E7, I fought to prevent her from being raped. Not only was she raped, but also the rapists lied and got me demoted to E3. The Chief of Staff hands the Commanding General a copy of the court-martial. The General pulls out another file from his desk from his criminal investigations Division and looks at our supervisor asking for his input. Our supervisor tells the General he tried to disprove what he feels to be false charges, yet the cards were stacked against him. The General asks him if he believes I am innocent. Our supervisor tells him the reason he asked to let both of us work for him was because he felt enough salt had been placed on this man made wound. At this, the General excuses the Chaplain's clerk and asks him to have our Colonel waiting in his secretary's area. He calls for his secretary to have five chairs circled his desk, one on each side with the remaining three sitting in front of his desk. Afterwards, he opens his special criminal file and hands papers to us for our review. These papers report that all four who accused me of assaulting them were all now in prison for raping other women. These reports leave me speechless, as Sonia, and I sit here staring at the Generals. Our supervisor informs the Generals these reports do not surprise him in any way. He knew they were rapists the first time he saw them; however, the military does not make their decisions based on his recommendations. With this, the DCG (deputy commanding general) asks him how he feels about my demotion. He tells the General my demotion made a joke out of justice and is a black mark on the army. The General asks me how I feel. I tell him that this was a small price to pay for the one whom depended on me for protection. Sonia reaches over and kisses me. Our supervisor tells us to be good. The Chief of Staff remarks this is a qualified exception; however, try to keep this G-rated since our Commanding General (CG) has a poor heart. The CG tells us we need to discuss one more subject before he dismisses us. He looks at my supervisor and asks why he did not make sure we were in uniform before reporting to his office.

The Chief of Staff jumps in by asking us if we know how disrespectable it is to be out of uniform in front of a CG. Our DCG, a two-star General confesses that even he double-checked his uniform before coming to this office. My supervisor and Sony scan me; however, provide no improvements. I inspect myself and apologize to the Generals for being so unworthy of being in the

Army. The CG stands up, bangs his hand on his desk, and tells me he disagrees and needs a sharp Master Sergeant to handle his officer assignments. He hands me another folder and orders me to read it aloud. I begin reading it discovering it is my promotion orders to Master Sergeant, signed by the number-one General in the army. The DCG and Chief of Staff pin the new rank insignia on my uniform. I commend them on how perfectly they centered them on my collar. The CG motioned for our Colonel to enter and congratulate me. The CG informs us that Personnel and Finance were already on board with this and recommended that I take Sony out to eat. The Chief of Staff looks at Sony and tells her to soak me for a fine dinner and take advantage of my new Master Sergeant's pay. I hug her and make sure the Generals know that she will be fed wonderfully from this day forward. The General now asks our Colonel why he told us not to cause any more trouble. The Colonel informs the Generals that he did not want anything to happen that would endanger our readiness, teamwork, and fighting spirit. The CG tells him that those who work in this building represent him, and when his people are treated disrespectfully, his commanders will soon adopt the same nasty habit. He has told his subordinate units that to disrespect his people is the same as slapping him in the face. His showdown with them today has reinforced this claim. The Colonel comes out and apologizes to me for not making himself clear. Sony reassures the Colonel that we did not report this to the General. My supervisor explains to our Colonel that he did all the talking to the Generals when they asked them about this, and that he told these Generals, he believed our Colonel feared the reservists would wait until later and ambush them and wanted us to keep it as calm as possible.

Accordingly, we enter the elevator to drop back to the first floor. The Colonel thanks us for our support and promises to disapprove our Major's request to have Sony discharged. Sony thanks him, as does our supervisor. The Colonel tells us to return to our front desks and for our supervisor to send another private to the front desk. He will get everyone together in the training room for a special awards ceremony. We return to our station, as it takes some time for me to realize that I got a promotion on top of my previous rank reinstated. Later, our supervisor comes out and tells us we need to go to the training room. Once there, the Colonel calls me up to the stage, announces my promotion, and invites our coworkers to congratulate us. The spirit of celebration flooded through our section, as soon our duty day was finished. A group of reserve Sergeants brings in a keg of what they call special wine and a bag of plastic cups. They explain this is a peace offering for the misunderstanding this afternoon. The Colonel authorizes everyone to have a cup of wine before leaving. The reservists pour the wine into the cups, a cup for each person they counted. After pouring this wine, they depart with the wine keg, explaining they still have much work in preparing for their deployment. Sony informs me she believes something strange is about this. She also tells me we will not drink this wine, because she does not want to spoil our dinner. We chat with the others while they are drinking. The party begins to liven until people begin choking and falling to the floor dead. Sony and I rush to the Generals explaining the reservists have poisoned our section. They call the military police and order the Garrison, and all other units on post collect their arms and come to our defense. The Generals order this Division to attention and walk with us as we try to identify the ones who delivered the wine. We slowly find each of the four as they spread themselves out among the different units. The Generals had these men face their execution. He had this authority since we were in a wartime situation, and these four had killed most in a critical section. He now was faced with a complete staffing and would need to pull people from other units on the fort, to include the NSA (National Security Agency). Sony and I changed into our civilian clothes, and ventured to a special restaurant. The small orchestra was playing romantic songs; therefore, Sony and I began to dance. We began to kiss as she started to fade. I hated to see my Master Sergeant's insignia dim from my view. That which I lost, I got back and more. The hero got the girl in this one.

Being fired

I roll in my bed and begin dancing once more, sadly this time I dance alone. Looking in front of me, I saw a group of people running back and forth, as if I were watching a video being fast-forwarded. I yell out asking what is happening. Suddenly, I saw these people running in reverse and finally stopping. I wonder if whatever is running or controlling me has an elevator that cannot make it to the top floor. Afterwards, it hits me that I am at least a part of production of these events; therefore, I must hold my peace. I walk in our office building as I pass our owner's desk. He is laughing with many of his subordinates. I chuckle lightly and continue walking pass my coworkers to our reception desk, where two coworkers, I usually chat with stare at me strangely. I ask how my special cupcakes are doing. They tell me much better than I will be doing soon. I challenge them to clarify what they mean. These two working women explain they believe our owner is going to fire me today, over maybe not fire, but will definitely no longer give me assignments. Our assignments generally lasted for one week, thus no assignment would mean no work for that entire week. I decided to go up to our office and go ahead with what I usually did this time of the week, and that was to plan my next assignment recruiting advertisements. Meanwhile, a sales woman comes rushing to my office telling me the co-owner needed my help in the attic. The co-owner was the owner's wife who can be harsh at times, if not bipolar. One thing was for sure, when she called for someone to help her, that person stopped everything and responded.

Accordingly, I was mystified that she was in the attic. This was usually what we would consider janitorial or another lowly title. Either way, up the wooden ladder, I climbed until I got above our second floor and carefully walked out into the large opened and unfinished room. I yelled for by boss to tell me how to get to her. She did not respond; therefore, I turned on my flashlight that was on my iPhone and scanned this large open area and saw some steps, which I carefully walked across the loose floor. A creak from a floorboard that wishes to wobble each step I take. I breathe a sigh of relief when the board becomes firm and not sucking me into the floors beneath it. The steps are questionable; nevertheless, I walk up four more floors finally reaching the top. I never realized the inside had this many floors above it. Accordingly, I spot my boss and confess to her; I have at no time been up here. She confesses they did not tell anyone about this. I ask her how she made it up the steps from the hallway that runs pass my office. She laughs and then reveals to me the steps extend down to her office. There is a closet in her restroom and in that dark closet; behind where she hangs her coats is a door that leads to the stairway. I ask her why they do not refinish this and rent this out as office space. The downtown location would be appealing. She explains they believe it would cost too much for the income it would produce. They can list this as a selling point when they sell this place. I ask her why we are in this empty part of the building. My boss reports that we must find several important papers, or copies of an insurance policy. I ask her if the insurance company had these papers. She now confesses they believe these papers to have been falsified. She asks me to spread out these boxes enabling her to search through them quickly. Fortunately, she found these papers in the third box I had pulled down for her. Subsequently, she told me we could go now. I asked her if she wanted me to put the boxes back. She tells me not to worry, since they will not be here much longer. Afterwards, she asks that I keep what she told me secret.

I testify that I have always kept my word with her. She agreed that her husband is constantly boasting about my trustworthiness. I immediately ask her why there are rumors I will be fired. She reveals this building is to be sold, and then they will file bankruptcy. She reminds me this is in great confidence. She reminds me to clean up in the upstairs restroom before being called to the owner's office. We journey back to our respective offices, and I clean myself and not much later, I receive the call to come see the boss. I walk into his office as the smile and happy personality, he unleashed on everyone today vanished. He started reading the statistics, such as sales by new recruits, and it appears my fresh hires were not performing as these unknown hires from the other recruiters. Next, he tells me how much money he feels I had lost for his company, money they needed vitally to stay in business. Accordingly, he asks me not to return unless I want to be a sales representative. After all, I did not want to be a salesperson, as their pay was totally contingent on sales. No sales meant no pay, which was not my way. I walk to my car and prepare to go home. My car has decided not to cooperate with me and failed to start. Accordingly, I surmise that when it rains, it pours. Naturally, the first thing that happens after being fired is my car would stop working. I lift my hood and begin troubleshooting. This is something beyond me; therefore, I will need to have a towing company tow and fix it. I decide on a company about twenty miles away and make the arrangements using my cell phone. About one hour later, the owner, his wife, their three children departs their business. This is rather strange, in that two of their children work for this company. One of my coworkers, who was also one of the owner's children asked me if I needed a ride. I told her I lived too far away from them to catch a ride. She explains that she will be working in one of our distant offices and can pass through my village if need be. I thank her revealing to her; I believe she is a lifesaver. She tells me we have some minor work at her parent's house first, no more than two hours tops. This sounded reasonable to me, in that she was saving me a costly taxi ride. We arrive at the owner's house, and pull into an area behind the house I never knew existed.

Subsequently, we continue down the dirt road through a thick forest into a meadow with a large old barn standing tall as to brag about the years it has existed. We collect items from their house and store them in here. The mother in this group explains this barn is on a separate deed they are not including in the bankruptcy. They have registered this as no trespassing territory and posted the appropriate warning signs. The bankruptcy contains a standard statement protecting neighboring lands from invasion of their privacy and searches. I did not want to get into too much detail, as I told my previous coworkers; I needed to find another job. They agree I am not the lone one that must also find another job. I knew this would be an adjustment for them as well, although their parents demanded from this what they expected from us. I could never argue they received preferential treatment, when considering we gain special favors from our respective parents; they at least had a right to something. I decide to stay out of this and to move on in a new direction. Once returning home, I began searching for a fresh job, this time entertaining working in other directions and towns. A month passed, when one day I received a call from the owner asking me to meet him in his office. I am puzzled, believing that stage of my life was history. Nonetheless, I go to his office and find out what he wants. I notice our receptionist is at the front desk busy as usual. The owner explains that he recalled my predecessor to work for him; however, he is no longer associated with this company. I ask him what this has to do with me. He explains my previous position is available if I want it. I inform him time is needed for me to discuss this with my wife, and I will call him soon. I walk out of this building feeling fine inside, in that I will not call them to regain my previous position. Only I fool returns to his folly. A large storm hits our area, as I travel at merely ten miles per hour. I must further cross over a high bridge and great river. The winds rock my small vehicle as a few times I can feel my car wanting to rise. I decrease my speed during these lifts to add weight to my car as the wind pushes down as well. Fortunately, I made it over the bridge claiming never more to cross it.

Accordingly, this gave me the impression that I belonged north of the river. I continue driving to my home, when my car slides off the road and rests beside a quickly rising creek. I slip out of my passenger window and crawl to my house. Once I make it back up the hill to the highway, I attempt to stand on my feet. I find a sturdy then pole and use it as a can, and stand on my legs. Consequently, I begin walking up the steep hill that opens into my village. Realizing the weather is making it extremely difficult to drive I leap into the ditch beside this highway each time a car passes me. Fortunately, there is not much traffic tonight. Finally, I make it to my back door and enter my dark house. My family tells me our electricity is out, and they are cold. I light our gas oven and then bring our gas grill from the back porch into our living room, resting it on the towels to protect our carpet. I ignited our grill, thus it would not be long in our house would be holding much heat and fiery light. I change into dry clothes and prepare a lot of left overs as my evening meal. We elect to sleep in our heated areas tonight as the destructive winds continue to beat against this cherry wood strong house. Later in the night, I hear someone trying to break in our back door. Immediately, I grab my shotgun and a few knives. When these men break into my house, I shoot the first one with my shotgun, killing him instantly. Afterwards, I grab the two knives and begin stabbing the second man, who is pulled out of my house by his friends. They flee from my land, as I open my back door with my reloaded shotgun at my side and push the dead trespasser out onto my back porch. I secure my back door with a spare lock I had. This lock worked, except I had no key for it. We would need to use our front door, which is not the end of the world. The next day, I see my former boss's wife driving into my driveway. She asks me where my car is. I tell her it will be delivered to me soon. A friend was going to pull it out with his tractor. She asks me when I will return to work. I ask her not to tell her husband; however, I would not be returning. Saddened, she gets into her vehicle and leaves. The important thing that I know is by asking her to keep this a secret, her husband will know before she leaves this small village. I start laughing as the thunder begins to dim as my home begins to fade. I held onto my integrity as another world vanishes around me.

The funerals

Feeling my hands on a steering wheel, I emerge driving a vehicle, or actually a Hearst. Beside me, am I believe my coworker. I ask him how things are going. He chuckles and tells me to ask him when we finish the man in the back later tonight. Notwithstanding, I start to work, and will have to wait for any fun in this event. We pull into our building, and I help unload this body on a cart. My coworker asks me to start arranging things upstairs and discover what is happening with our boss, and he will take care of this corpse. I climb the steps and enter a hallway that contains our viewing rooms. They are absolutely trashed. I grab what appears to be a cleaning cart and begin working on the rooms. I remove the trash, vacuum the carpets, and polish the wood. Finally, I arrange the folding chairs where our guests can rest. It takes about two hours to tidy everything; thereafter, I put the cart in our janitorial room. Apparently, I have a knack for moving around this building, so while I stick to my instincts I should not make too great a fool of myself. Worse case, I will go back downstairs to my coworker, nevertheless, considering he is working on a corpse; I hold this as my last resort. Accordingly, I stroll the floor and discover our boss. I greet him while entering his office and inform him we wanted to know if he had any additional assignments for us. He smiles at me and reveals he has something special for us.

Subsequently, I dislike it when they have something special for me when I do not understand what is expected. He tells me I will be posted at the front door and brief our guests as they enter. I notice three caskets being delivered to the rooms I just cleaned. He hands me a card with the three names and the room number they are assigned. My boss explains most questions will be related to which room the funeral they wish to attend. About one hour henceforward, he tells me to start the service in the first room, thereafter go to the second room, and finish in the third room. After I finish in each room, a crew will take the casket for burial. My boss hands me three index cards, each with some notes to form my final message. I go to the front door and between greeting guests, I review the three index cards. Accordingly, I hope to give these speeches as natural and personal as possible. Unfortunately, I welcome a string of nasty and rude guests. Their remarks make the inside of me explode, yet somehow I hold it in place. Finally, a group gets out of hand, and I shut them up by reminding them someday they will be in one of the caskets here. This shuts them up quickly, and I have no more trouble for my remaining guests. Apparently, one person from this group is briefing the people outside before they come to my door. My boss stands beside me and tells me he heard what I said and congratulates me for using my head. This is why he hates being the greeter, as we know the pain and frustration from the loss of a loved one. My boss pats me on my back and tells me to begin my first service in twenty minutes, as he goes to his office. I continue to welcome our guests, who are either the extreme elderly, or college age. There are no children here, as this appears to be a constant among all families. Everyone appears to look their best, so I slowly walk to the first briefing room. Just before entering, I review it once more and put it in my shirt pocket, so if I forget it will be where I can grab it quickly. I have never heard a funeral home speech before burial.

I walk into the room unnoticed by the attendees. I place my card on the podium that I am standing. They continue to ignore me; therefore, I can see this will be a take-charge situation. The body beside me is the corpse of Mr. Smith. To keep this from being too personal I call him Mr. in place of his first name. I begin my message by telling them that I believe Mr. Smith wants me to say a few wonderful words on his behalf. This got their attention as they sit. I say a few words about how Mr. Smith thanks them for taking the time to say goodbye to him. At this time, the room becomes dark while I hear noise in the casket. The light quickly returned as I noticed Mr. Smith was sitting up and his face currently fostering a big smile. Now, I am starting to realize I am moving too close to the deadline. Subsequently, the strange thing is that everyone is dark black. Something has changed their race. The crowd begins to scream, yet, for some reason; no sound departs from their mouths. Realizing their voice was silenced; they formed in a circle around me and wrote a note demanding to be told why I did this. I inform them I did nothing to them; everything was done by Mr. Smith. I recommend if they want fixed, they need to get back on Mr. Smith's good side by apologizing for their rudeness and lack of showing him respect. I reveal that they can stand in front of him and speak their words and when they hear their voices return, they will know Mr. Smith has found favor in their words. Within minutes, they began turning back to white with their voices restored. Not all were transformed, because a few never were favored by Mr. Smith. He had his mark on these four, and he would not release his special curse upon them. I told this group my work with them and wished them a wonderful burial. Surprisingly, I received some marvelous hugs and handshakes as we exchange sincere goodbyes. I feel satisfied while seeing how those who do not appreciate who they are can find themselves striving hard to regain what they lost. I walk into the hallway, motion for my boss to take the room and proceed to my second funeral.

I walk into the second room, as all are sitting holding back their anger. They immediately ask me why I am late. I tell them I had some trouble with the previous group and had to wait for our SWAT team to eliminate the troublemakers. One of them told me that he was going to take the nasty out of my words. Straight from the beginning, I can see this group will be trouble. Oddly, the majority of this group is college age and therefore, does not hold fast to tradition. Once more, I place my card on the podium, introduce Mrs. Zackers to her family, and tell them to come up one at a time and say a few special words about her. One of the young women tells me this is my job. The room becomes dark; a thump in the casket and the light comes back to brighten the room. I am curious what surprise Mrs. Zackers has for us. Glancing over, I see that she is presently sitting. I get a dreamy surprise when I look out at the mostly female group, as they are all currently completely nude. I look at them and ask who the decent ones are now. Their men are hiding behind them. I start snapping pictures with my cell phone. The women complain I cannot take these photos. My argument is I can photograph anyone in my showing rooms. I appreciate what they are showing. The women ask me how their clothing will be returned. I appreciate their positive attitude. I tell them they must gain their clothing by pleasing Mrs. Zackers. They begin praising her and she slowly gives them back their clothing. Once they are clothed, I finish their small ceremony and walk into the hallway where I motion for my boss who this time is accompanied by one of my coworkers. My boss informs me he will do the final service, as this place experienced enough supernatural to last a century. He also tells me to leave my cell phone on his desk before I leave. My coworker takes the second group to bury Mrs. Zackers. I am relieved concerning my release from the final service. Afterwards, I sit in my office to rest finding myself more exhausted than I thought. I begin to fall asleep as this world fades away. I take with me the joy of watching those with the heads in the clouds being humbled.

The long ride on the interstate

I fade into a busy Friday afternoon and into an excited office. A gorgeous coworker comes in my office and asks me if I am excited in that we will be in our hometown later this night. Therefore, I ask her why I would not be excited. In my mind, I picture a weekend with her and cannot see, off hand, why it would not be wonderful, especially when considering how much enthusiasm she has spilled around us. I ask her to run through our plan once more to make sure we do not act mistakenly. She explains that two of our girlfriends, and she are going to our hometown for a one-week vacation. The snake in this garden is that our supervisor and his nasty friend will be crowded in van with us. She is thankful they will not be on our return trip.

They told everyone to eat a large lunch and bring their evening meal. She tells me they know their supervisor, and his friend will not bring an evening meal since they want to show them off in a restaurant until they apologize for not bringing their money. To offset this, they brought some diapers and laced two spare dinners with ex laz. I ask her why they did this. She confides the girls have determined they have taken all the 'crap' from them; they will ever take, and it is time for revenge. We load up hurriedly as we can hit the road before the scheduled time. Our supervisor, who wanted to get home quickly as well, got us released two hours early. This was the same as telling us we could obtain a one-hundred-mile jump, or get home two hours earlier. The girls set my supervisor straight when he tried to lag at the beginning. He was standing between them and their families, which is not a wise place to stand. My supervisor and his friend were placed in the back row with our luggage stacked in the limited open areas within the van. Considering, there were four females in this van; naturally, we loaded the luggage rack as well.

We soon were on the road and within a few minutes my significant other, or without question the head hen in this gang, issues the first warning to whom I label as Nastyboy. She promises to rip his tongue out of his head if he says one more word. My supervisor orders me to keep my dog on a leash. I remind him we are off post and that the rank was left. Additionally, I warn him that if he ever says anything disrespectful to my co-pilot, he and his nasty little diseased dog will be walking. I ask him if he wants to test me on this. He immediately retreats. I tell the girls to let me know if they even make a move that can be a hint at disrespectful. My supervisor tells me he will settle the score when we get back to base. I hold my peace waiting until we are halfway on our journey before I hold my court. Our van remains quiet as Nastyboy regains his confidence and demands we stop for dinner. We are now five hours into our journey, so I yell out that it is time for us to bury our differences and offer a peace prize. I tell the girls to give our guests the best of our food, especially to give them the superior treat my woman prepared for this trip. They pulled out two wonderful wrapped meals with cups filled with wine. I ask them to keep the caps to their wine cups close in case we are pulled over by the police. The line was laced with a special laxative to enhance the effects of the ex laz. Within ten minutes, they were begging us to stop. We find a gas station on a remote highway. As the side slide door opens these two men rush out of the van, taking their new raunchy smell with them. Once they wobbled into the restrooms, which we each recorded on our cell phones, we returned to the road. I sent a text to my supervisor that if he in any way tries to settle this score, we would publish our video of them wobbling to the restroom. My woman worked out a secret deal with the station attendants for additional filming from their security cameras. I knew my supervisor would try to rebuff our evidence, and once we received this special evidence, I told my friends this was the best one-hundred dollars I ever spent. The station emailed the video to us, and after securing spare copies, I sent my supervisor our update, especially since the station verified they had departed. We knew that Nastyboy and my supervisor were angry now, as I so much wished I could see the shock on their faces. Accordingly, I refuse to have mercy on them, as I did warn them. We return to the interstate and make a quick departure on the next exit to dispose of the sabotaged wine and food, more for fear; one of us might accidentally eat it.

We continue our trip making it to our hometown. Fortunately, one of the women in our gang has a father who is a judge, and thus obtains for us protection orders, just in case my supervisor gives way to his psychotic side. They also agree routinely to send their police and sheriff pass our houses. Two days later, my supervisor tries to break in the back door to my mother's house. My father quickly places his raccoon traps along the steps that go up to our second floor. Twenty minutes later, we hear both my supervisor, and Nastyboy screamed as the traps bit hold of their legs. Next, my father and I turn our lights on and at gunpoint secure these two intruders, while my mother calls the police. Happily, two deputies arrive within minutes and apprehend them, placing them in the county jail. The next morning our featured judge gave them a ten-year sentence with the first two years in solitary confinement. He upheld our request they be immediately banished so the military would claim they went AWOL (absent without leave) and after thirty days, label them as deserters. I felt bad for what happened to them, nevertheless; I knew they would have not only killed me, but my parents, and then continued through as many of the others as possible before they returned to our base. Even if a few lived to return to our base, they would soon be executed by them. I despise this feeling of guilt for saving my innocent friends and myself. Evil thinks not twice when it kills, yet the honorable cry before killing while simultaneously begging for yet any other path. I rejoice in using the judge and courts to spare their lives. Death is a fast end and as a punishment is too kind. Living in a cage for ten years should teach them about the wrong they have done. If not, then I will face the virtuous choice of whether they live or die. After returning from my deep thought, my mother asks that I join them at our table for a snack before going back to bed.

Accordingly, I welcomed anything to settle my nerves. As I sit, I notice a welcomed sight at our table. My significant other is at our table, in her nightgown, pouring our coffee. This tells me she is familiar with my family, as if a member of this family. She asks my mother how her husband did in this fight. My mother tells my wife, I was strong and brave. Surprisingly, I can now feel my ring on my left hand. Furthermore, I will have someone to add some stability in this strange episode. The atmosphere in our van changed from dead to alive when Nastyboy and my supervisor were abandoned. They sang songs and teased each, challenging the others to outwit them. I kept quiet, since these girls were hitting hard below the belt. Accordingly, I knew they would bury me instantly. Now that everyone is where they wanted to be, I ask my wife how she thinks her girls are doing. She laughs and tells me they are currently in their parent's houses, passed out from hitting every club in our county. This tells me they are close by, which I guess makes it good for us when we are away from home. Our weekend soon finishes; our three passengers arrive on time. About one hour into our return trip, we begin discussing the fate of Nastyboy. We continually debate if it is right they spend so much time in prison, and if we could have let them off with a warning. I argue strongly they knew these were psychotic killers. We have to live with this, as I tell them when you put this many lovely girls together, unless you are married to one of them, there will be trouble. I see a shine cross their faces as one shyly asks me if I think they are pretty. I tell them the sole thing that keeps me under control is my mammoth love for my wife. I must carefully word things so as not to defame them and pass a few compliments, which I feel they deserve. Without a warning, my car goes completely dead. The girls locate a tow company on their cell phones and within thirty minutes, the tow us into their shop. They test my car and tell me my car needs a new alternator. I ask them if they have one. Fortunately, they claim to be able to put new brushes and rewind the copper. They agree to have us on the road for two hundred dollars, including the tow. I happily agree, and three hours later; we are back on the road. We had to spend some extra time while they recharged our battery.

The garage double-checked my charging system to see if something else had damaged it. Everything checked out and as we prepared to hit the road these mechanics gave us snacks and soda for our trip. We were fortunate in leaving early so we not solely caught the garage open, but still make it home. We find ourselves eager to make it back to base, fearing the bad karma jinx us. My wife tells us to share funny things that have happened. This gave us a few laughs and made the time go quicker as we soon pulled into our base. The next day, our commander calls us into his office and asks if we can account for my supervisor and Nastyboy. Naturally, he did not call him Nastyboy; this is a label and the lone way we will ever think about him. The commander knows they departed with us, yet we did not deliver them to the drop-off point as promised. He asked me why we left them in a gas station. We had finalized our combined phone and the station videos, which revealed they had crapped everywhere and even on their clothes. I give our commander a flash drive, so he could view the video. After he watched it, I confessed that I feared making the girls sick, nor did I want to put such stink in my van. We had no doubt that their relatives would rescue them. I knew they had met with their relatives, so I asked the commander if those same relatives received them. He confirms they rescued them, yet the mystery comes when they purchased a blanket bus ticket. The blanket ticket allowed them to travel any bus they wished during a specified period. This also allowed them to float around undetected. I tell the commander that we never had any agreement for a return trip and that my supervisor always bragged about so many of his retired friends spotted around the country. I ask the commander what he would surmise from this information. The commander tells me they most likely went somewhere to be crazy for a few days and then come back to base. The commander asks us if we have heard anything from them. We claim not to have received any contact. The commander tells us he must report them Absent Without Leave (AWOL) and if they do not show up, declare them deserters. We formed outside the commander's office and returned to our duty stations, holding our wits until we could have a private conversation at some undetermined restaurant in town. Luckily, the remainder of the day goes quickly, and as I will shower for tonight's dinner, I begin to fade out of this challenging world.

The dead that live once more

A wonderful world materializes around me with a shining sun and blue sky. I am sitting at a splendid table in the middle of a green meadow surrounded by a superabundance of leaf-filled trees. We have a tall glass of tea on the rocks in front of us, as well as an assortment of fruits to snack in the center of the table. I count six young unfamiliar women at this table. I am guessing they are foreign by the manner they are talking, as their English is broken, and they have an uncommon accent. They are dressed in summer tee shirts and stylish female jeans, wearing no makeup and their hairstyle are piggy tails. This tells me they are living with their parents and are not yet comfortable with the current generation of teens, and filling more estranged than even their American counterpart parents. I make out one being from Eastern Europe, two from Asia, two from India, and one from middle Africa. I have enjoyed teaching English to foreigners for over eight years, so I have a natural feel for this. I begin by telling them today we are going to determine how their English conversation has improved, thereby I want them to tell me who they are and who they were. The first girl, the Eastern European's American name is Lizz (with two z'x) who comes from the Ukraine. Her family came to this area, as her father teaches Russian to students at Ohio University. He moved his family to this area, and commutes one hour per day so his family can stay among our German heritage rich area. Their parents met at a social function and elected to move to our area, which provided a pleasant source of additional income for my family. My wife and I both teach and spend much time with them, joining them in cultural functions as well. They are like our foster children since they spend time helping my wife babysit, cook, shop and so many more things that most people in this area believe they are our relatives.

The second smiley face, the one I believe is from Central Africa tells me her English name is Mary, and she is from Nigeria. She enjoys being on the track team and is our high school's fastest female, which brings more glory to her parents and homeland relatives, because our local area is still on the baseball, basketball, and football mentality. Nevertheless, our group attended all her events; in fact, all sports events these girls participated, as we believe they need this to define their team working and cultural skills. These events bond them with their teammates and therefore, with their community, which makes them a part of and not a part from this society. The next student identifies herself as Jerry and is one of the Asians as she comes from China. Her parents had high expectations for her and at first believed her accumulation of knowledge was the key. They later learned from their friends that they were receiving increasing decreasing benefits of this philosophy. Being more specific, their children performed as machines when young, soaking in all the knowledge put before them, yet later when the social and cultural forces consumed their generation, these forces hit them twice as hard, crippling their college performances. They elected to reduce the academic overload in their high school years and allow them to compete as Americans who are more complete. My major problem with this occupation is I am not naturally inclined to seek pleasure activities and non-productive activities. At first, I felt all this 'fun time' with these kids was a waste of time and soaking too deep, into what I believed to be my personal family zone. I later learned these kids were bonded and a part of our family. We would live in them the remainder of their days. I knew that as each went off to college, rivers of tears would flow in our house. We have over one-thousand who want to be in our next phase. I dread that stage, as we are may even consider building a private school. That will be ironed out in my future years.

We are devoting time currently to organize our training for a comprehensive future program. This is in the ground works now and solely down in our private time. We must survive this first part on the path before leaping toward the sky. The fourth student is an Asian from Japan, who goes by the English name of Terry. Her parents accepted the identical philosophy as Jerry's parents. Terry and Jerry spent much time together and were eager to enjoy the western civilization. They enjoy track and girls' basketball. We have been fortunate so far that these girls have not ventured into boys and dates. I speak freely about this telling them it is okay. Surprisingly, they refuse to date, claiming their friends told them the boys in this area were too much trouble. It always amazes me how they could have a room of parents saying it is okay to do something, yet a couple of their friends tell them it is not okay, and they would prefer to die rather than engage in that safe behavior. The truth is this has worked to our advantage, in that six teenage high school girls mixing with American hillbilly boys working with their advanced country hunting skills to take these girls as their prey. I will never underestimate my fellow citizens. The next one of my perfect angels is a precious young woman from Bombay; India named Carry. I think of her and Fairy, the other student from India, especially from Ranchi, as beloved in; I had to work so hard first to get them to accept their femininity. They were accordingly convinced in the mighty power of men. I had to fight hard resisting the uncontrollable respect they show men. The degree of overkill turned me off from their obedience. If the men in their culture do not take advantage of this honor, but instead strive hard to earn it, as they know specific responsibilities that accompany this power. I depend upon the other girls to reinforce the correct respect for men. They constantly play tricks with her concerning this male thing, yet fortunately; they solely play these tricks in our company and never in a social situation. They behave as close as blood sisters would. Smile and trial were our philosophy and a code we lived by as much as we could do. I can solely feel happiness as I scan each one of my girls. We are a family, and I have complete confidence in their attitude and desire to become professionals.

Nonetheless, they finished their introductions, and I felt comfortable their English was easily understandable and had enough slang and accent to fit into the American culture. We are taking a small break while my angels were eating fruit. Accordingly, this event was so pleasant I actually hoped this event would not end. I would not mind if this episode lasted for a long time. Just as that thought departed from me, the sky became black. My complete world was dark and silent. Consequently, the darkness departed as fast as it arrived. Something froze me while my mind contemplated going into shock. When what I see cannot be true, and what I touch is, weird I must question my sanity. My girls are frozen and when I touch them, they feel as if they are cold flesh. Their stiff faces reveal their eyes open with a far off stare; their smiles are the 'cheese' style. My cell phone rings, as my wife tells me to hurry home with our girls. Instantly, after she says goodbye, the light in my world is shining. I sit quietly in the absolute dark, when once the black the surrounds me gives way to the light of my day. Once more, I am greeted with a surprise. My girls have vanished. Now I know I am in big trouble, because I have no desire to stand in front of their parents and tell them their babies vanished. I rush to my house and inform my wife. As expected she blames me and tells me only an idiot would lose six teenage girls. We were in the woods when they vanished, which brought great stress on my wife. She complains that a wild tiger, bear, or dog with rabies could have gotten them. It is amazing how they cite the worst-case scenario. I explain to her; we need to start searching for anything that looks or feels different. Accordingly, I reemphasis they were frozen and then taken. We knock on all the doors in our small town, and many of the elders are joining us in this great search. Just the mention of these girls and everyone's hearts melt. Their reputation is four-star. I am wondering why this bad thing had to happen to such blameless young souls. My wife asks why I am so convinced we can save these girls.

Notwithstanding, I find the what, who, why, and even where combined with if, defines my current search dilemma. A friend calls our cell phone telling us reports are coming to the police about people missing under strange situations. Now, reports are arriving of people falling down dead. This new situation has everyone staying outside in large groups. They feel more secure being part of many, hoping the mere number of people can act as a deterrent. My wife receives a call from a friend in the next town that Lizz is laying on her porch. Our mob follows us as we race to the subsequent town to the house, which is a house on our side of the ensuing town. We arrive and find Lizz's body. My wife begins sobbing and mourning over the motionless corpse beneath her. I pet Lizz's hair and touch her skin. Then, it hits me that she has not started to decay. Stored gasses in her body should be causing a sort of bloating. I sniff her, and she smells like any person would and not as a human that died four hours earlier. This puzzle has me completely lost. Subsequently, I see a vision of Carry's top body as she tells me that she put a letter from her in my front pants pocket. Carry causes me to blink my eyes as she vanishes. I reach my hand into my pocket and sure enough; a letter is in my pocket. Carry has given the directions where the other five girls, including directions to where their bodies are. I tell my wife and the gang following us to join me. What others believe was by magic, I find the girls, and have all of them placed at our dining room table. By the third girl, I was followed by believers. Carry's note instructed me to have eight people holding hands and for us to say this three sentence spell. I must first memorize it, and teach it to our friends. I tell my neighbors the location of the bodies was correct, thus this well worth our faith. We did exactly as Carry instructed, as she was the first to awaken, then the other five awoke. Terry handed me a ten-line spell and told us we would need twenty people to cite this spell and that all who were missing would return alive. We did, as she told us, not worried if it was true or false. I asked Terry and Carry where they got these spells. They told me some good monsters of this other realm helped them find a way to return all taken from our realm. The parallel dimension tried to match the selections to make sure a high degree of compatibility. This was what saved our world, in that my girls were matched with virtuous, moral, and honest girls. I told my girls they were going to be hugged by everyone in our towns. They were now heroes and when their parents discovered these deeds, they danced and rejoiced on our streets. The excitement overwhelmed them. I was laughing so hard when seeing them dance that I began choking as my world faded sending me back to my other realm.

The land of the identities

I find myself missing my little angels, since I now am without a family. My new role has me as a teenage boy belonging to a tribe that is living on a mountainside. The air is slightly chilly, as the fog is slowly burning off our hillside. This much fog implies a river is nearby. Either way, the people do not appear alarmed that I am here. I see an elderly woman trying to carry her water. I ask her if I can carry the water for her. She reluctantly agrees so I follow her home and place the water on her counter. This elderly woman asks me for my name, and I tell her a recent sickness temporary took my memory. Accordingly, she asks me if I want to be her sister's grandson, who lives in the valley far from us. I ask her if she can tell me about this place. 'Granny' begins by telling me their village is divided into family clans. She has four sons and their families to help her. Their town is ruled by the Overseer, who knows all the evil spirits and those spirits who sometimes might help. Many times the virtuous spirits know of our hidden evils and thereby refuse to help. She asks me if I have an evil spirit, to which I tell her my slate is clean. Granny tells me that if I am not, the Overseer will inform us at once if he can sense it. Only those who serve the finest powers of evil can escape his detection. I ask her if there have been many who later were known to be controlled by these greatest powers. Granny tells us yes, and this is because of the great vast armies they rule. Nevertheless, this was pretty much what I expected, in this leader had an explanation for his failures and when covered both ways, no one can prove you wrong. Granny told me she had to take me to the Overseer first before I could live with her.

Granny guides me to the overseer's hut. When I meet him, I am caught slightly off guard by his normal peaceful look. His words were soft and filled with kindness. I told him it was such a great honor to meet him, as we hugged. Thereafter, he told my Granny that if her sister had any additional young men like me to ship them this way. We enjoyed a good laugh with that one. Accordingly, he looked at me seriously and told me that life with this tribe was dangerous, and we had to make sure that more than two people are trained in any special function. The major two positions were the Rituals chief and the Protector Chief. The Rituals chief is primary concerned with the proper honor given to the gods, such as for rich harvests, healthy bodies, many babies, and luck in war. The luck in war demanded that all the known gods be appeased in the manner the legends. The Protector Chief trains our warriors, ensures all are safe, care for the livestock and crops, and care for those afflicted by the evil or angry gods. I ask our Overseer who serves as the warriors. Granny tells me all the young men, until they take a wife. This is how they become motivated to help in procreation. I argue this is a tough choice to give young free men, especially with so much hunting available. They look at me as if I am strange thinking a man would rather hunt then get married. Nevertheless, I failed to account; they hunt for survival and with ancient weapons, these hunts were not enjoyable. I cannot image a life where there is not a fast-food place nearby as I am quickly noticing the difference running water can make for a life. Even though I am still fresh in this event, those around me have endowed themselves with their distinctive odors. I can understand how hunting can present such an overwhelming challenge for them. I realized extreme care would need to enlighten this tribe in the benefits to cleaning. I noticed they tended to shy away from me also; therefore, my deodorants and body soaps must have caused them concern as well. Granny presently guided me throughout this tribe introducing me to people she knew, which actually included everyone we met.

Sadly, I noticed the teeth were bad for most who lived here. The reality is that without the benefits of modern science, these people ate much raw meat, believing the gods forbid cooking meat unless for sacrifices. The sacrificial meat may be eaten the next day, which unfortunately was rich in bacteria that were detrimental to their dental health. Another factor helping to explain why animals were not affected to the same degree, as humans were in the animals consumed all parts of their prey, whereas humans merely consumed selected body parts. Accordingly, the animals consumed the bacteria fighting antibodies, whereas the humans discarded these tissues, without the knowledge that these contained the agents needed for their survival. It was too late for me to save these people, as they would never listen to me, unless I proved myself first to them. This would present me a challenge indeed. I told the Overseer that in my village, all people ate cooked meat. He asked me if they worshiped the evil spirits as well. I reported that I had never seen any worship evil. He called for his warriors to bind me and tied me to the tree in the middle of their village. Next, a group of villagers began dancing around me. Suddenly, they turned bright red as their heads exploded. Nonetheless, they continued to dance. The Overseer ordered his warriors to set these headless bodies afire. Granny begged the Overseer to keep his warriors away from her grandson while destroying the headless body of the slaves of the Possessor. The Possessor fills a person with evil spirits, making them slaves to the kingdom of the wicked. This small example proved to me that the Possessor was the force to avoid at all costs. The headless bodies soon burned and fell to the ground. Granny petitioned the Overseer to free me, claiming that if I were from evil, the possessed would have freed me. The Overseer argues the demons may have been honoring me, as their leader. Granny, who is hard to suppress once she has determined her position, argued if I had that power, I would have freed myself. The Overseer agreed this was solid logic, thus he would go to his tent and ask the gods for permission to release me. After he departed, Granny told me he simply went back to his tent to take a nap. One hour later, three warriors came to release me.

Granny rushed me back to her cabin. She told me we had a bigger danger than the Possessor was. I could not imagine what could be a greater danger than something taking over my body living inside me could. Granny begins to sweat causing her to grab a rag she kept beside her water bucket as she wiped her face. She motioned for me to sit down so she could talk with me. Granny explained to me another evil invisible punishing god they called the Abductor existed. He would take people causing them to vanish. When he takes someone, everyone in the village joined because the Abductor would solely take his victims if they were alone. No one knows where he takes him or her. Meanwhile, warriors banged on our door. Granny asked them to come inside and tell her what they needed. She pulled out a bag tucked in her kitchen pile and gave each of the five warriors a special cookie. Apparently, Granny's cookies are a highlight among this village. The warriors confess they compete over who gets to summon Granny for the Overseer. Granny points to her coat, which is on a chair beside her bed. She put her coat on, and we returned to the village, where many were standing with their weapons. The Overseer was placing his blessed water on the villager's heads. He applied his magic water to Granny's and my heads. While he applied the water to my head, a warm feeling came over me. The Overseer told us the Possessor was selecting people to destroy. Additionally, the villagers were claiming that two men were missing. These men had families, therefore, reinforcing the Overseer's theory. The Overseer had his village sing their fable songs about great mighty warriors in their distant past. This helped give rest to the anxiety that previously was crippling them. I grew to trust him quickly, and rejoice over the care and security he had provided for those under his care, including Granny. Accordingly, I rejoiced that my other events did not have a Possessor nor an Abductor. I was fortunate not to have encountered the Abductor, as I learn from all, I talk with; no one has seen the Abductor except for those abducted who have never returned. This is a sort of; it could not be proved or disproved theory. Granny tucks me in as I sleep on the floor beside her bed. As I drift into my sleep a strange noise of men laughing.

The cheaters

I quickly shut my eyes and opened them once more. I am in a car with two other young men, as we are drinking beer and blazing on the interstate. I listen to them talking, especially when one asks the other how far we are from St. Louis. He (red beard) verifies if the other (brown beard) still wishes to spend four days in St. Louis. Brown beard tells red beard the two extra days away from us will do his health a great service. Their continual drunken arguing was filling my mind with the information I needed. Some of what they were saying caused me concern. Brown beard argues with red beard that if he did not rape the three wives at the church camp. Red beard argues he did not know they were married, and he regrets having to go to their house and murder them. Red beard thanks brown beard for helping him with the final two. They thank me for driving their getaway car and for finding the home addresses of the wives. I feel tremendous regret that I could have been or may even now be a criminal. Red beard warns us that a police car is behind us. They begin handing me their beer bottles as I carefully bring them down in front of me and with my legs spread, I could lower them using my body to prevent the police in their car behind us from catching our transfer. Once we transferred the bottles to my backseat, I laid myself down to rest. In my rest position, I tucked the bottles under the car seats. The police car followed us for thirty minutes, and then passed us staring ahead as if they did not notice us. Either way, brown beard warned us these cops were acting too disenchanted with us, especially after following us for so long. Red beard claims they were trying to hide behind us, so they could catch speedsters in the other two lands moving toward us. Just to be safe, we got off at the next exit, emptied our trash and open beer bottles, filled up with gas and bought some breath mints, and of course another case of beer. Moreover, as beer drinkers do quite often, we used the restrooms. Here, we emptied our milk jugs; we used to store our urine, and rinsed them with water. If we did not do this, we would stop every ten minutes.

We found another road that would lead to an exit about twenty miles ahead. Nevertheless, we hoped this would keep the cops off our trail, if they were even on our trail. After returning to the interstate, we slowly worked our nerves back to the point where we felt comfortable. We painfully remained below the speed limit throughout the entire night. Red beard and brown beard discuss our mission in St. Louis. Apparently, two churches have angered the mafia, who now wanted them brought back under their control. Red beard tells him they have given them two machine guns. Brown beard complains why no beard, what they call me, ever has to use a machine gun. Red beard tells him the way 'I' shoot, we would be in more dangers from me, and therefore, they keep me in the getaway car to save their lives. Red beard tells us, if 'I' was not waiting in the getaway car, and escape route already planned. I confess to them that this beer has my mind being lazy on me. Why must he stay two extra days? Red beard tells me the police will be looking for three men; however, there will simply be two, and even at that, if one is laying in the back seat sleeping, there will merely be one visible. Red beard will be staying with his family for two days, then drive in a rental car, or maybe shave his beard and cut most of his hair, afterwards fly back on an airplane. We worked our way into St. Louis late the next morning. We ate some lunch, in the downtown area, so we could blend in with the locals. Next, we got us a hotel room the following exit on the interstate. We would take everything with us on attack day, even with Red beard's rental car beside mine. We would remove the batteries from our cell phones, just in case someone recognized them under their masks. They would also have a small rag rolled in each cheek, so if either one spoke, the voice would sound different. Our big night quickly came. We went to the two churches, as Red beard went into one church, and brown beard went into the other. I could see in the churches through their open windows.

Subsequently, I could hear what they said as well. Previously, red beard and brown beard reviewed why they had to do this; I believe to settle their conscience. Their reports claimed these two churches had closed satanic meetings. They were also stealing babies and sacrificing them. Fortunately, for St. Louis they only made one sacrifice each year. The reports generated by the kidnapping of two babies kept all parents on their toes not wanting the same fate. When it happened, the equivalent days the following year, the city was terrified, as many knew this was going to be an annual curse. During their regular meetings, they used animal blood. Another factor that brought fear to their denominations was the rate their groups were growing. If they did not do something now, the churches would have no more Christians. The time for the attacks was here. Red beard and brown beard were instructed not to look into anyone's eyes, or they could become bewitched. They took in their machine guns with silencers. We were fortunate the two services were running on the same schedule. The plan was to enter when they were doing their nude dances, which was before the sacrifice of the babies. In the shaved red beard, and a shaved brown beard rushed into their respective churches and began shooting their dancers. Naturally, they were wearing thin tight gloves so as not to leave fingerprints, which do not care where you go or live. They each had four magazines, each magazine with fifty rounds. As the dancers began to fall, they moved toward them to prevent any from escaping and make sure they did not get the babies. After emptying three magazines each, they came running to our cars. Red and Brown had their cell phones strapped on their foreheads recording their work. This was for the church authorities. We called the police on track one phones to tell them the babies were in the churches. Just as we predicted, when the police rescued the babies, they gave no attention except for removal and burial, for the nude satanic monsters. The police arrested the administrative personnel and ministers from both churches, claiming there was no way for them not to know about this activity. Red visited with his mother, monitoring the local news. His cousin was a volunteer firefighter; thereby Red could monitor the radio traffic. The police argued whoever cleaned this perversion were heroes. Red called us to meet at our secret place we called the Fish cove next Tuesday, which we called two.

Brown and I returned to our homes, to discover our secret still intact. I went to our denomination to see what records they had with our names on it, such as the payment. They had us listed as skilled carpenters and bombshell constructors. The church listed us as a thirty-man operation to justify our great fee. They skimmed money from other projects to purchase the supplies and used volunteer labor. This was to protect us for this cash process. The church warned us not to be flashing our money, but instead pay our living expenses by cash. This was the least of my worries, as images of those helpless babies whom we saved initially tormented me. Nevertheless, Red replaced this in my mind when he sent us the links to the TV and newspapers in St. Louis, which reported the 'mystery saviors' as we have been labeled by the press, reported how we not only saved these two babies, but also saved babies in the future. We learned the satanic worshippers abused their family members as well. Brown and I felt fine with our new hero status, even though we still had to conceal our identities. Red flew back to us, and we decided to move to a remote rural location. These areas tended to do most of their marketing with cash. We found a little church, so we could become a larger part of it. This is like being a big fish in a small pond. My life had changed, and I was so happy with what had happened to me. From listening to Red and Brown, discussing going into a church with machine guns while drinking beer and hiding from cops now to know we went face to face against evil and walked away saving lives of the virtuous. I needed an event such as this to see what I really was, deep down, inside me. Accordingly, I believe we have hidden fears about who we are. Leastwise, now I know that if I have a machine gun while drinking a beer, I might not be doing wrong. My world began spinning around me, forcing my eyes to close. I knew a new event was soon to be holding me.

The flood

My car is lightly rocking from the steady wind. I was driving my vehicle through this determined storm. The highway dipped through a valley with a stream before rising again two miles, passing over a small hill into our town. The water was rising quickly, as I could not see the road and thus determine how high the water was. I was trapped now, because if I turned around, there was another low straight stretch of five miles north that would flood frequently. I made it about halfway by driving extremely slowly, which allowed the water to keep on rising. I had to roll my window down to get out, since the water pressure from the flood waters had my door sealed shut. I crawled out of my window, falling headfirst into the water. Being sucked into the water, I grabbed my front wheel. Holding on tight, I planted my toes and pushed my feet even on the ground. I moved my body into the upright position, with one hand holding onto my passenger door. Once stabilized, I believed the current was peaceful enough to where I could make it. Rather than walk the straight mile, I would walk directly to the right bank and then walk up the hill, behind the school, afterwards across another side stream, which usually is a regular depth because it had large open fields along most of its path. After the creek, I would walk up the hill and cross the street to my house. I felt confident I could make it straight to the right bank, since I was in the middle, so each step will be going from the heavy current. I began walking away from the car. The current quickly knocked me off my feet. It was time to swim. The current was not truly that powerful; it simply caught me off guard. I made it to the right bank rather quickly since I was swimming away from the middle of the flash flood. I decided to walk along the bank, so I can get a better idea of our current condition. I spotted other cars abandoned presently. The road made a sharp turn from where my car stopped, thus I could not see these abandoned cars. I figured now the water was deeper in this part of the road. I walked up this hill, so I could drop down on the side stream in its easiest part. Once at my home, I joined my family on our back deck. They had flashlights shining them over our backyard. This flood was merely three feet from our back road. We did not worry about it because for it to raise any further, we would need the storm of the century. I slipped into dry clothes and went to sleep. Accordingly, after swimming in the currents I had no desire to see the water.

My worry was if my car is okay. I think it should be good, as it was still running when I decided to abandon. I could look far enough ahead to see it would be impossible. For the flood to hurt my engine and transmission it would have to storm hard for another two weeks, and by then I would have run a rope to it and pulled it out of the water. The next day one of our friends who had a tow truck and chains will pull my car. I was fortunate in this tow truck could lift my front end out of the water. We bring my car back to my house. I will get new oil for both engine and transmission next week and change it the subsequent weekend. Fortunately, I have two vehicles, so I will not miss any work. I put my car in the backyard, thus the sun will help dry it. I was disappointed with the amount of slush I will need to clean. Like most people in this area, I was curious about what damage actually occurred. We saw on the news a town six miles north of us was flooded, and houses destroyed. Most were old homes and not built solid. The amount of slush left that town in need of weeks of work. Our town was not affected because we built on three hills, leaving the center of our town for the highway junctions. The town two miles south of us did not hurt much, except for the bank as most houses were on their steep hill. Their largest harm was the slush in their front yards and waiting for the water to drain from the highway. The important issue was that no one was injured or died.

Subsequently, I got my sons to walk with me through our town. We walked across the street and up the hill to our far street, so we could look out over what was a wide valley. It was now a large mud filled pond. We were fortunate this flood was in the fall, as it was moving the top layer, spreading its nutrients over the sizeable cornfields that flowed beside the stream. My sons and I were playing with the dogs and cats who ran into the street to beg for some treats. The animals in our town were well fed, nevertheless, even with bellies completely filled; they became hams through their begging. We came across a house that sat on the far corner of our town tucked away behind trees. The women who lived here would take walks in the evenings around town. This reduced any mystery concerning who they were. They invite my sons for some homemade cookies. We begin chatting about the great flood we were surviving. One of the women stands up and throws a handful of peanuts into her yard. When she does this, about twenty cats came running looking for the peanuts. They tossed more peanuts, and the cats continued to eat them. They stopped sharing their peanuts within one hour, at which time the cats began fighting with each other. My sons and I were shocked as we raced to stand on these women's porch. A few of the cats were now blood soaked as they were fighting to kill withholding nothing. My second shock was when these two women began laughing at the cat's misery. We were trapped on their porch; thereby I could not get my sons away from this cruelty. I know that many times when a child sees something such as this, they will try to copy it on other animals. There is always the chance that someday they could progress from animal torture to human torment.

Accordingly, I yelled at the two women for setting such a terrible example for my children. I also told them I would alert others in this town about the dead or injured cats. We had carefully to work our way through her yard; furthermore, I had to use a stick to ward off the extremely ferocious cats. By the time we made it to the road, many neighbors had assembled. They began screaming at me accusing us of killing the cats. My sons started yelling back, denying our responsibility. This mob starts to cool down; they question me wanting to know what caused these animals to behave as if they had rabies. I confess to them the sole thing that could be attributed to the elderly lady's actions would be more of what they did not do compared to what they did. Explaining this, I tell them the aged women fed the cats three cans of peanuts; from what I remember seeing them remove the lids. Accordingly, I report the cats became aggressive when the peanuts vanished. Therefore, I cannot hold them responsible because they ran out of peanuts. The group began to argue until one man brought up a solid point. They argued it might not have been the peanuts, but an unknown poison or drug covering the peanuts making them aggressive. They point out to the fact the cats were eating peanuts, whereas maybe one or two might nibble on one to satisfy their curiosity. Additionally, they cite the way the animals all turned violent and went into their killing rages.

There was one more thing I knew not to tell them and that was they laughed when seeing the cats clawing themselves. I knew they would go on a witch-hunt, and these two witches would be burned at their stakes. My neighbors asked me if I had anything else to add. I suggested these cats be buried before the village's children started their post flood exploration. I did not have any cats; therefore, no one was expecting me to help in the cleanup. We walk back to my house when I notice five cars parked in my driveway. A strange feeling came over me, as I suspected my house was filled with trouble. This is not the placing my life in danger kind of trouble; it is the get your hand out of the cookie jar trouble. I walked into my living room, and it was packed with my aunts, or my mother's sisters. These aunts began drilling me about the dead cats claiming it was some way my fault. Nevertheless, I argued in my defense, yet learned they were holding hard to their position. My sons complained to my aunts claiming their father was innocent. Now, I went off on these aunts because they had terrorized my wife while waiting for me. They did the "Mikey; we are sorry," attack on me, which naturally left me speechless. My past favorable memories with my aunts included many holiday celebrations. Who can forget the cookies, pies, and candy, although not to the same level as grandmas? They turn to some funny events that happened in our past; such as the time, I got a bow and arrow for Christmas and shot an arrow straight up in the air. I failed accurately to calculate the return trajectory. Subsequently, the arrow went through the living room of our mobile home. Accordingly, they summoned me before them. They still remember my excuse, as I told my father; the arrow hit an airplane and boomeranged back through our roof. The reason I remember this is that my father simply asked me not to do this once more. My cousins believed that once everyone was gone, my father would punish me. Consequently, my father did the opposite, and merely asked me to help him repair the roof. Even I agreed this fair.

Unexpectedly, my aunts began singing 'happy birthday' while unveiling special cakes. I forgot today was my oldest son's birthday. This was the first time the family celebrated a birthday of a member in my immediate family. Nevertheless, supposedly they wanted a reason to investigate any damage from our flood. When they discussed their intention to visit my town, which is their hometown next to where they spent their childhood. My mother suggested that since it was my oldest son's birthday, we could use this celebration as a foundation for exploring the damage caused by the flood. Except for being blamed for the cat's misfortune, today might just work out peacefully. When we finished our birthday party and cleaned our house with their help, I decided to take another walk, this time by myself. I walked the opposite way this time going up my street, then turning left just before the two churches. While walking on the sidewalk, I heard a man counting to ten loudly. I spun around to see what was happening. I began walking toward these two men trying to tell myself that what I was seeing was not real. Subsequently, I rubbed my eyes and stared at these two men once more. Accordingly, I knew without a doubt, who these men resembled. I was confused and wondering if my eyes were telling me the truth. I saw President Nixon, and President Kennedy was engaged in a duel. They spun around on the count of ten, and both fired their pistols. I saw President Nixon be hit in his belly, as blood quickly began to soak his shirt. He fell to the ground, stopping his moving forever. This hit me in my stomach hard. I have constantly idolized President Nixon; feeling history gave him a raw deal. Watergate found him doing the same thing the Democrats had done for years. I did not feel like getting deep into this now; my hero was dead. My problem was my other hero was President Kennedy. Movies about the Kennedy's have always captivated me. I walked over to President Kennedy, who gave me his pistol.

Instantly I tossed the pistol into my neighbor's yard and told the President; I was not going to hold a pistol that killed a President. I was so thankful the day had turned chilly, so I wore a pair of gloves; therefore, my fingerprints were not on it. Accordingly, I laughed with President Kennedy asking him if he could see me trying to explain to the police why my fingerprints were on a pistol that killed a former President. I could see everyone laughing when I claimed that President Kennedy shot President Nixon. Then I looked at President Kennedy and confirmed that I would testify it was a mutual agreeable duel. I asked him why they were dueling. President Kennedy told me the loser of this duel would be the President who is assassinated. He would not have as a final image his brain splattered over his wife in the back seat of a car. The President told me because I saw the duel; I would have to relearn the new history. I asked him if he was President now. JFK looked at me as if I were a drug addict and told me he was President beginning in 1961 for two terms. I asked him what happened to President Johnson. He laughed at me and told me Vice President Johnson served beside him for two terms. I now realized that if JFK were not assassinated, then Johnson would not become President. I asked the President what was his greatest accomplishment. He stood up and proudly declared that winning the Vietnam War was his crowning victory. In this new history, the Americans strongly supported JFK, and he defeated North Vietnam easily, especially once Cambodia and Laos joined the United States, which prevented the North the ability to enter the South from its western boarders. I invited the President back to my house, and while we walked pass President Nixon's body, I asked JFK what was going to happen the President Nixon's corpse. He told me not to worry, because he was assassinated decades earlier.

With this, Nixon's cadaver vanished. Subsequently, I asked the President what happened to Watergate. The President told me the new history did not have a Watergate, but instead had a woman-gate in which President Clinton was impeached. JFK shakes his head and confesses to having 'enjoyed special company' ten times more than President Clinton had, yet he was smart enough not to be caught. He reveals that President Clinton should have made his brother the Attorney General, and such charges would vanish as quickly as they appeared. We went in my house, and I turned on my laptop as the President updated me on the many new aspects in history. Two hours later, he vanishes. My son comes into the kitchen and asks me whom I am talking with currently. I pretend as if I was asleep and tell him I was talking in my sleep. I feel myself sucked into the sky and drop back for another event.

Journey inside the body

Nonetheless, I lay in my bed having spent time with former presidents. The first thing I look up on my computer is JFK, to discover once more, there was a rainy day in Texas in 1963. I am in a scarlet red tunnel or sealed roller coaster, which goes in many directions but loose. This tunnel has thousands of what appear to be smaller side tunnels that branch out in all directions. I am sliding on a red ball, but also see white balls bouncing back and forth. About once per sixty seconds thousands on thousands of small mouths open and bite the red and white balls. During these brief periods, I lift my feet to prevent being eaten as well. Subsequently, thirty seconds afterwards, the mouths, which completely coats the circumference of these round tunnels and spit out a gooey substance that is cleansed in a temporary stream that washes this slush through these tunnels. Fortunately, a woman approximately half my size that later returns and introduces herself as Vita Blodkroppar comes to my rescue. She had a special staff that enabled her to latch to the side of this tunnel. She attaches herself to a red ball in front of me and sits in such a way that we are facing each. I introduce myself to her and confess to her that I do not know where I am. Something came over me advising I tell her the truth. I believe that her being so small and alone gave me the confidence to keep everything above board.

Vita Blodkroppar reveals that we are defenders against disease. This is one of the most sought-after jobs among the virtuous dead. Curiosity overtook me; nevertheless, Vita told me we must exit through an upcoming door. She grabbed my hand and pulled me through the door. Vita reveals to me that most of our work is done in the veins of our host, and we must exit here to bypass the Liver and Kidneys, and then jump back in just pass the Kidneys. I followed her, and once more; we were in the blood flow. We pass through the lungs where air bubbles pack our open area. The walls turn to millions of mouths, which fight over the air bubbles. Our roller coaster got a powerful boost as we raced through the heart, which filled our mouths with air, closing the vein walls once more. Suddenly, Vita turned blue scaring me half to death. She told me to get prepared to exit; we were getting out at the next door. I was completely confused, yet knew that Vita was the way for me to go since she has won my complete trust as if by nature. I followed her through a maze that worked its way throughout the cells. Cells were large balls of gush that squeezed tightly within its organ. Vita knew how to wiggle her way through them. We worked our way into the organ when we run into two pink cells. This is the first time I have seen pink cells. The normal color of cells in this organ is blue-green. These pink cells stand out, and many more are reproducing themselves. Vita begins to cry. I ask Vita why she is crying. Vita tells me this body is in serious trouble. I am puzzled; thereby I ask Vita if she can explain to me what the big deal is with these pink cells. I think the pink cells may need some food, oxygen, or dispose its wastes. Accordingly, I ask Vita if this situation can be fixed. She looks at me and reveals these cells are reproducing. I ask her if this means they will be sent to the veins and replace dead cells throughout the body. Vita tells me these cells are strictly for this organ. I tell Vita these are too many cells in this organ, thus it is stupid they are reproducing without any control. Vita agrees this is the problem. She asks me to reveal to her what the condition is when cells begin to reproduce out of control. My mind goes blank; therefore, I tell her I have no idea. Vita drops the bomb when she informs me this is cancer and by the rate of growth, this body will die within one year.

Vita tells me our work is done here. I ask her why we do not work until this body stop. Vita explains that staying in the body until the end would be ideal; however, we are so short on vein patrols; therefore, when the end is probable, we exit. I ask Vita what I should do or where I need to go. Vita reports to me that she is my trainer, and I am to stay with her. She will determine when I am qualified to body patrol on my own. I complain to her that I was dumped into this body with no training or briefing. Vita tells me this is the preferred way to indoctrinate, because it builds a bond between the trainer and trainee. Accordingly, I confess I had trust in her just about instantly. The fear of not knowing anything, then suddenly someone who was not threatening yet knew how to survive was like a cup of water in the middle of a desert. Vita instructed me to hold her hand as we exited this body and entered into another. She enlightens me that our assignments are controlled by spirits thus, when we finish one mission, they transport us to our unknown undertaking. We arrive in our new host instantaneously and begin floating in its veins. I question Vita when we can know our objective. She reports this is for us to discover, and she will show me how to determine our priorities, as a body patrol continuously has exploration as a major function. A problem I always had was lack of confidence that I have mastered a new skill when learning it. I probe Vita for an estimate, on how long we will be together as a team. Vita tells me the absolute minimum is two years. Feeling as if I lost ten tons of pressure, I lean over and kiss Vita telling her thanks. She jumps back and slaps me in a reflective manner.

Suddenly, Vita jumps up, materializes a spear, and rams it into a dark man who came out of nowhere. She never released her spear, driving it into the mystery man, subsequently pulling it out and stabbing him repeatedly. Afterwards, the man and Vita's spear vanished. Vita tells me we just killed a virus. Vita tells me we must do a complete search for both bacteria and viruses before they do any damage. Accordingly, she tells me when I confront our enemies simply think spear and start stabbing. We can never release the spear. Vita warns me to be careful and never stab our host's flesh. We floated through this body, until I saw a giant shinny blade flash before me. Vita tells me to stop, because some external force has just cut this body. She warns me that we need to get out of here now. We move up the vein about one real body inch, which far our minute size is around ten feet. Suddenly, white balls begin to flood the cut area. They pack themselves tight in this area. Vita tells me the white balls will attack anything that tries to enter the body. Vita tells me these white balls expand when in contact with outside air. Normally they are the size of dust. When the air came through the cut, they launched their defense. Vita wanted us away from the cut zone, so we would not get trapped inside the white balls, which horde themselves tight. We make five rounds through the body before determining this body is healthy. Suddenly, a wide metal pipe slides into this body before releasing purple square balls. The square masses crumble apart. These small pieces are being consumed by the cells it comes in contact. Vita tells me I am lucky, because I just witnessed an immunization. Vita explains these purple square masses will continue to fall apart until they are invisible. They will eventually be in every cell. Via believes this body received a Tetanus shot to prevent infection from the knife wound. I never knew how the body functioned and now that I understand, I cannot tell others, or I would be labeled as crazy. I tell Vita I am tired and need to rest. She takes me to the door just before the Kidneys. Subsequently, we wiggle through cells to an area filled that has larger jelly cells. Vita explains we are on body fat, which is the softest material the body has. Accordingly, we will have comfort when sleeping. I laid down on my spongy fat cell. Consequently, I sense myself expanding. All I can think about is trying to find a way to say goodbye to Vita.

Zeta

My journeys have been far and many tough, yet somehow I had prevailed. I judge my success by the overall definition of my character. I had core principles that were now united from the deep to the extreme limits of the sky. How hard could the wicked torment me until I fell? I counted myself blessed in that I have not fallen prey to these cannibals. Such tribulations arrive in sheep's clothing and evolve into deadly wolves. When hands transform into swords, personal justice prevails. When the swords of hands work with the swords of the tongue, it will chase the sharpest horns of those beasts of the deep. I planned for another round of my escapades if such preparation is conceivable. As in a roller coaster ride once the railcar begins the true danger is in exiting the safety of the seat that held is captivated passenger. If I knew what lay ahead of me, I might have had my eyes sewn open.

The feedings

The thick fog proves difficult to negotiate. Fortunately, each step I take the fog weakens slightly. Nevertheless, I trip over some broken debris falling face-first on the ground submerged once more in the fog. This time, my recovery was instant as I jump to my feet standing erect with my head focused well above the descending fog. The tan sky and dirt-covered buildings fail to surrender an impression of life. Scanning my surroundings, I see shattered buildings with hundreds of small streams of smoke ascending to the sky. I question what these could be, therefore, becoming a slave to my curiosity enter a small, partially destroyed the structure to behold, a woman with three children hovering around their little wood fire. Her son detests me and tells his mother a 'clean' is at our door. This mother grabs a knife and rushes toward me. I step to the side, using my foot to trip her while simultaneously grabbing the knife from her hand. I grabbed her knife fearing she could hurt herself if she landed on it. Her two small daughters begin begging me not to hurt their mother. I reassure them; they will not be harmed by me, except for self-defense. I look at their mother and ask her to stop trying to kill me. She tells me to show I trust her; I should give her my knife. I compromise that I should give it to her oldest daughter. I walk over to a broken table along their back wall and lay the knife on it. When in the rear portion of the mother rushes into their house to hover over her children. I walk back to the doorway, while her son rushes over to grab the table knife. The woman identifies herself as Sara, asks me why I am here. I tell Sara this is not the first time someone has asked me this question. I explain that I have suffered from a strange accident, which has erased my memories.

Sara continues her questions by asking me if I am married. I tell her I have a family, wife, son, and daughter. Her daughter asks me what my daughter's name is. Accordingly, I confess that I cannot remember. I had tears, unknown to me, flowing down my cheek. The child takes a small piece of paper and wipes my face with it. Her mother yells, "Lsis get back now." I thank Lsis for wiping my face and tell Sara that Lsis is in no danger. I ask them why they have a campfire in their house. Sara reports this is how they cook and keep warm during the day when scouting for food. I ask Sara where they go at night. We meet at the old theater. She explains the theater is the only structure in town that still has a roof. Sara asks me what I remember about the world. I confess to having a complete blank. Sara tells me she does not know much about what happened, because she never concerned herself with such things. I was not solely one thing, as many different people tell distinctive stories. Accordingly, her husband as most young men in this town departed and has not returned yet. Sara added the 'yet' suggesting she still had hope. Her lone priorities were food, shelter, and security. There were times when gangs would raid their theater and steal their food. They must fight hard to hold onto something, if possible. They still live, which means they have not lost a battle yet, because these fights are to the death, as the raiders do not take women and children, because the burden of feeding them is greater than any possible benefits. If they are not stealing, it meant they could not feed their current population. Her son asked Sara if we should go to the theater now. Sara stares at me and shakes her head, indicating yes. We assemble outside the house while Sara collects the bounty, they gathered that day. We walk down the middle of the street to the second intersection and then begin walking the street on our right.

The houses were battered badly; windows busted out, and most appeared as if someone took baseball practice on the walls. The strange factor was how all had their roofs removed impeccably. It is similar to something cutting them perfectly with a power saw, which with no electricity was not likely. I asked Sara what happened to the roofs. Sara confesses she never saw the surgery of the roof, but heard many tales that were similar. Stories abound that a mighty empire existing under the oceans needed this building material and sends their giant armies across the world. Something used gasses that made people sleep for two weeks. When people awoke, their roofs were gone; nonetheless, their food reserves and population remained unaltered. Sara reports that most believe this was from the invisible sky people, so they could monitor ground life. I asked Sara why these sky people would wish to monitor the ground people. Subsequently, I realize we are inside the theater surrounding by Sara's cohabitants. They answered on her behalf, the tales claim the sky people fear the ground savages will once more rise and try to destroy the world. I ask these people how they know the ground people destroyed the ground life the first time. An elderly man, that all called Gramps answered this legend is written in the great book of the world before ours. I asked Gramps if he had seen this book. Gramps reports he saw this book as a child in a decaying city in a land 300 walking days to the South. Sara asked him if they traveled beside the ocean. Gramps confessed they walked away from the ocean into the mountains until encountering a long river, which led to a great sea. I continue my questioning by asking Gramps to explain how we know the stories in those books hold the truth. Gramps asks me how we know anything not seen through our eyes as genuine. Accordingly, I confess that such cannot be known. I would wait until such could be known before I would declare it as truth. Gramps agrees nothing is greater than this philosophy.

Gramps extends his hand as I graciously thank him for hearing my words. Sara introduces me to those who sleep in this theater. Accordingly, I find myself astonished in the bonds of these people. I confess to Sara that this bond is nearly divine. Sara explains they had fought together so many times as she has saved many and many have saved her. Next, we proceeded to the stage where tables were covered with food. These tables were different from those I remember. Someone cuts the legs, reducing their height to approximately eighteen inches. Sara explains they lack chairs, therefore, lowered the tables allowing those who eat to sit on the floor. I noticed tables had plates with food evenly spaced. Sara guided me around the table until she stopped and told me we were to sit here. I notice two plates evenly spaced and three plates in front of our dishes. Sara invites me to sit down, as her children come to her one at a time. She dispersed the three plates to her youngsters. Sara, as if she could read my mind, explains the children eat by themselves, allowing the adults to discuss survival strategies. While sitting before my plate, I noticed a sword beside mine and a bat beside Sara's. Gramps sits on my left and explains raids have occurred during their evening meals. I glance around the theater seeing no children. Subsequently, I ask Sara where the children are eating. She reveals their children eat and sleep in the basement, which enhances their protection. Gramps adds this teaches the children how to function without their parents. Nevertheless, I agreed it was more important to protect the children. I ask Sara where they got this food. She explains each day particular foods appear in unique places. They have discovered the locations where the food is made available and collect it each day. I marvel how this manna is shared. The providers are unknown, thus they do not seek domination. Nonetheless, I ask them if they believe this normal. Gramps argues, without this food; they would quickly dissimulate and die. It is solely through their agreement that they remain united. The providers have not attempted to dominate or request any form of repayment.

Consequently, the plates contained balanced, healthy food. The group discussed possible enhancements to the theater's defense. I noticed that all the available food was eaten. Sara explains that for most in this tribe, this is their sole meal of the day. One woman from each side collected the empty plates and stacked them at the table end. Sara invited Gramps and I to join her with some conversation. Subsequently, I heard beating on both front doors and the back door. Sara tells me we must go to the first front door. The habitants flowed to the three doors forming an open horseshoe in each. I asked Susan why they left so much space, allowing the raiders to enter easily. Gramps explains they need to have these raiders, inside so they can kill them. This was a calculated ambush. Then the door before us broke open as dirty savage looking men came inside screaming.

We began picking them off one by one from all parts of our horseshoe. The savages had no room to maneuver as their dead began following each other. I prided myself in killing five of the savages. Others were not as lucky because our final tally revealed, we lost eight people while killing 127 of the raiders. Afterwards, we carried these bodies outside about thirty yards from our theater. Through being a part of defending this theater, I felt it was my new home. Gramps and Sara, thank me for fighting with them. I completely concurred with their ambush style as it did open their enemy for slaughter. Thereafter, I asked Gramps why we carry the bodies so far from the theater. Sara was not with us, since the women did not help carry these corpses. Gramps explains others from the raiders' tribe will come back here later to take their dead to their lands for their ceremonial burials. Accordingly, I question how the families of these raiders know the bodies will be publicly displayed. Gramps reveals this is a custom in all lands and to disobey this could bring great suffering. After we removed their dead from the theater, we carried our dead, placing them in a house beside this theater. Gramps reports we shall bury them tomorrow. For now, they place them in a house, without a roof, so the sky people can know our losses. Gramps confesses they sole thing they can pray for is that additional strong kind men, such as I, would enter their fold.

The following day three of our scavengers came back excited in they have found a new home for us. The tables were filled with food; therefore, we must go to this place. Our scroungers return without food. This convinced the elders whom we must travel to our new home. We rapidly assemble, especially with the help from their horns. One of the scavengers led the first group to our new home. Men of the tribe went to the outer places where people spent their days blowing their horns. The elder left a note on the table explaining where we were. To help them, we would tie colored ribbons on small poles to identify our path. We would keep the ribbons the same color, and when we ran out of that color, we would put a ribbon of the new color beside it. Our count revealed two members were still unaccounted. The group needed to get to our new home before nightfall; therefore, we departed. The second scavenger guided us. Meanwhile the third scavenger with two men followed behind tying the ribbons for the three stragglers to trial. Surviving the massive amount of confusion, which goes hand in hand by traveling with women and children presented a monumental challenge. The elders exhibited great compassion and patience in appeasing to the unexpected and recurring problems with this movement, as we completed this one-hour walk in just under three hours. Gramps believes we solely could finish in just three hours because they surrendered to their hunger. I agree in that I am dreaming of food as well. Accordingly, Sara stays beside Gramps and I, with her three children helping her. Subsequently, I compliment Sara that these kids as being the best behaved. Gramps jokes to Sara that these youngsters are recruiting their new father. I smile at Sara and confess her children are performing effectively toward this end.

Our new home was an abandoned three-story hotel. The ground floor had offices plus a large restaurant, which still held the tables and chairs. Gramps shouts with excitement that we may now eat when sitting on chairs. Sitting on the floor brought pain to his legs, creating great discomfort. The elders discovered the perfect basement beneath us. It had additional rooms and a dining area, with some exercise rooms. They released the children to select the rooms they wanted. We found comfort in the tables; both in the main lobby and this basement were loaded with food-filled plates. The children instinctively knew where to sit. We inspected the rooms, as for now all would sleep on a bed. Our doors had a special six-inch thick steel door that locks from the inside of it. The ground floor has no windows, and its outside is solid rock with nails that would eject when pressure was placed against the wall. We believed our security was assured while in this new home. Sara and I once more share our sleeping area in a room together. Two rooms share the same shower and bathroom. These are called sweet mates. Gramps gets the room next to us that he shares with another of the elders. We agree to keep our bathroom doors open. Sara's room had two separate beds, which implies I must buy the cow before I get any of its milk. This is for the best, as I would be so embarrassed if Gramps was to catch us. We get our first comfortable night's sleep, and receive another special surprise when we discover we have a wonderful breakfast. Our tribe joins around our table as we congratulate the three stragglers, and the third scavenger guide returned last night. An elder asks them how they got inside. Their guide tells us the door was open; therefore, they simply walked in and closed the door. We gaze at each another, wondering how the door opened by itself. Gramps rejoices claiming that something is working in our favor. The elders led us in songs as we celebrate our perceived deliverance.

I find myself confused as to why we are secured and feed. It is as if we were livestock. Gramps explains that whoever is doing this for us is giving us life, as we would surely have died long ago. Sara asks if anyone has seen his or her children today. An elder pacifies us by suggesting they do not want to depart from their comfortable beds; however, recommends we wake them up, so they can eat their breakfast. Several mothers rush downstairs to yank their children from their beds. Suddenly; we hear them screaming. We rush down to meet them and determine why they are screaming. Sara yells to Gramps and me her children are not here. Accordingly, every adult is summoned, and we begin our detailed search. We find no children, nor evidence of a struggle. Several mothers report the children have their gathering bags. They also discovered the basement door was opened, and similar to our upstairs doors had an inside steel door. The children must have opened these doors. One mother argues someone must have come inside to provide our breakfast. Gramps asks why the children did not receive their breakfast. This intensifies the mystery causing the elders to sanction our sole effort today is to search this area for our children. We return that evening hoping someone has good news. The opposite develops since no one has found any evidence our children traveled through this area. Our mood is solemn during our evening meal. We did not understand how we could accept that our children had vanished. We did not know if they were in a better place or dying. Sara sits beside me depressed as if she was carrying the burdens of the world on her back. Gramps asks me to give Sara the breathing room. He believes she is strong and will survive this misery. She lays her head on my shoulder when I feel tears rolling from her face to my chest. I place my arms around her, and then pat her head. The tribe agrees we will sleep together in our dining area to prevent any additional mysterious abductions. I feel how important the children were to this tribe. Sara's missing children flood her with misery, especially not knowing their current condition. I hear her cries throughout the night, as once more I drift off to sleep. Afterwards, I wake up alone. Sara, Gramps, Lsis, the elders, our hotel is gone.

I begin walking the streets looking for anything that resembles where I was. Accordingly, I determine this is a different place. This town shows no signs of war destruction. The homes look pleasant, except the yards were not mowed. After walking around the streets for two hours seeing no people I begin to feel sad. I wonder if I am being punished for not showing more compassion toward Sara. If I were, then this would not be justified considering I heeded to the wisdom of Gramps. Fortunately, my brain turns on, and I realize that Sara, Gramps, and the gang are not in this episode. I have jumped into a fresh event. Usually, I receive a transition notice when jumping into new situations. Another unusual factor is how I remember the people in the previous situation. Surprisingly, two women come out of a house and motion for me to join them. Cautiously, I walk toward them looking for any sign of deceit. I remember a proverb that warns about women in dark alleys. When I arrive in front of them, we exchange our introductions. They tell me their names, Jane and Judy. They ask me why I am walking around as if I am lost. I explain that I am lost, and I do not remember anything. Jane comforts me, revealing the eight people in this group will protect me. Subsequently, I ask Jane and Judy why they want to help me. Judy tells me to look around them. I do as she requests. Afterwards, Jane challenges me to inform her how many people I saw this day. I report they are the first people I have seen. Jane enlightens me that few opportunities exist here to meet new people. Judy adds that if they had wanted to harm me, they would have done it when I was walking pass the large white church. Realizing I walked pass the white church over two hours ago. They have been watching me having so many opportunities to kill me.

Accordingly, I elect to trust Judy and Jane. We enter her home as I am greeted by the remaining six people. I am surprised that they merely had two men in this group and can now understand why they would want a third man considering the difficulty in protecting six women. Each member welcomes me and gives me something to eat, such as crackers and small cookies. Judy and Jane hover around me, as they appear to be staking their claim on me. The group recognizes this claim, in that they discovered me and took a chance on welcoming me. Judy explains that many times a warrior or criminal will pass by their house. They carefully go upstairs and remain quiet until they leave. A special rule they live by requires they always make sure the downstairs does not appear to be occupied. When they cook their meals, they clean the dishes as they were dirtying them. They take no chances, as one small mistake could cost them their lives. I ask them where they get their food. Five of them have jobs working in the tunnels. Their tunnels provide an underground passageway throughout their town. The center of town, beside their police and local National Guard unit, which one of the two men who lives here belongs, has the grocery store. Cargo ships bring food through this area every two weeks. The National Guard unit goes to the ship and purchases the food and supplies we need. This town trades the coal and salt they mine through their underground tunnels. I ask Jane how many people live in this town, in which she reveals almost 1,000 people currently live here. Judy adds that before the great plague, over 50,000 people lived in this town. Judy continues by reporting they had to burn not solely the bodies from this town, but from the rural area surrounding the town. Most of the farms released their livestock knowing that when they died, these animals could starve. The town has a generator, which keeps a large cavern they dug underground refrigerated. They harvested enough animals to pack this cavern with meat. Occasionally a farm animal will come through town looking for water, as the town inspects this beast to make sure no wild animal with the plague has infected them, and if clean, harvest the animal. I ask her how often an animal comes through. Jane explains they keep water in special containers in town. This is well water, thus has no chemicals. The animals smell the water and while taking a drink most of the time steps in the concealed traps surrounding the container. Subsequently, my two homes were beginning to merge, as one minute I was in the hotel, afterwards theater, returning here. Flashes of the children being harvested began to confuse me. The sole thing I knew was, these people were melting me, and I did not want to be around for any bad news.

The shifting

I rush to my car, hoping for certain sanctuary from the awful animal smell. During my original escapes, I would seek the adventure to the end. Afterwards, I just as soon get out of it and jump into a new one, hoping it to be better. My transfers are smother now, as a new world emerges around me. My car and the world around me are lightly rocking from the steady wind, while I drive my vehicle through an unremitting storm. This highway dipped through a valley with a stream before rising again two miles, passing over a small hill into our town. The water was rising quickly, as I could not see the road and thus determine how high the water was. I was trapped now, because if I turned around, there was another low straight stretch of five miles north that would flood frequently. I made it roughly midway in driving extremely slowly, which allowed the water to keep on rising. I had to roll my window down to get out, since the water pressure from the flood waters had my door sealed shut. I crawled out of my window, falling headfirst into the water. Being sucked into the water, I grabbed my front wheel. Holding on tight, I planted my toes and pushed my feet even on the ground. I moved my body into the upright position, with one hand holding onto my passenger door. Once stabilized, I believed the current was peaceful enough to where I could make it. Rather than walk the horizontal mile, I would walk straight to the right bank and afterwards walk up the hill, behind the school, then across another side stream, which usually is the regular depth because it had large open fields along most of its path. After the Creek, I would walk up the hill and cross the street to my house. I felt confident I could make it straight to the right bank, since I was in the middle, so each step will be going to another place from the heavy current. I began walking away from my car, and as unexpected failed to discover a swifter undercurrent, which rolled over the ground for the first six inches of depth. The total depth was a little of over two feet. My adjustment was to run to the shore, landing on my toes realizing I would miss my target point, which was no big deal. This strategy worked until I was five feet from the shore and my foot landed on a slippery snake causing me to fall into the water. I simply swam to safety, being fortunate the current flooded elsewhere. Subsequently, once on the rain soaked ground I began to run toward my house following my preplanned route. My heart raced for joy when I have my house in view.

Rushing to my front door, my son opens it, allowing me to continue straight into my living room. My wife hands me two towels, wiping me to no significant benefit. I rush upstairs to my bedroom to change into dry clothes. The joy of dry clothes, replacing wet clothes is even significant in this realm. With my wind no longer preoccupied with the chill of soaked clothes, I realize we have visitors. I decided it was time to repair the desperate portrayal I just painted for our guests when I rushed passed them. I notice many strangers in my house and ask my wife to introduce them to me. She gives me a strange look, as if I have lost my mind. I explain the raging currents I just swam through to get here, and that certain patience is needed under these current circumstances. My wife tells me this result from the Jim Beam I have been drinking. I emit the sole response a husband can ever release in defense with the prime objective to be a cease in the conversation, such as "Yes, Dear." I scan our 'guests,' to determine my next course of action. I begin by explaining my adventure getting back home today. One of the elderly men offers to help me retrieve my vehicle now, since he has a tractor. He warns that leaving the vehicle in this water overnight may totally damage it, although retrieving it currently will require replacement of the engine and transmission fluids at a minimum; the vehicle should eventually dry out, although extensive deodorizing may ultimately remove the stench of the floodwaters. I tell him I would be especially thankful if he could help me. He jumps up, heading for my back door. I enthusiastically follow, as we go out of my back door. Standing on my back deck, I notice a slew of tractors in my yard. My rescuer smiles at me and reveals the only way to travel now is by a tractor. These farmers came from the hills to see if anyone on these low grounds would need a little help. They had completed all the rescues and when they learned from the neighbors, I have yet to return; they accepted my wife's invitation for selected hot soup and coffee and volunteered to wait until my return.

I confess my gratitude for their kindness. We leap on his tractor and head back to the flooded chaos I just departed. The man, who identifies himself as Jed, is wise to travel along the shore as best he can. Jed explains we can withstand the currents, yet he does not want to push his luck. I agree this is not wise to challenge these currents. Fortunately, the Creek's current is mild over the bridge that leaves our town. The bride is just high enough to cut the current to where the hill on the other side forces it to back up satisfactorily to ripple and provide a wall of water to redirect the full force behind the current. Once we are over the bridge, Jed stays on the main highway, explaining to me the road provides a much more stable foundation to drive on than the lower muddy banks to the side. I report the currents hit me hard when I got out of my car and went toward the shore. Jed explains this was because the highway sets above the ground beside it and this centrifugally creates these currents. I realize Jed may not be current with the laws of physics, nevertheless; he has the knowledge of the hills, which is of considerably more benefit in this situation. We always say to do it the way that works is much better than to test a new way that may not work. Notwithstanding, we arrive at my vehicle, and Jed turns his tractor around, so we can chain my vehicle to its back. He dives into the water with his chain and soon reemerges telling me it is time to head home. He is shivering from the cold water, yet drove us back home and into our driveway. I tell him we must get him into various dry clothes and will unhook my car later. As we rush into my front door, the women have a robe for Jed to change into and tell him to through his wet clothes into the dryer. Meanwhile, we enjoy our evening meal, which is dawned with farm vegetables, many of these wives canned from their summer harvests. They even included a few of their thick steaks from a recent butchering. We were having a feast tonight. As we prepare to eat, our phone rings. Another person needs help, thus two men leap up and departs. I explain they may have to move my car out of the way first. They nod their heads and quickly exit.

I sit and begin to eat. Next, I feel a sting in my eye, thereby quenching it to prevent any possible damage. When I reopen my eyes, I discover our guests have vanished as I am now sitting with my family eating dinner. I notice it is sunny outside, and my car parked in its normal location. Realizing any questions will only revoke hours of return questions and detailed explanations, most who would come from the seat of my pants. I save myself all this agony by eating my barbeque pork and vegetables as if everything was normal. I believe it would be a great time to give up my bourbon. Notwithstanding, I sneeze and when I instantly reopen my eyes, the farmers and our feast reappear. My wife asks me if I am okay. I tell her a meal such as this must be shared with my bourbon. She gives me my special glass, mixed with diet coke and an abundance of ice cubes. I do this to water the alcohol and thereby reduce the intensity of my intoxication. Today, I hope it will reduce my sneezes and any eye itches. I can accept either world I appear within, yet crave the stability offered by the continuing existence in one dimension or world. Strangely, I have no memories in this current world. This jeopardizes my sanity, yet I give it no great concern, as I will soon have enough Jim Bean in me to erase these concerns. For now, the game is survival, and considering those among us now appeared to be respectable people, I see no need to become defensive. Accordingly, I ask any of my guests if they would like a little bourbon. They all refuse my invitation, reporting their need to be sober if any more cries for help should fall on their ears. I understand this, as it is their purpose for visiting our town in the valley below them. Little did I realize; more surprises awaited me.

Subsequently, the two rescuers return and are sent to my bathroom to get out their wet clothes. My dryer will be working double time today, as a small price to pay for the peace of mind, knowing our neighbors will be saved if need be. We continue to wait for the dryer to dry their clothes when they, as couples, begin to change colors. One couple is green, another blue, yet even another pink. They all change colors, creating a living rainbow in my house. I appear as the lone one to notice this oddity. Everyone else behaves normally; notwithstanding, they are asking me if I am okay. They are such kind people, willing to help asking nothing, except acceptance, of which they deserve. I feel like the bad one here, only in that I am not doing as much for my neighbors as I can. Consequently, I comfort them by claiming to have had a troubling day, and that I think I may have too much anxiety pinned within me. I ask if I may join the next group that is called out to rescue. I figure the raging currents are better than shifting worlds and colors, plus any additional always-unexpected surprises. They agree, although most do not expect any more emergencies. Currently, they each change from one head to having two heads. This upsets my stomach, not so much for fearing them, but more from not being used for two-headed people. Lives forget to teach me about this special feature.

The oddity about my two-headed friends is when they talk, one head will speak a sentence, and the other head will speak the next sentence. They rotate back and forth until finished. Consequently, one woman asks me why I always turn my head back and forth when she talks. Embarrassed, I tell her that I am not used to such mountain beauty, which can also cook. To comfort her and keep me from swallowing her father's shotgun, I add that her beauty is only surpassed by one, and that is my wife. I lightly bang on my belly and add this proof of her cooking. The group begins to laugh. Presently, when I am speaking, I keep my face fixated between the two heads, letting my ears handed the shift from the conversation. I go out on my front porch, which had a roof and sat on my chair to smoke a cigarette. A few of my male guests come outside and light their pipes. They raise their own tobacco, and it smells great. I notice one hand takes the pipe from each head to the other during their process. I guess this allows each mouth to enjoy the taste. My adventures continue, as my house begins to rise. My guests continue their conversations as if all was normal. Meanwhile, I notice we are now above the clouds and the rain. Accordingly, my guests notice the rain has stopped and told their spouses the rain has stopped, and it is time for them to leave. My heart thumps throughout my chest, as if it wishes to explode. We walk back into my house as the men round up their wives. The first couple heads out the back door, as I inform my wife, I will see them out of our rear porch deck. I ask her to make sure each gets what they brought plus their share of the leftovers and something special for helping us. They refuse to accept anything from us. I secretly agree I have no idea what to get a two-headed green man. Should it be different from a two-headed blue man? The Oranges leave first, as I name them according to their color. I hug the wife, as the hug is brief considering the two heads through me for a loop. I shake the husband's hand, giving the couple thanks for his or her life saving rescues.

They casually walk off the porch and fall into the clouds below. I hear their screams, which alerts their inside friends. The pinks come out currently asking me what the source of the screams was. I tell them it came from the oranges. Mrs. Pink explains they must have slipped on the ice in my driveway and asked my wife for some salt. The Greens stand beside me as we bid the Pinks farewell. The Pinks walk off the porch and immediately fall into the clouds, which float below us. They scream as well. Mr. Green tells me they are leaving at once to help the Pinks. I give him my son's aluminum bat that we keep outside, which he gladly accepts. They rush off into the open sky before the scream as they fall. The Blues come out now, asking me what is happening. I tell them it is not safe for them; therefore, they must wait. Mr. Blue informs me they will immediately rescue their friends. My wife tells me she will go with them. I tell her she is staying here, in case the water rises higher and I must take the kids to safety. Mrs. Blue tells my wife that I am correct in that she must care for her children, which is her highest priority. The Blues drop off into the clouds that surround our house presently. This leads me to believe we are dropping. I noticed the Blue's screams were louder than the previous ones. I guide my wife back into our house, which locking our back door. This will have no effect on my family in that they know how to unlock it. It will keep strangers from entering. Then I think again, what sort of strangers float in the sky, yet, then again, how many two-headed orange women do you run into? I notice my house vibrating and hear some settling in sounds. I walk out on my front porch and notice we are seated on the ground once more. I look at the highway in front of me and begin screaming at what was before me.

My wife rushes out to my side and begins crying, while telling our children to get back inside, adding that they may get soda from our refrigerator. This is too great a deal for them to pass, pulling them into our kitchen. Subsequently, we must find a way to deal with what is on our road. I use my cell phone to call 911. They offer to send fire trucks, ambulances, and law enforcement. The 911 operator asks me to give her a number estimate. I tell her eight. This looks to be the greatest disaster in our local history. My neighbors rush to me and ask me what happened. They are scared also, considering the spread in this awful splash runs on the road in front of their houses as well. Our neighbor from across the road begins yelling, wanting to know why we have eight strange-looking people plastered on our road. Even I do not know why they had to land in front of our houses. Our female neighbor, which lives in the yellow house beside me, and goes by Karol, asked me why these people had two heads and were colored in colors, which are abnormal. Adam, the neighbor on the opposite side from Karol confesses to having never seen pink or orange people. I wonder why whatever brought them to my house and made these changes had to kill them in front of our house. The police arrive and begin checking my house. I ask them if they have a warrant, and they show me that they do. In fact, the judge is in their inspection group. It never surprises me how they believe to know who the guilty person is immediately and concerned themselves with simply proving guilt. Their initial attitude has pissed me off, as I motion for my wife to join me. I whisper in her ear not to talk about the house being in the sky. She tells me that we were never in the sky; we simply had some thick fog from the Creek below our house. I tell her that is okay to tell. We agree to tell them that as they left and around our house, they screamed. I explain this to the deputy who questions me. He asks me why I did not go outside to see who was there. I explain to him that this is why I pay so many taxes, so the police can protect us. I report to him that if he is done smelling my underwear and picking on the innocent, then he should try to discover what killed these people.

Each theory they developed on methods of how I committed these murders had no proof and actually involved outrageous feats, such as one where I flew over in an airplane and through them out, while still piloting the low-flying plane. The agony in this dream was financial, in that each time they came up with these atrocious charges and came to arrest me; I have to pay a lawyer to argue in the arraignment and come up with more bond so to stay out of jail. After the third time, we filled three lawsuits against the county and state for false arrest. We filed against the state for negligence. Additionally, I wanted to put selected pressure from above on the county. One day, a scientist came to our house and after looking at our foundation, told me they believed our house was elevated, and that a protective force for these eight citizens decided to have them executed. I wanted to explain that our house did float in the sky, yet my lawyer told me the police would bring hundreds of additional charges against me, and this was something I did not want to be involved. We were fortunate in our first case against the county, winning it is four days. This was the once where they claimed I flew a plane and dumped these creatures on the road in front of my house. I remarked these creatures killed themselves in front of my house because they knew the sheriff was too lazy to look for them. Either way, the jury decided in ten minutes this was a false arrest and awarded me twenty million dollars. I figured to use this money to harass our local sheriff, such as provided lawyers for everyone they arrested. They had a tendency to hit the poor people harder knowing they could get away with more against them. The final analysis was, these people were alien beings and had broken a no-contact rule by visiting me, and thus their superiors elected to execute them. I went with it, as it moves the blame from me, and I could not come up with any better explanation. Something wrong happened to cause such lovely people to fall to their deaths. If this was true, I had some serious concerns in that they would cause us to befriend them first. The scientists believe this is, so they can study our responses. I sit at the table currently with my wife, and prepare to count our money and make a budget on spending it. It does not come out as high as we hoped because they are repaying it in twenty years. While scratching my head, I look up and see the sun shining from above my head. This means daytime is coming, and this adventure is ending.

Neighbors

My daytime world has afforded me trustworthy neighbors. We have yet to exchange words, and for the most part, go about our business. The lone event that puts us all in the same place was the colored two-headed people who splashed in our street. I am rejoiced as I now stand on a clean street in front of my house. I notice a strange-looking man coming out of Karol's house. The man greets me with a good morning neighbor. This tells me some things are different now, and I have to dance on the needles until I figure out what is happening. George, as he calls himself, complains about how nothing exciting has ever happened here. I comment how nothing is better than something terrible is. Getting on the map from the blood of others is not my cup of tea. George claims he does not want someone to die; however, if they must die, why not here and make us famous. Having first-hand knowledge about this, I explain that I hear such things usually involve detailed police investigations and hungry reporters snooping into everything. George agrees that we do not need any more trouble in that our previous wives have brought enough tears to us. At present, this is a mystery for me now; therefore, I excuse myself telling George I need to tinker in the house for a while. Rushing into my house, I find some newspapers in what used to be our master bedroom, yet is now set up like an office.

Our bed and dressers are gone. Nothing is in the room that was here previously. I notice my son's sofa bed in this room, with a blanket crumbled on it. I walk back to my son's room to find one of my daughter's bunks placed here with my dresser, and a wooden wardrobe moved to this room. This was the lone complaint I had concerning this house was the lack of closets, having just one small one at the top of the stairs. I did leave the TVs in their respective rooms. It looks like I have stored my family's personal items. All traces of my family are absent. Walking back to my upstairs office, I notice a table with newspapers on it. I glance through them searching for clues, and the information; I discover breaks my heart. Apparently, my wife and children were with George's wife and children in their van when an inebriated driver hit them, killing all in the van as it immediately exploded. The drunk driver died a few weeks later from burns, which covered ninety percent of his body. These memories are coming into my mind currently sending chills over me. This is the first time I have ever dealt with a death in my immediate family. I never realized how much they truly mean to me, and I do not want even to entertain this thought. I wish there was a way I could have checked out of this nightmare, yet unfortunately; I have yet to master this skill. I am taking previous memories into the new challenges, which is my concern with the loss of my family. I marvel that George has the nerve to be around me, although rationally I realize he is not to blame. Subsequently, I saw ugly accidents on our highway previously, nevertheless, as all others do, never thought it could happen to us. I wonder what sort of person is blown out of their mind and races down a highway. I confess to having been blown away a few times in my life, yet when I did not feel in control of my vehicle, I got off the road and slept until sober enough to drive legally. Getting home the next morning was much better than risking arriving home months later with broken bones and other lifelong serious problems. I decide to get downstairs, where I notice my dining room is different. This was my home working area. I now have the wall covered with family pics. I have removed much furniture opening up the living areas. I do not know if this were wise, as I would think, the emptiness would create a deeper feeling of loneliness. Maybe I wanted to feel lonely, who knows. My contemplation is broken when I hear George screaming at my front door.

I rush to the door and open it. George rushes pass me and tells me to get on my steps. He shuts and dead bolts my front door and follows me to my steps telling me to go up higher so we are protected from my large living room window. We sit about two thirds up these steps as he scoots next to me. I ask him what is going on now. He explains that Ben, my neighbor on the other side claims someone took one of his cats, and he believes it was us. I ask him why Ben would blame us. George explains, because we constantly complain about them getting into our things. Accordingly, I hear Ben banging on our front door. He threatens that I must leave my house someday, and that he will get George and I in the end. I ask George what we should do. George takes out his cell phone and calls the sheriff. He explains that Ben is threatening to kill us once more. The sheriff tells George that he has a deputy not far from us, and he will be there in a few minutes. Meanwhile, we are to stay inside presently. George explains the deputy will arrest Ben, put him in jail and that in a few days, after verifying his cat has returned, we will once mare call and tell the sheriff we have decided not to press charges. I ask George that maybe we should reconsider this time, in that Ben keeps on doing this; he is a danger to our town. What will we do if he gets one of us someday? After all, he is an experienced hunter. Somehow, I knew this. George reminds me that if we have old Ben sent to prison, we would be shunned by all in this area. I can understand the logic in this. Ben does something different this time and actually shoots through my front door. Fortunately, this is a solid door and except for a few holes holds itself together. I am not too happy about the five hundred bucks it will cost to repair.

I tell George Ben will pay to have my door replaced and installed, or he will do time. This time it has gotten out of hand. Suddenly, we hear other people screaming and bullets fired into my other windows. One shot comes in from my large living room window and hits two steps below me. If that would have been a shotgun, we would be filled with bouncing bee bees now. Subsequently, a shot comes through my top-floor hall window and bee bees from this shotgun shell splatters everywhere. Fortunately, the angle was so high that most hit my hallway ceiling and ricocheted throughout the upstairs. This was a narrow escape; nevertheless, George explains this is the best place for us to wait, because we do not know how much they will be shooting. George jumps on his cell phone and tells the sheriff this time we are receiving multiple shots and are in grave danger. The sheriff tells us they will be here in just a few minutes from his helicopter. He warns his deputy who is now on the scene that Ben has a gang this time. Fortunately, when the deputy arrived, a few of our neighbors had their rifles waiting to ride with him. He told them that he could not bring them with him, yet if they could establish some back up for him on the other side of the street; he would attempt to draw Ben and his crew onto the highway and get his team to draw down upon us. They assume their sniper positions as the deputy parks his car in front of Ben's house and turns on his lights and siren. He then walks to the front of my house and asks Ben to come out and talk with him. Ben comes up to the deputy, as he has so many times before. Luckily, the deputy and Ben were co-workers, many years earlier. The deputy asks Ben if he has anyone helping him this time. Ben reports that three of his drinking friends are with him. He calls them to join him in front of my house. Two come stumbling up, causing the deputy to ask where the third one is. The men laugh, explaining their mate is passed out in the back yard.

The deputy asks the men to surrender their weapons. Ben surrenders his; nevertheless, the other two men refuse to surrender theirs. One of them takes a shot at the deputy, who dives back across the highway into the open yard on the opposite side of the street. The four neighbors open fire and easily fill the two men with bullets. Meanwhile, Ben rushed across the highway to help provide cover for the deputy. Afterwards, deputies began appearing from all around my house, as the helicopter hovers above us. The deputies apprehend the passed out man in my backyard handcuffing him before he awakens. They also secure the area and verify there are no other hostiles in the area. Once secure, they call for George and me to join them in the street. I come out and ask the sheriff to take pictures of my broken front door, plus living room window, upstairs hallway window and the destruction in my house. He assigns three deputies to document the damage. I walk with the sheriff to Ben, who is handcuffed in the back seat of the deputy's vehicle, while

I tell Ben that until my house is repaired, he will stay in prison. Ben attempts to work his way loose, as if he is going to strike me. His deputy explains to Ben that he had better strive to get back on my good side, or he could spend the rest of his life in prison. At this time, the deputy takes Ben and his intoxicated friend to jail. The arrested his drunk friend as an accomplice with intent to murder, in that he was passed out in my backyard with his rifle beside him. The ambulances have now arrived to take the two dead men to the coroners. Most everyone who lives in our town presently circles around my house. One of my neighbors asks what will happen to Ben. The sheriff tells them that he is pressing the charges this time, because Ben's actions resulted in one of his deputies being shot at, and this is the line of no return. George looks at the neighbor and asks if he believes it is permissible to shoot up another man's house. Ironically, Ben's cat comes purring at my leg. I pick the cat up, give it to the sheriff, and tell him to show it to Ben before he sends it to the animal shelter. Afterwards, I order these people to go somewhere else, unless they want to repair my house on behalf of their hero Ben. I was surprised that all repairs were finished on my house before sundown that day. Ben worked for a construction company, who jumped on this fast to keep down the publicity.

I invite George in for a little coffee, as we prepare for peace while my house is being repaired. Ben's co-workers asked why Ben exhibited so much violence against me. George reassures them that we have never done anything to hurt Ben's cat, as they witnessed today in the manner, this cat purred around my leg. The lone thing we ever did was complain to Ben about what his cat was doing, which was destroying our property. George explains the primary reason we complained to Ben was that many of the other neighbors here, were not as forgiving as we were. We all agreed that Ben had changed ever since the death of his wife, and his oldest daughter within one week. This was truly sad, in that death seemed to have found a new home on our street. Ben's co-workers warn us that several of our neighbors in this town are speaking ill about us. I look at George and reply that since we have lost our wife and children, they must believe we have too much happiness in our lives. George tells me not to worry about this, there are a few good neighbors, and that is all we need. If too many of them like us, we would go broke buying birthday and Christmas gifts. This way, we can barbeque in our back yard and have the satisfaction of knowing it is causing them slight misery. I agree our neighbors shot two men who had a desire to kill us, although their reasons were legally defined as defense of a deputy. George reminds me the deputy was here to save us. This long day finally ends, as I notice Ben's construction company upgraded my door and windows. I see no benefit in defaming them, as they are as innocent as I am in this ordeal. I walk into my son's prior room and see my daughters top bunk bed (twin size) waiting for me to sleep. This is extremely different from our preceding king-sized bed that I shared with my wife. I lay down as my tears begin to flow like a river. I have never faced this previously.

Fortunately, I begin to spin and this world vanishes. I wake up in our new king-sized bed; we have bought since the first one needed replacement. Joyfully, I see the sun appearing, thereby; I will have some day life to shake off this miserable experience. Sadly, this is not arriving soon enough for me. The night lingers while a few cats decide to fight outside my window. The mating rituals of cats can be disturbing at best, especially with the elongated whines as if in total agony. Then I realize it has been almost two decades since I have dated. I wonder whether I will sound as bad as these poor cats when I go prowling once more among the neoteric generation's jungles. Seriously, earlier this evening I asked George what we are going to do about finding fresh wives. He reminded me that we should spend time healing the wounds inside us before we move on into new relationships. We cannot hope to begin a novel relationship when we are trapped in our preceding one. No woman wants to lay in a bed with a man who cries all night for a deceased previous spouse. These women do not fear the living, in that they have a chance battling against them. Nonetheless, they cannot fight a ghost or martyred memory. George was correct. I had to fight these memories, which were hounding me now. The hope my lost family members could be exchanging new communication with me, such as talking to me from the dead. I know this is not likely, and even though possible, it is not probable. This is my mind working against me, or attempting to feed the dying hope that has squeezed my heart without mercy. My dream body can feel my tears as they drip from my eyes, roll down my face, and then soak my tee shirt. Accordingly, I hold to anger against this pain because I believe my family is worth a river of tears. This small bed finally begins to spin, which alerts me change is coming.

The judge

I survive one more day in my peaceful daytime world, spending the entire day with my family. Consequently, I realize that having them another day is revealing rivers of miracles. It amazes me how humanity can create great technological things, nevertheless, still has vastly limited knowledge about the functioning of the human body. My exhaustion plummets me into a deep sleep. I feel a smooth wave of tranquility flow through my nighttime soul. Just as I begin to take a deep breath, enjoying the harmony of this new place, I notice something that changes my serenity. I am sitting in a courtroom, with George sitting beside me. Many of the people sitting in this courtroom were fellow neighbors who were nothing more than acquaintances; nevertheless, so far they are not hostile. When I take my daily walk, several waves, others sit on their porch and stare through me. I consider ignoring better than aggressively challenging. The judge and defendant's seats are empty. The prosecuting attorney and his aides are prepared. Next, the judge comes into the courtroom as the bailiff calls for everyone to rise. Everyone rises, then the judgment seats. After everyone sits down, an attorney with Ben beside him came walking into the courtroom. The judge jumped up, as did everyone in the courtroom, except for George and me. A man beside me begins screaming for us to stand up now. Two men behind us, lift us up on our feet. We elect not to struggle or intensify the situation. We hold our peace as those around us divert their attention back to the courtroom. I ask George what sort of courtroom is this. I have never seen the defense have so much power as this. Ben stands up, turns around looking at me, and declares that I should be the one sitting in his seat. The judge tells Ben to relax, because they will find a way to put me in that defendant's seat. This quickly puts a lump in my throat.

I ask George why we came today. He explains the sheriff asked us to be here to back up his deputy's testimony. The defense calls Ben to the stand. I never heard of a case where the individual charged ran the courtroom. This was scary indeed. Rumor had it that Ben had more anger against the sheriff than he had against me, since the sheriff showed him, his cat and then gave it to the animal shelter, which ended putting it down forever. Ben vowed eternal revenge when he heard this. Fortunately, my neighbors told him that his cat purred around my legs. Ben knew that George, and I would provide a little catnip and treats occasionally. We did that, for the most part, to lure him back into his yard, as we never gave him the treats, unless we were in his yard. I did not want to motivate him to camp out in my yard. I constantly wondered why I was not fond of that cat, yet suspect most likely; it was because of my intense dislike for Ben. I have been around cats long enough to mask my genuine intentions because if they believe you do not like them; they will hover around you. Somehow, that cat could read our true minds; nevertheless, he would not forgo his catnip and treats. I suspect that cats, like people, think differently when their bellies are empty. I return my focus to the matter at hand. The judge reads the charge and each time he mentions Bens' name everyone cheered. Ben had control of this courtroom, much to the bewilderment of George and me. He did not do anything special around the community, except drive into town after work, shunning all who came around him. This forces me to ask George what we did to make these people so angry. George replies that all we had to do was breath and appear to mourn over the loss of our families. We still held contempt because no one in town, except for a few of our wives' closest friends, showed any remorse or concern for our bereavement. I was shocked when the girl scouts and 4h clubs came soliciting at our door. We felt as if they believed we had a disease or through secret evils deserved our fate.

George and I both kept a full suitcase in our trunks as part of our contingency fast evacuation plan. We each also kept a crossbow and two containers of arrows that came with it. We live too close to a state border and therefore, cannot keep firearms in our vehicles and travel over state boarders. I often wonder why we stay in this town, even though a part of me claims this is to hold onto my previous family life memories. This makes some sort of sense; however, that would be at the subconscious level, which should predominate now. Somehow, this is not as great of a concern currently, as I can see Ben looking over at us. It is only a matter of time before he unleashes on me. He is most likely exploring his options to decide when best to attack. Considering, I am not as lost in this episode as I usually am, realizing I just jumped from an earlier part. Nonetheless, I have yet to determine the true underlying cause of this friction. George believes it stems from his old European heritage and racism against the Asians. Ironically, his German ancestors caused the same, if not more, grief as the Japanese, as my wife was. This is hard for many westerners to realize the variations in the Asians resemble the variations in the Europeans. A Frenchman is as much British as a Filipino is Japanese, just as a snowball has as well a chance in Hell as I do in this courtroom on this day. The sole chance I have today is that I am not on trial. I appreciate George's advice that I keep my cool, which I must agree. A victory in a battle today would have little effect on the outcome in the battle ahead of us. Any ways, I want to get a feel for what Ben has planned. I wonder how psychotic he is going to get in each stage of this waste of life. We recognize the sheriff is merely the first hurdle on the road we must negotiate. A strange-looking man came running through our courtroom. He was yelling at people and quickly gained control of all who were here. He appeared to be concerned that the court had not built a special cage for George and me. The judge explains that police officers are guarding the doors, and that he has muscle men sitting around us.

Nevertheless, the man begins to yell at the judge, as Ben stands up and tells him to wait outside this courtroom. The man at once obeys Ben, as everyone, including the judge, applauded him. I hear the men behind me tell his friend that this is yet, but another example of the high moral character of Ben. The applauding continues, as many begin standing while they are clapping on Ben's behalf. George and I also stand before Hercules, who is sitting behind up puts us on our feet. We pretend to clap and merely lip serviced our cheers. Even though infinitesimal, we wanted to make sure not to be contributors to our own fates. Ben finally stands up and motions for everyone to be quiet. The audience and judge obey his most-recent command. I wonder how I was stuck living beside this lunatic; nonetheless, I find it harder to place the sole blame on him. The people who surround him are feeding him. I wonder what I would do if I had a mob of people begging to obey my every command. The judge finally calls this court in session as Ben takes the defendant's chair, and two police officers come back to me when the lead one bends over and whispers in my ear to follow him. I get up on my feet and walk behind him, as the second police officer guarded me from behind me. They escort me to a dirty chair positioned center of the courtroom in the wide open. The police officers report, aloud, to the judge the agitator is seated in the guilty man's chair. The courtroom natural applauds, creating within me a desire for a future event in my town where I can torture each one of them. This is not as any courtroom should be, forcing me to accept this mad house as my temporary existence. The trouble with the provisional part is that this temporary is now. Once it becomes before, I will be relieved, or at the minimum work harder to keep it in our history. Considering that, I must stand tall and defeat this now; my testing moments presently manifested their desire to engage.

The judge ordered his quest for justice to begin. I wondered what fantasy world he lived in, because this room had everything but justice. Ben looked at me and asked why I constantly tortured his cat. Accordingly, I told him that my sole contact with that cat was to provide stress relief and treats to offset the horrifying neglect he unleashed to that poor creature. George stands up and seconds my statement. The judge tells George this is a court trial and not a procedural hearing. Ben stands up and tells the court, this is the proof of how George and I live lies and are solely interested in defaming him. The prosecution asks that I not be permitted to lie in court. My attorney tells the judge that Ben is the lone one to lie in this court so far. Ben asks the prosecution that if the judge does not allow me to speak, how he can prove to the jury about the extent of the lies and attempts to deceive the jury. The judge orders the attorneys to sustain and let Ben continue proving his innocence. I turned to the judge and asked why I was here, as there is no evidence throughout the world that could ever prove Ben innocent. The judge asks me to tell the court what happened that day. Accordingly, I begin by telling the court that Ben had other crazy spells, and this time combined his threats with actual gunfire. Ben asks me why the sheriff did not take any pictures of my shattered windows. I told the judge Ben's company agreed with the sheriff if they replaced the windows, he would let Ben slide on that part of the charge, with a promise that if he ever did it once more, these charges would be added. The company sealed an agreement with the sheriff, including signed statements with photos of the damage and physical evidence of the broken windows. Ben asks me what happened to this evidence. I told Ben that I did not monitor the internal administration of the sheriff's office; however, I am sure they would cooperate with even a corrupt court. At this time, Ben officially accuses me of lying about these shots. I ask Ben if he shot two of my windows. He stands up proud and tall and denies any of my windows were shot that day. I felt so relieved that he denied any of my windows were shot and thus claimed no windows had been damaged. At this, I walk to the jury and ask them to open some dated emails on my phone. Ben, who was foolishly convinced I had no evidence allowed me to show this to the jury.

Fortunately, for us, our neighbor from across the street took pictures of Ben shooting my house and emailed them to George and myself. Considering that, George opened his copy of the email, and we viewed these pictures and downloaded them to his spare laptop, he kept in his attack, we elected not to open my email. The jury opened this email and looked over the pictures. The judge then demanded to see the email. The jury member forwarded this email to his fellow members and next gave my phone to the judge, who looked at it, pushed a button, and afterwards asked where the pictures were. I asked the judge how he knew there were pictures on my phone. He stuttered and explained he heard the jury talk about seeing pictures. Thereafter, one jury member tells the jury, this is the judge's lucky day, because he will email him another copy. The prosecution became angry that evidence has been exposed to the jury that is not favorable to Ben. George asks the judge how such a guilty man can find justice. The judge tells George he will find the answer for that question when I stand trial. I shake my head in disbelief, yet must accept at least the injustice that is in the open here and not hidden like a secret as in most other courts. I am appalled each day when I see the injustices and corruption in the judicial system in my daytime world. The foolishness of a few greedy police officers can doom the life of an innocent man. This is a prime reason I am exercising much patience during this process currently, in that I truly want to find the legitimacy behind Ben's perception. I know when two people look at the same thing; each may have a different view of what they see. It appears that so many in my community share Ben's view, which is a mystery to me.

I turn and ask Ben why he has treated my former family and me so unjustly. Ben claims that he had tried accordingly hard to accept the wicked ways of George and me, nevertheless, must accept the views of the others who live in our town that I am too malicious to reform. I decide to withdraw my offensive and play it conservatively until I get out of this challenge. I hold many views against the power of the American government as they have stripped away too many of our rights. Understanding the realm of this issue is beyond my adventures in unconscious. I am finding the openness of the prejudice to be refreshing. I consider it a sense of security in the judge has yet to be hostile. Nevertheless, this was about to change. Ben tells the judge he is done with me, that since I continue to lie, it might be better to let me think about my evil ways before my confession. The judge told me to take my seat and for the bailiff to call in the sheriff. The sheriff comes in with TV crews from two area stations, plus dozens of reporters. The judge told the reporters to get out of his courtroom, or he would declare them in contempt and sentence them to long prison terms. The sheriff tells the judges not today. Notwithstanding, he walks up to the judge and hands him an official order from the State's Adjutant General. The sheriff looked at Ben and told him to sit in his seat beside his attorney. The sheriff then looked at Ben's attorney and asked him if he would tell the court what happened that night. The sheriff explained the event as it happened. Ben continued to disrupt the proceeding by objecting. Finally, the sheriff looked at Ben and told him he would get his chance to talk, and if he interrupted him one more time he would arrest him for obstructing a police officer. Ben asks the judge if the sheriff can do this. The judge told him he did not know; nevertheless, he recommended that Ben sat down and stopped interrupting the sheriff. The sheriff told the judge and news reporters that I had no business being here and that George, and I should be released. Afterwards, the sheriff released his frustration on Ben.

The sheriff told Ben that it was only a matter of time before they get him across the county lines and then send him to a federal prison. Ben smiled at the sheriff and told him to keep on dreaming. The sheriff hands Ben a judgment that his construction company be dissolved and that anyone still associated with it in two days be sent to prison. He also hands Ben a subpoena to appear in a federal court located in our state capital in two weeks. The judge asks the sheriff why the federal government is interfering with local jurisdictions. The sheriff explains that some homes in West Virginia, with many in Ohio are complaining about receiving threats if they did not purchase this unwanted construction. Ben's lawyer explains to him that by going over state borders, the federal government could take jurisdiction. Ben asks him about the subpoena. His lawyer explains they will talk about that later. The sheriff takes George and me with him as he leaves the court. The judge demands he leaves them there. The sheriff tells the judge that he no longer needed us as a witness, and since they are not on trial here, he will give us a ride home. The sheriff makes us a strange offer. He recommends we get out of our hometown for a few months for our own safety. He tells me that his neighbor died last year and that his estate needed someone to stay there and make some small repairs, supplies at the estate's responsibility. George and I thought this might be a good idea. The farm is five miles off the highway and tucked off the country road with merely a small path back to it. The sheriff asks us to give him a list of things that need to be secured in our homes before the yellow tag them as crime scenes. He also asks for a list of clothing and volunteers to bring any perishables, such as leftovers in refrigerator and fruits. We made our lists as he sent his deputies to secure them for us.

We got word later that week that by some great mystery, Ben was found not guilty of the charges. Most commentators attributed this to the pronounced justice in our county. Unfortunately, for Ben the state highway patrol with some federal marshals took him to our state capital, where he was convicted for tax fraud and sent to prison. He sold his house to pay for legal counsel. We vanished during this social event, thereby keeping ourselves disassociated. The judge was also convicted and sent to prison. George and I worked our way back into our homes. Life was different now in our hometown, as most neighbors simply avoided us in their shame. George and I readjusted rather harshly. We could solely feel pain and death around us. It did not help that two men were shot in my front yard. Consequently, it is almost as if I can sense them being in my yard. Each night I could hear them scream, as they continually call out my name to save them. This tortures me in that how could I save men who would kill me on sight. George and I were victims, yet things worked out fine for us in the view that we were on the road to recovery. I wish consequently, that this road was not so long, and it would not be over so many events. Ben sent me a letter apologizing. My minister, or should I say the minister of one small church in our town recommended that I keep a low profile and ignore the letter. If Ben writes an additional letter, we will deal with that when it happens, if it actually happens once more. Somehow, the sanctuary farm the sheriff provided offered enough distractions to divert my normal concentration on my self-pity, as George would label my behavior. I had not realized it has endured this long. I am not the first to have faced this type of life event, yet I am truly sad that I hope to be among the last. Subsequently, I realize that healing is a process that takes time and effort. Suddenly, I was going to, for the second time; during my life learn how to walk. Accordingly, I looked at George and asked him if he was glad to be back in town. He looked at me as if I had lost my mind declaring the farm, we were temporarily safeguarding was at least 100 times better than our small lots in this town. He so much enjoyed feeding animals and playing on the tractors. I knew other events lay ahead of me, and my time here, was ending. I lay down; hoping tonight would be the first night.

Delusional leaders

The world around me began to spin. Unlike the previous transitions, this time I remained stable as the world spun surrounding me. Then it began to slow down as an office appeared around me. I was in a large office that had diagrams of the surrounding Pentagon. Correspondingly, I find myself in an Army uniform. We are not wearing our battle dress uniforms, but instead Army office uniforms, which, for the most part, was dress pants and a light-green shirt. I look at my desk and see my name and rank. It reads Major General Hendershot. This is wonderful. I look around this office area and see that my desk is the first one, such as a receptionist. Behind me are five desks, all occupied by Command Sergeant Majors. I am learning this by walking around this office. Our office has four offices that branch off it, all occupied by four Generals with command titles about a mile long each. I also see an empty coffee pot, and decide to go ahead and make a fresh pot. This habit I picked up during my work career, because I usually arrive in my office before any others. Subsequently, I need time to settle in before the rat race begins. I see a disturbing title in front of my desk, which reads 'Chief of Staff.' Appropriately, I can think that to be a 'Chief of Staff' for four Generals who command so much must be an awesome challenge. I am also smart enough to know not to touch their Command Sergeant Majors (CSM). I look at my calendar and see that I have some meetings today. Fortunately, I recorded which rooms these meetings would occur. The first four-star comes in and says good morning. I notice he walks over to one of the CSM's desks and takes a folder, which is centered on that desk, to his office. Wow, the CSMs perform a function. One of the CSMs comes in and asks me if I am ready for the breakfast bar. I say yes, and off we go. The military has this numbering system to label the rank. The E represents enlisted and O represents an officer. The number is the rank or number of promotions counting the automatic first promotion from civilian to military. Even though he is an E9 enlisted, and I am an O8, that E9 has a big O10 protecting him, and I will slip under that umbrella.

Accordingly, I believe this will be a perfect opportunity to get some information out of this CSM, whose last name is Barker.

CSM Barker orders our food as I offer to pay for it. When we sit at our table, CSM Barker asks me if everything is okay. I smile and probe him about why he is asking this question. CSM Barker explains that I always pay with my dinner's card, and today I paid with cash. He asks me for my billfold and takes out some cards, showing me the ones to get in our office, building, and car lot and lunch area. I thank him and ask him why he is showing me these. CSM Barker tells me that I am different someway today. I shake my head and compliment him by telling him he should be a General with his keen perception. I give the excuse that I hit my head hard last night and am not completely here. CSM Barker tells me to listen carefully to what he will advise me. If I am stuck on something in the office, I can write a quick note, and he will tell me what I need to do. He reveals to me that we have no real functions. The meetings we sit in on, we simply pass any notes our Generals give us. Their staff will give me, or lay on my desk any notes for the General before they go to their meetings. He explains that we have extensive staffs to support us. We walk to my desk where I see four hotlines. This CSM warns me to pick up the phone, look at the extensions' list, and push the button to whom I need. We do not want to disturb the Generals by hitting the wrong extension. This seems like a safe precaution to observe.

Notwithstanding, I review this information with CSM Barker. I simply go to the meetings and before the meeting; someone will bring me the appropriate folder. That is the procedure, and how it is supposed to work. If something happens, and the General cannot go to a meeting, I am supposed to attend the meeting on his behalf, and that General's CSM will cover my meetings. In case, more than two Generals are absent; their CSM's handle their meetings. CSM Barker tells me not to worry about any of the other CSMs. He will brief them, and everything will be all right. We cover each. I ask him why they are so supportive of me. He explains that occasionally, an officer will come in to flex his muscles. They need me to run interference for them. I have saved them on many occasions, by telling the Generals the truth. Naturally, those who make asses out of themselves in this office are signing their death warrants. Nevertheless, for some unknown reasons, some commanders come in here forgetting they get their power from above, and that which goes up can come down, and it comes down a lot faster than it went up. I attend my first meeting, and read the notes from the appropriate General. The meeting went smoothly. Afterwards, I walk back to our office. The minutes for the meeting will be placed on my desk to review before I sent it to the General. Afterwards, I return to our office, the CSM's greet me in the hallway. I ask them why they are in the hallway. CSM Barker tells me the Generals are drinking, so we stay back out of their business. I ask them if we have any meetings. He tells me that we never schedule anything for Wednesdays as we label it General's time. This is when they get together and socialize sharing their ideas and plans. They actually do get much work done as it results in more coordination and cooperation throughout our force. After a few drinks, they spill it all with each another. They do support it and no one, not even a president would challenge four Generals. CSM Barker adds that this is not the reason they were waiting for me in the hallway. They are going to go and eat a big lunch, because the Generals will invite us in for their afternoon party. They eat now so better to hold their liquor when drinking with the four-stars that afternoon. Even though we are under a blanket of immunity with these leaders, it is best to have some form of self-control.

While enjoying the party in the afternoon, I walk out to use the restroom and see a young soldier sitting in a chair in front of my desk. When he sees me, he asks if I can help him. I motion for CSM Barker to help me. He comes out to talk to the soldier while I use the restroom. I come back in and ask the CSM what we should do. He recommends that I sign for them and when I date it, put (Wed-Bkr) in front of the date. If it ever comes back to the Generals, they will know I signed it Wednesday afternoon and that CSM Barker approved it. That works for me. I signed it and he soldier was soon on his way. I made it through my first day, and the CSMs offered to show me our living quarters. For security reasons, our families could not live with us on this assignment. There are two dividing qualifications for quarters, the first one is four-star Generals, and the other one is 'all others.' My room or apartment is across the hall and between our four CSMs, so this works out well for us.

We play some cards and order some food as they teach me how to find the numbers for any support requirements. We cannot order out because of security issues, so the government provides everything for us through internal market outlets with below fair market prices, which is great considering everything is checked for poisons and any other support threats. This also helps keep our wives comfortable in that they know no one comes in or out without permission from the Federal Bureau of Investigations (FBI) or Central Intelligence Agency (CIA). We have chips implanted within us that when we leave our building, without clearing it with the FBI and waiting for our security escorts, our wives and local law enforcement are notified. All law enforcement notifications must be cleared by a four-star not in our evaluation chain. This is quite embarrassing. I ask them what happens if we make a mistake. They explain the FBI and CIA agents are extremely understanding and bend over backwards to help us if we are on the level with them. Reporting us creates tons of paperwork for them.

Consequently, the bottom line is that they are working hard to keep us safe with the side effect of seclusion. While we are relaxing, CSM Barker shows me a copy of the form I signed today for the soldier. His original orders had the signatures removed. Barker tells me there is a small cell in the military that is attempting to reassign people they feel will report them. I asked him how we helped that soldier today. Barker tells me we reassigned him to a special security force that will protect his family as we gain all detailed knowledge. Furthermore, they always submit these unique requests to us on Wednesday, so if anything hits the press, the Generals are protected. I ask them what if it comes back to me. The CSMs tell me not to worry; as long as it has one of their initials on it, I am covered. Everyone knows I am not going to get between a General and his CSM. Next, I ask who protects them. The CSMs tell me not to worry; they have one hundred places to point their fingers. The important thing is that we are in the chain to smooth any hiccups. The danger of discovery is in these glitches in the system, and no one below will mess with a two-star Chief of Staff, supporting four powerful four-star Generals. No one wants to go up against them. The important thing is for each level to know as little as likely, so when some step is compromised, as little damage as possible will cause others to face harm. When we address security leaks in the Pentagon, we are speaking of dangerous threats to worldwide security for the world's population. The way these senior soldiers explain this actually sends some chills throughout my body. This secret, guerrilla ambush style of fighting is fearful at a minimum. The thought of someone kidnapping me and then dissecting my fingers, poking out my eyes, made me curious whether this job is one I should be occupying. With this thought in mind, I ask these office mates if our families are safe.

They reassure me that our families are safe in that we are not associated with any sensitive information. Our Generals make sure of that. Their J2 or J6 outfits staffs brief them in their sections as no sensitive information can leave their secure sections in a written or digital form. I made a trip to my refrigerator and grabbed another six-pack for my guests and another Pepsi Max for myself. Due to cholesterol levels, I shy away from alcohol, and of course; I am gazing for another star or eventually two more. My current position is a ticket punching position in that I have an exception on my evaluation in that all four Generals sign my evaluation and add comments, with their appropriate initials beside it. A special advantage is that two of these Generals once held the position I am currently filling. I believe one of the keys to my success in this position is working with these four CSMs, especially considering I am not in their evaluation network. This proved not to have any effect on the event we were soon to find ourselves undergoing. While watching a military adventure movie we naturally discussed how we would have done it differently. I usually wait until they advance their arguments to decide which one makes sense to me. To keep the fire burning, I try to rotate on whom I agree with, to keep them on their toes. I get up to use the restroom and give them a chance to plan a strategy against me. Fortunately, I am usually able to stay just one-step ahead of them. While in my restroom, I heard my doorbell ring. I did not give any concern, in that my guests have lived here longer than I have and know what is happening. Additionally, considering I am still lost in this event, it is best I avoid as many situations as possible. This may have been one situation is should have took part in, although the sole thing, I would have done different is to ask questions. This trip to the restroom would turn out to be extremely costly.

When I return to my living room, I discover the CSMs standing along my wall with their hands handcuffed behind their backs. Furthermore, I notice three men with guns sitting on my sofa. I casually walk over to my recliner, sit down, and unceremoniously ask them why they are disturbing my evening. One of the men stands up and tells me I have offended him in that he does not feel welcome. I tell him he must learn to live with hurt feelings because I never welcome scum in my house. He walks over in front of me, while his two partners are laughing and waves his gun in my face telling me, he will fix me to where my appearance would look worse than any form of scum yet to be seen. I slow slide my pocketknife out onto my chair and snap it open. As his spit hits my face from his words, I slice his neck from right to left grabbing his pistol and immediately shooting the other two men bull's eye in their heads while they were still laughing. Somehow, they got off a shot each, yet their partner's body, which was now bleeding over me, took both shots, allowing me to shuffle his dead body to the side. I walk over to one of the two men I shot in the head and took the keys from his pocket. I believed he had the keys since he just wore a tie. My CSMs ducked to my floor, a response I concur with seeing that they were handcuffed. Accordingly, as I am unlocking their handcuffs, I ask them why they ducked. They confess their belief was that I was a dead man, as they never saw a General fight previously. Notwithstanding, I ask them how these men got inside my apartment. CSM Barker explains they said they were from the pizza department of our food court and had three pizzas I had ordered. I ask them where the pizzas are. They explain that before they could see if they had the pizzas they had their pistols sticking in their faces. One of the CSMs calls the building security. When security arrived, I asked them if they had any reports of gunfire. They told me such reports were ignored because some people play their TV's loud and action movies tend to blare from just about every room. If one were not careful, he or she would think a live battle zone surrounded them. The investigators finally arrived and began processing the crime scene. We were fortunate, in that this was Friday night, so we do not have to get up early.

Subsequently, they question each of us separately, not letting us speak to each other until they questioned us completely. Finally, they recognize my innocence and heroic deeds. They removed the bodies, yet checked my complete apartment, rumbling through my clothes and attempted to depart leaving my apartment in shatters. I yell for the five of them to stand at attention. They try to explain to me that they do not have to obey me. The four CSMs explain to them that I am a two-star General flag officer, and if they want to challenge this, they could face a General court martial. The leader of this group calls his commander who orders them to do as I say. Their commander, a colonel, rushed to my apartment and introduced himself officially apologizing for the initial disrespect of his men. I could see his men double timing to spit shine my apartment. I sat down in my recliner while the CSMs treated me as if I had the power of Hitler. They put on a show that I knew would bring me laughs for the remainder of my life. The colonel asked me if I wanted the blood stains cleaned from my furniture. I told him that since it was government property and damaged in a homicide case, it would be best if the trained criminal investigators remove any biological or blood based material. He quickly agreed, which, in principle, was solid. If they are looking for evidence, they should be the ones to remove any crime material. I told the colonel that I wanted a 'perfect' ten-page report from the five men on military curtsey and traditions. One extra thing is that they cannot include any issue or factor in more than one report. They are to report to me Monday morning in full-dress uniform with the colonel and reports.

I ask my CSMs if I might have come out extra hard. They told me such military formality should be inbred into all soldiers. The true benefit will be through the way they spread this news to all their fellow comrades. This will do a lot to enhance military courtesy training; as such stories, spread like wildfire and are committed to memory. I wonder if any of the formal leadership may frown on this. CSM Barker tells me now General will ever condemn another General for commanding the proper protocol. Appropriate protocol is not a General, who kills three terrorists who have bound four CSMs. This is when a Goliath swooped down and saved the backbone of the force, he commanded. Generals were quick to jump on this bandwagon, emphasizing the importance of these senior-enlisted advisors. We received a message Sunday that our office was closed on Monday, and we were to report to our dominant General's house. Once we arrived there, we were taken to the Secretary of Defense's private estate where they gave me a special reward. The three terrorists whom I killed were wanted by the CIA and FBI. I wondered how they could roam in our intensely secure living area. This forced a serious, comprehensive overhaul of the current security system. I suggested that we wore our pistols until security is reestablished. The Secretary agreed, as one of our Generals complained, they would have to be kind to me now, in case I became angry and decided to have a shootout in the Pentagon Corral. CSM Barker told me he had never seen our Generals so proud and believed that our office was moving into a new era of comradeship rarely enjoyed by a group with hence much power. The CSMs warned me that I would not be walking around by myself much longer, as many felt safer being around me. The greatest feeling I have now is the pure respect the officers and enlisted gave me in our work environment. We are, for the most part, fierce warriors suddenly riding a desk. This takes some getting used to, from being a big fish in a tiny pond to a little fish in a large pond. Suddenly, I found myself swimming in a small pond that was getting smaller each minute. The day turned to night as I once more could hear my snores. My journey among the stars was final. They were a wonderful group of co-workers.

Naughty neighbors

I reappear in my recliner, sitting in front of my TV watching a new episode of the Vikings. I always favored the History channel, and finally they have a series that I find interesting, as wonderful entertainment, which feeds my thrill of the mysterious Vikings. I know they were tough people, yet I also know they came from Scandinavia, and settled in such places as Greenland. Understanding this verifies they lived in some chilly places, and the lone time I enjoy cold is in the summertime. For the first time in many events, I am with my wife, son, and daughter. I find it so refreshing having a family event, especially having had to deal with Ben and George, encounters of the extreme of what I find comfortable. What is even more special is that we live in one of my childhood homes in a neighboring county seat. I am thankful, in the last few trips to my house in Ohio have left a lot to be desired. These experiences relieve me of any anguish in a decision to relocate to the West Coast. The house we are currently living in was a childhood home, in which a lifetime dream of returning to it was realized. Our primary concern was our children enjoy the better opportunities available everywhere else in America. As I stroll through this home, I notice we have our suitcases in our rooms. This is our family summer vacation-home, which, when thinking about it; I would go crazy if I had to stay here throughout the year. We have furnished this home by taking advantage of auctions and yard sales. We want it to have a touch of home, yet at the same time a touch of its own. Besides wonderful porches, the front door opens into a large, high hallway, which leads to the stairs that go to the second floor. The right side of the initial floor has our master bedroom, guest room with a restroom between it and an eat-in kitchen in the right corner of the first floor, which leads to the back porch. A wonderful pantry connects the kitchen and dining room with a door that leads to our large basement. The left side of the bottom floor has a den, living room, and dining room, with giant doors that can divide them or open them into one great room. The second floor, not counting the basement, has four bedrooms, one bathroom, and a large waiting area that we have set up as an upstairs family room. We converted a substantial part of the attic into a third-floor family loft, with pool tables and a ping-pong table. This is more or less a place for the grandchildren to spend their private time.

Our living room has two windows, yet our house sits up high enough that our windows focus between my neighbors first and second floors. We felt our privacy was protected, yet I still prefer to keep our lights dimmed. Our house is within ten feet of our neighbor, who works the afternoon shift at a nearby nursing home. This works out good for us, in that we can enjoy family time with our curtains open. We close them in the mornings and after midnight. We decided to have some local pizza tonight, which I guess most fresh that is would be created locally. This night was different, in that I saw two faces looking in our window. I carefully slid out of my seat, and through the den since I left the dividing doors open, grabbed my Japanese decorated sword, and went out of my front door. As I rushed out, I saw the two men running for their car. I ran as fast as I could, nonetheless, quickly realized they were getting away from me. Therefore, I flung my sword at their back window. The sword spun halfway, so it hit their rear window parallel at just a perfect angle to shatter one of the shield's layers. Fortunately, for me, it only takes one layer to create visible damage. I ran up the street, grabbed my sword, and immediately called 911. After this, I rushed to my car, because when I saw them take a left at the end of my street, I knew they could be heading out of town, and once they get out of town, it would be so hard to find them. I could get just far enough behind them to make it to the top of the back road that ran along a Creek in the field forming a border of this small city. This gave me a vantage point to see if they were going out of our village and taking a route that ran up a high hill to the vast rural part of this county. By ruling this improbable, I could advise the village police to concentrate on our village and the sheriff to concentrate on North Street that led out across the interstate. The sheriff could plant some deputies at our village exit to the north and the next exit about five miles south. They had to prevent them from getting on the interstate, which would open the United States for them.

Although everyone searched diligently, except for me as I rushed back to be with my family, the peeping toms evaded capture. Our family decided to keep our blinds pulled down at all times and to install motion detector lights and a silent alarm security system from a security company. I contacted the county officially to mark our border boundary and hired a local construction company to build a high fence around our property, plus a large garage with an underground tunnel to our basement. I hate having to make these improvements; however, apparently we are in danger of being perceived as having some money, and therefore, the section of society that believes they do not have to work to provide for their livelihood, but instead as leaches to suck the financial resources from their rightful owners. I believe they are scouting for jewelry, bonds, Certificate of Deposits, passwords, or other potential financial recourses, actually anything they think can produce a workless gain for them. The thought of this burns me, especially as we donate too much to charities, that help support another section of the needy, yet this group survives and what it shared with them. That part, I can respect. Everyone is hit or could be hit with a devastating hurdle in the race of life. Now, I have to think about protecting what we have and how to defend my family. I marvel at how safe, we are when staying in our Asian homes, yet to come back to my high school hometown and must sleep behind walls with my rifle.

Accordingly, we were forced to keep the family together always, with everyone under observation by at least two other family members. Nevertheless, a few weeks later, I heard some glass shattering and then some screaming coming from our guest room. I grabbed my sword and rushed to the room, swinging my sword just in time to land a solid deep cut in one man's leg. He still made it outside, where I had to let them escape. This is where the law is designed to make sure the thieves are protected, and the victims are hand tied. If I shoot them, even though they are inside my tall security fence, I will be charged. I am forced to call the police, who will most likely allow them to escape once more. This time, we can hope they will have to go to a hospital for stitches. The police took pictures of my shattered window, as they were trying to document my invasion. They questioned the way I had mousetraps between my outside screens and double pane windows. I told them that only those who were trespassing into my house would face these traps. The police told me I should post warnings. I told them that would be a cold day in Hell, to get their heads out of their butts, and catch these thieves. This is beginning to weigh heavy on me. I purchase a handgun, and wear a holster while inside my home. One night, while sleeping, I look up and see two men with pistols pointed in my face telling me it is time for me to share my valuables with them. This time, they caught me off-guard and wasted no time pointing their pistols in my wife's face. They knew by controlling my wife; they could control me. We do not keep valuables in the United States, as we get better purchase deals in Asia and do not want to waste money in customs. Notwithstanding, we enjoy purchasing fake jewelry and have assembled a wonderful collection. I led my hillbilly bandits into my den and unlocked my safe. We kept our counterfeit jewelry, plus phony track able money orders in our safe. Our security company gave us these fake bonds and money orders, which had traceable metal strips in them that reveal the GPS location through satellite technology. This is a new technology, which I hope will surprise these thieves, when they try to hide from the police to gloat over their ill-gotten bounty.

I pretended to be so afraid and submissive. Their eyes almost popped out of their heads when I opened my safe. The fake diamonds reflected marvelously from the flashlights, as we kept the lights to the den off, since the den had three large front windows and the thieves were afraid someone could see and identify them from the street in front of our house. They acted as if their ship had finally come in, and they had discovered their riches. I was amazed at how fast they claimed this as their property. This disturbed me that they could so easily dismiss their social responsibility to respect the property of others. I know that if someone stole from them, they would demand the government dedicate an enormous among of resources in favor of their recovery. Notwithstanding, they filled their bags and joyfully exited my house, and took a shot at my wife who dropped at once. They had to break our deal, in that we gave them our property in exchange for our security, and they had to take that. Fortunately, the gunfire set off an audible alarm that motivated the thieves into escaping instantaneously. Nevertheless, when they rushed outside as I proceeded temporary to dress her wound. As the thieves exited my security fence, they were met by the police who were notified by my home security. The three men foolishly attempted to shoot their way to their freedom. Two immediately fell to the ground while the third one surrendered. The first ambulance appeared and foolishly when to load one of the criminals. I became angry and demanded they take my wife initially. The police agreed, especially when they realized I was recording this on my cell phone. The two thieves complained. Therefore, I asked them if they wanted me to handle them as they treated me. To add to the suspense, I asked the ambulance driver to tell the next ambulance to take their time before arriving here. To add to the suspense, I handed them a twenty-dollar bill and told him to have them stop by and have a pleasant breakfast before returning.

The police took my property as evidence. Because the court date was pushed out so far in the future, I foresaw a problem. We would have to postpone our annual migrations so to be available during the court trial. I make some form of adjustment; I ordered a helicopter to land on the special pad I built in our garage, and moved my family to our summer Canadian ranch. I will commute back and forth until I send my family to Asia for the winter. I am indecisive and commit to the fact that I must be an overburdened victim for the government to gain satisfaction the offenders have received as much social protection and reward as possible. I have so many times wished the law enforcement wages were based on the tax dollars paid by their criminals. I endured through the trial process until the defense demanded to see my wife to prove she was shot during the invasion. My lawyer told the defense that if they cannot read police statements, medical statements from emergency personnel and hospital officials, they are in trouble. We put on a stand to this charging the defense of purposely harassing the victims and as such denied every deal offered by the government. I declared that after three attacks, these criminals would do their time. At the same time, I sewed them twenty two times in civil court. I also initiated a public campaign against these criminals, painting them as part of a government-protected network. This was sufficient to put enough fear in the public to force them to apply pressure to the courts, through motivating the media frantically to follow this event. It took one year to receive their convictions. I won all the civil cases, fixing it so I at least broke even with the court and hospital bills. My wife did recover, although no one in my family wanted to return to this terrible place. I sold this childhood memory, deciding the area was not safe to live. When I saw the for-sale sign appear, my world began to dim. Another what should have been a happy event resulted in another challenge to avoid a disaster.

Eta

I wanted to call my siblings and reveal the great improvements I made to our childhood mansion. I believed they would enjoy the improvements as much as I did, before the high-rise security fence, which blocked our otherwise boring view. Although it was traditionally boring, it was a childhood memory and as such something, that would have been respectable to preserve. Nevertheless, the choice between memories and my family member's lives, the choice leaves the memories empty-handed. The prime reason that I must forfeit this opportunity for inner family glory is they would most likely declare me insane. I achieved one special treat in that I finally got the third floor in our childhood home. I always believed it was such a waste of space not reclaiming this uncovered space. The thought of falling through this flooring and dropping into the high space above the open stairway connecting the first and second floors, was not something I looked forward to experiencing. My dream is still to travel through a house that has appeared during many of my dreams. This house has stairways that keep appearing, and as I go to another, I discover a new set of steps before me. I have learned to tuck more of those adventures into the depths of my being. One thing I am learning is that as I age, the number of these mystery episodes is increasing. Nonetheless, my consolation is the pleasure in reliving these events, which adds some stability to the rocky waves that time, itself, sends to my shores. I witness my ship pulling into my dock and once aboard begin to sail out into the sea of my night world. I like this style better than the spinning world or dimming lights' transitions. I hope the boat will add stability to my revolving worlds. I may even be able to sink a few of the worlds I did not appreciate into the floors that cover the deep unknown realm far below the surface. Accordingly, I decide to scout on this new temporary home between my worlds and challenges. The deck is wide and spacious with high lofty sails. I initially deemed it strange that merely I was on this ship, until reaffirming this is my unconscious and based on my insanity or crumbling castles in my sky. The sea is smooth and sky filled with so many stars. I wonder many times, which is the longest distance, the distance to the stars or depths of the unconscious. I see an island ahead and a boat rowing toward my ship. Two men yell for me to swim to their boat. Electing to go with the flow, as best possible on the open sea as it passes an island, into the sea I jump.

The teacher

I forgot that most times when jumping into water, the initial sensation is arctic. I know cold and I know freezing, nevertheless; I always believed that frozen water was ice. There is no ice in this water, yet it is cold. One of the men on the boat yells for me to swim faster, and the chill will give way to the heat of my body. I wondered how there can be heat in my body if I am chilled currently. Rather than debate his wisdom, I knew the faster I swam the quicker I could get in his boat and out of this water. Fortunately, they were rowing their boat toward me. Within five minutes, I was in their boat as they wiped me and wrapped me in a snug blanket. It was now that I began to notice the island that we were quickly approaching. Subsequently, one of the men pointed to my ship. We sit amazed at how my ship has positioned itself parallel with this island, as if to tell me there is no need to hurry. The men ask me where the crew is. I tell them they most likely are eating and preparing to relax while I am gone. Consequently, I knew if they thought my ship was empty; they would try to board it. What Captain would want to lose his ship? Meanwhile, I knew to keep my poker face strong, while through my mind, I was reminded of my weakness; I have by tending to jump out of a frying pan and into the fire. I decided to toss a wild card to validate my poker hand by declaring my crew was loyal to me and would do whatever it took to make sure I was safe. This went over smoothly as this boat's crew told me they understood this and was dedicated to ensuring a successful educational performance for me. I wondered why they are so concerned over my academic needs. This almost feels like a lecture that I routinely give my children. Nevertheless, we were soon on the island and walked inland past the high trees that sealed the beachfront. After walking a few hundred feet, I saw a wonderful tall two-story schoolhouse. I recognized it was a school from the sign above the main door, which said 'Island School.'

Accordingly, approximately thirty adults, with twenty of them female, which was easy to identify considering everyone was wearing swimming gear. One of the women came forward and told me, "Welcome to our friendly island school, James." This caught me for a loop in that I had yet to identify myself. I ask her how she knew my name. She revealed that my ship told them. I thanked her for being honest with me. This is when I seriously thought about questioning my sanity until I realized that this is the world on the other side, so maybe ships do talk. When I get back on board, I am going to ask my ship why it does not talk with me. With this in mind, I am curious about what I need to learn. Another woman comes to me and introduces herself as Julia. She reports that she was born on this island, and they rarely receive new visitors. Julia warns me to be on my best behavior in the classrooms because the instructors take this serious. They tend to get too deep in their subject, expecting their students to feel the same enthusiasm. Julia reminds me this does develop the greatest minds. The vast majority of their graduates leave the island. I asked Julia that if, so many left the island, how are there still so many here? Julia smiles and tells me the sea seems to give them new people. I ask her if I am to be one of those who came from the sea. Julia reassures me; they were all told I would be a visitor, because I came from another dimension, which did not permit permanent residence on her island. Julia has a peaceful smile that blends with this tropical paradise. Ironically, I find myself not at ease because everyone is smiling. I accept this is much better than the angry faces I have so often been surrounded. This disparity stems from not knowing them. Julia studies me quickly explaining anything that appears to confuse me. Julia informs me that I need to stay close to her during my visit here, for my safety and maximum enjoyment. Her warnings are sinking in my mind, nevertheless; they demand some caution on my part as well. We enter the classroom, with one wall filled with windows from the front to back. The windows are open, allowing a comfortable breeze, which keeps us cool and relaxes us with the peaceful chatter of the singing birds. Julia leads me into the classroom, as my experience is about to begin.

Julia sits beside me in the center of the front row. She explains this will show my enthusiasm and desire to learn. The instructor, a tall old bald-headed man walks in, looks around the classroom, and makes a few marks in his notebook. Julia reveals that Mr. Sharp knows all his students and can take the roll instantly. Any student who is absent, he will contact their parents to verify why. Mr. Sharp welcomes me to his class, hands me a book and tells us what pages he will cover today. He reveals to me that he will exempt Julia and me from today's questions. I think it is kind that he exempt Julia, as I realize she may have done much work to prepare for my visit. Mr. Sharp begins his history lecture. Scanning through this book, I notice the years go from 20,000 BC and 3,000 AD. It explains, there was a great war that destroyed most of the world and dissolved all the governments. This book is extremely interesting, especially since it has taken almost 900 years to revolve into a world of thousands of small city governments. I also learn this island is an independent state, in that all islands govern themselves. I find myself embarrassed that my country began the war, based on pressure from large businesses having their overseas property capitalized. Greed verses need was the factor that destroyed a world. Some metropolitan areas are marked off-limits to all people. They feared radiation-covered surfaces. Mr. Sharp walked over to in front of me and began telling this class that people like me destroyed the once thriving world. I tried to argue that my family kept to themselves, and we were not rich. So much of our money went to taxes, licenses, and fees. Mr. Sharp questions me on what I did to prevent the Great War.

Accordingly, I explain to Mr. Sharp that my world has yet to reach the war he is referring to in this class. Mr. Sharp declares, as does the book in front of me that a Martin Hendershot invaded a missile sight and fired the initial nuclear bomb at the Iranians. He was part of a 10,000-person demonstration, which broke through the security at the sight and fired the missile. I reassured Mr. Sharp that I did not know this Martin; nevertheless, if he had 10,000 followers to a remote mountain sight, then there must have been a sound reason. Mr. Smart tells the class the Iranians bombed Israel, who struck back hard. The Iranians were on the verge of collapse. The launch of the missile from the Americans pulled the Russians into the counter strike. Many European nations and Asian nations went after the Russians. Once they had the Russians arguments over territory created new wars, including a war over the Middle East and the riches that lay with the largest oil reserves. Mr. Sharp is animate that a Hendershot started the downward spiral. He demanded that I accept this blame and beg him and this class for forgiveness. Notwithstanding, I refuse to apologize. Mr. Sharp tells me not to return to his class in the future. He sees death and destruction when looking at me. Several other students petition on my behalf. Mr. Sharp criticizes these students for supporting me. He tells them they are a poor example for the modern world, and that after discussing this with their parents, he will expel many of them. Julia explains that Mr. Sharp cannot expel students, that power is left for the parents, who, by the way, can also terminate him, therefore he will need to be careful how he approaches this. Mr. Sharp demands that I stand in front of the class. Julia follows beside me. Thus, he tells Julia that she may sit down in her seat. Julia refuses to return to her seat claiming her instructions were to be at my side at all times. Furthermore, she reminds Mr. Sharp these instructions came from the high council and that disobeying the high counsel would result in a painful punishment for not just her, but also for anyone who made her violate their instructions. Mr. Sharp agrees and informs Julia she may stand beside me. Once in front of the room, we receive our surprise.

Shockingly, a few students begin throwing things at me, calling me a baby killer. This did not set well with me. I look at Mr. Sharp and declare he is the baby killer because he is killing the minds of the innocent young people this island trusted him to educate. He his killing their thirst for knowledge and for the truth, and as such is a criminal in the fullest sense of its definition to include stealing the faith given him. Mr. Sharp threatens me that if I do not go and take my followers with me, he will beat us with a big club he pulled out from his desk. Julia, plus ten other women, and I immediately exited the classroom. As we walked out, Mr. Sharp rushed out behind us screaming at the top of his lungs declaring that I am a demon and came only to lead the innocent astray and find new children to kill. I yell back that he is insane. Another teacher yells at me to hold my peace. I tell this other teacher that if he does not know what he is talking about to stop talking. The students do not need to know that Mr. Sharp is not the lone idiot who is deceiving the young children. Julia and the other women tell this other teacher that Mr. Sharp has gone crazy and she was going to the counsel to report this, and if he did not back off they would report him as well. This teacher noticed Julia was wearing a red shirt, which is a symbol that she is on an official assignment. Accordingly, I was beginning to wonder if this great brother in the sky was enough to keep us alive before we made it out of this school today. Mr. Sharp was shaking many students causing them to lose their conservative postures. Suddenly, oranges began flying pass our heads. I screamed for the women to leave out the back door, so we would be running away from the source of the oranges. Once the women were safely pass me, I began to follow them. Julia was furious that I had placed myself in possible danger. Notwithstanding, I look her squarely in the eyes and inform her that when women follow me and as in this case, follow my instructions, they will receive the best possible protection I can provide them. The women began clapping and Julia, knowing I was serious about this, reached over and kissed my cheek.

Naturally, her kiss mellowed me as I ask her if she knows a place, we can hide until things settle and it is safe for them to return in public. The group recommends we go to the cave on the outskirts of their village. I asked them if being trapped in a cave so close to town was a wise thing to do. Julia explains we will not be trapped in the cave, and need to get their quickly. She appoints six women to take me to the cave. Julia reveals that she and four women will collect some food for us. I ask her how much food she plans to get. Julia informs me they will bring two days' worth, as she reassures me this will be plenty. We split and go our separate ways. My group takes me to the cave, which has a strange small opening that I was barely able to crawl pass the first ten feet. Fortunately, the women went in before me. Considering I did not know anything about this cave and they did, I saw no reason to go against their recommendation. As I begin wiggling through the tight tunnel, I seriously question if this was a wise idea. This tight tunnel curves about five feet in and straightens approximately ten feet later. The final five feet evolve into an upward crawl, which finally opens into a large open cavity. The curving tunnel and upward flow are instrumental in disguising this open cavity. The group started a small fire. They explained a small fire was and light this cavity while at the same time would not burn all their air. I saw a small light above us. They explain there is a hole in the ground above them. The smoke from this fire seeps out that hole, which fortunately exits in an area that has a constant breeze therefore the smoke dissipates quickly guarding this location. I asked Cindy-one, because they are all called Cindy how they get the wood in here, and what happens when there is no wind. Cindy-one explains they walk on the top of the hill over this cave and drop the wood through the hole above them. She continues by reporting there are many smoke holes throughout this island, because they do have an active volcano below it. Another Cindy asks me not to number them, just to call each one Cindy.

Julia comes crawling in with her Cindy's and some food. They report the villages are angry and taking Mr. Sharp's side. Julia believes they will begin their search in the morning. It will take that long for Mr. Sharp to spread his message and get the people angry and mad. I ask her if they cooled down during the night. Julia reports that Mr. Sharp will stir their fire in the morning. I ask Julia if we should try to escape. Cindy reminds me we are on an island, and as such, there are not so many places to run. Our greatest defense is to eat well and sleep early today, which will give us a solid jump in the morning. We will wait to see which way the villagers go, and then travel in the opposite direction. With this, I invite them to travel with me on my ship. Julia asked me if they would be secure on my ship. I told her they would belong to me, and I would keep them beside me, so they will be safe. Cindy asks me if they need protection from me. I smile at them and reply they will only need protection if they are male. Julia stands close to my side and explains they are all women, and made so elegantly that I will find no other better than even the worse one in my concubine. One of the Cindies asked if they are all in my concubine. Julia tells them that only those who stay may play in the concubine. Accordingly, Julia declares that if any do not want this reward, they should leave now. They chat eagerly among themselves and declare enthusiastically they accept the honor of these positions. I explain to them, there will be no courting or socialization until we get to my ship. Our primary goal is to make it to our sanctuary alive. Nevertheless, I ask Julia if there is a way to some boats from this cave. A Cindy reports she knows a shortcut that will have us to the boats in less than one hour.

Subsequently, Julia explains most of the ships are in the ocean fishing now. They will bring their boats in just before dark. Approximately two hours past dark will be a fine time to row to my ship. Julia further declares they will arrive just behind the trees that border the beach one hour before nightfalls and locate my ship. Once they locate it, they will wait until it becomes dark and then study the moon and stars, and more importantly, they will plot their course based on their compass. Out of curiosity, I ask her why they will study the moon and stars if they have a compass. Julia explains the moon, and stars are for if we get lost in the sea, missing my boat. Julia confesses that it is so difficult to measure the distance traveled in the dark. I remember that I can talk or communicate with my ship through my thoughts. Therefore, I warn my ship that I will be bringing eleven females on the ship. A strange message comes in my mind, asking if I thought about the food and water requirements. I tell my ship to use its magic and provide the provisions. My ship asks me where I will be. I hold Julia's hand and tell her to think about where we will be on the island to depart for my ship. A few Cindy's, who know the terrain, as they know the back of their hands, also join our circle. My ship thanks me for the pinpoint location and projected time of arrival. It also tells me not to worry about crossing over the sea, as it will provide the boats and cannon air support to protect us in our crossing. My heart almost stopped when Julia thanked me for the boats and protection in the ocean. Notwithstanding, I stare at her as if I see a ghost and verify she just heard the voices in my head. Julia confesses she did not hear any voices; however, she did feel my ship talking to us. This flooded my soul with a new sense of peace, in that for the first time, in my life through both my realities; I had someone else in my mind with me. It could be premature to speculate someone in addition is in my mind, it could be simply she can hear my ship as well. Either way, it is wonderful to know that someone else is as insane as I am by also hearing my ship talk with me.

Accordingly, Cindy asks us what we are discussing. We look at her and profess we are planning for our safe future, hoping it will be one with at least the next few days without pain and excessive suffering. Cindy wishes me luck in that they all yearn for Julie and me the best possible luck in that endeavor. I can now hope not to be alone among my challenges, and even perhaps something stable while flipping between the new worlds. Julia recommends we start our escape currently, since the ship will get us an overhead cover fire, the noise from that will easily alert everyone about our escape. Therefore, to wait until night, would simply make the escape harder for us, as risking boating in the dark when a safer alternative is available. We agreed with her, as Julia told one of the Cindies to lead us through the cave tunnel network. We fired up our torches and began our trek, going up then turning, dropping down to walk along an underground river, the taking a cave tunnel back up to the surface, with a few side tunnels providing the connection. Julia had complete faith in my ship and brought this confidence to life as she led us out of the maze of cave tunnels to the side of a hill that proceeded to the beach. Fortunately, for my nerves, the opening is semi-concealed by trees and high brush. We exited the cave and entered the forest. The initial pleasure we experienced was breathing fresh air with the sea taste in blended within it. The sunrays as they rain through the branches above us return warmth to our skin. There is something about the darkness in caves, which bleeds chill into the bones. When we reach the beach, the islanders surprised us. Apparently, when my ship reset its coordinates, the fishers reported this to the villagers who immediately put all the pieces together. They grabbed their bows and spears and rushed to the beach. Julia, as a precaution climbs one of the tall trees to determine the situation and to give my ship some eyes to plot its cannon fire and fires. Julia tells my ship, there are too many targets, and that we cannot make it to the sea alive.

My ship begins firing its canons and arrows temporary pushing the villagers back. Julia scans the battlefield as my ship fires at each target instilling fear in the villagers, as they are confused over the sharpshooting they are victims. Julia motions for Cindy to climb up to her and explains to her; they must rush to the boats now, while she keeps watch. Julia additionally tells Cindy to have me stand on the beach and wave my arms when they are to begin their run over the sands. Julia knew the ship could see me waving my hands and would give us the fire. My ship was firing solely arrows and spears now dropping the villagers as one would flies. This forced the villagers to retreat, planning to attack on the flanks. As they regrouped, Julia rushed down the tree and ran to the water and then into the water and began swimming. The ship released one of our two boats we rowed from the shoreline. We boarded the ship; thereafter, it rushed a boat with a rope attached to it toward Julia. Julia swam fast, considering she swam every day. Once she met the small boat, she climbed in and lay down flat. By now, the villagers were shooting arrows into the sea. Julia was swimming underwater, coming up behind waves to breath. Accordingly, as she lay in the boat now, my ship pulled it by the rope that connected them. My ship was sailing out into the ocean presently. My ship pulled Julia's boat, as it had done ours, up on the opposite side of the shore. We welcomed her on board our ship. Cindy came rushing up to reveal she found a dining room filled with dinner on the tables. Realizing we were hungry, and now far enough from the island, there was no need to worry about an attack, we rushed below deck for our feast. The food loosened up the women as they were attempting to guess what would lay in their future. At this time, my ship introduced itself to the Cindies. At first, they were petrified, notwithstanding Julia told them not to worry, for she had been talking to the ship. Cindy asks Julia if the ship sees everything. I tell her it does. Next, they ask if the ship is male or female. The ship tells them she is feminine. The Cindies are relieved, because now they can bathe, use the restroom, and change their clothing. I pretended to be alarmed and asked them what about me. They laughed and reported that I would have Julia with me. I looked at Julia and asked her if this was true. Julia winked at me and reported that I knew this.

The high dive

After finishing our meals our ship invited us to its deck. We discovered twelve chairs with small end tables alongside them and a large glass of wine, beside a bottle. Julia thanks our ship for being so generous. Each glass of wine brought forth more laughter and wilder challenges. I enjoyed listening to them sing and dance. My ship tells me not to stay up to late, because I have another adventure in the morning. Our party eventually died out, and we all proceeded to our rooms. This being our first day on the ship together, we wanted to stay with each other. I entirely had a few hours more than they did and that were merely on the deck. The rooms had names on them, and were identical, since they made me inspect the rooms before entering. They constantly boasted about their superiority, nevertheless, inspecting these rooms was a job they were more than enthusiastically motivated to give me the lead. Knowing this, and wanting to keep peace with the group, I simply behaved as this is completely normal and got them settled, when I discovered there was a large master bedroom with my name and Julia's name on the door. This was interesting, as I reminded my ship that I am married. My ship reminds me that even though I am sleeping with Julia, I will solely be sleeping. I looked at Julia and told her sorry. She slaps me and tells me that she never does anything until two years of serious dating. I tell her I make the women wait three years. Julia tells me this is not true, since I am married. She claims married men jump on every opportunity. My ship takes my side by telling Julia that I am a faithful husband. I tell Julia that I am not a saint, and that I need her support, as I fear the challenges will become greater.

Julia winks at me and confesses to knowing my mind. When traveling this deep in the unconscious the line between minds becomes blurred. We laid in our wonderful large bed after changing into comfortable pajamas. Julia thanked me for saving her friends and her. I remind her they were the ones that saved me. Julia confesses they dreamed about getting free from that island or a prison as they saw it. I remind her that she told me before class yesterday most students graduated and left the island. Julia confessed no one left the island. The elders told her to say that many left so as not to alarm me concerning the abuses the tribes suffered. I complemented them on how great they had tricked me. Consequently, they all looked so content that I was seriously thinking about moving to their island. I reveal that at first I believed it strange when so many were helping me, nevertheless, when Julia reported the elders had appointed her to watch me, then the pieces came together in my mind. The eerie part was when Mr. Sharp went crazy on me. Julia agrees he even scared her. She reports Cindy believes Mr. Sharp did this to force her friends and her to escape, hoping we would make it out successfully. Julia further professes Mr. Sharp placed fear in their hearts. Accordingly, I agreed when Julia told us, they would begin their search in the morning I wondered what his strategy was. As a result, I hoped he was giving us a chance to escape, nevertheless; I had to face the possibility that he suspected we would make a move for the shore and was keeping his force centralized for easy mobilization. Consequently, I added the island was behind us for now. I asked my ship if Julia or any of the Cindies would join me on my escapes. My ship informs me that it does not know as she receives only its instructions, which, for the most part, is support on my behalf.

I decided to walk up the steps and view the ocean from the ship's deck. While walking up the steps I immediately appeared on a high dive jumping board above an empty pool. A strange woman appears behind me on the board and yells for me to jump so she may jump. I look at her and inform her the pool is empty. She walks by me pushing me to the side. Unfortunately, there was not enough side to be pushed as I fell from the board. Instinctively, my hands gripped the side of the bouncing board. The woman jumped from the board, as I heard her scream for help and then her body splashed into the concrete floor. The spring from her jump challenged my grip, yet somehow I used the upward motion of the board's spring to aid in lifting my legs onto the board. It was more as my leg went up, or in reality, raised its position relative to the board as it dropped. The momentum permitted me to get both legs on the board, and when positioned shifted my right hand to the board as I released my left hand to slide over the board and gripped the left side. Once I caught my breath, I looked down and saw the body of the woman who pushed me splattered on the empty pool below us. I could not believe this woman was so foolish. Apparently, the audience below me also did not think she jumped voluntarily. I heard them yelling; there is a man on the board who pushed this woman to her death. Nevertheless, I yelled down that she pushed me. Afterwards, I ask that anyone who saw this to testify. No one came forward. The group became angry because a few agitators were mingling throughout the group demanding justice. At this time, a vision comes through my mind revealing that I pushed this woman to her death. I knew this vision was false, nevertheless; I cannot believe an artificial vision would invade my mind. An eerie sensation is chilling my body. Based on the current thoughts in my mind, I am a criminal. A question that floods my mind is currently wondering if it is possible that I am a murderer. No human can erase what he or she did the previous day, the sole thing he or she can do is pay for those actions today and each day until death frees them.

Subsequently, three more men join the present hostile group that is passing judgment on me. What makes these men different from the others is they have sport rifles with scopes. To my sad misfortune, they begin firing on my board. By what I believe to be a miracle, the board is bouncing the bullets causing them to ricochet to the pool's surface. I saw a few people rushing trying to avoid the bullets. Three were not so lucky, as I saw them drop. As the bullets hit my board, they cause it to vibrate sending sharp stings through the board. Although the stings may not be deadly, they create strong distress within my mind. Accordingly, I try to slide back to the base of the board. This is a slow ongoing fearful process. One of the shooters relocates on the steps of a nearby building and now shoots at me on a parallel plane. His third shot hits me in my arm, which jolted me enough to propel me off the board. The pool floor rushes toward me. This was one of the few times that I faced death in my nighttime adventures. As I approach the pool floor, the pool vanishes and with it, the angry mob this was shooting at me. Subsequently, I softly hit the bottom dirt of an underground tunnel. Initially, it was far from daytime, and then the lights began to chase away the darkness. Strangely, the woman who pushed me on the board appeared tied to a pole. Another odd variable was the blood that was dripping from my arm. I brought the injury from being shot with me. I notice a knife on the tunnel's floor. I walk with the woman and ask her why she pushed me. She reports she was trying to save me from the mob. She decided to jump believing I would be right behind her, not believing I could hold on to the board. Consequently, she asked me to cut the rope that bound her to a pole inserted centrally in this tunnel. I grabbed the knife and freed this woman. My logic was simple, someone or thing put the knife there beside a woman who needed to be freed. She appears to know what is transpiring. Without this intelligence, I could face unnecessary dangers. Additional consideration acknowledged she would have easily killed me on the board, especially knowing she was kamikaze and merely had to hold on to me as she leaped from the board. I am extremely shocked she did not take me down with her. Notwithstanding, I ask her why she did not take me with her. She confessed to trying; however, I was sweating so much that her hands could not grip me.

I confess that spinning on a high dive above an empty pool has a tendency to make me perspire. She affirms that she felt sorry for me, having to see her body splattered. It was important to present this illusion to shake up the mob that was forming. I tell her they did such a good job shaking them up that they used me for target practice. Subsequently, she explains the reason the guardians tied her to the pole was they feared she might hurt herself as she suffered watching me be shot with rifles. I assure her she was not the sole one suffering, as the bullet that hit my arm got my attention quickly. I ask her to introduce herself, as she says her name is Ann. Next, I ask Ann, who was the ones that tied her to the pole. Ann explains I do not want to know. Just at that time, strange noises began echoing through this tunnel. Ann begins to shake stuttering, James; they are returning. We need to get out of this place. I ask Ann how we can get out of here since I do not know where we were. Ann agrees that she also does not know where are; however, knows we should not be at this point. She tells me to follow her. Ann dashes into one of the small side tunnels. I follow crawling behind her. I question her if she knows where this tunnel ends. Ann explains she has no idea; she just knows it goes away from where we were. My mind wonders why I am following this nut. Just as I think she is crazy, the tunnel opens up into a medium-sized room. The benefit was that we could stand on our feet, which for me was welcomed. Ann asks me if I have difficulty crawling in the tunnels. I tell her I have been crawling with women in underground tunnels too much recently. My greatest concern was over not knowing where we were going.

Accordingly, Ann updates me concerning her reason for selecting this tunnel. Earlier, she has noticed a weak breeze coming through the small hole when she was tied to the pole. She also noticed the guardians ignored it. I ask her about the guardian's appearance. Ann explains I would not believe her, and she hopes I never see them. The important thing is that they had not harmed us, and actually opened the bottom of the pool for us to pass. Next, Ann says the word that I hate so much when people are telling me something and that is 'but'. Ann claims that we do not know their true purpose, and should be in as favorable position as possible before meeting them once more. Ann pulled out her cell phone. I asked her if she is going to call for help. Ann winks at me and explains there is no way she has a signal here. Instead, she uses the flashlight to make sure she is safe. She scans our cavern quickly and then turned it off to save her battery. Ann hears a noise and whispers for me to stand still. Afterwards, she grabs my hand and guides me through another side tunnel. Fortunately, this tunnel was high enough for us to walk on our feet. After walking for approximately one hour, we once more entered a large cavern. This cavern surprised us, when we discovered one side was open. The stars looked wonderful. Meanwhile, there was no moon on this night. Ann claims this could be to our benefit, and that we should take advantage of this by getting away from this cave. I challenge her that if we do not know where these guardians are. Ann reminds me the one thing we do know is the guardians are in the cave, and it cannot hurt to have some distance from the cave's entrance. I agreed and decided to lead the way this time. Ann expresses joy in her belief that I knew where I was going. I told her she was following a blind man by following me. My goal was to get somewhere in one piece. Ann confides that she does not believe she could do better.

I find a building and rush into it, as dawn was approaching. Ann was right behind me. I grabbed a broken mop handle and quietly opened each door to the hallway to inspect the rooms. Ann laughs telling me the mop will have no effect against the guardians. With this in mind, I explain there could be a possibility the guardians do not know this. We can rest assured they have not witnessed to many humans hunting or fighting with broken mop handles. The mystery was soon over, as I realized Ann was correct in that I did not want to see these guardians. I ask her if these are guardians. Ann tells me yes, and that we need to get out of here. These creatures just about made me vomit when I looked at them. They appeared covered with their rotten, decayed flesh and horrendous smell. I realized this smell was one of our defensive assets. I notice they cannot run as fast as we can; however, these things are everywhere. They are chanting, "James and Ann are killers and must be executed." I ask Ann if she murdered someone. She denies having done so. I tell her I never murdered anyone, nevertheless; something tried to plant some memories in my head, to which I have fought hard to eliminate. We continue to run, finding a two-lane paved highway with state traffic signs. While running down the road, what I believed my salvation came driving toward us. Ann and I stop, wanting to alert these police officers of the danger we face. Instead of rescuing us, they turned on their lights and sirens stopping in front of us. Next, they jump out of their vehicle, pointed their pistols at us declaring we were under arrest. They order us to the ground and handcuff us. I ask them why they have arrested us. They look at each other and laugh, herd us to their car and take us to their station. Once in the station, they place us in different rooms and begin interrogating us. Three of them gang up on me. I turn on my cell phone and ask for a lawyer. This angers them, nevertheless; they continue to badger me. The sole thing I repeat over and over that, I want a lawyer. After a little more than one hour, we hear a bang on the large window that covers one complete wall. The investigators pause and leave the room.

I sit within my room alone for another hour. Then, a man walks in and introduces himself as my lawyer. He informs me that he can get a deal, where they will reduce my charge and get only thirty years in prison. I told him he was crazy, and that I never committed any crime, which would require even one day in prison. My lawyer explains the police told him Ann had agreed to testify against me. I told him that Ann would never purposely lie and by law if the police told him this, based on discovery, he could demand a copy of that confession. He stares at me and agrees. I tell him to go get that report. Accordingly, he leaves my room and walks in Ann's interrogation room. He asks Ann if she wants a lawyer. She quickly affirms this. Thereafter, he tells her to stay silent. Then he asks her if she has agreed to testify against me. Ann declares she would never make such a statement.

The investigators become angry with this lawyer for asking this question. The lawyer tells Ann to follow him, and they leave the room. He opens my door where the investigators snuck back in to question me. My lawyer tells the investigators to prepare for the charges he is pressing because the investigators interrogated me without him being present. I jump up and walk to Ann asking her why she is going to lie for these beasts against me. Ann reassures me; she said nothing to the investigators, claiming she took the fifth and exercised her right to remain silent. The lawyer guides us to the shift leader's desk. We began the paperwork to press charges against the police for violating our rights. The desk sergeant initially refused to start the paper work. Nevertheless, our lawyer turns on his cell phone and begins recording, when the desk sergeant reconsidered. Our lawyer pressed charges against each of the eight investigators involved and then for false arrest. We walked out with our lawyer, who told us we would not be going in there again, except as witnesses.

Thereafter, we proceeded to the TV station to make our statement. The press jumped on this, especially since our lawyer gave them copies of our complaints. The media flooded the police station. After this, our lawyer asks where we are staying. Ann invites me to her apartment, which since I did not have a place this was a lifesaver. Suddenly, the guardians begin to cross the road. Our lawyer pushes a few buttons, and his vehicle began to fly over the road. He tells us that he knows a cabin in higher mountains that will be safe for a few days. He asks us if we have any cash. I reach in my pocket and pull out three hundred dollars. Having no idea why I have this money, I give it to the lawyer. He explains we need some more gas and a couple of weeks of groceries. He stays close to the tree line and finds an open stretch where he returns to the road. We drive into a nearby town, where we fill up with gas. He also buys three five-gallon gas cans and fills them with kerosene. Next, we head to the grocery store, where he tells us to get whatever we wanted, especially since his cabin had large refrigerators plus freezers. We got our supplies, in which he stopped by a sporting goods store, purchased an assortment of bullets and two sleeping bags and two thick blankets. We jump in his car, and once we are out of town; return to the tree lines. Our lawyer explains he stays close to the tree lines so his green car will blend with the trees. The guardians tend to search in the sky and ground separately. They ignore the tops of trees, since they have no way of climbing along the treetops. Approximately twenty minutes later, we land in front of his cabin. The cabin is exclusive in that no roads connect this cabin with the reminder of the world. There was a large steep cliff about four hundred feet in front of this cabin. This space was covered by forest. He carefully landed his car dropping through a small opening between two trees, as the thin branches brushed against his car. He slowly drove his car to the cabin. When we reach the cabin, he asks us to help to unload his car. Once unloaded, he cut some branches to camouflage this vehicle under some nearby trees. Then he put the excess kerosene in a small storage cellar he dug into the side of the hill behind the cabin. After settling in, we assembled around the table where Ann has prepared our dinner.

One bite and complements flooded from my mouth about the quality of Ann's cooking. Our host agreed with each word that came from my mouth. Ann tells me not to make so many complements, as all she did was take it from a can and add a few spices. Our host, as I call him Mr. Host, because I did not want to press into his personal life believing that by allowing him to keep some of his privacy, he may be more at ease with me. If I do not pound him with questions, then he should not be so inquisitive concerning Ann and myself. Providentially, Mr. Host expressed no interests in our cause. He worried more about our security. Ann thanks him for helping us and then asks out of curiosity, why he is helping us. Mr. Host explains he had no choice, as he could not leave us to the police, and if he has a chance at winning our case, in the event, they are foolish enough to take us to court; he must keep us away from them. I ask him if he believes they will take us to court. Mr. Host (Lawyer) explains they have no valid charge, nevertheless; he expects they will create some false charges and offer a deal if we drop our charges for discovery violations. Ann smiles and clarifies we solely pressed our charges to have a few cards on the table, so we can make a deal. Mr. Host agrees that if you do not have any cards on the table, you are out of the game. I smile at our Lawyer and profess it was our lucky day when he took our case. Ann supplements my praise by adding the flying car, and hidden cabin was a priceless bonus. Mr. Host confesses this is the first time he has had company in this cabin. He further believes this to be a special time. I ask him how we can know if anyone is attempting to invade us. He explains, there is a cave that connects his storage tunnel to a hole at the top of the high hill above us. We can come and go to this lookout point, where we may inspect for miles surrounding us. From that position, we can have almost one-day advance notice, unless they attack by airplane, which would not matter.

Nevertheless, I went to our lookout point and saw no one trying to invade us. I went back to our cabin to give my mates the all clear report. Then, we hear knocks on our door. Mr. Host gives Ann and me our rifles as he answers our door. When our door opens three guardians come rushing in our living room. Ann and I begin firing. We aim at their heads, hoping that cracking their skulls may disorientate them. Accordingly, we know that hitting their rotten flesh covered bodies would have a minimal effect. Mr. Host grabs his ball bat and smashes their skulls for the final blows. Afterwards, I rush to our door and spin around telling Mr. Host; we have two more guardians in the yard. I pump two rounds into each of their heads while our lawyer rushes to them and smashes their skulls. Thereafter, he informs me there is a cliff about two feet east of us, and that we should toss these bodies over the cliff, as the result would place them a few difficult miles from us. He explains we can put them in the trunk of his car and slowly drive to the cliff. Next, we tossed the five skeletons over the cliff. After hiding his car once more, we walk back into our cabin. Mr. Host recommends we sit on the front porch and quietly discuss our potential options.

He further reveals that even smashed guardians have a tendency to return. This is why it was so wise to toss them over the cliff. Ann asks if there are more of them on this hill. Mr. Host claims it is not likely, as they usually travel in a combined group to increase their fighting abilities in conflicts, especially when considering how slow and clumsy, they are. Furthermore, since they are covering more territory, they are spread thin. Mr. Host believes that when they discover the five crushed skeletons, they will saturate that area to exact their revenge. Most times, the guardians launch their searches from a straight line. Considering that it had to take these five longer to get up here, the flanks to their lines must be well ahead. Subsequently, since we tossed these five terminated guardians behind their search line, it could be a long time before they return. When they retreat, they should be exhausted and thus not motivated to search on top of this desolate hill.

Mr. Host takes us on a small trip to a local store. While on the way, he explains we need to have an occupation to look sociable before the court. He claims to have a friend who owns a local store and owes him a few favors. We pull into a small country family store. Ann asks if he is sure, they have positions for us. Our lawyer tells us that if he does not, he will make them. The owners were a senior couple, who struggled with each movement. Ann and I quickly went to work, organizing and cleaning their store. We noticed a few kids come inside the store, fill some bags of food, and walk out. Ann and I at once chased after them. After catching them, they immediately threatened to tell their parents about us. Ann tells them we will save them the trouble and demands they tell us where they live. They refuse; therefore, we take them back to the store and asked Mr. Host to contact the local justice of the peace for us. Mr. Host, whom we now renamed Leroy, short for Lawyer, so as not ironically to add to this confusion, warns the parents of these children are wild rednecks, and that it would be best to avoid them. Ann refuses to release these boys and tells them that when their fathers arrive, they will be kissing their rifles. One of the boys offers to visit a nearby relative and get the money. Ann warns this boy that if he pulls any tricks, his friend will die. Leroy tells him that he will collect some dead guardians and plant them on their farms. This catches the boy's attention. We release one boy who brings back a bag of money. I ask the boy if he believes this will pay for what they took. The boys confessed this was not the first time they forgot to pay, and they believe this will settle their accounts. Ann asks them how they know this. They confess they saved the money their parents gave them for the groceries. Leroy thanks them for their rehabilitation.

We gave this money to the elderly owners after releasing the boys. I questioned Leroy if he believed we could trust these boys. Leroy affirms we have no danger, especially since the mountain money, is so easy to identify and such rare coins were plentiful in the bag they gave us. Ann wonders how we can specify this came from the boys, considering everyone shops in this store who lives in this area. Leroy shows me the bag and reveals this bag has their family emblem outside it. Ann asks him why he is so wise. Leroy replies that only the wisest may become lawyers. Neither Ann nor I challenged this statement, especially considering every action he has taken has saved us. I go to the back room to repack the shelves, only to discover their entire storeroom empty. Accordingly, I return to the store and ask the owners where they keep their inventory. They explain they have no inventory, nor any cash, and they sold their farm and put that cash into their inventory. Ann asks them what they did with the cash from their sales. They shyly agree this is what they forgot to do and that is to collect the money. Leroy shakes his head in disbelief probing how they could forget this. The husband claims he thought his wife took the money and concentrated on packing the customer's purchases. His wife claims she was involved with the packing, because of their age took both to pack the groceries, therefore, she thought her husband handled the cash, to include doing the tax record keeping at the end of the day. A shocked husband claims he believed his wife was doing the reports, and if they have not been doing their reports, they are in deep trouble. Leroy tells them not to worry because he will represent them. He also volunteers to finance their restocking solely if they keep Ann and me in the store interacting with the customers. Leroy made the calls and scheduled the resupplies, which would begin flowing in the next day. Ann and I knew we had some work ahead of us. Leroy recommended that we make sure any who enter the store have some form of payment. If they have no form of currency or cards, they have no need to be in the store.

As suspected, the next six customers had no money and as such, we made them exit. There was a pause for a few hours. After wards, customers began to enter, and of greater importance had cash. Leroy came to pick us up after we closed the store and took as back in the mornings. These were long days, with the store opening at 9 AM. and closing at 9 PM., Ann and I had plenty of time to chat among ourselves. I was trying to determine what Ann's role is in my dream. She was spreading her wings over me, shielding me from as much danger as possible. We attempted to present a strong serious image for the customers, especially since most were rough looking hillbillies. One afternoon, our luck ran out when a group of six men took us to our storage room and began hitting us. They hit in my mouth and in my right eye. Consequently, I did not worry so much about me being hit; it was the blood flowing from Ann's face, which angered me. Next, I took a hard it in my stomach, which temporarily took my breath. When I regained control over myself, I heard some shots as bullets were flying around us. I saw our captors trying to take cover by hiding behind some crates. I saw a bottle of ketchup and busted it on the floor. At once, I grabbed the head of the abductor closest to me and cut his neck open with the broken ketchup bottle. Subsequently, I snapped his neck, grabbed his riffle, and picked off the five remaining hostage takers. They spread themselves out among the boxes trying to hide from the shots coming from the front. This made it easy to pop them one by one. Auspiciously, I hit each one in their heads, since I did not want them to warn the others. Accordingly, I yelled for whoever was shooting to stop because the coast was clear. Next, I turned my attention to Ann, who was passed out on the floor. Therefore, I picked her up and rushed her to the front of the store. After lying Ann on the counter, I rush toward the front of the store and lock the door. There were still one man and two women in the store.

Now extremely suspicious of all the locals, I ask the remaining customers promptly to finish their shopping, pay, and then leave. The man tells me he has not paid for anything in this store for his previous three visits, and he is not paying today. I fire a bullet into his head, and he drops dead instantly. This made the women angry, especially when one declared I had just killed her husband. After telling them I was so sorry, I shot them in their heads. Without any delay, I repositioned these three in our inventory room so it looked as if they were in a shooting match with our captives. I planned to tell everyone how he saved us. I took the pistol from the man I just killed and shot each of our six torturers in the front of their heads standing them so their bodies were leaning forward. My story concluded with how I killed the remaining captor to save Ann and myself. Henceforth, I rushed back to Ann and began treating her bruises. Next, I began pressing her lightly to test for any possible broken bones. I was so happy when I verified she did not have any infringed bones. The raiding men beat on Ann's fleshy parts. Apparently, they were more interested in defacing her appearance than doing any permanent bodily damage. The owners brought us some pain pills and lotions. Leroy was surprised when he came to take us back to the cabin. He recommended to the owners; they keep their store closed for a few days to give Ann and me a chance to heal. They agreed, therefore, Leroy took us back to his cabin, where he planned to nurse us to a manageable pain filled condition within a few days. Ann was struggling hard to regain her fight posture. I believe she did not feel well about not being able to defend herself. Notwithstanding, I can understand her position, since we had many obstacles to overcome. Thus, I was looking for a few days to get myself back in a fighting condition, even though while in this condition I did have nine kills under my belt. Unfortunately, the mountains had a few more curve balls to toss at me, trying to catch me while I was partially handicapped.

Strangely, while nursing Ann, I found myself missing Julia and the Cindies. I have been on this adventure for many days already, and do not see any relief for a while. The next morning I went outside to gather some twigs to start a fire in our fireplace. At the same time, as I was gathering these thin chunks of wood, the ground became flooded with mice. Naturally, I threw the wood into the air and began running for the cabin's door yelling for Leroy. Leroy took one look and rushed back inside his cabin. He reappeared with a spray can as he began squirting the ground. The spray irritated the mice causing them immediately to scatter. I lost any sense of courage and jumped around as a chicken without a head trying to avoid the fleeing mice. Leroy calls my name providing me with a position to flee toward as he stood on the porch's edge. He slowly worked his way toward me, yelling when my path deviated from our reunion. The wind blew enough of this spray to burn my eyes, thus I kept my eyes closed, and hands over them as my ears were locked on the words that come from Leroy's mouth. Once Leroy noticed my difficulties, he redirected his spray area to herd the mice to each of my sides leaving a clearer path for me to advance. Unfortunately, a few mice leaped on me biting fiercely. I quickly mastered the skill of grabbing them while chocking them. Once I chocked them enough to force them to release me; I flung them off to the side. When on the porch, Leroy began to concentrate his spraying. After he had soaked many of the fleeing mice, he tossed a match on them. Considering the spray was highly inflammable, our yard lit up, as would a bond fire. The spray dulled the senses of the mice and as such caused them to react in total chaos to the intense heat that burned those who surrounded them. Leroy rushed the remaining spray inside his cabin to prevent it from feeding the fire that raged in our front yard. As the rotten smell of the burning flesh of mice made the air vow to my stomach, we use our spare clothing to seal the air within our cabin.

Just as quickly as our dangers increased somehow, our fortunes have returned in just enough proportion to create an illusion of possible recovery. Our raft through this raging sea came this time in the form of rain. Rain was common on this mountainside, as it pours just about each day or night. The night showers danced from the slate Leroy had on his cabin's roof. The dancing raindrops battling against the cool breeze added the words to the showers. It was as if there was a quiet, peaceful orchestra entertaining us. On this day, the rains came in the last afternoon and in time to prevent the flaming mice from starting a forest fire. We received an extra-long down poor this night, which assisted in washing the burned mice remains from our yard. Leroy's pain pills allowed Ann and me to sleep well this night. Leroy searched to discover any recovery, we may have made throughout the night. Our healing was progressing normally, to our delight, although Leroy said that we needed at least two weeks to recover to a fighting condition. He did not worry so much about our ability to heal. Leroy worried more over the return of the guardians, or other strange hazards and even our court trial, as it would be possible that other perils could surround that trial. Leroy warns that just the innocent and honorable face danger in the courts, because the wicked speak with a false tongue and sees with evil eyes. Leroy was searching deep in his mind trying to discover a place where we could hide. Leroy and I discussed so many possible options over the next few days. We talked outside on the porch, because Ann was recovering from worsened wounds than was I. Her appearance was worse than her injury; therefore, we decided to give her some extra breathing rooms so as not to overstress her.

One afternoon, while chatting with Leroy three large hunting dogs came rushing toward us. Instinctively, we grabbed and fired our rifles killing the three dogs. As if we could read each other's minds, we continued shooting until the three dogs lay died. Even though our rifle shoots could be heard at least ten-minute walk in all directions surrounding us, Leroy acknowledged there was a possibility the hunters did not hear it. In fact, he said they could have been searching in caves, or in one of the hundreds of valleys in this area. Another probability could be the dogs were far ahead of them. Leroy claims the hunters start early, and by this time during the day are dragging their feet. Either way, we would find out soon enough.

Accordingly, I ask Leroy if he can guess how many hunters are in this gang. Leroy smiles and reveals there are four, maybe five tops. I was surprised at the speed and confidence with his answer. Leroy noticed by the confusion written across my face, I needed some other form of verification. Leroy smiles and then clarifies that each hunter has a dog, and they always keep at least one dog with them, which is usually the oldest dog. It is common for the eldest dog to have a partner, which is also an older dog to hang together. Kind of two old dogs can function as one younger dog. Leroy clarifies the prime danger from these dogs is their bark and smell. They would naturally pose a threat if engaged in a fistfight with the owners, so Leroy recommends we shoot the hunters first, since the dogs will not leave them if they fall on the ground. Once more, he stressed the greatest danger is the advance dogs, which were now dead in our yard. Leroy suggested we played possum tonight, by making a campfire in the valley below us and scatter twigs everywhere. The twigs will allow us to track their steps in the dark. We put everything into play, took our position in the trees after walking in circles surrounding the tree below us. Leroy claimed this would confuse the dogs and keep them in the close range for our scopes. Fortunately, this was a full moon night allowing us to see the ground clearly and enough dark to camouflage us in the trees. We waited throughout the night, considering Leroy believed they would hunt until they found their dogs. Moreover, to this end, they did. Approximately three AM the aged dogs detected the dead dogs we planted around the campfire. The dogs must have been too distorted from discovering the old dogs that they gave no attention to what was above them.

Leroy and I shot the first two in the center of the tops of theirs hats causing them to drop immediately. The remaining two hunters foolishly hid behind some trees causing their backs to face us. This was not a time to debate over shooting someone in the back since our survival was in question, and these hunters were attacking us. It took us four shots to finish the remaining two hunters. We hit them in their backs causing them to fall backwards to the ground at which time we hit them once more in their stomachs causing them to release their weapons. Their movements confused the dogs who were dashing around the campfire barking loudly. I hesitated to shoot the challenged dogs, nevertheless, Leroy's desire to survive was greater than mine causing him to apply his effective shooting skills and drop the final two dogs. Our foes, at least for this day were defeated. We beefed up our chests filled with courage and pride; death came after us, and we skillfully entrapped them. I felt bad for chocking in the final round as I had. Leroy sensed this and told me he was proud of my performance. Thus, I changed the subject by wondering if Ann was safe. Leroy laughed and commented that even if the dangers were foolish enough to challenge Ann would get a thumping not easily forgotten. Leroy reminded me Ann was not in her normal condition and therefore, may need our protection more now than previously. Living with so much unpredictability was beginning to shatter my realm of security. I was looking around each corner expecting the unexpected. Fearing something bad may happen and then spending each day barely overcoming these encounters close to death by sending others to their death. I needed something to hold on to, so I can move forward.

Leroy comforted me by assuring me he was here for Ann and me. Notwithstanding, after thanking Leroy for helping us once more asked him why he was helping us. Leroy comes clean to me by confessing he believes there are too many dirty hands in the law enforcement and the judicial system. Initially, he believed we would have a few harsh words in the court, exchanging our charges for acquittal, receiving a couple of warnings from the judge and sent on our way. Leroy agrees it may be wise for us to retreat and questioned me if I knew of a safe place for us.

Strangely, all through this episode I remembered my Cindies, Julia and ship. The ship was as close to my other existence in the land of hunger and pain that my mind would venture. Accordingly, I explain to Leroy, I have a ship that has been in the sea, yet unfortunately; I do not remember where it is located. Leroy informs me that he might know where it is. We will stay on his small hill for a few days, allowing Ann to recover, and then we will search for my ship. I felt this would be finished with favorable results. Exhausted, once more I slept on the cabin's dirt floor. I slept here by choice, since I believed by sleeping on the ground that I could better hear the steps of any dangerous intruders. To my extreme happiness, I heard no steps. My first order of business was nursing Ann, who is recovering brilliantly. Her spirit and determination is my inspiration, which would help me throughout my future tribulations. I decided to do some reconnaissance throughout this secluded area. The fresh air and splendid sounds from the birds turned this walk into an exploration journey. This place offered an abundance of paths created by the wild animals who struggled for their survival in this lovely area adorned by its small streams conveniently located within the forests. My route, created by connecting several random paths soon provided me with an effective way to scout the various lands surrounding our sanctuary.

The next afternoon, while on my relaxation walk my solitude was broken by six soldiers who surrounded me. Hoping they were friendly, since the military is not supposed to be used as police, I invited them to my house for some coffee. The senior ranking soldier in this group asked me if I had roommates and living close on this side of the mountain. The way he asked me unleashed within me a powerful sense of urgency forcing me to exercise precaution. I knew of a cabin about three miles back that rested beside a soft stream. I tried to convince Leroy that this would be a pleasant place to live, being tucked away in the low lands. Leroy disagreed, explaining it was so much harder defending depressed lands than defending highlands. Nevertheless, their ranking sergeant told me their first priority was getting me to safety. They would be scouting that area once more after I am safe. At this time, while pretending not to know, I asked the soldiers about this so-called current danger. They report, there are some crazy gun maniacs killed several people in the store and were now shooting hunters. I explain I knew about the store, nevertheless; I did not hear about hunters. The sergeant informs me they found them about four hundred feet downstream from me. One of the soldiers comments that I should have heard the shots. I explain to him that unlike life in a fort, life in these mountains requires hunting expeditions and food gathering trips. He asks me what I am doing presently. I tell him it is none of his business. I declare that I do not like it when people stick their heads in my butt. Notwithstanding, he took a swing at me. I ducked and landed a punch in his face at which time the soldiers separated us. Their sergeant told them not to ask any more questions. The important issue presently was getting me to safety. This prompted my question concerning how they were to keep me secure. The sergeant brags how the military can provide the best security possible. To minimize the current friction, I agreed enthusiastically over the military's security fame. Next, I probed about an update on our destination. These soldiers informed me that I did not need to know where the path led, it was more important that we stayed on the path.

The soldiers relaxed, which allowed me to joke with them while we traveled. Later, we came to a camouflaged door at the bottom of several steps tucked against a steep cliff, yet still hidden by tall trees. They were careful to ruffle the leaves to erase any tracks. I wrestled with one soldier hoping to leave some mark on the ground, nevertheless, the harder I struggled, the more soldiers jumped on to retrain me. I realized that once they put me in the cave, it would be almost impossible to escape. I lost this battle and soon found myself way down inside the Earth, tied from head to foot on a pole drilled into the rock floor. It was extremely damp and chilly soaking deep into my bones. Considering that I was bound to this pole and had no movement, except enough, barely to breathe, I could not generate any motion to create warmth. I complained to the soldiers who handcuffed my hands behind the pole and one of my feet to a floor hook. This permitted movement, which generated body heat. Unfortunately, it did not create enough warmth, thus I had to supplement this somehow. Desperately, I chose to flood my mind with some pleasant memories. Memories of Ann and Julia poured into my mind. I envisioned them walking into this cavern, which as they turned into a room. The bare rocks and walls transformed into flowers all rich in their bloom. The dungy smell of death and emptiness dampness evolved into a paradise of powerful perfumes. For the first time since capture, I experienced a sense of joy. This experienced vanished as fast as it arrived when I felt the soldiers hitting me while yelling for me to awaken. Suddenly, their ugly faces replaced Ann and Julia's faces as reality once more reminded me this situation was not good. While the excited soldiers were tormenting me, they began to hit my face and busted my nose causing blood to flow. This thrilled them so much they leaped in eagerness hoping to do more harm.

While losing their sense of control the small handcuff keys fell out of someone's pocket and hit my foot. When it hit my foot, I at once recognized it, and quickly scooted it back under my foot. With this, I pretended as if my broken nose had rendered me unconscious. It is so difficult not screaming or reacting to punches to appear cataleptic. These soldiers quickly lost interest and went back to their area where they most likely kept their alcohol. They must be getting drunker by the moment by the volume of their erratic singing. I worked one key between two toes on my free foot and lifted my heal above my kneecap where my fingers grabbed hold of it. Next, I unlocked my right wrist cuff freeing my right hand, which quickly unlocked my left hand. I fell forward and then twisted myself, so I faced my feet and unlocked the cuffs with the other key freeing my feet. I had a score to settle now. Therefore, I carefully began to scout this cave. I knew the sergeant ran a tight ship, thus he would have his weapons accountable in one area. Within a few minutes, considering the limited space this underground prison camp possessed, I found where their weapons were stored. I filled a bag with hand grenades and ammunition, grabbed a holster belt and pistol, and slapped a rifle over my shoulder and a machine-gun with a box holding 1,000 rounds. This machine-gun was heavy; nonetheless, it had three legs, which provided a stable foundation holding the weapon's weight permitting the shooter to kill with ease. My purpose for this was to kill those who captured me. I can merely hope that 1,000 large bullets can hit six targets. My primary fear was they may not all be together. Logic told me that by being cuffed and with a secure entrance, there should be no reason why they would be separated. The latter proved true, as their drunken singing allowed me to position my machine-gun dead center in their entrance.

They had a fireplace, close to the entrance, most likely so the smoke would not choke them, which blinded them from seeing outside their drinking cavity. I counted all seven and decided to kill the ones on the sides first, thus herding them on top of each another. Accordingly, I realized this massacre must be swift, and not even knowing it, I fired the first shots, three shots, and three hits. The remaining flopped on each other in their drunken confusion. I pumped hundreds of bullets on them. Soon, the sole movement was their bodies absorbing these large machine-gun bullets. Afterwards, I decided to let my weapon cool down and see if any were still living. I saw flood flowing from each body. With this new sense of independence, I slowly plucked five more shots into each soldier, concentrating on their heads. Subsequently, I watched them for ten minutes, detecting no movement. I took a small hatchet and checked each one to verify they are deceased. Too many movies have the dead victim return, so I wanted to make sure this did not happen to me. I spread the bodies in a sitting position with their backs to the cavity's walls. Once more, I pumped bullets into each body. When I departed from this cave, I wanted to make sure there was no doubt they were dead. Another decision was pressing my mind for direction. Should I bring the machine-gun back to the cabin? It would be heavy, yet would guarantee our cabin would be safe, and fit in Leroy's trunk, then give my ship some extra punch. I know that we will face attacks while back on my ship, as our enemies are coming out of the woodworks. I had to take advantage of anything that could keep us alive. I began pushing this wheeled container out of the cave. I studied the hills around me noticing the types of trees and recognized the general area I was currently. I followed the paths and within three hours, was pushing my container over some small paths that guided me to our cabin. When I knock on the door, no one answers. I call out my name and alert the occupants I am coming inside. To be safe, I pulled my pistol. I had a key to the door, unlocked it, and immediately rushed inside. Next, I found myself under fire and started shooting in the direction of the fire, hitting the mystery man in our cabin. I walk over to him, when Ann screams out for me to make sure this killer is dead.

Accordingly, I walk over to this man and shot him once more through the top of his head. Afterwards, I walk in Ann's room, finding her tied to a chair. Subsequently, I untie her and help put her back on her bed, so she could return to her recovery. Ann predicts she can travel within a few days. She laughs, explaining the Leroy and me simply need to escort her to Leroy's car, which must be next to our porch. Notwithstanding, I ask Ann where Leroy is. She believes he is setting traps and trying to confuse the other three men who attacked them. Ann explains the exhausted villains should be returning within a few hours. With this return in mind, I stockpiled my container in Leroy's storage tunnel. Next, I took my machine-gun and another 1000 rounds, plus the remaining bullets from my earlier execution of the soldiers and set me up a solid position just inside the forest line that surrounds our front yard. This position offered me a range of fire, which covered most of our yard. The trouble would be waiting until the three were in the open area, since I did not want one to hide back in the forest. As a security measure, I bring an extra rifle and two pistols. Just as Ann predicted, the three men returned. Lucidly, one was injured requiring the other two to escort him back to the cabin. This was perfect, considering the bullets from this machine-gun will go through three men easily from this range. When they were halfway between the cabin and forest, I began firing my machine-gun. The first bullet went through all three dropping them instantly. With all three on the ground, I began pumping bullets into their legs and then their torsos. They were goners, considering these bullets went through their bodies leaving large holes. Suddenly, I heard a familiar voice call for me to hold my fire.

I look to my left and witness Leroy entering the yard. He begins to verify the three bodies were dead and then tells me we are safe now. I begin to carry my weapons back to the cabin. Leroy gives me a shocked look and asks me if I invaded an Army base. I put my machine-gun, ammo, and rifles on our porch and invite Leroy to walk with me to our storage area. Once there, I reveal my container, explaining I kept it here in case the raiders made it to the cabin. Leroy is excited about these new weapons, claiming we will be able to survive a few large battles with this arsenal. We stashed these weapons in our cabin and then went back in the yard to bury the four bodies. Leroy comments that soon, this hill will have too many bodies buried under its surface. I tell Leroy we need to move on within a few days, especially since Ann feels she can travel soon. Leroy agrees, and then asks me where I have been vacationing for the past week. I point to my crocked nose and open my shirt to reveal the bruises explaining I was a prisoner held by seven soldiers in an underground fortress. After hearing a noise, Leroy spun around and with his rifle shot a rabbit running through the trees. Leroy tells me we will eat wonderful tonight. I helped him prepare a special reunion dinner as we treated Ann as the queen, which she truly was. Ann complained because I put six pistols on our table, two for each of us. Halfway through our dinner, our cabin door flies open as four men come rushing. Leroy, Ann, and I grabbed our pistols and began spraying bullets dropping these men to the floor causing them to gasp for their last breaths. Leroy complains over needing to bury more bodies. I ask him if we can simply place them in his storage cave. He refused to allow this, citing he planned on returning here in the future and the last thing he wanted to see or smell was the rotten cadavers in his escape tunnel. Ann handed us each one shovel and said we needed to hurry and finish before sunrise. This time Leroy told me, we would put all four bodies in one hole behind our cabin about one hundred feet into the forest.

Accordingly, we quickly dug a hole about three feet down, spread the bodies in the hole and refilled the hole with dirt, and then jumped on it packing the dirt. Next, we replaced the top sod layer. Leroy was always careful to remove the first four inches of soil containing the sod and stacked it evenly. He believed it was important to give the sod as much support as possible, considering once the grass reestablished its hold nature would do the rest. I agreed the faster a gravesite returned to normal, the less unexpected dangers would manifest themselves. I never question if this was true or not, because my goal is to be long gone before verifying the validity of his claim. The next morning I woke up to an itching face, as I immediately began sneezing merely to hear Ann asserting at me for spitting in her face. I instantly apologized swearing it was an accident. I knew not to deny doing it, since my focusing eyes could see my spit on her face. She thanked me for brushing my teeth this morning. Thinking over her comment, I found some comfort that at least I did not blast her with a dirty stinky mouth. Hoping to find a defense, I probed Ann to explain why her face was above mine, and her hair flopping in my face. Leroy asks me if I am really complaining over what Ann did. I told them I was not complaining, just that I wish I had been prepared. Ann laughs, and then replies that if I were prepared, then she would be in danger. While we all begin laughing, I smile, and to regain my male ego, I winked at Ann and replied, "You know it." Leroy pauses for a second and then tells Ann he is jealous now over the extra attention she is giving me. Ann tells Leroy not to worry; she was simply telling me today she was ready to travel. She was tired of merely having our ugly faced to look forward to each day. Leroy informs me that Ann must have gone crazy, because few women are blessed with our beauty. I wholeheartedly agreed that solely an insane woman could think as this woman before us is thinking currently. Ann begins throwing cups at us. Thankfully, they were wooden cups.

Subsequently, Leroy and I agreed we needed to find a place to get rid of Ann, so we can find a woman worthy of our greatness. Ann began throwing our things outside, thus Leroy, and I stored them in his car. Not long thereafter, she began throwing her things outside as well. Ann finished cleaning out our cabin while Leroy and I loaded the weapons I brought with us. Leroy said for us to leave the pistols available, in case we meet any hostiles while traveling. We planned our route on Leroy's hand drawn map while eating lunch. Leroy knew of a large sea that was passed the mountains. The difficulty he predicted was getting his car over the high mountains. The terrain was too steep to drive and the mountains were too high to fly. The air was too thin for his engine to keep this car in the air. He remembers a few old men who spoke of a pass through the mountains. They used it as a trade route, therefor Leroy believed their tales. His plan was to travel higher about one mile from the mountain slopes. He believed we would be able to identify this passage. This strategy would weed out most of the dead-end paths. A worst-case scenario we end on a few dead-end attempts. Finally, we began our voyage. I felt a loss of security as our hills turned into small bumps way off in the distance. The forests below flowed throughout our horizon. Even though they appeared similar, I could sense different worlds created by their inhabitants. I could just hope the righteous people were stronger than the wicked people were. What I now find scary is how each area, as even did I in our hill, feels like its own complete world. The loss of our world, even though brief, embeds a feeling of homesickness. Leroy asks us to keep an eye out for any towns. He plans to stop at every possible gas station so we have a full tank when we go through the pass. He knows the land on the other side of the mountain has extremely few inhabitants, and therefor-limited resources. We found a gas station and refueled. Ann and I hustled a few candy bars. The chocolate was to calm an urge to fall into the hands of temptation. Sometimes doing something bad feels so good.

Accordingly, it was early evening on our first day and we still had not found the magical pass. Leroy lowered his car into a small meadow. We gathered some wood and started a campfire. Leroy recommended we sleep in his car. We were enjoying the outside and the stars around our campfire. Ann got the crazy notion to start singing, and soon Leroy and I joined her. This was actually the first time we enjoyed ourselves in a celebration. Sure, it was not a holiday; however, we were hungry for our new future or promised land. Notwithstanding, our future would not solely be on land, but instead ride the waves of the open sea. When I watch how Ann laughs and waves her hands with overflowing jubilee I find myself slipping back onto my ship with Julie and my Cindies. I know I must make a decision concerning the parameters of our relationships. Consequently, there is the paradox of why I would even desire a deeper, longer-term relationship with any woman in my dark world. The moral issue would then be, 'who would be my true spouse? Can a relationship established in an invisible dimension void of any matter be physically binding? Another question deals with the transcendent issue debating if it is possible to sin in this night dimension deep inside my mind?' Nevertheless, fearfully I wonder which dimension is closer to my soul. This night dimension resembles the spiritual realm with their joint absence of matter and freedom from the limitations of time and space. The lone manner in which I can guess what age my escapades are in is by the type of buildings, clothing, and available objects and the frequency of their occurrences. The older a technology is, the more of it that is distributed among society. Examples include telephones, radios, TVs, computers, microwaves, and cell phones to list merely a few. Tonight, we did not worry about technology, even though I am assured that flying cars are not common in my daytime dimension. There is something about a star lighted night, with a partial moon, the bright North Star and a crackling campfire, no matter what dimension, that provides a serenity that is one solid haven for harmony uniting the soul and nature. Ann and I used extra caution not to elaborate on this experience, fearing Leroy would once more guide us on one of his, 'enlightened roads of his philosophy.'

We slept in Leroy's car that night, thankfully free from any outside noises. The forests have so many new songs for each valley one travels. I can see the songs from the sky, yet I cannot hear them. Even though I cannot hear them, I can strangely feel them. What I feel is refreshing, nevertheless, unknown, thus I cannot give it much attention. As the ground moves aside from us, so does the feeling. The old fades away as the new comes into focus. Leroy recommended we loosen up and stretch our muscles before what might be a long day in his car. Leroy decides to get our blood rolling by declaring he heard me call out Ann's name in my dreams last night. I knew this was false in that I never had dreams in this alternate dimension. Ann joins this harassment by confessing she has known for a long time that I have the uncontrollable burning for her. Ann trapped me with this statement, because if I deny her statement would be a lie, nevertheless, to accept it would advance our relationship too fast and to a level, I am not prepared to encompass. The pressing issue now is that I will not hurt Ann's feelings. She has made too many sacrifices on my behalf to be treated so cruelly, therefor it was time to think through my pants. I looked at them and asked, "Is there any sane man who would not burn inside at just one sight of Ann, or after becoming acquainted would not cry out her name throughout the entire night?" Leroy jumps on-line with me quickly by agreeing completely. Ann accepts this compliment with the same enthusiasm as a wife would with a new credit card in a shopping center. Notwithstanding, Ann filled our car with her excitement, which made time fly for us. Our hope took a few punches as we eliminated a few of the deeper dead-ends.

Subsequently, early in the afternoon we discovered another possible pass. We just about decided to ignore it; nevertheless, Ann argues the one stone left unturned could be the stone that brings the end to our mission. She refused to be part of a half-assed mission. Ann got my attention fast; causing me to alert Leroy that if we are going to find my ship, we must make sure the passage is not behind us. To do this, attention to detail must be our rule. Leroy said nothing while he turned his car into this narrow pass. The passage had steep cliffs on each side, and ran horizontally, not rising but constantly remaining level. After a few miles, Ann asks Leroy why we are flying and not simply driving on the ground to save fuel. Leroy lowers our car onto the road and continues driving. He explains that since his car can rise up as a helicopter would and fly. This meant it did not need a runway to fly. He preferred using the road as a runway in that it did not use as much fuel. To our advantage to pass seemed to wiggle its way through both mountain ridges, as if it was a flat calm river. Fortunately, Leroy had a compass and after each wiggle in our path, we seemed to travel east. The passage took two hours to complete. Two hours to travel ten miles was actually a great success. It would have taken an extra week to circle the mountain. More importantly, that would have been a week of dangerous exposure. This was a well-guarded secret, which not only offered perfect cover, but also made our voyage as if we were invisible. We were presently flying over the vast forest below us. Leroy told us, fortunately, the sea was to the north, therefor the distance from his cabin, and the pass was flowing toward the sea. We found a new renaissance for our hope as it regained control over our minds. As early evening approached, we found a small town with a gas station. After filling our tank, we went to the town's restaurant and ate as if we had not eaten in months. Ann claimed it was the spices and oils they used to prepare this food that fulfilled a taste that had been dormant in our months for quite some time. After eating, Leroy drove his car for about twenty miles, where he found a side road, which offered a place to hide our car. We made a fireplace about 100 feet from the car. Leroy wanted us to relax from a day in his car and to prepare ourselves psychologically for the sea ahead of us.

He asked me about the deck of my ship. He figured to do what he called a hover-controlled drop on the center of the deck.

I knew we would not be able to put his car below deck, so I recommended that Leroy park closer to the captain's cabin on deck. He agreed with me, and then returned to looking for the sea. Leroy asked me how we would find my ship. I told him I hoped my ship would find us. Leroy reports we will be in my hands within a few hours. He qualifies his prediction by telling us we will be at the sea before lunch. Leroy decided to take us a few thousand feet higher, so we could see the far horizon. Today, time was moving slower than normal. I knew once we saw the sea, time would once more join us. Forty-five minutes later, we saw a darker blue in the horizon. Leroy verifies it is the sea as he slowly begins a controlled descent, as he now wishes to fly just above the trees to minimize our exposure. Once we are over the sea, the risk of exposure will be minimized. His primary fear would be going too far out and not have enough fuel to get back. He comforts us by assuring us his car is water tight if it sank beneath the water; nonetheless, our concern then would be how long our air lasted. It would be best to avoid that situation. Ann and I agreed. Unexpectedly, we found ourselves flying over a meadow. I felt naked without all the trees below us. This was the first time we exposed ourselves in months. Leroy told us to keep our eyes open, yet not to worry, because with so few people living in this area, the odds of danger around this meadow would be equal to finding a needle in a haystack. Just as he said 'stack', we began to receive gunfire from the forest that surrounded the meadow.

Instinctively, Leroy lowered his car into the meadow taking advantage of the high grass. He flung open his door, grabbing a rifle from the back seat's floor. I followed suit by leaping out of the other door, and Ann followed me. We divided the 360-degree circle that surrounded us into three sectors, and began spraying our targets. We spent three hours fighting this what turned out to be a group of six men. Fortunately, four of the men were in Leroy's sector as he displayed his surprisingly superior battle skills. I got a lucky shot into a thick tree killing a hillbilly sniper hanging on a high branch. Leroy rolled over to Ann's sector killing her foe who displaying a disproportionate sense of confidence as he foolishly walked across the meadow while firing at Ann. He provided an easy target for Leroy, who simply held his position waiting for the killer to move within his range plucking him with a shot straight to his head. When the shots ceased coming our way, Leroy bravely walked through the woods and began searching for any other attackers. I told Ann to cover us, as I rushed through the woods to begin my reconnaissance. Soon, we secured our area, yet Leroy told us it was too late in the day to venture over the sea. Undoubtedly, we might have become disorientated, and instead go deeper into the sea, rather than toward the shore; we would be in deep danger of an unpleasant danger of demise. Ann asks him what the difference between day and night is, as with both once we are in the sea, we cannot see the shore. Leroy explains that in the daytime, we have the sun as a directional fixed point. Ann asks about the stars at night. Leroy confesses not to understand the stars at night. All he hears leaves him to think the determination of points and directions would take too much time and distance to establish a desired course. I confess to Ann that I have no idea what he is saying, nevertheless, he has not done us wrong yet, and we need to remember, all he is doing is voluntary. Leroy laughs and tells us he hopes we can chuckle just as loud when we see his bill. Ann changes the subject for us by asking why these strangers were shooting at us, especially considering we were not signifying any threat of hostile actions.

Leroy explains our foes were hunters and not warriors. Ann's face became overshadowed with a puzzled expression causing her to ask Leroy what these men were hunting. Leroy tells us these men came to have us for dinner. Ann replied that if they wanted to invite us, all they had to do was ask, as everyone should know how to make hand gestures to communicate. Leroy smiles and subsequently clarify they wanted to have us as the main entrée for their meal will be us. Leroy then asks Ann if she has any recommendation for their chefs about how to prepare her. I tell Leroy they need to fry Ann at their highest heat for hours to burn out all her meanness. Ann leaps on me playfully slap me telling Leroy, she is going to update them to fry me first, this way they will be poisoned sparing Leroy and her. Leroy confirms we were saving our butts from the frying pan during this last battle. I laugh and say this must be why Leroy killed five of the six hunters. Leroy chuckles and reports that if he did not shoot them, they would have killed Ann and me, because he needed the conversation during the long days while driving his car. Accordingly, I agree with him. Therefore, I offer to find us something to eat for dinner while Ann volunteers to prepare our campfire. Leroy cautions me to avoid bringing back any of the hunters, because his mother forbids him to behave as a cannibal. I tell him my mother must have gone to the same mommy's school that he went. Leroy recommends I do my hunting with a bow, so we can observe noise discipline. He saw no use inviting any additional guests for dinner. I was fortunate to snap a small bore, which made a wonderful meal for us. We cooked all the flesh, planning to nibble on the leftovers during the next few days. Leroy said we would sleep outside tonight under the stars, as a prophecy concerning our rich future, free from any prisons. This had an excellent tone to it.

The next morning, after eating our leftovers and privately fertilizing the forests, we ventured into the air going into the sea. I closed my eyes and called out for my ship. We drove for about twenty minutes from the shore when I saw a small white glittering object in our horizon. I called out to my ship hoping for some sort of response. Within minutes, I heard a voice that felt as if a memory from another life. Julia tells me to stop whining and clarifies they do not see my boat. I explain that I am with some angels now and preparing to swoop in from the sky. Just as we received her words, my ship began shooting at us. I yell to Julia to tell my ship to stop shooting at me. Julie yells for my ship to stop at me. My ship tells her it was simply shooting at an unidentified flying object. I scream out to my ship; I am in that unrecognized object that is flying toward him and to cease-fire and prepare to be boarded. Cindy reports the only thing they see in the sky is a car. Julia tells the Cindies that cars drive on roads and do not fly through the sky. Another Cindy reminds Julia this is not our dimension, and thus we do not determine the accepted realities. With this in mind, Julia asks me, just out of curiosity, if I am riding in a car that is flying in the sky. I confess that I am in the car, yet to maintain my reputation of sanity and normality, I report this is not my car, but instead belongs to my lawyer. Julia laughs and then calms the situation by informing her shipmates there is nothing to be unexpected from lawyers. It is best to learn from the sharks and to avoid these vampires of the courtroom as much as possible. Leroy smiles and tells them they can laugh now; he will laugh when he takes their check for his bill to the bank and cashes it.

Tears in the sea

My ship extends an invitation for us to board. Julia asks me how we plan to board. Leroy explains we will land on the ship's deck, unaware of the restless winds closer to the surface. Even I was caught off guard by this as our vehicle began lightly spinning, then flipping out of control. This totally caught us unexpectedly; Ann begins screaming, while our vehicle begins misfiring. I ask Leroy what is happening. He claims no longer to have any control of their vehicle and the wind is bouncing from the sea up under our hood chocking out his engine. Ann tells him to pop his hood. Leroy explains if he pops his hood, it would offset the balance of their airborne condition, which could send them higher and then dive into the sea. Leroy had no control over his vehicle since all power went out of the engine. The spinning was making me dizzy and scaring my ship, because we were spinning toward it. My ship informs me the incoming vehicle cannot be controlled and its trajectory guides it straight into the ship's hull as a dangerous weapon that can sink it, killing all aboard this ship. I look at Leroy, who confirms my ship's predictions and further tells me I need to save my ship taking into account that if we hit it, we are dead. Nonetheless, there is no need for all to die. Accepting what Leroy was recommending, I told my ship to protect itself. Julia tells my ship to use precaution on how it neutralizes us and predicting that we would be in the sea, she ordered the attack.

Cindies to prepare the boats for a possible sea rescue. My ship tells us to duck down in our seats as it begins shooting at my vehicle. My ship hits our trunk with its first shot, and then as our vehicle changes from a horizontal spinning to a vertical sharp descent, the second spray shot rips the ceiling from our vehicle. We can see the sea rapidly approaching. Leroy yells for us to remove our seatbelts and that just before sinking we need to leap from our car. It was now I realized why my ship skillfully shot off the roof of our vehicle. It was thinking about us escaping from our vehicle as we sank. Unfortunately, when it blew our trunk, the initial blast separated the trunk from our vehicle. Once separated, the heat ignited the grenades and other explosives propelling them in all directions, to include my ship. As my vehicle meets the water, the right half engine of our engine rips at my ship. This temporary slowdown created by the friction of our car hitting my ship gave us a chance to leap from Leroy's car. Before we hit the water, Leroy tells us to swim away from our vehicle toward the front of the ship. As our heads popped up, ropes with lifeguard vests were tossed overboard.

We were pulled over beside my ship and taken up one by one. I sent Ann and Leroy up before me. Once I reach the deck, I discover Ann, Leroy, and one Cindy to greet me. For some strange reason, I expected more to greet me. I ask Cindy where everyone is. She explains they are trying to fix the ship's damage from Leroy's car, and we must rush down to help them. We meet Julia on the third deck who asks me to help her; Leroy got the first deck to help the girls and for Ann to work on the second deck. We must work fast as the ship is taking on water. Julia explains the cracks are currently small; nonetheless, if not reattached the boards will work loose. Time is too important now. I asked what our ship is doing to help. Julia shows me a bucket of white thick wall sealant. Julia showed me eight cracks and asked me to seal them. While sealing them, I heard some more cracks manifest themselves. We were almost keeping up with it when I heard a loud explosion. I ask my ship to tell me what happened. My ship reports that some explosives from my car are creating fires. He warns the shots are creating fires, which, if not quenched quickly will burn the ship. Julia tells me to wait here; she will start fighting the fires with our fire extinguishers and reassign Cindies as needed. Soon they are fighting the firsts leaving Ann, Leroy, and me on the cracks. This is starting to make me angry, as each crack sealed creates new cracks. It is almost as if a crack must break through. I yell for my ship to move closer to the shore. Subsequently, screams echo throughout my ship as Leroy comes running upstairs crying how his crack has broken, and that we must abandon ship. Julia comes running in warning the fires are out of control and that our escape boats are damaged. We need to prepare to escape. They have axes and hatchets. Julia tells us to beat down a door and toss it overboard to use for a raft. They may have enough already, yet now are tossing supplies and extra doors. Julia predicts my ship will be resting on the ocean's floor within thirty minutes. I could not believe what I was hearing. How can so many things turn out so bad? We are in survival mode presently. Everyone was working alone tossing whatever may be of use overboard.

We were tossing food and clothing over when my ship warned everyone to get overboard and underwater away from this ship. We did as instructed and began leaping. I notice Ann is not with us. I yell for her. She screams back, she will be up in one second. My ship is releasing a solid alarm currently declaring everyone must be overboard. I warn Ann now is the time as I rush for the deck. Just as I hit the deck, a huge flame encompasses me. To my salvation, a hand grabs me and into the air, we go, barely ahead of a large explosion. When we hit the water, pieces of my ship began to shatter filling the air and surface. My home between escapades was gone. Leroy pulls me down into the water while huge objects begin splashing above us. Leroy releases me under a few large pieces of wood. I know enough to lift the wood just sufficient to get some air. Unfortunately, with the air also comes the sound, as I look over and see Ann, skin burned to a crisp and left arm missing. She was dead, which was to her benefit when considering her body was nothing but a cage for pain; she would be experiencing nothing but horrifying pain. I rapidly looked elsewhere, because this is not the final memory, I want concerning Ann. My ship quickly went under taking its infernal with it. Now was the time to see who survived. Julia three of the Cindies had serious burns. Leroy secretly tells me they will not make it long. I am trying to put this together, wondering why the first continuity of my episodes has to turn into a blood bath. Something just is not fitting in this puzzle. We swim around gathering what is still afloat while not noticing how the waves are pushing us away from land and not toward the shoreline as we hoped. What I thought was good luck was now turning into disaster. My two alternate worlds met in cooperation; nevertheless, something turned this into a nightmare. Once the sun was up, one of my Cindies asks me where the shore is. Leroy tells me we should be on land, and the tides have turned the opposite direction. We are in serious trouble now, in that no one thought to bring water. Cindy tells us the water would have sunk therefor was impossible to save. The sun was baking hard on us today. A few more Cindies died, as they were nursing severe burns. For the first time in my recorded escapes, I could feel pain. This is unusual. Now is the time for me to, for the first time, to start worrying.

Worry is new for this dimension, in that I always had the trump cards that if the heat got too hot, I could simply awaken. I have woken up so many times in this extended nightmare. When you lose two people that bond deep inside, who are enough to cause me to entertain this dimension as my preferred primary domain. Suddenly, sharp fins begin swarming around us. Leroy tells us they are determining our ability to defend ourselves. Nevertheless, four of my Cindies begin screaming of something eating them. As I go to jump on a board, something bites a chunk of leg. The intense pain virtually pulls me into my daytime realm. The key word is 'almost' as I soon discover I have some more debt to pay against my misery charges. I look over and see Leroy dying in front of me. He reports the sharks got both of his legs as he begins to sink. I make it on my flimsy board, and while looking around me and merely see two Cindies on their boards. One is lying motionless and is verified as dead by the last Cindy. I am now beginning to wonder if the ocean can actually support this many sharks. The fins are everywhere instilling their terror. I was so unaware how fast they turn into a live flesh eater filling the air with razor-sharp rows of teeth. I look over at my last shipmate only to see her door crack from the sharps driving their heads into it. Cindy falls into the water, and is consumed before she has an opportunity to scream for help. This is not funny since I am once more, alone. I put my head down on this board and began to cry. I can never remember crying this hard. This cannot be fair. I foolishly believed I had found a new home in this dimension, even though it was filled with constant dangers, I was a member of two teams, and this was to be the chance the merge these two teams into one large family.

I knew this was the end of something special. A part of me was dying. I simply lay on my board, as the sharks continued to swim around me, yet strangely were not biting. I recognized they could smell the blood pouring from my leg. I am tired of feeling, hurting, and struggling. I have cried so much I wonder if I have any more tears to shed. Such feelings and miseries reminded me of any place, which I merely had to awaken to exist. It would be a long while before I eagerly rushed back into this realm, nor, for that matter, want to return to the day realm. I am questioning presently whether each realm is for the living or a prelude to the peace of death. My goal now, is once I return to my day world to stay there for as long as I can. Previously, a goodbye was merely a prelude to a hello in my other realm. From this point on, I will think carefully before addressing my introduction.

Index

The other adventures in this exciting series

Prikhodko, Dream of Nagykanizsai
Search for Wise Wolf
Seven Wives of Siklósi
Passion of the Progenitor
Mempire, Born in Blood
Penance on Earth
Patmos Paradigm
Lord of New Venus
Tianshire, Life in the Light
Rachmanism in Ereshkigal
Sisterhood, Blood of our Blood
Salvation, Showers of Blood
Hell of the Harvey
Emsky Chronicles
Methuselah's Hidden Antediluvian Abridgment
American States of China

Author Bio

James Hendershot, D.D. was born in Marietta Ohio, finally settling in Caldwell, Ohio where he eventually graduated from high school. After graduating, he served four years in the Air Force and graduated, Magna Cum Laude, with three majors from the prestigious Marietta College. He then served until retirement in the US Army during which time he earned his Masters of Science degree from Central Michigan University in Public Administration, and his third degree in Computer Programing from Central Texas College.

His final degree was the honorary degree of Doctor of Divinity from Kingsway Bible College, which provided him with keen insight into the divine nature of man. After retiring from the US Army, he accepted a visiting professor position with Korea University in Seoul, South Korea. He later moved to a suburb outside Seattle to finish his lifelong search for Mempire and the goddess Lilith, only to find them in his fingers and not with his eyes. It is now time for Earth to learn about the great mysteries not only deep in our universe but also in the dimensions beyond sharing these magnanimities with you.

Printed in the United States
By Bookmasters